Praise for
Rebecca Brandewyne's
PASSION MOON RISING

"An extraordinary novel of high adventure and epic romance from the pen of the incomparable Rebecca Brandewyne. Laced with exquisite delicacy as well as sparkling brilliance, this poetic chronicle is . . . a telling allegory of the human condition. . . . Written with an ethereal beauty and spellbinding intensity. . . ."

—*Rave Reviews*

"*PASSION MOON RISING* is one of the most extraordinary books I've read. It is historical, allegorical, and fantasmagorical . . . thought-provoking as well as entertaining."

—*Rendezvous*

"In *PASSION MOON RISING*, Rebecca Brandewyne has gone into a realm of writing and imagination that she has never ventured into before. . . . When an artist masters her craft, it is only natural for her to venture forth and experiment in new areas. . . . We feel that Rebecca Brandewyne is off to a fine start."

—*Affairé de Coeur*

"A remarkably imaginative book."

—*Publishers Weekly*

Books by Rebecca Brandewyne

Passion Moon Rising
Beyond the Starlit Frost

Published by POCKET BOOKS

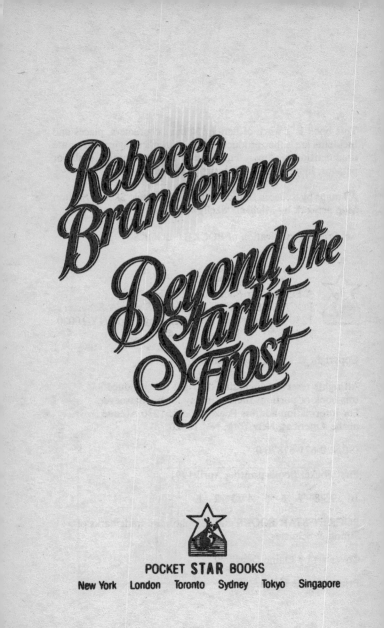

Rebecca Brandewyne

Beyond The Starlit Frost

POCKET STAR BOOKS

New York   London   Toronto   Sydney   Tokyo   Singapore

All maps by Rebecca Brandewyne and Michael "Skelly" Skelton
Map artwork by Michael "Skelly" Skelton

An *Original* Publication of POCKET BOOKS

A Pocket Star Book published by
POCKET BOOKS, a division of Simon & Schuster
1230 Avenue of the Americas, New York, NY 10020

ISBN: 0-671-67876-0

First Pocket Books printing April 1991

10 9 8 7 6 5 4 3 2 1

POCKET STAR BOOKS and colophon are trademarks of
Simon & Schuster.

Cover art by Elaine Dewillow

Printed in the U.S.A.

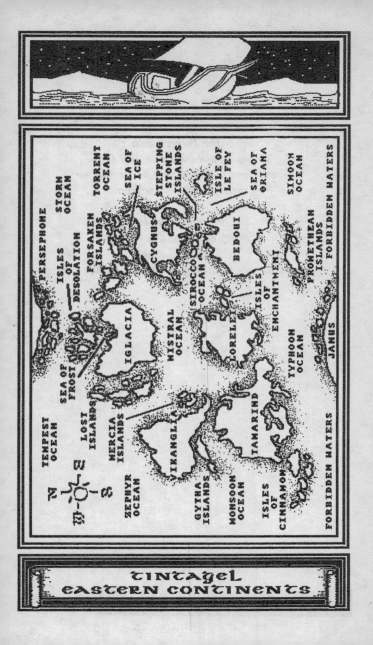

TINTAGEL
EASTERN CONTINENTS

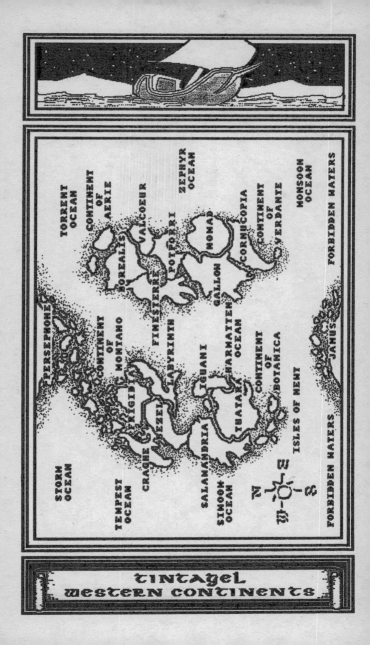

TORRENT OCEAN

CONTINENT OF AERIE

PERSEPHONE

BOREALIS

VALCOEUR

FINESTERE

POTPORRI

ZEPHYR OCEAN

NOMAD

GALLON

CORNUCOPIA

CONTINENT OF VERDANTE

MONSOON OCEAN

FORBIDDEN WATERS

CONTINENT OF MONTANO

LABYRINTH

FRIGID

JEZEL

IGUANI

TUATARA

HARMATTEN OCEAN

CONTINENT OF BOTANICA

FORBIDDEN WATERS

JANUS

CRAGHE

SALAMANDRIA

ISLES OF NEWT

STORM OCEAN

TEMPEST OCEAN

SIMOON OCEAN

N W E S

FORBIDDEN WATERS

TINTAGEL
WESTERN CONTINENTS

The Players

THE ROYAL HOUSE OF LOTHIAN
Rhiannon Olafursdaughter, set Boreal; later known as the Lady Rhiannon sin Lothian, set Vikanglia

THE ROYAL HOUSE OF TOVARITCH
The Lord Iskander sin Tovaritch, set Iglacia

THE ROYAL HOUSE OF ARIEL
The Lady Ileana sin Ariel sul Khali, set Cygnus; the High Princess of East Tintagel; wife to the Lord Cain (a Sword of Ishtar quester)

THE ROYAL HOUSE OF KHALI
The Lord Cain sin Khali sul Ariel, set Bedoui; the High Prince of East Tintagel; husband to the Lady Ileana (a Sword of Ishtar quester)

THE NUNNERY OF MONT SAINT MIKHAELA
The Reverend Mother Sharai san Jyotis, set Bedoui; the High Priestess of Mont Saint Mikhaela

Sister Amineh san Pázia, set Bedoui; a twelfth-ranked priestess; mentor to the Lady Ileana

**THE MONASTERY OF MONT
SAINT CHRISTOPHER**

The Reverend Father Kokudza san Dyami, set Tamarind;
the High Priest of Mont Saint Christopher

Brother Ottah san Huatsu, set Tamarind; a twelfth-ranked
priest; mentor to the Lord Cain

**THE EASTERN RULERS FROM
THE ROYAL HOUSES**

The Lord Balthasar sin Ariel sul Ariel, the High King of East
Tintagel

The Lady Nenet sin Khali sul Khali, the Queen
of Bedoui

The Lord Xenos sin Ariel sul Ariel, the King of Cygnus

The Lord Tobolsk sin Tovaritch sol Kharkov, the King of
Iglacia

The Lord Lionel sin Morgant sol Draca, the King of Lorelei

The Lady Pualani sin Gingiber sul Gingiber, the Queen of
Tamarind

The Lord Faolan sin Lothian sul Lothian, the King of
Vikanglia

**THE EASTERN RULERS FROM THE
COMMON HOUSES**

Master Radomil san Pavel sol Antoni, set Iglacia; the High
Minister of East Tintagel

Mistress Elysabeth san Villette sol Franchot, set Lorelei; the
High Electress of East Tintagel

THE QUESTERS

Anuk, a lupine of Iglacia

Yael Olafursson, a giant of Borealis

Chervil, an elf of Potpourri

Anise, an elf of Potpourri

Sir Weythe, a swordsman of Finísterre

Gunda Granite, a gnome of Labyrinth

Lido Lodestone, a gnome of Labyrinth

Moolah, a merchant of Bezel

Kaliq, a mercenary of Bezel

Hordib, a mercenary of Bezel

OTHERS

Ulthor, a giant of Borealis (a Sword of Ishtar quester)

The Lord Gerard, the Prince of Finisterre (a Sword of Ishtar quester)

The Lord Parrish (called "Perish"), a necromancer of Finisterre; brother to the Lord Gerard

The Lord Fiend of Salamandria, the Imperial Leader of the UnKind

The Lord Ghoul of Salamandria, the First Leader of the UnKind

Contents

NEW STAR
Already Seen
1

THE RISING
The Ice Prince
19

MORNING STAR
Beyond the Starlit Frost
97

DAY STAR
ShapeShifter
167

EVENING STAR
Shadows of the Blue Moon
241

xiii

CONTENTS

NIGHT STAR
The Darkness
301

THE FALLING
The Sacred Scroll
351

DARK STAR
The Moonbow Lights
429

Beyond the Starlit Frost

The heavens were unfurling to release the night,
The twelve signs opening all their pearly gates
To let the stars out slowly,
Like a prophecy long foretold,
A part now already seen.
Deep within the Piney Woods of Yukon Valley,
From conifers, the snowy owls,
With plaintive cries, were calling
And counting every flicker
Of the skies' illumination;
And the Moonbow Lights shimmered,
In colors bright,
Against the melanotic welkin.
The Eternal Bell chimed midnight,
As though it struck a galaxy away—so distant—
And two Mont-Sect cloisters answered it the same.
The luminaries glowed
Soft like the mist along the narrow wynds;
And Lothian Hold twined across sleet-dappled plains.
Beyond the starlit frost, Tovaritch Fortress,
In which the mysterious obelisks stand,
Towering, cupolaed,
Each based upon its antlered hreinns,
Guarded that fair fane, Iskander's bride,
ShapeShifter, Chosen by the Light.
The Passion Moon was rising,
And shadows of the First and Blue
Had filled up all the planet to the brim,
Limning yonder castle
In some enchanted incandescence,

Compelling her who gazed with passionate desire
To shiver and shatter
And find an Ice Prince
Who hungered for her soul.
To kiss him was to bring away
His rime upon her lips.
Her body trembled at the thought.
Her aura froze; still, he engulfed her with his own.
The seal of the Sacred Scroll lay broken;
And somewhere, the Darkness drew near. . . .*

---

*Poem adapted from *Aurora Leigh,* Eighth Book, by Elizabeth Barrett Browning.

NEW STAR

Already Seen

It is not enough for one who has been Chosen to lift the thin veil that shrouds Time Future and to gaze deep into the fires and the mists of summoning, the silver pools, the polished mirrors, and the crystal spheres of portent, or to read the ancient cards and the tea leaves of omen, in search of the Signs of the Things to Come. One who has been Chosen must also be able to look back, and see clearly, the Shape of the Things that have gone before in Time Past, and to heed well the many lessons they teach.

To fail in this Bounden Duty is to fail in all things, for then are the mistakes of history made again and again, and worsened each time by the Knowledge and the Power amassed in between, so what rises like the Phoenix from the ashes is once more ashes in the end, swept away as though it never were. And where, then, lies the profit? What, then, has prevailed but ungovernable, eternal Time, where the legacies of all things are written —tragic in their futility if unread, unremembered?

But is it not inevitable that all things come full circle, ye may ask, and rightly? Yea, for that is the way of the heavens and of the earths. But is not the circle ever-changing, even so, I ask? Are not the new, greening leaves of the ageless oak tree different each spring from those of the last? Yea.

And so I say unto ye that the one who is no wiser at the circle's end than at its beginning is the fool of all fools and, having wrought no change for the better in the circle's ceaseless turning, deserves condemnation to whatever Fate, Time's hand-

maiden, may choose to bestow. And so it is that one who has been Chosen must look not only to Time Future, but also to Time Past for Truth and Understanding—and must never forget that even the oldest and mightiest of oak trees may be toppled by a single wild wind. . . .

—Thus it is Written—
in
The Gift of the Power
by the Sorceress Saint Sidi
san Bel-Abbes set Mosheh

Torcrag, Borealis, 7274.12.25

HIGH ABOVE THE PLANET TINTAGEL, THE MOONBOW Lights shimmered, embroidering a thousand strands of color upon the black-velvet tapestry of the night sky. About the three glowing moons the Lights twined satin knots and, with silken threads, boldly stitched together the countless silver stars strewn across the heavens. At the bottom edge of the firmament a fringe of incandescent ribbons trailed from the brilliant tapestry the Lights wove, streaming to the earth far below. There, they tumbled down the thickly forested mountainsides and played like sunbeams through prisms among the many icicles encrusting the branches of the conifers that rose, tall and spirelike, upon the vast expanse that bordered the northern tundra. Delicate as a spider's web, the Lights spun and threaded their way through the resinous trees, dappling the snow-laden ground, making it gleam like stained glass and seem to shift like the patterns of a kaleidoscope. With the glimmer of wraiths, the grace of fairies, the Lights flitted and fluttered across the cold white terrain, scattering mist and moondust in their radiant wake as, at long last, they came to dance in the flames flickering at the heart of several gray stones that ringed a large, solitary fire.

Here, a circle of giants, each wrapped in a fur cloak, sat solemnly upon animal skins spread earlier upon the hard-packed snow. It was the winter solstice, the longest night of the year; and once, this had been an evening of ceremony and celebration in which the giants of the land of Borealis had honored their gods. But now their old gods no longer existed for them. Now they worshiped and believed only in the Being who was the Light; and this was an evening of ritual and requiem, in which they mourned their brethren whose Time of Passing had come upon the Strathmore Plains one year ago this night. Yet the deep sorrow the giants felt was mingled with their extreme pride in the valiant thousand strong of their number who had died to save their world. For if not for the stalwart courage of their dead brethren, the whole of Tintagel would have been lost to the Darkness, the nothingness.

Now, as the Lord Jorvik, the chieftain of the tribe of the giants, glanced at the still faces of his people illuminated by the fire, he saw they were waiting expectantly, and he knew that the time for the bittersweet tale had come. The realization preyed heavily on his mind, for the story was tragic and, worse, had as yet no real ending; and this last was a fearsome thought. But at least now he and his people knew how to battle the Darkness, the unspeakable evil that had invaded the shores of their homeland, Borealis, and beyond. There was hope in that. Still, how many more lives would be given in the fight? Jorvik did not know. Too many, he suspected. Finally, heaving a deep, grievous sigh and feeling keenly the weight of his many years, the aged chieftain spoke.

"Tell us, Ulthor," he directed, his stately voice

echoing in the silence hitherto broken only by the whine of the wind wending through the mountains, the muffled rustling of the evergreen trees of the Piney Woods, and the crackling of the fire. "Tell us of the Strathmore Plains."

"Yea, tell us, Ulthor," others among the giants then took up the call. "Tell us of the Strathmore Plains. Tell us, Ulthor. Ulthor! Ulthor! Ulthor!"

The voices rose and swelled until they clamored as one for the story the giants had heard but once before, shortly after the culmination of the events it recounted, the story that had turned the tribe from their ancient gods, and this evening into what it had become. It was a painful tale to hear, an even more painful tale to tell; and for a moment his throat choked so with emotion that the giant Ulthor feared he was unequal to the task that had been laid upon his shoulders. Then he recalled his brethren, slain to the last warrior upon the Strathmore Plains, and determinedly he gathered his heart for the telling. His brethren had not failed him then. He would not fail them now. Flinging back his long mane of red hair, he slowly stood.

At the sight of him silhouetted against the Moonbow Lights in the ebony sky, a mighty roar burst from the ranks of the tribe to reverberate through the mountains and the forest. Then the cheering and chanting gradually faded as, one by one, the giants assembled around the flames fell silent. For what seemed a long while Ulthor stared at those congregated about the fire, noting how many faces were missing, faces that had been present last year—before the Strathmore Plains. Tears of which he was unashamed stung his eyes as he forced down the lump in his throat and struggled to master his feelings. Then finally he began to speak—quietly, but still, the wind carried the sound of his voice to the ears of all.

"I am not a bard but a warrior," he uttered simply, "so I have no gifts of the tongue, and my words are not richly musical and eloquent, but the poor, rough, unlearned words of a plain soldier. Still, it is I, Ulthor of Borealis, who tells this tale. I tell it because I was there upon the Strathmore Plains, and so it is my right. But more than this I tell it so those of Time Future will know and remember what came to pass one winter solstice in the land of Finisterre.

"It is for many—unnamed and unknown—who were there also that I speak; for our dead brethren, a thousand warriors strong, they who remained undaunted unto the end of their lives. It is for the swordsman, the Prince Lord Gerard of Finisterre, that I speak, he who, wrongly accused of murder and banished from his homeland, was once known as Garrote the Dispossessed, and who was the boon companion of my youthful traveling days. It is for his elfin wife, the Princess Lady Rosemary of Potpourri; for her brother, the Prince Lord Tarragon of Potpourri; and for my own lady wife, the gypsy Syeira of Nomad, that I speak." Ulthor gazed down lovingly for an instant at the woman who knelt at his feet, her dark sloe eyes shining with tears and pride. Briefly he laid his hand upon her long black hair, thinking of all that they had been through together, that bound them to each other as surely as their love did. Then he continued. "It is for the Bedouin, the Lord Cain, the High Prince of the six Eastern Tribes of Tintagel, that I speak, he who bore so bravely the hideous beast of the Darkness that lay coiled within him, and who conquered it, despite unbearable agony to himself. But most of all it is for the Cygninae, the Lady Ileana, the High Princess of the six Eastern Tribes of Tintagel and wife to the Lord Cain, that I speak, she who is the truest of the Defenders of the Light, who risked all she knew and loved so we and our world might be saved,

7

and for whom I would give even my life if she asked it of me.

"It is a long tale I will tell, of those born of the Royal Blood and of those Common, but great and noble men and women all. Unafraid, they stood fast against the most horrifying Darkness ever to come upon Tintagel, either before or since the Wars of the Kind and the Apocalypse.

"My part in this story is small, for mostly it is the Lady Ileana's tale, she who bade me tell it far and wide, and whose trust and faith in me I keep by speaking. So listen now and I will tell to ye, as best I can recall, what is written in *The Book of Eden* of the Holy Book, *The Word and The Way,* which the Lady Ileana quoted to me, lo, these many long nights past and charged me on my Sacred Oath to remember; and what came later, the Lady Ileana's quest for the magic Sword of Ishtar, of which my knowledge is from her own lips, also; and what came later still, what I saw, with my own eyes, upon the Strathmore Plains one year ago this night—what I, alone of all our dead brethren, lived to return to Borealis and tell. Listen, I say, and heed my words well, for they have lessons to teach. Hear now, then, my tale."

Ulthor paused, ordering his thoughts and words, and even the Piney Woods seemed hushed and breathless, waiting. Only the bleak wind soughed—a whisper, a moan, as from a thousand ghostly giants. Gone but not forgotten, they would live forever in the hearts and minds of their brethren, brought to life each winter solstice, around the tribe's communal fire. Aware of this, Ulthor, when he again spoke, pitched his voice low, his tone reverent.

"In the Beginning, aeons ere there was aught we know or have even dreamed of, there was only the Being. It was alone in the cold, empty darkness we call the nothingness, a titanic ethereal essence that stretched to the very ends of the heavens, for all that ever was or ever would be was within It. Yet It did not even know if It was real, for there was naught else to confirm Its existence.

"The Being wished to know whether It was; and so thinking, It summoned Its power from every breadth of Its never-ending reach. Like an aura, the Being began to glow, darkly at first, then brighter and brighter, shimmering colors—like the Moonbow Lights that mark this night—streaming from Its center until at last It exploded, scattering Its force across the nothingness to illuminate the darkness, to fill up the emptiness, and to warm the coldness.

"The Being was pleased by what It had created, for though Its tremendous burst of energy had first generated Chaos, from this It had wrought the stars and the planets and, most of all, Order as It had fixed them in the heavens, along with the suns and the moons that, henceforth, would bring day and night.

"After this the Being caused upheaval upon the planets so the seas were divided and the land was revealed. Upon this It sowed the seeds of Its might, and these grew to cover the land with earth and flora; and then the seas, the land, and the heavens became filled with creatures. The Being saw that this was good, and It blessed all the creatures, for they were a part of It.

"Still, this was not enough. So presently, as It had made the others, the Being created two more creatures, and these It made in Its image. These two creatures, which the Being called the Kind, It placed upon the land, beneath the Tree of Life and Knowledge born from the seed of Its power. Then lightly the Being touched the tree, and upon its branches the Fruit of Free Will burst into bloom.

"The Being wished to know the truth of Its existence, and It knew that in order to discover this, It must give the Kind the freedom to choose between the Light that was Itself and the Darkness that was the nothingness. If the Kind chose the Light, then the Being's existence would be confirmed. If the Kind chose the Darkness, then there would be only nothingness.

"In time the Kind ate of the fruit from the tree, and so the Seeds of Free Will were planted within them and took root; and the Kind learned that, unlike the creatures of the seas, the land, and the heavens, they had been given the freedom to choose their own LifePaths and Destinies.

"As time passed, the Kind mated and begat children, and these children begat more children, until the planets were peopled with the Kind; and these became the Tribes, for the Kind were many and, over the ages, grew to be different from one another.

"Some of the Tribes worshiped the Being who was the Light, though they called It by many names. But there were others who chose the Darkness, the nothingness, and so the Being sent messengers to the planets to tell of It; and these became the Keepers and the Prophets.

"But still, some of the Tribes did not believe in the Being, and they disrupted the Harmony of all It had created; and the Darkness began to attain power. The ethereal essence within those of the Tribes who chose the Darkness metamorphosed until it was no longer as the Being had fashioned it. These creatures so changed became the Demons Fear, Ignorance, Prejudice, Hate, Greed, and Apathy—the minions of the Immortal Guardian's antithesis, the Foul Enslaver, and that which sits at Its left hand, Chaos.

"Because the ethereal essence of these Demons had altered, they were no longer a part of the Being who had made them, and the Way to return to It, to become One with It, as they had been in the Beginning, was lost to them forever; and what had once been good within them was corrupted and turned to evil.

"Soon the other Tribes became infected by the wickedness of those who served the Darkness, and mistakenly they began to believe that their name for the Being who was the Light they worshiped was the only name by which It could be called or known. So, in the Name of the Light, the Tribes began to war among themselves, shedding the Blood of Life and destroying those who did not believe as they believed. Many civilizations passed into the Darkness, the nothingness, nevermore to be. This was the Time of the Tribal Wars.

"Through Its messengers the Being admonished the Tribes, telling them that this was not the Way or the Truth of the Light. But they did not listen. At last, disheartened, the Being again summoned Its power, and the heavens were filled once more with Chaos, as they had been in the Beginning. This was the Time of the Cataclysms.

"But still, the Tribes did not heed the Being's warnings; and over the ages they turned from Its ancient teachings to a new learning, in which they sought to discover the key to the energy of the Being and to make it their own. They did not understand that only fragments of Its force had been revealed to them. They thought themselves possessed of the Being's secret.

"With their newfound pieces of knowledge, which they called Technology, the Tribes of each planet began once more to war among themselves. Great explosions shook the land, and the planets were devastated by the destruction wrought, as the Keepers and the Prophets had foretold. This was the Time of the World Wars.

"Again, through Its messengers, the Being admonished the Tribes. But still, they refused to listen; and they continued their pursuit of what could be fully known and understood only by those who had become One with the Being in the End, as had been promised to all those who believed.

"With their Technology the Tribes on each planet discovered the existence of those on the other planets; and because all, in their ignorance, were afraid of the others, in the Name of the Light, the Tribes of the planets set out to destroy one another. The worlds collided. Fire and ice such as had never been seen before swept across the planets, consuming them, and all were devastated by the destruction wrought, as the Keepers and the Prophets had foretold. This was the Time of the Wars of the Kind and the Apocalypse.

"All things come full circle.

"After the Apocalypse, all was as it had been in the Beginning, the Tribes scattered and unable to move physically through Time and Space as they had before. Many were so changed that they were unrecognizable as the Kind, and indeed, they no longer were, for they had regressed to creatures such as they had been before the Being had gifted them with Its ethereal essence, and with the Fruit of Free Will from the Tree of Life and Knowledge. Others were lost forever, their worlds having passed into the Darkness, the nothingness, and having ceased to exist.

"Those who survived were few. These were the Tribes whose belief in the Being had never faltered, who had wielded the Swords of Truth, Righteousness, and Honor against the Darkness so the Light would not be extinguished but would continue to burn, no matter how faintly, shedding Its rays of hope and promise throughout the universe.

"These were the Tribes who experienced the Time of the Rebirth and the Enlightenment, when Faith, the Keeper of the Flame, appeared and spake again of the

Way to the Being, the Immortal Guardian of all things that ever were and ever shall be, the Light Eternal that forever holds the Darkness at bay so long as even one of the Kind believes that the Being is.

"And this time, on Tintagel, the Tribes heard the Word—and they listened. So it is written in *The Book of Eden* of the Holy Book, *The Word and The Way*, which the Lady Ileana quoted to me.

"Now, it came to pass that in the East of our world, two cloisters were established to honor, serve, and defend the Light; and for centuries, heeding the lesson taught by the Keeper Faith, the Kind lived in Harmony, and all was well. But an ancient Prophecy foretold the return of the Darkness; and in time the Druswids, the Chosen trained at the two cloisters, looked into the fires and the mists they summoned and saw the Signs of the Things to Come. And they knew that the Prophecy had spoken truly, that the Darkness was once more upon them, a Darkness more terrible than any they had ever before seen, though they could not discern Its shape, only Its growing strength and power.

"So the two Ancient Ones of the cloisters, Takis san Baruch and Gitana san Kovichi, each performed the dangerous Ritual of Choosing and brought forth from the heavens two SoulMates—a Son of the Darkness and a Daughter of the Light—each to balance the other's Power of the Elements in a perilous union against the coming evil. These two SoulMates so Chosen were the Lord Cain and the Lady Ileana.

"In the mighty windjammer *Moon Raker*, they sailed to the West to search for the magic Sword of Ishtar, with which the Prophecy ordained they must battle the Darkness. But during their crossing of the seas, they were set upon by a leviathan octopus and their ship was sunk. Only the Lord Cain, the Lady Ileana, and a handful of the hundreds who had accompanied them survived to reach the shores of

Cornucopia. There, they were befriended by the tribe of the dwarfs, two of whom agreed to act as their guides here in the West.

"But these two dwarfs, Bergren Birchbark and Jiro Juniper, were not alone in offering their assistance. Many others, myself among them, also knew there was a wrongness in the land, for we had spied the diseased minions of the Foul Enslaver and battled them; and so eventually we, too, joined the Lord Cain and the Lady Ileana's quest as they journeyed hard across the continents of Aerie and Verdante, of which our homeland, Borealis, is a part.

"The Wheel of Time turned—all too swiftly, we feared. But finally the Lord Cain and the Lady Ileana came to the land of Valcoeur; and there, at the Citadel of False Colors, the Lady Ileana drew from the crystal flames of truth the magic Sword of Ishtar to wield against the Darkness.

"But now the monstrous beast of evil placed within the Lord Cain during the Ritual of Choosing, so he might recognize and become a force even more horrible than the Darkness Itself, was fully roused. And so when we came at last to the Strathmore Plains of Finisterre, he stole, by means of trickery, the Sword of Ishtar from the Lady Ileana, and he turned its magic to the left hand of the Darkness.

"It was the winter solstice, the longest night of the year, and the snow lay thick upon the Strathmore Plains, where the minions of the Foul Enslaver were massed, an army of thousands, black as night, scaly as reptiles. Once, they had been Kind. Now, infected with vile disease, they had metamorphosed, had become UnKind, SoulEaters; and at their head was Woden, once a giant of Borealis."

Here, a collective, sharply indrawn breath hissed through the tribe at the deadly betrayal by one of their own. At their reaction Ulthor nodded tersely, his red-bearded face set sternly.

"Yea, it was he, Woden of Borealis," he declared again gravely. "From the ramparts of the castle at Ashton Wells, which overlooks the Strathmore Plains, I saw him and knew him for our own, and my fury and my shame were great.

"That first night the Lord Cain alone of the Kind stood upon the Strathmore Plains. He alone met the charge of the UnKind. But by then such was his awful, awesome Power born of the Darkness that, unscathed, he slew them by the hundreds, while we watched from the keep and the Lady Ileana warded us, and the boundaries of the Strathmore Plains, too, with her own Power, which she could not turn upon the SoulEaters, for it was born of the Light.

"For two days, then, the dreadful battle raged, and the slaughtered of the UnKind littered the frozen ground. But still, the Lord Cain stood strong, for the magic Sword of Ishtar had increased his Power tenfold, as the death of each SoulEater increased it, also.

"Then, at the dawning of the third day, the Lady Ileana collapsed, drained of her Power, and the aura of warding she had stretched across the Strathmore Plains vanished. We thought then that we were lost, and all Tintagel with us, for the UnKind would have overrun the world, infecting us each and every one with their putrid poison, corrupting us, body and soul. And our hearts were heavy and sore. But before I had gone to Ashton Wells, I had begged the Lord Erek, he who was then chieftain of our tribe, for help against the SoulEaters. And now, from the veil of morning mist that cloaked the land, an army marched down from the north, our brethren, a thousand warriors strong.

"'*Uig-biorne, märz ana! Uig-biorne, märz ana!'*

they cried over and over. 'War-bears, march on!' "
Ulthor uttered fiercely, proudly, tears trickling down
his cheeks at the memory of the gallant giants stoutly
striding row after row onto the despoiled Strathmore
Plains. His voice cracked, but at last he composed it
and went on. "We cheered them! Oh, how we cheered
them—and regained our heart for the fight as they
shouted their battle cry and fearlessly attacked the
UnKind.

"The SoulEaters were not proof against the maces
and morning stars, the sledgehammers and battle-axes
of our brethren. In desperation the perverted creatures cast away their shields and weapons, and with
their unnaturally sharp teeth and claws, they tore like
rabid animals into our brethren and—and—" Ulthor
broke off abruptly, passing his hand across his stinging
eyes, as though not only to wipe away his tears but the
grisly, appalling memory of how the thousand warrior
giants had perished. Finally he continued.

"When it was done, every last man and woman of
our intrepid brethren lay dead upon the Strathmore
Plains. But their glorious sacrifice was not in vain, for
they had taken every last SoulEater with them. Only
their UnKind leader, Woden, and the Lord Cain
remained. Though the First Moon had risen, the night
was blacker than black as they faced each other
murderously, their eyes glowing with a diabolical red
light. What followed then was a duel so abominable
that I have not the words to describe it. So I will say
only that in the end, with the Sword of Ishtar, the
Lord Cain stabbed Woden straight through the heart.
Woden's body exploded at the impact of the thrust;
and as it did so, the ghastly black sky opened without
warning, and in the heavens, much to our disbelief, a
gruesome maw of jagged teeth gaped, such as never
seen before or since. Then, right before our eyes, a
savage whirlwind formed and swept down to the

earth, violently sucking up all in its path. Only the Lord Cain was not taken.

"Alone on the Strathmore Plains, then, he stood, a menacing, macabre sight, the Darkness Itself; and with despair we thought that he would surely now turn on us himself and destroy us—and all Tintagel with us.

"The Blue Moon had joined the First Moon in the sky, and now, upon the horizon, the Passion Moon began to rise as the Lady Ileana, who had recovered and left the keep, walked toward him, unafraid; for in that moment she was the Light Itself, our only hope, our only salvation. I speak no lie when I say that we upon the ramparts were breathless, waiting, frozen with terror, for we believed that the Lord Cain was now so transfused and transformed by the Darkness that he would kill even her, his beloved SoulMate.

"But the Kind are always given a choice, for this is the Way and the Truth of the Light. And the Lord Cain's deep, abiding love for the Lady Ileana, his SoulMate, proved stronger in the end than even the heinous beast within him; for there was one all-important part of him it did not have: his heart—and therein was the Lady Ileana's Light. So the Lord Cain chose her; and at insufferable anguish to himself, he conquered his Darkness, and we and Tintagel were saved."

Ulthor fell silent then, and the rest of the tribe were silent, too, for there were no words for what they felt. After a time, one by one, they slowly stood. With a multitude of pine branches they fed the flames of the fire until it blazed even brighter and higher; and then, their right hands clenched and pressed to their breasts, in the highest tribute of all to those who had died upon the Strathmore Plains of Finisterre, they began to sing the requiem that honored their dead heroes.

In voices loud and strong and clear, the giants keened, until they drowned out the wailing wind, until the forest and the mountains and even the very heavens, where the Moonbow Lights shimmered, rang with their splendorous song of mourning, and their rejoicing for the Light.

THE RISING

The Ice Prince

ISLES OF CINNAMON
AND TAMARIND

Chapter 1

*The last and hardest test to determine whether a
Chosen novice is Worthy to take the Final Vows
and to enter the halls of the Mont-Sect cloisters to
become a Druswidic priest or priestess, to have the
mark of the sun or moon set upon the brow, and to
be given the Collar of First Rank is this: to
summon the barge and to guide it through the
mists to the shores of the cloister of training. If this
cannot be done, the Chosen novice shall be deemed
Unworthy to take the Final Vows, and the gates of
the Mont-Sect cloisters shall be closed to that
Unworthy One forever.*

—Thus it is Written—
in
The Books of the Lesser Mysteries
Volume I

The Southern Shore of Tamarind, 7274.12.25

AFTER A LONG AND DIFFICULT VOYAGE, THE SMALL, ELFIN-
built ship *Spice of the Seas* had dropped anchor at last
off the southern coast of the continent of Tamarind.

Then, with great care, a dinghy had been lowered so a man and a woman could row alone to shore. Now the man and the woman—Druswids both—stood silently upon the rocky black beach that stretched just beyond the Hills of the Incas to the sea.

Unlike in the land of Borealis far to the North, where it was winter, it was summer here in the South, but the tropical night was dreary. The wind that billowed in from the Monsoon Ocean was chilly, and drizzle fell from the clouds massed in the sky, dimming the light of the moons and the stars. Shivering slightly, the woman, a priestess, drew more closely about her the djellaba she wore. The cloak was woven of lightweight Finisterrean wool, dyed an icy violet, and she was glad to have it; for much of what she had begun her travels with three years ago was now lost to her. Still, she had survived to return home. That was all that mattered.

She glanced expectantly at the man, a priest, beside her, waiting for him to summon the barge that would take them through the blanketing mist to the Isles of Cinnamon and Mont Saint Christopher. She might have called the boat herself, but as the monastery was not her cloister, it would have been presumptuous of her to send for the *Hawk Hymn*. Still, puzzled, she wondered why the man did not.

Wending its way through the huge fronds of the towering palm trees that lined the coast of Tamarind, the hazy light of the three moons illuminated his still, bronze face. She noted fine grooves, which had not been there three years ago, about his eyes and mouth, and her heart ached for him. The cloisters they both served had asked too much of them, she thought. It was not right, what had been done to them— even worse that it had been done in the Name of the Light.

The silence stretched between them, and still, the

woman waited—and still, the man did not summon the barge. She continued to wonder why, and then finally, even before he spoke, she realized he was afraid. *Afraid!* She wanted to weep, for his courage was that of a thousand men—none knew that better than she—and this inner doubt was not of his making.

"*Kari,*" her husband said quietly, in the Bedouin language of his tribe. "I do not know if I can call the boat."

A year ago he would not have admitted his fear to her. But they had both changed, and now the bond between them transcended all things, even Time itself. Though she had been born unto the tribe of the Cygninae, the woman knew the harsh tongue of the Bedouins as well as she knew her own lilting one, and she answered the man accordingly.

"Ye are strong, *cid,*" she uttered softly, earnestly, "stronger than what lies within ye! Ye have proved that! And I am here, as always. Never again shall I leave your side. This, by all that is holy, I swear."

The man gazed at his wife for a very long moment, his black eyes speaking for him all the love he bore her and for which there were not words enough at his command. He had always been laconic and brooding, and after what he and she had been through together, these characteristics had become even more pronounced. But his wife understood, and not for the first time did he send a prayer of thanks to the Light that she was his.

He had not used for a year the vast Power of the Elements that was his. He had not wanted to use it. But now he must—and so he was afraid, afraid that by doing so he would waken that which lay within him, conquered but not slain; for how does a man kill an inborn part of himself?

Turning, he stared out over the midnight-blue Monsoon Ocean toward the Isles of Cinnamon that rose darkly from the frothy waves, trailing like a spiny tail away from the dragon-shaped continent of Tamarind and cutting an oblique into the horizon. The isles were named for the redolent evergreen trees whence the spice itself came and that grew in abundance in the rainforest that enveloped the large main island—Bark Island—and the smaller islets. Yet in truth, the man saw the isles only in his mind. For now, as always, they were concealed by the cool, thick, rolling white-gray fog that was carried northward on the wings of the bitterly cold winds that blew up from Janus, the southern polar cap. It was for this reason that no ships approached the isles and that no one dared attempt to land upon them from the sky. Thus was Mont Saint Christopher effectively isolated. To reach the monastery, the barge *Hawk Hymn* must be summoned.

Very slowly the man pressed his hands together at his breast and bowed his head so it touched his fingertips and his chin rested upon his thumbs. Then, after taking several deep breaths and closing his eyes and ears to shut out his surroundings, he willed himself to call up his Power.

In the beginning it did not respond, and for a moment he thought he had lost it, and he did not know whether to rejoice or to grieve. But then sluggishly, like a muddy river, it started to flow through his veins, pounding harder and harder until at last it roared in his ears. Despite himself, the man's heart leaped with exultation in his breast as his Power surged through him, filled him, then suddenly burst from him in a wild, glorious, fearsome, silent cry whose name was Triumph.

The soundless shout pealed across the ocean. Through the mist it rang. It echoed over the isles, to the heart of Bark Island, to the monastery, and shook the very halls within, terrifying the Druswids who heard its clamor in their minds and did not understand it, shocking to the marrow of their bones those who did but disbelieved. The man felt them all reel and recoil, stricken—all but one—and a grim, sardonic smile that did not quite reach his glittering black eyes twisted his carnal lips. Deliberately, as though to demonstrate further the potency of the Power at his command, he split the spine-chilling shriek in two, softening and sweetening that which reached the solitary one who evinced neither terror nor shock at sensing his presence, but with all his heart rejoiced.

"Ottah! Ottah!" the man called out in his mind to that lone one.

And proud and strong and clear, the answer came: *"Welcome home, my son."*

At that, abruptly overcome by emotion and knowing that his message had been received, the man broke off the TelePath and looked up, spreading his palms wide before dropping his arms to his sides. His wife spoke not, but her pale, luminous Cygninae eyes shone with pride and a razor-sharp relish at his victory, and he knew that she had heard and felt and understood: For what had been done to them, for what they must now live with, there was a ponderous debt owed them—and tonight it would in part be paid.

Earlier, through undetected scrying, they had discovered that the four from whom they would exact their price were all gathered at the monastery, a fortuitous happenstance. Of their return the man and the woman had deliberately sent no word to these four. Now, despite their meeting having been shattered—violently and without warning—these four were rapidly collecting themselves and preparing to receive the two they had presumed lost or even dead these three years past; for the Power of these four was considerable, also, and they were not easily cowed. All this the man and the woman knew.

Still, even sooner than they expected, as though borne on the wings of magic, there appeared on the horizon a small, ancient boat gliding noiselessly over the ocean, its angled bow, sides, and stern fashioned to resemble a hawk. Made from the wood of the massive shadow oak, the barge was black as a moonless night. A single square sail billowed from its mast. Six young, hooded Brothers manned its long oars, faces hidden deep within the folds of their cowls, the hands that protruded from their bell-like sleeves appearing disembodied against their dark robes and the darkness itself.

As they neared the shore where the man and the woman stood waiting, the somber priests drew in their paddles. Then, heedless of their belted cassocks, they disembarked, wading through the swirling water to haul the boat onto the beach.

Once ashore they spoke neither to the man nor to the woman, but were mute as though they had taken a vow of silence—or had had their tongues cut from them. As none who manned the *Hawk Hymn* had ever done before when fetching a summoner from the shore, they dropped as one to their knees upon the slick black shingle, heads bowed, hands clasped, as though they expected some swift and dreadful fate to befall them. Plainly the Brothers were awed by the man who had called the barge in such a manner From the depths of their hoods, they cast at him frightened glances, and even the highest ranked among them trembled before him.

But they were innocent of any wrongdoing, and the man's wrath and retribution was reserved for the guilty four. And so, much to the priests' surprise and relief, he did naught save turn to help his wife into the boat; for she was heavy with child and clumsy as a result. Then he himself stepped in, and after making sure she was comfortably settled, he took his place at the prow.

Scarcely daring to believe their good fortune, the Brothers stumbled to their feet. They pushed the barge back into the water, then scrambled over the wings of the hawk that formed its sides, resuming their positions at the oars. Slowly the *Hawk Hymn* headed toward the open sea and the Isles of Cinnamon.

As the boat skimmed over the foaming waves, its sail flogging in the wind, its paddles, manned by the priests, moving in perfect unison, the fog draped it in a veil as thick and white as death. Others, blinded, would have shivered with fear as the mist enshrouded them. But those in the barge had no need to see. Sure now of his Power, the man guided the boat unerringly through the fog and past the deadly coral reefs that ringed the isles.

His ink-black hair flowed like the long, silky mane of a faesthors. The woolen burnous he wore fluttered black as a raven's wings about his still figure, making him seem not of this earth, but of some dark netherworld. Rain and spindrift sprayed upon him, so his bronze skin glistened in the moonlight as at last the barge broke free of the mist and Bark Island loomed before them.

As before, the priests waded into the water and dragged the boat up onto the golden beach cleft by long, gnarled fingers of obsidian rock. Without waiting for the Brothers, the man and the woman set off upon the path that wound its way from the shore to the heart of the island. There, in a verdant glade at the base of the enormous snowcapped volcano Yama-Magara, the meticulously designed and stoutly constructed high-walled monastery of Mont Saint Christopher stood.

Centuries old, it had been built of solidified magma wrested from the earth, then hewn into square blocks and polished until it shone like the volcanic glass with which it was studded. At each corner of its four battlemented walls was a square, crenellated tower. The structure itself was quadrangular in shape, the church at its center surrounded by the wings. A square, gold-domed bell tower thrust up from the steep, pitched roof of the chancel. The gable-roofed wings were three stories tall and lined on all sides with mullioned casement windows of amber glass that appeared to stare like the gleaming yellow eyes of smilodons through the rainforest. In the mornings, when the rising sun was high enough in the sky to look down upon the edifice, the lozenge panes caught and reflected the brilliant red-gold rays, making the monastery seem like a powerful black lupine springing from a shimmering pool of liquid fire. It was a perfect onyx for the golden-green setting that held it.

The man and the woman were expected; and now, as the Brothers guarding the gatehouse caught sight of them, the heavy iron portcullis was raised, and the huge wooden doors that barred the monastery slowly swung open on creaking hinges to permit the two Druswids passage through the arched portal. They crossed the public courtyard, then entered the cloister, where they were met by yet another priest, older and less afraid than his Brothers, though no less silent and wary. Inclining his head in solemn greeting, he indicated they were to accompany him.

The folds of their garments whispering in the hush, the two followed him down the narrow, winding corridors of the monastery, torches, set into iron sconces upon the walls, lighting their way. Finally the priest paused before a stout door and knocked upon it. At the terse "Come," he turned the knob and opened the door. Then he stood aside so the man and the woman might step into the dimly lighted chamber beyond, where the four who sat within waited—and wondered anxiously what the arrival of the two who now approached them portended.

> *The Wheel of Time turns relentlessly, irreversibly, unstoppably. And so, as surely as one thrusts a spoke into the Wheel, the spoke shall return to thrust that one.*

—Thus it is Written—
in
The Teachings of the Mont Sects
The Book of Laws, Chapter Four

Inside the Reverend Kokudza san Dyami's private sitting room were he and the three other highest-ranking Druswids in the world. But though their Power was mighty—and their combined Power was even mightier—and they, more than anyone, knew above all how to mask their emotions, only one of them gazed with perfect equanimity at the man and the woman who entered. Only this same one exhibited neither surprise nor outrage that instead of kneeling, as they ought, the man and the woman stood unflinchingly before the four convened in the chamber.

Indeed, Brother Ottah san Huatsu was hard-pressed to conceal from his three angry and uneasy colleagues his respect and admiration for the two who had journeyed to the far side of Tintagel—and had lived to return and tell of it. This was a feat unmatched by any who had gone before them; and although Ottah and his colleagues had despaired of, yet counted on, the man and the woman's success, none was unaware that their having achieved it now made the two of them a force to be reckoned with, greater than that of the four who hitherto had been the greatest force in all Tintagel.

The thought both humbled and frightened Ottah's colleagues, and they, grown arrogant in their supreme Power and authority, were not accustomed to being either. Yet now their emotions were those of persons who, driven by ambition, have knowingly created a gargantuan monster to conquer the world—and who, too late, have realized they themselves are part of the world on which they have loosed it. Triumph was theirs, yes—but at what price? In doing its work their monster had grasped the fact that it must call none master. It was no longer subject to their bidding. Now only Ottah did not fear it.

The tension in the air was so thick that all present felt as though it could have been cut with the ceremonial arthames they each carried at their waists, a symbol of their Druswidic Power and rank. No one spoke. No one moved. It was as though the room were frozen, like a vignette somehow set apart from the scheme of reality or like a photograph from Time Before. The woman who stared at those who had so ruthlessly dispatched her to the far side of Tintagel three years past had seen such a picture once, long ago, an image captured forever on a strange piece of paper by some forgotten—mechanical—means of the Old Ones. Born of instinct, a twinge of guilt assailed her at the remembrance. It was forbidden to speak of such things, forbidden even to think of them. Yet the photograph, or what remained of it, had been there, in the library of Mont Saint Mikhaela, where she had trained as a Druswid, its image blurred, its colors faded, but there, despite its being accessible only to those who had been admitted to the Greater Mysteries. At the thought ire overrode her guilt. Possessing artifacts of the Old Ones was against the laws of the land—though the Druswids were above all laws except those of the Light. Yet these, too, the Druswids had, like the Old Ones, broken in the Name of the Light and, in doing so, had set themselves above the very Light they served.

There must be an accounting for that.

Now, as though he sensed the woman's musings, Ottah rose from his chair, shattering at last the stillness of the chamber. Lovingly he embraced the man who stood before him, the man who had been as a son to him.

"'Tis good to see ye alive and well, Cain," he said simply.

The Lord Cain, the High Prince of East Tintagel, returned Ottah's hug fiercely, his throat tightening with emotion at his mentor's understanding and unconditional acceptance of him—of what he had been, of what he had become, and of what he now was: a man who must fight every day of his life to keep chained the hideous beast of the Darkness that lay coiled inside him, a beast the Druswids had caused to be a part of him forever, a beast whose full wicked fury Ottah's three colleagues now feared that Cain would unleash upon them.

A muscle twitched in his set jaw as slowly Cain drew away from his mentor to face them. They had nearly destroyed both him and his beloved wife, the Lady Ileana. At the thought it was all he could do to hold his rage in check—and the beast at bay. A perceptible shudder racked his body as, sensing how he seethed inwardly, the beast stirred and flicked its spiny tail. The eyes of Ottah's colleagues widened with alarm. They flinched, horrified. Though they only guessed what the beast, in concert with Cain's Power, was capable of, they had no desire to have their suspicions confirmed. Cain's harsh laughter echoed in the room.

"What is the matter, Sharai?" He sneered at the

Reverend Mother Sharai san Jyotis, the High Priestess of Mont Saint Mikhaela, for against her he harbored a special grudge. Her tongue had lashed him insultingly once—unjustly—and he had not forgotten it. "Are ye not as pleased as Ottah to see me? Do ye not wish to know what ye and the rest wrought within me? The beast I must live with every day of this LifePath—Nay, ye are but wasting your art on me!" His voice was scathing as, thinking to test the limits of his Power and, if it were not as formidable as she and her colleagues worried, to gain control of him, Sharai suddenly employed a small but effective magic that made her appear all at once to tower over him terribly, like a titan. With this arcanum had she once, long ago, deceived and intimidated even him, a twelfth-ranked priest. "Ye must know I am now far beyond being fooled by such tricks!" Cain spat.

So saying, he himself conjured much the same spell as Sharai—except that instead of merely looming even larger than she, he seemed to turn into a colossal black dragon as well. Duly chastened and dismayed, Sharai dwindled at once to her true size, and Cain laughed again, crimson flames roaring from his scaly throat.

"Cain," his wife, Ileana, chided gently, laying one hand upon his arm. "Cain, ye do but rouse the beast with this."

Abruptly, knowing she was right, he resumed his normal appearance, and all in the chamber breathed a little easier. It was clear that Ileana, at least, wielded some influence over her husband, even if none of the rest did; and this helped alleviate their dread. Unlike Cain's, Ileana's Power derived from the Light. For this reason the others thought her incapable of harming them—or of permitting her husband to do so, either, though they misjudged her in this.

Still, feeling somewhat surer now that he and his

colleagues were in no immediate danger, the Reverend Father Kokudza san Dyami, the High Priest of Mont Saint Christopher, dared to question Cain.

"So, Cain, among us all only Ottah is to be forgiven —is that it?" he asked.

"Within the limits of his knowledge and despite the way in which ye hampered him, Ottah prepared me as best he could for what I was to face. He alone is deserving of forgiveness among ye. The rest of ye sent me, and Ileana, too, ignorant to our fates, and would have seen us both dead rather than tell us the truth of your machinations—and all in the Name of the Light!" Cain's voice was bitter at the irony.

"Yet ye are alive," Sister Amineh san Pázia pointed out.

"Had Ileana loved me less, had I loved her as little as ye, Amineh, the mentor whom she trusted and who betrayed her, ye would *all* be dead now, and I would be a monstrosity the like of which ye cannot even begin to imagine! And had I become such, Amineh, had I not conquered the beast with which ye and the others, in your zeal, saw fit to vest me, Tintagel would now be a world devastated by the most horrifying Darkness ever to come upon it, a Darkness much worse than even what Ileana and I found and faced a year ago this very night!"

"Ye have seen the Darkness foretold by the Prophecy, then?" Kokudza queried sharply.

"Yea, we have seen It," Cain replied grimly, the strain and exhaustion of the past three years now plain upon his face, "and survived It and defeated It in battle. But we did not win the war, and therein lies the rotten core of what confronts us now. Despite all your hopes, it is not victory we bring ye, but warning: The worst is yet to come—and I am a far more dangerous champion than even ye, who made me so, believed; for the beast inside me thrives on the Darkness, and it is all I can do even now to keep it caged. If ever it should master me, nothing in the world will prove strong enough to defeat me—and *I,* who am become the Darkness then, will ravage all Tintagel!"

At that a deathly stillness once more enveloped the room as those within it digested the full import of Cain's words. All save Ileana, already privy to the pitfalls of her husband's Power, were stricken, for though they had glimpsed some inkling of this knowledge previously, to hear it confirmed was terrifying. Before, that such a fatal possibility existed had been speculative and remote. Now it was real—and it was here. Though Ottah's dark eyes were pitying, the rest viewed Cain askance, as though he might suddenly go berserk and slay them all. This time, however, he did not laugh at their trepidation.

"Yea," he jeered softly, "just like the foolish Old Ones, too late do ye consider the results of your actions. Too late do ye grasp what, in the Name of the Light, ye have loosed upon us all!"

It was Sharai, ever practical, who broke the silence that followed this dire pronouncement. Yet even though she sought to placate him, her regal voice was stiff, unaccustomed to apology.

"Cain, if we have done wrong—and it seems we have—then I am sure I speak for us all when I say we deeply regret it. We acted as we thought best to defend the Light, and perhaps in our fear and our fervor we were indeed, as ye claim, like the Old Ones, blind to a better way. But what is done is done; and no matter how much we might wish it, none of us can change Time Past. We must look instead to Time Future. It is that—if, as ye say, the worst is yet to come—which must concern us now." She indicated two chairs by the hearth, where a small fire burned to take the chill from the gloomy night.

"Come. Sit. We would hear of your years on the far

side of Tintagel and of this terrible Darkness that threatens us all; and we will listen and learn and be guided by your and Ileana's knowledge and advice in the matter, I swear." Sharai turned to Kokudza. "If we could order a light repast, perhaps? Cain and Ileana have journeyed long and far, and they are no doubt hungry and tired. Ileana is with child, too. . . ." Her voice trailed away as she studied the beautiful, silver-haired woman who stood before her, eyes steady and accusing, chin held high, arms folded protectively over her burgeoning womb.

A child, Sharai thought—and in her distress and apprehension, she was not alone. *How foolish we were not to have considered that possibility. How foolish, just like the Old Ones, have we been, indeed.*

Ileana's lavender eyes did not lower respectfully, nervously, as they once would have done beneath the Reverend Mother's dark, penetrating glance. Instead, she met Sharai's gaze coolly, as though issuing a challenge. Like her husband, Ileana did not forget that though both Sharai and Amineh loved her well, they had once betrayed her. Because they had believed that Cain and Ileana's physical joining was necessary to defeat the Darkness, they had drugged her and given her, a virgin, to him, regardless of the beast inside him, which she had sensed and feared then.

Now, despite the apparent capitulation of those in the room, their seeming willingness to heed her and Cain's counsel, Ileana still did not put it past any of them, especially the Reverend Mother, to seek some way to poison her—not to kill her, but to abort her child, lest it prove to be an anathema, born of Cain's tainted seed as it would be. Fury and fright rose within her that their determination to defend the Light at all costs was such that it might stretch even to harming her child.

"Do not even think *somehow to rid me of it, Sharai,"*

she coldly warned the Reverend Mother telepathically. *"Be very sure that for my child's sake, I will not stay Cain's hand if he should choose to lift it against ye—as he surely shall if ye should dare to touch our child."*

It was Sharai's eyes then that fell before Ileana's. Satisfied that her threat had not been taken lightly, Ileana sat down in one of the chairs before the fire, slipping off her djellaba and accepting gratefully the cup of palm wine that Cain had poured from Kokudza's sideboard and now handed to her. A cold supper was brought from the kitchen, and she and Cain ate hungrily, for they had missed the food of the East. Then afterward they spoke at length of their travels and of the battle that had taken place one year ago this night on the Strathmore Plains of Finisterre.

"So, ye see," Cain said when they had finished their story, "we dealt the Darkness a bitter blow, yea—but not a mortal one. We did not learn whence these diseased minions of the Foul Enslaver—these Un-Kind, these SoulEaters—originated. They may have come from the continents of Montano or Botanica; and if so, it is possible they have already conquered the lands there, swelling their ranks beyond counting—a thought that even I, who have fought and defeated them, find chilling, because I know that, even so, it will not be enough for them. For if there is one thing certain where these twisted abominations of the Kind are concerned, it is this: They will not rest until they have marched upon the whole of Tintagel, infecting us all and corrupting our souls, so the Way to return to the Immortal Guardian, to become One with It, as we were in the Beginning, will be lost to us forever!

"Like all living creatures, they are driven by one primal need: the preservation of their tribe. I believe that this vile disease with which they are infected, which causes the body to undergo this appalling metamorphosis from homo sapien to saurian, must somehow render either gender or both sterile during the mutation process. Otherwise, they could breed naturally to reproduce, and they would not need to take so many prisoners or to attack even animals—in which the transformation is gruesomely unsuccessful, by the way—in an effort to create more of their number. And so, like parasites, they prey upon us. And we . . . we must find their heart and strike at it—before all Tintagel is doomed!"

"What do ye propose, Cain?" Ottah inquired slowly, his face grave. "If what ye say is true and there are few ways currently known to us of killing—much less curing—these UnKind, then it seems that even an army of Druswids would have little hope of prevailing against their vast numbers—and that is not even taking into account the fact that the seas are treacherous and that the crossing of them is fraught with many perils. If the mighty windjammer *Moon Raker,* the greatest ship ever built, could sink . . ."

"Then what chance would the lesser vessels that now remain to us have of safely reaching the West?" Amineh completed the question.

"Little or none," Cain stated soberly. "That is doubtless why none of our other emissaries ever came back. Those ships that succeeded in reaching the far side of Tintagel were probably lost during their return voyage. It was only by the grace of the Light that Ileana and I survived."

"Then, I ask again: What do ye propose, Cain?" Ottah reiterated.

"I propose this: that we send a lone Druswid over the northern polar cap, Persephone, to the West, to find the heart of the Darkness, to infiltrate Its ranks, and to learn everything there is to know about It, so we may determine how best to deal with It."

"Why, that is madness!" Amineh exclaimed,

aghast. "What Druswid could possibly hope to survive in the arctic? What Druswid could possibly hope to spy upon these UnKind, these SoulEaters, to pass undetected as one of them, when they are, as ye say, no longer Kind, but have metamorphosed into saurians such as never before seen?"

"There is one such Druswid," Cain insisted, though pain shadowed his eyes deeply at the knowledge.

"Ahhhhh," Ottah breathed, in sudden understanding. "So, my son, ye are not after all without some comprehension of our plight and of our grief when we sent ye and Ileana into the Unknown, are ye?"

"Nay, Ottah."

"Yet even so, ye would still send your best friend, Iskander sin Tovaritch, into the very heart of the Darkness, would ye not? For it *is* he of whom ye speak, is it not?"

"Yea, Ottah," Cain replied unhappily. "It is he, and however reluctant I may be to do so, I *will* send him, if he will go."

"But of course he will go!" Kokudza burst out. "He is, indeed, the very Druswid—nay, the *only* Druswid —for the job; and as such, he shall do as he is commanded by the Mont Sects."

"Nay, Kokudza!" Cain grated, his dark face set harshly. "There shall be no more of that! That is part of the price ye will pay—all of ye—for what was done to Ileana and me. Ye will send no one else ignorant to his fate. Iskander is to be told the truth. He is to be allowed to make his own choice—or so help me, ye shall know what it means to rouse the beast inside me, I swear!"

Even Ottah blanched at this threat as he thought of the havoc Cain might wreak upon them—heedlessly, once caught fast in the grip of the beast inside him. It was a risk they dared not take.

"I will summon Iskander, Cain," Kokudza agreed

at last, with ill grace. "But it is ye who shall tell him of your knowledge. It is upon your shoulders that the results of his decision shall rest! And know this, Cain: If, because of your insistence upon burdening him with what is better left unknown, Iskander refuses the task ye would lay upon him, then ye, and ye alone, will have doomed Tintagel as surely as though ye yourself destroyed it!"

"Amen," Cain rejoined softly. "So be it."

Chapter 2

From the time I was small, I knew I was different from the rest of my family, in ways that, no matter how much I wished otherwise, set me apart from them.

Though I was born in Borealis, the land of the giants, I was not a Boreal, but a Vikanglian. My blood parents had come from the other side of the world, from the East, of which the giants knew only bits and pieces. During their journey across the continent of Aerie, my blood father and his companions had been set upon by reivers and slain—all save my blood mother, who somehow managed to escape and whom I have always thought must have been exceedingly brave and resourceful. For alone in a strange land and heavy with child, she nevertheless managed to make her way to Borealis, where the kindly giants found her and cared for her.

It is to my deep sorrow now that I never knew her, for she died giving birth to me, living just long enough to gasp out the name she had chosen for me. And so it was that I was reared by the giants, as though I were one of them. But I was not, and as I grew older, I became increasingly aware of the differences between us.

At first I did not understand why it was that I

would grow no taller, no larger, that I should always be much shorter and smaller than the rest of my giant family (though I know now that among my own tribe I should have been considered a fine specimen of a woman); and it was not until I complained bitterly to my giant mother, Freya, of my lack of stature that I learned I was not her blood child, was not, in fact, even a giant at all. I was an orphan, of a strange, little-known tribe, the Vikanglians, from the East.

My world fell apart that day; and ever after, though I knew that my giant family loved me well, I felt in my heart that I was alone, an alien in an alien land—though it was the place of my birth and all I had ever known. I became consumed with learning who I was, what I was. But my giant parents could tell me nothing further, for they knew little more than I about the East—and I knew nothing at all.

They gave me all my blood mother had possessed when she had come to them; but as this consisted only of some unfamiliar, worn garments and a small casket, in which was contained a scroll written in a foreign language that none of us could read, her belongings were of no use to me—though I kept them just the same. For it was after I first opened the casket and touched the scroll inside that I was changed.

Now, of course, I know that it was then that my Power, long dormant, awoke within me. But at the time I was ignorant of what stirred to life inside me; and I was terrified, as was my giant brother, Yael, who witnessed my initial transformation. How well I recall it even now, after all these years.

We were hunting, Yael and I, and I was running alongside him, morning star in hand, when, for some reason, I mentally likened myself to a grace-

ful hreinn galloping across the tundra, as I had often seen them do. No sooner had the thought occurred to me than something wild and strong and fearsome suddenly burst from within me, as though I had exploded; and for a few moments, it seemed as though I actually became the animal I envisioned I was.

I fainted, and the next thing I knew was Yael's face as he bent over me, anxious and afraid. We spoke little of what had happened. We convinced ourselves that we had only imagined it, that I had been giddy from running, that Yael's eyes had been deceived by the brilliant sun reflecting off the snow.

But in my heart I knew that it was not so. In my heart I knew that, however briefly, I had somehow metamorphosed into a hreinn, that I was not only an alien among the giants, but perhaps an alien among all tribes—cursed with a Power I did not understand and did not want.

Though a young woman, and beautiful—or so Yael had often told me—I felt myself an anathema, an abomination; and because I loved them, I began to withdraw more and more from my giant family and friends, lest I somehow taint them with the unnaturalness of my being.

—Thus it is Written—
in
The Private Journals
of the Lady Rhiannon sin Lothian

The Piney Woods, Borealis, 7274.12.26

AS SHE WAS OFTEN THESE DAYS, RHIANNON OLAFURS-daughter was alone. She had gone deep into the dense Piney Woods to hunt game, something she did more and more of late. It was not that her father, Olafur, or her brother, Yael, were not fine hunters, perfectly capable of providing meat aplenty for their table, because they were. It was simply that ever since she had discovered she was a witch, Rhiannon had felt a need to distance herself from her family and friends. Though they loved her well, they now feared her, too; and sometimes, behind her back, when they thought she did not see, she knew they made the ancient sign against evil. The knowledge wounded her deeply, but still, she could not blame them for being afraid. How could she, when she scared even herself?

Oh, if only she could go back to the days when she had been ignorant of the fact that she was not a Boreal, but a Vikanglian, Rhiannon thought, when she had believed her growth merely stunted and she had felt sure that eventually she would be as big as her giant mother, Freya. When she had not known of this strange Power she possessed, that sometimes made even her brother, Yael, who was closer to her than anyone else alive, eye her askance, torn between his deep love for her and his dread that she was not quite . . . Kind.

But she could not turn back the Wheel of Time. At the realization Rhiannon sighed heavily. Not for the first time did it occur to her that perhaps she ought to run away so her family would no longer have to be burdened by her—a witch. But then she thought of the UnKind, the SoulEaters, who even now, after the battle of the Strathmore Plains, were occasionally glimpsed in the land, and she shivered. To fall prey to them was a fate worse than death, and what chance would she, alone, accursed, stand against them? Besides, even if it *were* safe to travel, where could she go? To the fairies of Valcoeur? To the elves of Potpourri? To the dwarfs of Cornucopia? She was as different from them as she was from the giants. Even the

Finisterreans, the Nomads, and the Gallowish, all of whom more closely resembled her physically, were not the tribe whence she had sprung. And what means had she of sailing across the seas to the East, virtually unknown to the giants? To that faraway place, Vikanglia, her true homeland? None. It would be better to forget she had ever heard of it.

But Rhiannon could not forget. Indeed, the tale told by Ulthor around the ritual fire last night, the tale of the battle of the Strathmore Plains, had only honed to a keen edge her secret fervor to learn more about the East. Now, as she knelt in a peaceful glade upon the southern bank of the River Snowy, she dwelled at length upon Ulthor's story. The High Prince and the High Princess of East Tintagel, the Lord Cain and the Lady Ileana, had possessed Power, too, Ulthor had said. Perhaps it was not unlike her own, Rhiannon reflected. Perhaps among others of her ilk, she would not be considered a witch.

At the thought she reached into her rucksack for the small casket that had belonged to her blood mother and that she had carried with her always since Freya had given it to her. Now, as she opened it and drew forth the scroll inside, Rhiannon wondered, as always, what was written upon the parchment. It was embossed with an elaborate seal of red wax, now broken, and the language inside was like nothing she had ever before seen. No matter how hard she studied the foreign characters that formed the words upon the page, she could make no sense of them. At last, heaving another deep sigh, Rhiannon rerolled the parchment and replaced it in the casket. The scroll was useless to her. She did not know why she kept it, except that sometimes when she touched it, images formed in her mind, images she felt held some significance for her; and so, for all that the scroll disturbed her, she was reluctant to part with it. Shivering slightly, she shoved the casket back into her rucksack. Then she glanced at the dreary sky, unlightened by the sun, Sorcha, which, here in the lower reaches of the arctic region, shone so fleetingly each day during winter, if at all.

Bloated grey clouds were massing on the horizon. A snowstorm approached, Rhiannon suspected. She really ought to return home to Torcrag, the dwelling place of the giants. Yet she was disinclined to go back, to answer the questions that would surely be put to her when she appeared without so much as a single rabbit for the stewpot; for then her parents would know that her hunting had been just an excuse to leave the lodge, and their feelings would be hurt. Oh, why did she have to be so different from her family? she wondered again bitterly.

Rhiannon gazed at her reflection in the dark icy river, noting, as always, how little she had in common with the Boreals physically. She had known eighteen years. Yet despite her being full grown, she stood nearly four-and-a-half feet shorter than the shortest giant she knew; and though muscular, she was small-boned, her frame delicate compared to those of the Boreals as well. Her face, lost amid a mass of long red hair, was piquant, all planes and angles, with high, slanting cheekbones. Rhiannon had never thought herself beautiful, though Yael did. She knew only that because she did not resemble the giants, she felt as though she bore upon her forehead the brand of an outlaw. Even her eyes set her apart. Unlike the blue of the Boreals', hers were golden-brown, like topaz, and had an unnerving, luminous quality, as though with them she saw beyond the ken of mere mortals.

A sudden footfall startled Rhiannon from her reverie. With the quickness of those whose survival depends upon their wits, she snatched up her morning star and sprang to her feet, assuming the half crouch of a warrior. Then, seeing that it was only her brother, Yael, she relaxed, a small frown knitting her brow.

"I should have realized that it was ye," she said by way of greeting him, "for ye alone know of my fondness for this place."

"Yea." He nodded as he stepped into the clearing. "Ye come here oft, Rhiannon, especially of late . . . ever since that day—" He broke off abruptly, as though he struggled to hold back his words. But they burst from him all the same. "Ye are avoiding me!" he accused hotly, his crystal-blue eyes hurt and angry. "Ye are avoiding us all! Why?"

"Ye know why, Yael," Rhiannon responded, her voice low, her eyes averted, her cheeks stained crimson with guilt and shame. "Ye know what I am become. Everyone knows, since it seems that although I am possessed of this Power to change shape, I cannot control the transformations, and all have now witnessed them. The Boreals think me a witch, Yael— perhaps rightly, for I think I must be so myself—and it is only because of your parents' love for me and their high standing among the tribe that I have not been named an Outcast."

"They are your parents, too, Rhiannon," her brother insisted, more quietly.

Sadly she shook her head.

"Nay, Yael, not truly, though they call me daughter and love me well, as I love them. In truth, they were but caring enough to take me in when my blood mother died, and ye know it. For is not that the argument ye yourself have used oft enough to persuade me to marry ye—that we are not blood kin?"

Now it was Yael's turn to flush and look away. It was true he had said as much to her once he had realized, in his adulthood, that his abiding love for her was not that of a brother for his sister, but that of a man for the woman he would take to wife. Now the words haunted him, and Yael wished desperately that he could call them back. But he could not, and his heart ached for her.

Over the past several months—since that ill-omened day of her initial metamorphosis—he had grown increasingly aware of how Rhiannon deliberately isolated herself from the rest of the Boreals. Now he was afraid she planned to run away, to embark upon the life of an Outcast that many in the tribe, fearing her Power, would have seen her named. He was afraid he would lose her forever. The land was rife with dangers, not the least of which was the handful of scattered UnKind that remained, despite the battle of the Strathmore Plains. The thought of Rhiannon in the clutches of the SoulEaters terrified Yael. The thought of her dead pierced him to the core.

Yet in truth, how could he blame her for feeling as she did? Among the Boreals only Ulthor, who had traveled far and wide and known others with Power, did not think her a witch, did not make behind her back the ancient sign against evil. But even Ulthor did not understand Rhiannon's Power. Because of this, her ability to transform into creatures other than what she was would have been frightening under the best of circumstances to the tribe. Now the Boreals, in their ignorance, could not help but equate it with the appalling mutation of so many Kind into UnKind and thence to wonder whether Rhiannon was indeed a witch, perhaps a minion of the foul SoulEaters.

In his heart Yael knew she was not. Still, though he did not pretend to comprehend the Power that had come to her, he wished she did not have it. It set her even farther apart from the rest of the tribe. But even so, it did not make him love her any less. He still wanted her as his wife.

He moved to take her in his arms, but with an upraised hand, Rhiannon forestalled his action.

"Nay, Yael, don't. Ye do but hurt us both with this love of yours for me. Now, more than ever, it is no good between us. I love ye as a sister loves her brother; and even if I felt more for ye than that, I could not wed ye now, not since I am become what I am. I would not jeopardize your standing in the tribe by having it said ye had taken a witch to wife."

"I don't care what others say," he muttered stubbornly.

"But ye would, Yael!" Rhiannon declared. "If they began to shun ye as they shun me, if ye became as much of an Outcast among them as though ye had been named such, ye *would* care! Ye do not know what it means to be different, what it means not to belong. I do—and I would spare ye the pain of that."

"But I love ye, Rhiannon! Gladly would I share your pain. Gladly would I leave here today, even, if that is what ye desire, and take ye wherever ye want to go."

"I could not ask that of ye, Yael," she uttered softly, deeply touched. "Besides, there is nowhere I wish to go except across the seas to the East, and there is little hope of that. Nay, I must simply learn to accept the fact that there is no place that I will ever truly belong, that I will ever truly be able to call home—" Her voice broke, and a solitary tear slid from one eye to freeze like a crystal bead upon her cheek, increasing Yael's wrath and frustration at his impotence to comfort her.

Cursing under his breath, he struck a nearby pine a mighty blow with his fist. Instinctively Rhiannon cringed as the *thwack* reverberated through the forest. A sprinkling of pinecones drifted like snowflakes from the branches of the tree, and a startled squirrel bounded from its knothole to chatter at Yael from a high limb. Briefly a smile touched Rhiannon's lips, for it seemed she could almost understand the creature. Then, dismayed, she shrank from the thought, as though by thinking it, she might somehow make it come true; for how minor a magic conversing with an animal must be if one were capable of turning into one, however involuntarily one did so.

Something electric stirred within her at the realization; an unwitting shudder racked the length of her body—signs Rhiannon had come to recognize foreshadowed the awakening of the Power she could not control.

"Leave me, Yael! Now!" she rasped, wanting to weep at the grimace that crossed his face, evidence of the hurt her demand caused him. But she did not wish her brother to witness the metamorphosis she sensed was surely about to happen. "Please," she managed to get out more gently. "Please, leave me."

It seemed at first that Yael would argue with her. Then abruptly he clamped his mouth shut, and casting at her a speaking glance more eloquent than words, he turned on his booted heel and departed, the boughs of the pines closing like a snowy owl's wings behind him.

Once she was alone, Rhiannon fell to her knees, shivering and gasping at the Power that pulsed within her, so strong now that it felt as though it would rip her asunder. Her head reeled; points of light, like tiny stars, exploded in a multitude of glittering colors before her eyes. A cry of utter anguish burst from her lips—but it was with the spine-chilling howl of a wounded polar bear that the woods rang as, against her will, her shape shifted, became a blurry mass of thick, sleek white fur and long, sharp black claws thrashing in helpless torment and confusion upon the ground.

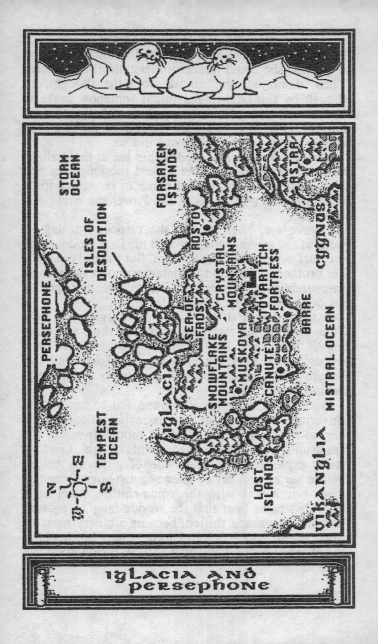

IGLACIA AND
PERSEPHONE

Chapter 3

Of the Known-Inhabited Continents, the northernmost tribe, the Iglacians, are the most physically isolated and so were the last to join the High Council established by the Survivors. Due largely to this physical isolation, which for many years hampered to its detriment communication and trade between Iglacia and the other five Known-Inhabited Continents, the Iglacians are a comparatively barbaric tribe. They are accustomed to a life of many hardships, born of Iglacia itself being composed primarily of tundra and thus lacking many of the natural resources to be found elsewhere on Tintagel. On a more positive note, however, the Iglacians have, as a result, developed an unequaled ability to adapt to their surroundings and are able to survive even in the wastelands of the arctic region.

—Thus it is Written—
in
Tundra Tenants:
A Study of the Iglacian Tribe
by the Anthropologist Sharif
san Al-Jabar set Zeheb

The Tundra, Iglacia, 7275.2.4

WHAT PASSED FOR DAWN IN THE SEEMINGLY INTERMINABLE winter darkness of the arctic region had broken, a faint light streaking across the horizon, pale as frost, barely differentiating day from night as it cast its shadows of grey and lilac and indigo upon the eternally frozen tundra. The ceaseless bitter wind of the north blew as though heralding the morning's arrival, and clouds of snow flurries whipped up by each gust intermittently obscured the vast expanse of land that lay before him—treeless, snow-covered, barren of all save the hardiest plants and grasses and an occasional animal that had adapted to the harshness of life in the arctic wastelands. Yet for all the relative inhospitableness of the tundra, Iskander sin Tovaritch knew, as he gazed toward the northern horizon, that the worst was still to come; for he had no illusions about the difficulty of the quest he had agreed to undertake.

Madness, Sister Amineh had called it. But then, so was wagering all on a single throw of the dice at Pharaoh, a risk Iskander was more often than not wont to take. Besides, if any Druswid could complete this journey alive, it was he. That was the plain, simple truth, unvarnished by any vanity on his part. He alone was uniquely suited to the task before him. He alone had a fighting chance to survive, born of his Power and knowledge.

Following his return home to Tovaritch Fortress from Mont Saint Christopher, he had spent a hectic month equipping himself for the many severe trials he would face. Still, though he had been sore-pressed for time, Iskander's preparations had been meticulous, for he had known that his very life would depend upon them. He had assembled the finest team of lupines in all Iglacia, and gathered from far and wide the supplies heaped high upon the sled on whose runners he now stood, surveying the bleak terrain. He was as ready now as he ever would be. He could either begin his mission or return south to tell his best friend—the Lord Cain sin Khali—and the others that he had changed his mind; and what, then, would become of all Tintagel? How could he do any less for his world than what Cain had done, despite the agonizing price he had paid for Tintagel's salvation? Iskander knew he could not; and so, though the burden he had shouldered weighed heavily upon him, he bore it unflinchingly. Cowardice was not in the nature of an Iglacian, especially one who was of the Royal Blood and a twelfth-ranked priest, besides.

"Mush!" he shouted through the thick wool muffler that protected his face from the cruel elements and, with fur-mittened hands, cracked his long, snakelike whip over the heads of his team of lupines.

With a lurch the beasts and the large, sturdy wooden sled to which they were harnessed started across the tundra toward the faraway Isles of Desolation and Persephone, the northern polar cap. Iskander's lonely sojourn had begun. He would not see another Kind for many long weeks now—never if he failed to survive the crossing of the Sea of Frost and Persephone, where a man was more likely than not to encounter his Time of Passing. Iskander was not afraid of death, only of what his dying—his quest unfulfilled—would mean to his world; for what was the fate of a single Kind when that of thousands hung in the balance?

The thought was ponderous as the weapon he carried in a leather sheath slung across his back—the magic Sword of Ishtar, given to him by Cain and Ileana, should he have need of it to wield against the Darkness. Made of metal fallen from the stars, the blade had been twice forged and so was invincible. Iskander sighed, wishing the same could be said of the one who bore it. But it could not. Despite all his Power and knowledge, he was mortal as the next man—a fact brought home to him all too markedly as the brutal wind lashed him, chilling him to the bone, despite the heavy sable cloak and many layers of fur-lined garments he wore. He shuddered at the realization that the cold would only worsen the farther north he traveled.

With his Power Iskander might have warded himself against the sharp bite of the whining wind. But this would have drained his strength, which he wisely concluded would be better conserved against unforeseen perils. So, instead, knowing that his exertions of maneuvering the team and sled would soon warm him, he held fast to the handles of the vehicle and urged the lupines on.

The animals were highly revered by the Iglacians and had been domesticated and bred by them for centuries. Neither wolf nor dog, but something more than each, the massive beasts stood fully three feet tall at the shoulders and were deep-chested and powerfully muscled. Because of their great size and strength, they were capable of covering long distances in a single day, even while hauling a sled as heavily laden as Iskander's. Almost without exception lupines were snow-white and blue-eyed, although rarely there appeared a melanism, such as the lead lupine of the team was—black-furred and silver-eyed, an anomaly in the tundra, where the species as a whole had originated.

Many Iglacians would superstitiously have shied away from the lead lupine, believing the aberration an ill-omened creature. But Iskander had purposefully chosen it, knowing that its distinct color would make it easier for him to keep it in sight and thus to act quickly should it flounder in a treacherous snowdrift.

So far Anuk, as he had named the animal, had proved a surefooted beast, keen of both eye and intelligence, and Iskander felt assured his faith in it was not misplaced. This was important, as mushers who traveled for hours on end were often prone to hallucinations and so were forced to depend on the lead lupine to guide the team without faltering. Iskander had put the animal through a series of rigorous tests to determine the extent and reliability of its training, instinct, and heart. With flying colors Anuk had passed all the examinations, demonstrating competence and steadfastness. Now, confident in Anuk's abilities, Iskander gave the lead lupine its head, and the team surged swiftly northward, the long miles he traveled eventually fading into even longer days as the Wheel of Time turned implacably on.

I have never known such feelings of aloneness and loneliness as I knew in those endless days that followed the beginning of my quest for the heart of the Darkness. Though a priest and therefore accustomed to solitude, still, I hungered more than I would have dreamed possible for the company of another Kind. But there was no one.

Though I knew that it was not so, in my mind I frequently imagined that the Wars of the Kind and the Apocalypse had wiped from the face of Tintagel every single Kind except me. It was an eerie, chilling thought; and more than once I almost turned back toward Tovaritch Fortress to reassure myself it still stood, ruled by my family, as it has been for centuries past.

But instead, I forced myself to laugh at my strange fancies; and to compensate for my lack of fellow Kind, I developed a bond with the lupines, especially the melanism, Anuk—little knowing then that he was to save my life on more than one

occasion and to become the truest friend I could
ever have asked for in my many hours of need.

No Kind could have served me better. If ever
there were an animal deserving of the highest
honor and respect, it is he.

—Thus it is Written—
in
The Private Journals
of the Lord Iskander sin Tovaritch

For several weeks afterward, this was the pattern of
Iskander's journey: He rose each morning and
promptly fed, watered, and groomed the lupines,
paying particular attention to the pads of their paws to
ensure that none was cracked or bleeding or had got
tiny stones or shards of ice wedged between them.
This was vital, for without the lupines he would be
forced to abandon his well-provisioned sled, and then
he would surely die. Once he had finished caring for
the animals, Iskander cooked and consumed his own
plain meal, then performed his hasty and limited
ablutions. After that he struck the small hide tent he
carried for shelter and loaded it back onto the sled,
along with the rest of his possessions, all of which he
tied down securely with strong ropes of rawhide. Then
he harnessed the team to the sled and traveled as
many miles as he could—hard miles, empty miles
that carried him farther and farther away from the
world he knew into one he did not.

At what he reckoned—lacking the sun to guide
him—was midday, Iskander paused to rest and to
check the lupines again and to eat a bite of the tough
jerky or the mixture of dried fruit he had stored in one
of his leather pouches. If he were lucky and spied
game, which was scarce, he hunted it, killed it, and
skinned it to supplement his stock of food, which,

though considerable, was not infinite and which, in his ignorance of how long his journey would take, he must ration strictly. Now and then he consulted his crude maps, pieced together from poor remnants of those from the Time Before, to estimate how far he was from the coast of the Sea of Frost, which he must reach before the slow, unpredictable, and thus, to him, dangerous spring thaw. Then he pushed on.

Using torches attached to the sled to light his path, it was not until long after the pitch-black darkness characteristic of the arctic winter had fallen that Iskander stopped for the night. He tended once more to the lupines. Then he pitched his tent and spread within it the pelts that served as his bed and blankets. After that he retrieved his belongings from the sled and settled in for the evening. With the blue fire born of the Power at his command, he heated between his hands the hearthstone he had prudently brought with him, aware he would lack the means to build a normal campfire in the arctic region. Then he prepared his supper, which, unless he had found game, was not unsimilar to his filling but seldom appetizing breakfast.

Sometimes, if he were not too exhausted, Iskander played a solitary game of Captain's Concubine or conversed with the lupines, his only companions. Anuk, especially, he spoke to often, finding more and more reasons as the weeks passed to be glad he had not permitted Iglacian superstition to prejudice him against the melanism—particularly as it was Anuk who warned him of the snow-tiger.

It was one night as Iskander was sliding the lid back into the grooved slots of the rectangular box that held the dice and playing pieces for Captain's Concubine that Anuk nosed open the tent flap and padded inside, his silver eyes glinting eerily in the blue light cast by the glowing hearthstone.

"*I came to warn ye,* khan," the lupine stated telepathically, addressing Iskander by the Iglacian title of lord. "*I have scented a snow-tiger in the distance. It prowls stealthily toward our camp. I sense that it does not seek just to satisfy its curiosity about us, but, rather, has hostile intentions toward us. It is the time of the long winter darkness,* khan, *and as ye have seen, game is scarce in the tundra,*" Anuk reminded him. "*For this reason I believe that the snow-tiger is no doubt hungry —hungry enough to attack a lupine, or even a man.*"

"Ye have done well, Anuk," Iskander praised the animal, reaching for the Sword of Ishtar that, when not riding his shoulders, lay always near at hand. He drew on his sable cloak and slipped into the harness of the leather scabbard. Then, picking up his targe, he said, "Come. Let us go and confront this menace, for at this early juncture of our journey, we can ill afford to lose even one of the team."

At that both man and beast stepped outside into the blackness, each momentarily blinded by the whorls of snowflakes that danced to the song of the wailing wind. Against the small, protective barrier formed by the tent, the rest of the lupines huddled, their thick white fur ruffling with each gust. But as he blinked the snow from his eyes, Iskander saw that none of the team slept. Instead, they stared watchfully into the darkness, their ears pricked forward. Now and then a soft whine or a low growl emanated from their ranks, evidence of their uneasiness. They, too, were aware of the ferocious snow-tiger's proximity.

Normally the creature would not have ventured so close to the camp or thought of trying to bring down a lupine, whose long, sharp canines, powerful viselike jaws, and propensity not only to defend itself aggressively against assault, but also to run in packs effectively discouraged even the most formidable of predators. Still, hunger, especially near-starvation, could be a capricious and thus deadly motivator, Iskander knew.

Slowly, warily, every fiber of his being tensed and poised for action, Iskander began to circle the outskirts of the camp, grateful for Anuk's presence as he searched for the snow-tiger, hoping to take it by surprise. At last Iskander spied it, and even he, who had seen the animals before and so knew what to expect, was taken aback by its size. His breath caught in his throat. Surely it was the biggest snow-tiger he had ever beheld—bigger even than the lupine vigilantly crouched beside him, ready to spring to his defense, if necessary.

The snow-tiger stood over four feet tall at the shoulders. Its long, white-furred body, striped with black, was lean and sinewy with muscle and scarred here and there from past battles, proclaiming it both a fighter and a survivor. The length of the silky white tufts upon its cheeks marked it as being several years old, further evidence that it would not prove an easy foe, as only the strongest and wiliest of beasts lived to any great age in the arctic wastelands. Its azure eyes gleamed in the hazy starlight, and its dagger black talons, outspread for purchase upon the snow, glinted as it padded silently across the white terrain, its cunning apparent in its crafty approach toward the camp. It was clear that had Anuk not been diligently patrolling the camp's boundaries, the snow-tiger might have succeeded in catching Iskander and the lupines off guard.

As Iskander's sable cloak and Anuk's black coat caused them to blend into the darkness, neither had as yet been observed by the snow-tiger. But both knew it was perhaps only a matter of moments before the blustery wind would shift, carrying their scent to the creature's nostrils. Iskander knew he must strike before that happened. Unsheathing the Sword of Ishtar, he swiftly summoned his Power.

Though Cain and Ileana had warned him of the mighty magic the blade possessed, Iskander was unprepared for the blast that rocked him violently as his Power burst from him in a dazzling aura of blue fire, inadvertently keying the weapon—and so suddenly and forcefully that it wrenched free of his iron grasp, spinning away like a silvery catherine wheel into the night. Higher and higher, it tumbled and flew, cutting a spangled arc across the heavens, until finally it righted itself and began to hurtle downward to stab and bury itself, point first, in the tundra. There, it vibrated so wildly that the music of its ringing metal echoed on the wind, and the brilliant light with which Iskander's Power had imbued it scintillated blindingly. At the impact of the sword's driving deep into the frozen earth, snow spewed in every direction, a geyser of crystalline white flakes that caught and reflected the starlight. Then abruptly the snow fell, and the blade stilled and dimmed.

Iskander dazedly became aware that the unanticipated potency of the weapon had knocked him to his knees and extinguished his aura, which would have shielded him from the snow-tiger. Now, unarmed and unwarded save for his targe, he faced the creature melting phantomlike from the blackness to charge straight toward him, fangs viciously bared, claws ominously splayed. In that instant Iskander felt as though he were but a heartbeat from death, and regret that his Time of Passing should prove so ironically untimely filled him.

His senses still reeling from the sword's keying, he had forgotten Anuk, however; and now, with a howl, the lupine bounded forward, a streak of black fur, to meet the snow-tiger's attack. Startled by the appearance of this unexpected opponent, the snow-tiger was unable to check its speed. The two animals crashed head-on, the impact sending them both sprawling. Quickly they regained their balance and, each going for the other's throat, came together in a mélange of fur and teeth and talons.

For a timeless moment Iskander stared at the two creatures, enthralled. The animals were nearly equally matched in size and barbarity, though its razor-sharp claws gave the snow-tiger an advantage the lupine lacked. Seeing this, Iskander recovered his wits and trekked hurriedly across the snow toward his lost sword. The blade had bitten deep into the hard ground, and it was with some difficulty that he yanked it loose. But at last he freed it.

This time, prepared for how the weapon would respond, he called up his Power more slowly, controlling how it welled inside him to surge forth in the protective aura of blue fire. Carefully he guarded against its igniting the sword and releasing the magic with which the blade had been vested by the Custodians of the Citadel of False Colors, whence Ileana had claimed it. Then, the unkeyed weapon and his targe in hand, he turned to confront the snow-tiger.

It was still entangled with the lupine, and such was the fury of their battle that Iskander found it hard to judge which beast, if either, prevailed. Hunks of fur drifted on the wind, and blood stained the snow crimson in patches. Seeing that, Iskander felt a sick hollowness assail the pit of his belly, for he knew that one or both of the creatures must be wounded, and he did not want to lose the lupine, which had surely saved his life. But until the animals broke apart, he dared not enter the fray, lest, with the unfamiliar, magical, and so, to him, as yet unpredictable sword, he accidentally slew Anuk. Chafing at his dilemma, his helplessness to assist the beast that had leaped so promptly to his defense, Iskander edged as close to the conflict as he dared, preparing to seize his opportunity quickly, should one arise.

Their snarls mingling chillingly with the *bain-sidhe*like cry of the wind that split the night, the creatures rolled and grappled their way across the snow, mauling each other unmercifully. The lupine's strength was in its traplike jaws, and with these it ravaged the snow-tiger cruelly. But finally a particularly powerful swipe of the snow-tiger's paw sent the lupine sailing. His every pore tingling with dread and expectation, Iskander moved rapidly to step into the breach.

Fear is a demon, he reminded himself, repeating silently the litany he had learned at Mont Saint Christopher. *It interferes with the processes of the mind so one cannot think clearly or rationally—if at all. I must face the Demon Fear and recognize it for what it is. Then I must conquer it by driving it from my mind and willing myself to concentrate on the Light. I will breathe deeply and think of the Light. I will think only of the Light.*

And so thinking, he advanced toward the snow-tiger. Deprived of its former prey, it gave a piercing shriek and flung itself at Iskander's throat, only to encounter the aura of blue fire that shielded him. The animal yowled with pain as tridentlike tongues of flame exploded at the contact, searing it, leaving a streak of smoldering blackness upon its fur.

Hissing and spitting, the snow-tiger fell back, and this time it did not make the mistake of charging into the blue barrier. Instead, it sought to circle Iskander in order to resume its assault upon the wounded lupine. Swiftly Iskander moved to place himself between the snow-tiger and Anuk; and again the canny snow-tiger, now sensing that Iskander would not be easily vanquished, retreated.

Shouting the Tovaritch battle cry, Iskander lunged forward, blade slashing. The weapon glittered strangely in the night, he realized suddenly, dismayed; for somehow, despite his caution, his Power had keyed it ever so slightly, and now it glowed and hummed with its magic. Pale blue fire crackled along its shining length, corrupted by a faint, ichorous green tinge that he had not anticipated—and that he feared. It was a wrongness in the sword, a holdover from Cain's loath but inevitable warping of its magic, his turning it to the left hand of the Darkness—a legacy of which both Cain and Ileana had been unaware, else they would have forewarned him of it, Iskander knew.

He was momentarily stricken by panic, for he did not know if it was possible for the taint to leach into his own Power, twisting it also to serve the Darkness; and he doubted his ability to fight that terrible threat, as well as the snow-tiger. His Power, while great, was not of the Elements, as Cain's was, but of the Terrestrial. It worked differently from Cain's, which, though not of his doing, was profaned, besides, by the hideous beast within him.

Iskander's brief indecision cost him dearly, for it gave the snow-tiger time to discover a chink in his aura, which he must shift continuously, creating gaps through which to wield his weapon. Not quick enough to maneuver his targe into place to shield himself, he cried out, agonized, as he felt the rake of the snow-tiger's talons tear deeply into his shoulder, bloodying him. The injury filled him afresh with apprehension, for the claws of a snow-tiger were hollow and loaded with a slowly paralyzing venom that resulted in death to its victim. Even now Iskander could feel the fiery sting of his flesh, which told him he had been injected with the snow-tiger's poison; and he knew he must kill the beast quickly so he could deal with the virulent gashes before they proved fatal.

He struck out with his blade, but the blow merely grazed the agile snow-tiger's cheek rather than taking the creature in the throat as Iskander had intended. But even as he cursed the animal's guile, he was forced to admire it, and silently he applauded the snow-tiger as a worthy adversary. Despite his Power, he would need all his intellect and skill to defeat it.

For a moment Iskander considered turning upon the snow-tiger the blue fire at his command, which would permit him to dispatch the beast immediately. Even as the notion occurred to him, he rejected it, however, knowing that the gift of the Power was not meant to be used in such a fashion. Those who so employed it soon found their souls minions of the Foul Enslaver, forfeit to Darkness, and the Way to the Immortal Guardian lost—perhaps forever. It was bad enough, Iskander thought, that he had unintentionally keyed the sword, freeing not only its magic, but whatever bane was Cain's unwilling bequest to it. Even now Iskander felt himself drawing upon the reserves of his Power to counter the balefulness of the blade, and he knew that his strength would soon be drained from him.

He swore at the treacherous snow that hampered his footing, the venom that seeped through his veins, inexorably numbing his body, and the Druswids who had vested Cain with the heinous beast of the Darkness that had befouled the Sword of Ishtar to begin with. Most of all Iskander cursed the snow-tiger, incited by its hunger into encroaching upon the camp and persisting, despite its own injuries, in its attack.

A multitude of deep punctures from Anuk's canines scored its flesh singed by Iskander's aura. Blood oozed and dripped from the right side of its face sliced open by the blade, besmirching the strands of the silky white tuft upon its cheek. Still, undaunted, the snow-tiger advanced.

Now, spurred by desperation, Iskander did not hesitate, but battled with all his might the creature that harried him. Scenting danger in the weapon that glimmered with a malevolent greenish light, the snow-tiger sidled just beyond the sword's reach, as though taunting Iskander. Its blue cat's eyes were narrowed and gleamed slyly, so he could almost see the wheels turning in its head as it contemplated how best to slay him. Because of his Power, Iskander could hear its thoughts in his mind, too, but they were so contorted by hunger, rage, and pain that he could not understand them.

Every now and then the snow-tiger rushed toward him, its mouth gaping so that Iskander could smell the fetid odor and feel the warmth of its breath against his skin. Time and again the animal lashed out with its talons at him, then drew back charily, its long tail undulating like a whip. Iskander knew that if it could, the beast would rend him limb from limb; and to avoid this dire fate, he altered his position constantly, his booted feet skidding and sinking in the snow, so that once or twice he nearly lost his balance and tripped. When that happened, his heart leaped to his throat, for he knew with certainty that if he fell, the snow-tiger would be at his throat before he could blink.

For hours, it seemed, Iskander and the creature stalked each other—while the snow-tiger's poison torpidly saturated his body, and the Sword of Ishtar grew brighter with the rancorous green light, despite how Iskander now fed it with his Power to combat the blight. To his despair he could feel himself weakening. His head spun, his eyes refused to focus properly, and despite the cold, sweat streamed down his face. Little by little, his aura began to dim; and the snow-tiger, sensing his escalating debility, pressed its offense, its paw probing tentatively the blue barrier that shielded him. A shower of sparks erupted at the invasion, and Iskander's circle of warding flickered and flashed wildly for an instant, giving the animal time to find another crevice in his defense. Only his clumsy but instinctive raising of his targe prevented him from being gouged again by the snow-tiger's claws.

They came down brutally upon the light, round buckler, scraping with a nerve-racking screech across the brass of which it was fashioned. At the impact pain shot from Iskander's wrist to his shoulder; and to his dismay the violent blow jerked the targe from his arm, sending the buckler flying. Jolted, he toppled back, landing so hard that the wind was knocked from him. In an instant the snow-tiger was upon him, shrilling horridly as it was scorched by his aura. But now there were too many rifts in the blue barrier for Iskander to seal; and he could feel the weight of the beast pressing him down as it struggled against the circle of warding to gain his throat, its maw yawning, slavering, its teeth poised to strike.

The Sword of Ishtar sang—a death knell—but for whom, Iskander, his nerves stretched taut as thong, was unsure until at last he managed to thrust the blade up, driving it deep into the snow-tiger's massive chest. Celadon light exploded in the night as the malignance of the weapon poured into the creature, making its body and Iskander's aura crackle like fox fire. Blood gushed from the mortal wound to flow in a river of scarlet upon the snow as Iskander quickly snatched the sword free, horrified by the evil that had touched him so briefly during its egress from the blade. The snow-tiger faltered in its steps, as though petrified. Then, a low gurgle emanating from its throat, it collapsed upon him, even as he felt the last dregs of his Power slip away. His aura winked out; and gasping for breath, feeling as though his heart and his lungs were about to burst within him, he flailed about like a madman until he managed to push the heavy snow-tiger off him.

Though some rational part of his being knew that the animal was surely dead, for a moment Iskander feared crazily that the Darkness contained in the weapon had somehow contaminated the snow-tiger so it would suddenly spring to unnatural life. Escape uppermost in his mind, he bounded to his feet, only to find himself impotent to stand. He stumbled forward and sank wearily to his knees, his weight driving deep into the ground the blade he still clutched tightly in his hands. Only his fists gripping the sword's bejeweled hilt then, supporting his body, prevented him from crumpling facedown in the snow.

For a long time after that, Iskander simply knelt there, panting from his exertions and dizzy from the onslaught of the snow-tiger's poison. But finally he somehow compelled himself to rise. With a warrior's instinct (for a priest was taught many things—and not all of them scholarly—at Mont Saint Christopher), he grabbed a handful of snow to wipe the Sword of Ishtar clean of the blood that smeared it, shuddering as he recalled that fleeting moment of incredible despite that had brushed him through his aura. Still, the blade seemed harmless enough now—cold and dark and silent—and Iskander thought he need no longer fear it, unkeyed as it now was. Besides, whatever had possessed it had been banished, he hoped as he sheathed it in its leather scabbard.

After that, lurching on his feet, he made his way toward the fallen lupine. It lay still, oblivious of its surroundings; and for an instant Iskander believed it was dead. But then, relieved, he observed its shallow breathing and knew that it lived—though barely. The snow-tiger's talons had scourged it badly, and like him, it was suffused with venom. Knowing he could not leave it, he hunkered down beside the lupine and, groaning, sweat beading his brow at the effort, hefted the husky beast onto his broad shoulders. Then he staggered toward the tent, pausing only to reassure the anxious team that the snow-tiger was now dead and that Anuk still survived, however feebly.

Once inside, Iskander laid the lupine gently on the pelts that covered the hide floor. Knowing that it was only a matter of time before he, too, fell into a coma born of the snow-tiger's lethal poison, he started to search frantically among his leather pouches for the store of medicines in whose use he was adequately skilled, having been taught various of the healing arts, too, at the monastery.

With mortar and pestle he hurriedly mashed a mixture of tangy winterroot, bitter hoarleaf, and sweet frostberries, which he placed in a pot of snow he set to melt and then boil upon the hearthstone. While the decoction was heating, Iskander uncorked a jar of aromatic healing balm, and after cleansing the lupine's wounds, he spread the soothing salve upon them. Then he treated the lacerations on his own flesh. Once he was done with that, he saw that the herbal infusion was ready; and he poured a generous amount into a cup and drank it little by little while he painstakingly pried open the lupine's mouth and spooned some of the liquid into it, also, stroking the unconscious creature's throat to make it swallow. After that he checked the animal for broken bones and further injuries. One of Anuk's rear legs was swollen with a knot the size of a ptarmigan's egg; but Iskander felt that the limb was only badly sprained, so he rubbed it with cool evergreen oil and wrapped it tightly with a bandage of linen, which he bound with a strip of rawhide.

Only then, knowing there was nothing more he

could do for either the lupine or himself, did he permit himself to give in to the pain and exhaustion that pervaded his body. Moaning, he sprawled head-long onto the pelts spread upon the floor of the tent—and fell into a deep, restless sleep of dreams and delirium, not knowing if he would live or die.

Chapter 4

I do not know how many days I lay frail and feverish, only half conscious, only half alive—too many, I suspected, knowing I must reach the Sea of Frost before the spring thaw. For even in my delirium the urgency of my quest preyed heavily upon my mind; so I did not rest well and frequently awoke, as I sometimes had at the monastery, with a feeling of dread that I had missed some important test upon which the remainder of my LifePath hinged.

In such moments I would rouse myself, only to realize that I was ill, that I had been poisoned by the snow-tiger, and that I lay in my tent pitched upon the tundra and was not in my cell at Mont Saint Christopher at all—though I heartily wished I were, for then I would have had someone to tend to my needs. But I did not. So at such times I would force myself to rise—to treat both Anuk and myself with the healing balm and to dose us each, as well, with the decoction that was the vile venom's antidote and that, even now, I scarcely remember preparing, though I know I must have done so, else we would surely have died.

Every so often one of the other lupines would enter the tent to check on us. But there was little they could do for us other than to guard the camp to ensure that no other predator wreaked havoc upon us, and to keep us warm with their bodies so we did not freeze to death when the heat of the hearthstone, unrenewed by my Power, finally dissipated. This, however, they did—commendably—which shall explain my sentimental actions toward them later, which otherwise must undoubtedly be thought by all Iglacian mushers as foolish in the extreme.

—Thus it is Written—
in
The Private Journals
of the Lord Iskander sin Tovaritch

ISKANDER AWOKE ON THE MORNING OF THE THIRD DAY, weak, disoriented, thirsty—and quite surprised to find both himself and Anuk alive. It seemed a miracle to him that they had survived, alone, poisoned, and helpless on the tundra as they had been. Slowly he got to his feet, wincing at his unsteadiness, at the soreness of his shoulder, and at the bitter aftertaste of the decoction that fouled his mouth. He felt unclean, and his nostrils twitching, he knew he smelled so. His muscles, joints, and leather garments were stiff with cold.

Squatting before the hearthstone at the center of the tent, he muzzily summoned his Power, which responded lethargically but well enough that he was able to heat the smooth, round rock. Presently a warm blue glow filled the tent. He was reluctant to leave it. But seeing that Anuk slept peacefully, Iskander knew that his first concern must be the rest of the lupines. Shivering at the gust of chill wind that assailed him as he pulled open the tent flap, he stepped outside, expecting to find that the team was half starved or else had deserted him.

To his relief he discovered that neither was the case. The lupines had, in fact, fended quite well for themselves in his absence. They had found the carcass of the snow-tiger and dragged it to the camp to feed upon, and several small bones Iskander recognized as belonging to ptarmigans and snowshoe rabbits lay scattered about as well. The team had even, he saw, brought down a hreinn, proof that they had ranged far in their hunting—and still returned to him.

Although he knew they had been well trained to serve their master, he was nevertheless deeply touched by their loyalty; for under the circumstances he would not have blamed them if they had instinctively reverted to the wild and run away. He praised them lavishly, then somewhat ruefully wished he had not as they all began to communicate with him at once, boasting of their deeds and inquiring as to his and Anuk's health. Their silent chatter echoed cacophonously in his still-clouded mind, and at last he was forced to beg them to desist. This they did, pink tongues lolling and white tails wagging with amusement and relief when one of the bolder lupines among their ranks remarked wryly that Iskander must indeed be cured of the snow-tiger's venom since he was starting to sound more like his usual self. Even he was compelled to smile at that, and seeing his good humor, the team erupted with a short round of their notorious barking, which sounded amazingly like laughter.

Little remained of the snow-tiger, Iskander saw. But the hreinn was a fresh kill, hardly cold, though he thought that the lupines must have hauled it some distance back to the camp. The carcass was as yet untouched, so his first order of business was to skin and butcher it and to give each of the team a generous portion of the raw meat, which they ate hungrily. The hide he rolled up and set aside for tanning later, along with the hreinn's majestic antlers, from which he would fashion tools and other useful items. Then he scooped up a pot of snow he would place upon the hearthstone to melt so the lupines would have fresh water, and returned to the tent.

Anuk was now awake and well enough to consume ravenously his share of the hreinn meat and to gulp a considerable amount of tepid water. He still limped slightly on his injured leg, but he determinedly pronounced himself fit to travel; and Iskander, wanting neither to hurt the lupine's pride nor to delay their journey any further than necessary, agreed they would start out at midday.

Iskander heated more water and, in the warmth of the tent, quickly stripped off his clothes, which were soiled with layers of dried sweat from his fever, as well as the stains of his travels. He sponged off his body, thought about shaving off the grizzly beard he had grown during the past several weeks, then decided against it, knowing that it protected his face from chafing in the arctic wind. Then he changed into clean garments, after which he felt much better. He cooked and devoured several chunks of the hreinn meat, along with some of the mixture of dried fruit in his leather pouches. Then he set about striking the camp.

What Iskander could carry of the hreinn meat, he loaded onto the sled. The rest he carefully wrapped in hide and buried in a hole that, with his shovel, he dug deep as he was able in the tundra. He marked the spot with a piece of wood that he had hacked from the sled. This was the pattern he would follow from now on, gradually shortening the sled as his supplies were used up, and caching what provisions he could along the way, so they would be there, waiting for him, to keep him alive during his return trip should he survive his quest.

Iskander still felt a little light-headed and shaky.

But like Anuk, he refused to allow this to deter him, though he suspected he would need to halt earlier than usual for the night. Still, even a few miles of progress was better than none, he thought grimly, ignorant of how long he had lain delirious in the tent and worried that perhaps even as much as a week had passed. If need be because of his weakness, he would tie himself to the sled so he wouldn't fall off, he decided. He simply must press on.

Once the tent and the rest of his possessions were packed and strapped onto the vehicle, Iskander harnessed the team to it, pausing to give Anuk a friendly scratch behind the ears and to reassure himself that the lupine really was in a condition to travel. He had rubbed Anuk's leg again with the evergreen oil and rewrapped the linen bandage tightly to help brace the limb. But still, he fretted about the lupine's placing so much weight and stress upon it so soon. Iskander insisted on being informed at once if Anuk found himself too tired to go on.

Then softly, his heart filled with deep appreciation for the lupine's quick and courageous defense of him against the snow-tiger, Iskander said, "Thank ye for saving my life, Anuk."

"As ye surely saved mine, khan," the lupine replied gravely, not unaware of all that Iskander, despite his own delirium, had done for him.

Unbeknown to both man and beast, it was the beginning of the strong bond they would forge between them, never to be broken so long as they lived. After giving Anuk another affectionate pat, Iskander took his place at the rear of the sled, positioning his booted feet carefully upon its long runners.

"Mush!" he cried, cracking his whip above the heads of the team.

The lupines broke into a steady trot, and the sled slid inexorably northward across the tundra.

And so the days passed, one much like another, until they numbered a great many on my tally stick, upon which I kept track of them; for this, too, was a part of my duties on my expedition. We of the six Eastern Tribes knew little of the northernmost tundra of Iglacia or of the Isles of Desolation or of Persephone, the northern polar cap, which lay beyond the Sea of Frost; and these I was to map more accurately as to distance and terrain.

The farther north I journeyed, the clearer it became to me that the maps with which I had been provided upon undertaking my mission were woefully inadequate, the miles miscalculated, the few solitary landmarks misplaced. Thus, to guide me, I had to rely principally upon the polestar, called the Prophet, that rose like a silver beacon each evening in the night sky.

Sometimes when the wind blew fiercely and the snow flurries fluttered like the Weeping Wraiths few but the Chosen ever glimpsed, the polestar was scarcely visible, and I longed wistfully, if a trifle guiltily (though I did not think it mechanical), for a device of the Old Ones—a compass, I recall its being named—which I had read about in the archives of the library at Mont Saint Christopher, and which had possessed some magnetic property that had enabled it to tell direction. But this, like so many other things since the Wars of the Kind and the Apocalypse, was now lost to us. So I was compelled to make my way north as best I could—and to hope that the path I chose to travel was the right one.

—Thus it is Written—
in
The Private Journals
of the Lord Iskander sin Tovaritch

The day arrived at last when Iskander's sled was short enough that he no longer needed the entire team to pull it. To another Iglacian musher this would have meant one thing—and one thing only: It was time to kill the two rearmost lupines, whose meat the musher would himself eat or cache for future consumption, as lupines would not feed on their own kind. In his head Iskander knew that this was the wise and practical course of action, particularly with game being so scarce and his provisions decreasing daily. But when he thought of how faithfully the lupines had behaved, his heart rebelled against the age-old custom.

As he led aside the two rearmost lupines, they whined anxiously. Iskander gazed into their sad, frightened eyes and realized that somehow Tyki and Sitka, as he called the two, were aware of the fate that befell lupines on a long trek. Thus the fact that they had not abandoned him when they had had the chance was even more moving. He knew then that he could not slay them.

"Do ye think ye can make your way back to Tovaritch Fortress?" Iskander asked the two quietly as he knelt beside them.

"*Yea,* khan," they responded as one, the hope that lighted their eyes tugging at his heartstrings.

"Then I would like ye to carry some messages home for me," he announced. "Wait here."

Iskander strode to the tent, where, with quill, ink, and parchment, he wrote three letters—a loving missive to his parents to let them know he was well (he saw no reason to worry them by telling them of the snow-tiger's attack); a report to Cain on the progress of his quest, as well as the difficulties he had encountered, including the affliction of the Sword of Ishtar; and a brief description to the Lord Tobolsk, the King of Iglacia, of all he had learned of the northern tundra thus far during his travels, also enclosing a map, upon which he sketched, as best he could determine, the route he had taken to this point. Then, in case one set of letters was lost, Iskander made a copy of each of the three scrolls. When he was finished, he rolled them up and sealed them with hot white candle wax, into which he pressed his signet ring, which bore both his initials and the Tovaritch coat of arms. Then he went back outside, where he securely tied one set of parchments each about the necks of the two lupines.

"Ye have served me well, Tyki and Sitka," Iskander told them. "Now, serve me likewise in this, also: The messages ye carry are important. See them safely delivered to Tovaritch Fortress."

"Have no fear, khan," Tyki answered soberly. "We are not ignorant of the fact that ye have broken a long-standing tradition of Iglacian mushing by granting us our lives, for which we are most grateful. We shall not fail ye in this, your last request of us. So long as I or Sitka survive, your messages will reach Tovaritch Fortress."

"Then may the Light be with ye on your journey," Iskander said.

"And with ye, also, on yours, khan, wherever it may lead ye," Sitka replied.

With those words of parting, the two lupines headed southward at a steady lope. Iskander watched them silently until minutes later they disappeared from sight, swallowed up by the veil of snow that drifted across the land.

At least if he did not live to fulfill his mission, he had done something useful by sending home the detailed accounts of his travels, he thought. He hoped that the two lupines did indeed reach Tovaritch Fortress, even as he remembered that none of the strong, swift messenger-hawks dispatched by Cain and Ileana from the West had ever arrived at their destinations of Mont Saint Christopher and Mont

Saint Mikhaela, leading the Druswids to believe that Cain and Ileana were dead.

At the memory of what his best friend and that friend's wife had suffered the past three years, a shadow momentarily darkened Iskander's visage. At least he had not been sent unsuspecting to his fate, unaware of the obstacles he would face. At least he had been given time to prepare for his quest, to assemble the team of lupines that, with their bravery and dedication, had more than proved their worth. They were not Kind, but even so, he could not have asked for any better companions, he thought.

But to the gladness of his heart, as the days passed, Iskander came to learn that his sparing the lives of Tyki and Sitka had caused the rest of the team to become even more devoted to him. Somehow they all knew that by permitting them to live, he was now forced to ration his stock of food even more stringently than before. Because of this, the lupines were even more diligent in tracking down whatever game was available, and Iskander's fears that he might starve because of his sentiment were soon allayed.

As time marched on relentlessly and the sled grew increasingly shorter, Iskander continued to free the lupines two by two, entrusting each with further messages for delivery to Tovaritch Fortress. By the time he reached the Sea of Frost, only twelve of the team remained. But they were the strongest of the lupines, and he knew he would have need of that strength as he traversed the Isles of Desolation and Persephone, the northern polar cap.

That night Iskander stood for a long time at the edge of the Sea of Frost. To his vast relief the brine had not yet started to thaw in earnest, but was still largely frozen. A hard layer of rime, sparkling like diamonds beneath the stars, encrusted its surface; and as he gazed out toward the Isles of Desolation and Persephone in the distance, he wondered what lay beyond the starlit frost, what waited for him in the West of Tintagel. He did not know. He could only guess, based on his rough maps and the tales of Cain and Ileana.

It was these last that gave Iskander pause, even made him consider yet again, however briefly, forsaking his quest and turning back. He could not even begin to imagine such malignant creatures as Cain and Ileana had described to him. Yet despite his not having beheld with his own eyes the perverted saurians, Iskander knew they were all too real. He had seen the corruption of the Sword of Ishtar; he had felt the terrible evil it had absorbed during Cain's wielding of it against the hideous creatures. Iskander shuddered to think that though the battle of the Strathmore Plains of Finisterre had been won, perhaps the war itself had yet to be waged; and he marveled at his own temerity in daring to brave the heart of the Darkness.

As he pondered his mission, Sister Amineh's outburst when he had agreed to undertake it rang once more in his ears. *Madness!* Even the icy wind that ruffled the fur of his sable cloak seemed to whisper the word: *Maaaaadness, maaaaadness.* Yet were not all Kind, at one time or another, a little mad? he wondered. Was that not what, in the end, had driven them to the Wars of the Kind and the Apocalypse? For what sane mind could have participated in the destruction of so many of the Tribes and their worlds? What sane mind could have condoned the use of the deadly nuclear, chemical, and biological weapons that had brought about universal ruin; the weapons that were, if Cain were right in his speculation, ultimately responsible for the creation of the noxious disease that had lain dormant for so many centuries afterward, then finally burgeoned to bring the mutant UnKind, the SoulEaters, into being? Iskander did not know. It seemed a sacrilege to him to want to lay to waste all that the Immortal Guardian had created, the gifts that the Being had bestowed upon the Kind.

More than anything else it was this that had convinced him to undertake this journey. Iskander knew that, as a True Defender of the Light, he could do no less. Still, he could not help but wonder what fate held in store for him.

He glanced up at the polestar, the Prophet, as though it somehow knew the answers to his many questions. But the silver orb was silent as the Sea of Frost.

Only the wind spoke—and its cold voice offered him no comfort.

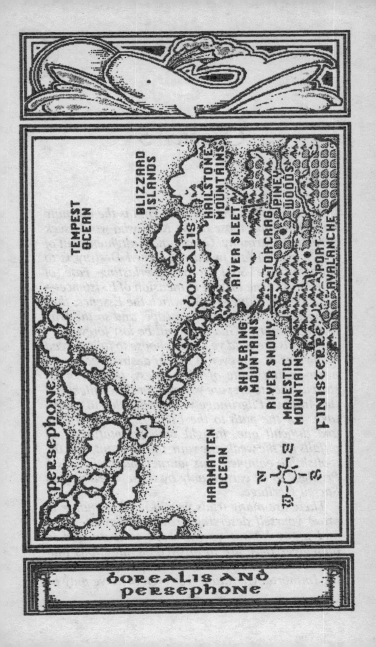

BOREALIS AND
PERSEPHONE

Chapter 5

To be one with the Light Eternal is the ultimate ambition of all those of the Kind who would seek Perpetual Harmony, Grace, and Enlightenment of the Spirit. To fail in this Ordained Destiny is to condemn the Soul to an Everlasting Fate of LifePaths in the Primal Dimension of Existence—the Physical Plane—from which the Essence, thus trapped, will be unable to escape; and so the Way to the Immortal Guardian will be lost forever.

If this is the road ye would choose to follow, read no further. If, however, it is your desire to achieve a never-ending State of Blessedness, then ye must start at once to prepare yourself for the challenge of the Arduous Pilgrimage ye have decided to undertake. For the path to the Light Eternal is a long and difficult one, fraught with temptations and pitfalls for the weak, the vain, the ignorant, and the foolish. To complete this journey successfully is a Privilege to be earned only by those Worthy of its Sacred Heritage.

There are many trials ye will need to endure to prove yourself deserving of this Hallowed Trust, and many lessons ye will need to learn and to remember if ye are to answer the questions that will be put to ye by Rocca, the Keeper of the Gate to the Immortal Guardian. For even there ye may be *turned away, deemed as yet Unfitting to enter the Most Precious Realm of the Light Eternal.*

Ye thus stand warned of the adversities of your task.

If ye are now still ready to attempt your search for the Imperishable Truth and Final Understanding, and to embark upon your travels to the Immortal Guardian of all things Ceaseless and Universal, then ye have already learned Lesson I: Have the courage to try.

—Thus it is Written—
in
The Teachings of the Mont Sects
The Book of Lessons, Chapter Three

IT WAS A THUNDEROUS BOOM THAT ECHOED ACROSS THE tundra, as though the earth had suddenly cleaved in two, that woke him. Startled wide-awake, Iskander leaped from the pelts upon which he lay and rushed outside the tent to see what was the matter.

In the pale band of light cast by the morning sun, he observed what had been concealed from him last night in the darkness: Numerous small cracks marred the rime that encrusted the surface of the Sea of Frost, making it resemble a crazed mirror; and what he had previously mistaken for shadows or snowdrifts were actually slowly widening rifts in the ice. To his horror he found that the sound he had heard had been caused by a huge fissure forming to reveal a length of cold, dark, foamy water. Inexorably the ice was expanding and rupturing.

The spring thaw had begun.

Iskander rushed back to the tent, where he quickly fed, watered, and groomed the lupines. Then he packed his belongings as swiftly as possible, gnawing on strips of jerky as he worked, not bothering to cook breakfast. After he had finished loading his possessions onto the sled, he harnessed the team to it. But instead of assuming his usual position at the back, on the runners, he took from the vehicle a long pike he had brought with him and strode to Anuk's head.

"We have come late to our crossing, khan," the lead lupine noted worriedly. *"It will be difficult—and dangerous."*

"Nevertheless, we *must* try, Anuk," Iskander rejoined, his jaw set as he looked out over the splintering Sea of Frost. He grimaced as another horrendous boom shook the land and a second large schism appeared, waves sloshing over its sides. "But take care. Watch closely where ye tread, lest ye fall through the ice and we all be swept away by the current to drown."

"Yea, khan," the lupine said.

Tentatively they started off, Iskander leading the way. With his long pike he tested every step of the ice to be certain it was solid before he and the team set foot upon it; and he listened attentively for rumblings that would warn him of further disseverances. This made for slow going, to say nothing of the fact that several times he and the lupines were forced to skirt unsafe patches of thinning ice. Still, Iskander and the team persisted, journeying steadily northward. By the light of the moons and the stars, they pressed on even long after nightfall, for Iskander was fearful of camping on the shifting ice; and at last, to his great relief, they reached without incident the first of the Isles of Desolation.

He did not know its name or even if it had ever borne one. But in the tent that night, as, by the light of his few candles and the hearthstone, he updated his maps, he marked the island as "Haven," for to him it was so.

Each morning, the sun shone a little longer as his travels continued—at a snail's pace. Iskander fretted, afraid he would be compelled to abandon the sled before he reached Persephone. This, he knew, would mean leaving behind almost all that remained of his supplies and putting to sea in the skiff he carried. He did not want to embark upon this course of action unless it proved absolutely necessary. The many seas of Tintagel were treacherous, and the boat was small, scarcely ten feet long and three feet wide, composed of a strong but light wooden frame over which hide was tightly stretched and sealed. It was not meant to venture far from shore. But he would need it to traverse the Sea of Clouds, which now he could not count on being frozen.

Across the cracking Sea of Frost, Iskander guided the team from one island to the next, never remaining any longer than necessary upon the thawing surface of the once-solid brine beneath his feet. But finally there came the day when they must cross an especially wide stretch of ice, and he was filled with dread and foreboding when he gazed upon it.

It was clear to him that it was even less stable than what they had already covered, for it was riddled with crevices and with more than one great chasm, where the sea roiled, spewing spume high into the air. It was when they were nearly halfway across that the ominous groaning of an impending fissure started. The hackles of the lupines rose, and low growls echoed down their ranks as a terrible shudder ran through the ice, flinging Iskander to his knees and sending half the team sprawling. With difficulty he scrambled to his feet, glancing about wildly, not knowing in which direction to turn; for all around him the ice shook so that he could hardly keep his balance. A terrific boom sounded, almost deafening him; and to his alarm he saw the ice behind him begin to split wide apart, with a speed he would not have believed possible. Like jagged tridents of lightning serrating the sky, waves swelled across the ice, rushing toward him and the lupines.

His heart pounding furiously in his breast, Iskander raced to the rear of the sled and mounted its runners.

"Mush!" he yelled hoarsely, his whip snaking out above the heads of the team. "Mush! Mush!"

The lupines needed no further urging. Instinctively they took off at a dead run, driven to the precarious speed by the certain doom hard on their heels. The sled bounced and skidded crazily across the ice, but somehow Iskander managed to keep it upright as it slid forward pell-mell. The terrain over which it passed was a blur before his eyes. But he only clutched the handles of the vehicle more tightly and, shouting, spurred the team to an even faster pace, while behind, the ice shattered violently and the arctic sea roared.

The wind rose, draping a veil of snow across the land, blinding him and the lupines. But still, they pressed on, Iskander praying that Anuk would not falter, would not plunge through the deceptive rime ahead into the glacial sea, dragging the rest of the team and the sled with him. But some sixth sense seemed to guide the lead lupine like a beacon as it shot across the quaking ice, zigzagging to avoid snowdrifts and rime of which it was intuitively suspect.

Behind, the tremendous cracking filled the air. But, all his concentration riveted on controlling the sled, Iskander dared not glance around to see how far they were from the crevasse that yawned toward them rapidly, intent on swallowing them whole. His blood thrummed in his ears. His hands were numb from the cold and gripping the handles of the sled so fiercely. Once or twice, when it hit a particularly rough patch of ice, he nearly lost hold of the vehicle completely. But gritting his teeth, he clenched his fists even more tightly around the handles and, somehow, hung on.

Just beyond, narrowing his eyes against the flurrying snow, Iskander could see that the terrain inclined, as though a colossal white turtle shell sat upon the ice. The shape was both familiar and welcome, for to his vast relief, he knew they approached yet another island. Moments later the team bounded up the rise, and jarringly the sled struck hard ground. The impact was such that it sent the vehicle careening wildly, and Iskander could no longer govern it—or even retain his grasp upon it. Pitched off, he tumbled headlong onto the frozen earth just before the sled turned over and crashed into a snowbank, snapping not only the ropes that secured his supplies but several lengths of harness, also, as the team was wrenched to a sprawling halt.

After a time, trembling from the aftermath of his horrific ride, Iskander stood unsteadily, his knees nearly buckling beneath him as he spied the enormous schism that stretched clear to the island, where whitecapped waves now broke against the shore. His belly heaved as he realized that had the island been a few more yards distant, he and the lupines would have been engulfed by the Sea of Frost.

The team got to their feet, creating a misty white cloud around them as they shook the snow from their thick fur coats, then stood motionless, waiting patiently for Iskander to untangle them from the snarl of harness.

"That was a close call, khan," Anuk observed as Iskander approached.

"A *very* close call," Iskander agreed, breathing hard and rubbing his fur-mittened hands together briskly to restore their circulation, "and I'm of no mind to suffer another today. After the harrowing experience we've just been through, we deserve a rest. Besides, I've got to repair the harness. So, despite that we've some hours yet till twilight, we'll make camp now. See that sizable land mass in the distance, just beyond that last stretch of rime?" He pointed northward to where huge cliffs of snow towered like the battlemented walls of a castle. "That's Persephone. By my reckoning, we can be there by noon tomorrow—and right now that's soon enough for me."

Once Iskander had finished freeing the lupines, he tossed aside the lengths of broken harness, then turned his attention to the sled, from which his neatly loaded provisions had been sent flying when it had smashed into the snowbank. Sighing heavily, he bent first to gather up his scattered supplies, carefully inspecting each leather pouch to make sure its contents were undamaged. Of primary importance was his store of medicines, which he was relieved to find intact. After that he examined the skiff and was dismayed to discover that one of the sled's runners had somehow punched a hole in the side of the boat. He would have to mend that. Fortunately he had plenty of cured hide that could serve for a patch, and he also carried a small jar of pitch for sealing purposes. The sled itself was unharmed. Panting at the effort, Iskander righted it and, so it would not be swept away by the incoming waves, dragged it farther up the slope of the island's rough shore. Then he set about pitching the tent.

I fixed both the harness and the skiff, and after—thankfully—crossing without difficulty the last stretch of ice, we came finally to Persephone, the northern polar cap. Here, too, was evidence that the long winter darkness was ending and that the spring thaw was under way. Massive bluffs of snow loomed above us, and periodically great banks would slide into the Sea of Frost, so geysers of snowflakes and spindrift sprayed high into the air. I was overwhelmed by the sight, and I felt myself small and insignificant in the face of this colossal upheaval upon the earth.

I shortened the sled again and loosed two more of the lupines. Without the harness and sled to encumber them, they would be able to traverse safely the Sea of Frost, I felt sure. For like polar bears, lupines are strong swimmers and well protected from the chill of the arctic brine by their thick fur and a wide layer of fat beneath; and despite the spring thaw, there would still be plenty of ice floes for them to rest upon in the sea if they tired. From the ice floes as well, the freed lupines could catch fish and other small sea creatures to eat along the way, so neither would go hungry, either.

Before the two left I wrote more messages to be dispatched home. Then, as I had all the rest, I thanked both lupines for serving me so well, and I bade them have a safe journey.

After that I harnessed the others to the sled; and after searching for a short while, we found a natural track that led up to the top of the snowy ridges. The going was rough, but my faithful team did not fail me; and at last I stood upon the uppermost shelf of the cliffs, whence I could see for miles in every direction.

I am not ashamed to admit that an immense feeling of pride and triumph swelled within me then. I was, so far as I knew, the first Kind to set foot upon Persephone since the Wars of the Kind and the Apocalypse centuries past; and for one *utterly thrilling moment, I felt myself supreme in all the world.*

—Thus it is Written—
in
The Private Journals
of the Lord Iskander sin Tovaritch

Before setting out across Persephone, Iskander buried another hoard of food and marked it with a stake taken from the sled. From now on he must ration his provisions even more strictly, he knew, in case he survived his quest and was not able to obtain adequate supplies in the West before starting home. He felt he would be wise to prepare for the worst.

Other than his limited food supply, Iskander had no reason to hurry now, so he was able to travel on in easier stages. He headed west, keeping always within sight of the coast, as he could not afford to lose his sense of direction in the interior region of the northern polar cap. Besides, he did not know what he might find in the inward reaches of Persephone. Janus, the southern polar cap, was rumored to be unstable, and so it was forbidden to trespass there. But for all he knew, ancient folk lore might have confused the two polar caps. It might, in reality, be Persephone that was capricious and therefore dangerous.

After several days of trekking, Iskander, much to his surprise, spied below him a herd of vanillan-seals lolling upon the snowy beach. Knowing that this was too good an opportunity to pass up, he slipped down the bluffs to the shore, where, with the unkeyed Sword of Ishtar, he slaughtered three of the unsuspecting animals. He skinned and butchered the carcasses, carefully wrapped the meat of one in its hide, then buried and marked it. The meat of the other dead seals he laid upon one of the two remaining white pelts and dragged to the top of the ridge, where he cut several large chunks for the lupines, who, like him, were on short rations and so tore ravenously into the sweet-flavored flesh. Then Iskander cooked and ate some of the tender, succulent meat himself. After that, retrieving the pelt he had left below, he loaded both skins and the remainder of the meat onto the sled. He would not have to worry about food now for many days. His spirits lighter than they had been since the beginning of his expedition, he considered the unexpected vanillan-seals a fortuitous omen.

Indeed, his trip did seem to go more smoothly after that. His only trouble was that the maps he had were so poor that he was uncertain how far he must circle Persephone before putting to sea in his small boat, in order to reach the continent of Montano. The islands off the coast of the northern polar cap all looked one much like another, and many were not even noted on the maps. He dutifully added and marked them, as well as making whatever corrections were necessary to the rest; but of course this was of no help to him currently. In the end he decided that when he was down to a month's worth of supplies, he would take to the sea.

However, it was but some days later, when the sled became so short that he was forced to turn the skiff sideways to carry it, that Iskander knew he could not go much farther by land. He had released all but the last two lupines, and what remained of his food would not adequately feed him and them both much longer. He would have to turn them loose and haul the sled himself to conserve his provisions. But although the female, Baklova, took off at once, Anuk stubbornly refused to depart.

"Nay, khan, *I will not leave ye,"* the melanism declared fiercely. *"The arctic is a harsh land in which to try to survive, especially for a man alone. Nor do ye*

know for certain what awaits in the West for ye. Ye may have need of a friend ye can trust. I would be that friend, khan. Please. Do not send me away."

Iskander was deeply touched by the lupine's loyalty; and in truth, he knew in his heart that he would be glad of Anuk's company and protection. Still, he warned, "There is not much left to eat, Anuk—and the worst is yet ahead of us. In the end ye may be sorry ye stayed."

"Together we will manage somehow, ye and I, khan," the lupine insisted, *"and no matter what, I would never come to regret my decision to continue in the service of one who deliberately broke with the tradition of Iglacian mushing to spare the lives of me and my team—at the risk of his own."*

"Well, then, let us not stand here all day, Anuk," Iskander said gruffly to conceal his emotions. "Come. Together we will pull the sled as far as we can before we must take to the sea."

And so it was that man and beast trudged on; and though the vehicle was heavy, its weight seemed lighter for their sharing of it.

But all too soon there came the day when it was clear that if they were to have enough food to reach the continent of Montano, they must abandon the sled and put to sea. Iskander buried and marked the last of what supplies he felt he could safely spare. Then he cut blocks of snow from the frozen earth until he had a hole large enough into which to place the sled. The blocks themselves he used to shelter the vehicle, so when he left it, it was contained in a crude square igloo. After that he dragged the skiff down to the coast and loaded it. Then he and Anuk climbed aboard, and Iskander raised the small sail. Within moments they were under way upon the Sea of Clouds.

Afraid to venture too far from shore, they hugged

the islands that ringed Persephone and that, according to Iskander's maps, stretched to Montano. So long as they kept the islands in sight, he and Anuk would come eventually to their destination, he hoped. Still, the arctic current was swift, and the ice floes that often impeded their progress did little to assist him in steering the boat. Both the wind and the spindrift were bitterly cold as well. More often than not soaked and chilled to the bone, Iskander came to feel that he would never be warm again. Miserable, he and Anuk huddled within the confines of the tent Iskander had managed to partially erect at the stern of the skiff, only the blue fire of the hearthstone preventing them from freezing to death.

It was some days later when, to Iskander's horror, they were caught in the grip of a southerly current too powerful for them to battle. Helpless, they could do naught but watch, stricken, as they were carried out beyond the Sea of Clouds into what Iskander realized must surely be the Tempest Ocean. His heart sank, for he felt then that they were inevitably doomed. Strong waves lashed the boat, threatening several times to capsize it. But somehow it miraculously remained afloat, drifting rapidly across the ocean.

For miles in every direction, Iskander could see nothing but water. Then, much to his surprise and relief, a few days afterward there appeared on the horizon a chain of islands so tiny that he did not wonder they were not marked on his maps. Grateful for this prospective salvation, he made hastily toward the islets, thinking that perhaps they were part of the larger chain that stretched to Montano. He spied a giant land mass far off in the distance, which seemed to confirm his speculation, and he decided he must have trekked farther westward around Persephone than he had realized.

The farther south they traveled, the warmer the

temperature got, too, though it was still too cold for comfort. But Iskander felt that he could bear anything now that the end of his voyage looked to be in sight. As before, hugging the coastline, he followed the islets southward.

He and Anuk had nearly reached the huge land mass when the storm struck. It blew up without warning, the dismal grey day turning in an instant, it seemed, even darker and drearier. With a howl the wind rose, catching the waves and hurtling them violently against the skiff, nearly swamping it. With each forceful gust the boat soared upon the foamy crests, then swept forward into the troughs of the sea. Iskander and Anuk could do nothing but press themselves flat against the bottom of the vessel and try to keep from being washed overboard.

The tent was gone, carried away by the initial onslaught of the squall, as was the slender mast, snapped in two by the roaring wind; only tatters of the small square sail remained. And though Iskander had strapped the provisions down tightly, now they, too, were ripped from the skiff—torn from the thongs that bound them and pitched helter-skelter into the roiling ocean. His two wooden water casks bobbed like corks upon the swollen waves. His many leather pouches streamed like flotsam across the sea.

Gargantuan forks of lightning split the firmament. Thunder boomed like some titanic hammer upon an even bigger anvil, and rain pelted unmercifully from the bloated black clouds massed in the heavens. Iskander held tightly to Anuk and the side of the boat—and prayed with all his might for deliverance as they were flung hither and yon by the fury of the tempest.

Then suddenly a horrendous wave towered above them, a wall so great that Iskander knew that it had death written on it. For a terrible eternity it hung over them, poised like an executioner's ax, before it smashed down, driving them fathoms deep, it seemed, beneath the ocean's surface. Dimly, as though from far away, Iskander felt both Anuk and the skiff wrenched from his grasp. Then the water closed over his head, filling his lungs to bursting, and he knew nothing more.

MORNING STAR

*Beyond the
Starlit Frost*

Chapter 6

*It was I who found the stranger—and perhaps
the Immortal Guardian, in Its Infinite Wisdom,
meant it to be so. I do not know. I know only that
when first I saw him, my heart turned over in my
breast; for though I knew that others, like myself,
outside the tribe of the giants existed, except for
Ulthor's wife, Syeira, the Nomad, I had seldom
before with my own eyes beheld such a one.*

*I shall never forget the sight of the stranger—a
man—lying there upon the snowy beach, more
dead than alive, cast up by the storm from the
depths of the sea. He was still wet with brine, so it
looked as though he were wrapped in a cocoon of
snowflakes; and because of the many fur garments
he wore, I could see naught of him but his face. But
despite its pallor, this was so beautiful to me that
for a moment I believed I must gaze upon some
ancient, pagan god, no mortal Kind at all; for
between his black brows was set the kiss of the
heavens, a strange Tyrian-crimson sunburst, like
no mark I had ever before seen upon man or
woman. Surely this alone was proof of his favored-
son status, I thought.*

*His long, shaggy hair was black as a midnight
sky during the seemingly endless dark time of the
winter, with two unusual but striking wings of*

silver at the temples. Like ravens in flight, his black brows swooped above his shuttered eyes fringed with black lashes so long and thick that they cast crescent smudges against the high bones of his lean cheeks. His proud, straight nose looked as though it had been chiseled from granite, without a single flaw. Beneath was set his full, sensual mouth, lips slightly parted, as though he yet breathed, I realized suddenly, praying that it was so.

Spellbound with wonder, I slowly knelt beside him and, after turning him over, pressed my head to his broad chest, relieved to hear the faint beating of his heart. It seemed a miracle to me, but somehow he was still alive. I did not know why I should be so glad of that, he being a stranger to me. But still, an immense joy filled me at finding that he lived. For some unknown reason I felt that his survival was an auspicious omen.

Yet even I did not know then how, as a tiny stone tossed into a stream sends its ripples to the farthest shore, the stranger's life was to touch my own—so inevitably, so intricately, and so irrevocably, changing it forever, so I should never again be the same.

—Thus it is Written—
in
The Private Journals
of the Lady Rhiannon sin Lothian

The Western Shore of Borealis, 7275.4.38

EVER AFTERWARD RHIANNON OLAFURSDAUGHTER WAS TO think how fortuitous it was that with the ending of the long winter darkness and the coming of the spring thaw, she and her brother, Yael, had gone west into the Shivering Mountains to hunt not only for fresh game, but for the medicinal early blooming wildflowers and herbs that grew only during the spring, in the cracks and crevices of the rocky crags.

It was from her vantage point upon the westernmost peak that Rhiannon chanced to spy the solitary man who lay so still upon the beach far below; and blowing her hunting horn to summon Yael, she began to make her way down to the shore, a frown knitting her brow as she wondered at the identity of the prone figure. Whoever it was, she thought he was surely hurt or ill or perhaps even dead. Yet she was puzzled, too, for except for her and Yael, she knew of no Boreals this far west; and though she had observed the man from some distance away, which she knew had made him seem smaller, he had, even so, not appeared to her to be a giant.

Perhaps he was a Finisterrean trapper and trader, Rhiannon mused, though if so, she could not imagine how he had come to wind up on the coast; for after passing through the Groaning Gorge of the Majestic Mountains, he ought to have traveled east to Port Avalanche or Torcrag. Still, it was possible he had lost his way, she supposed.

But at last, as she approached the man lying upon the beach, Rhiannon saw at once that he was unlike any of the tribes she had so rarely seen before. His clothes were of hides she did not recognize, and as she noted the damp brine that encrusted his garments, she realized that the man had come from the sea. Further evidence of this was to be found in the wreckage that strewed the shore, the remains of some sort of a small craft, she judged.

Slowly Rhiannon drew near and knelt beside him, marveling at his black-and-silver-bearded visage. He was so handsome that for a moment her breath caught in her throat. Tentatively she touched him, turned him, laid her head upon his chest to discover that he lived. An odd, unexpected happiness welled within her.

Urgently Rhiannon blew her hunting horn again, wishing that Yael would hurry. Then she began to examine the unconscious man more thoroughly, gently peeling back the layers of his furs, so foreign to her. She had just placed her hands upon his body to probe for internal injuries when a ferocious snarl shattered the silence. Alarmed, she glanced up to find herself staring into the face of what she thought must be the largest timber wolf she had ever seen. Her heart leaped in terror. Cautiously she rose to a half crouch and began to back away, dropping her wooden trug filled with wildflowers and herbs, her hand inching its way to the morning star she carried at her waist.

Still growling threateningly, the animal warily advanced, black fur bristling, silver eyes gleaming. But to Rhiannon's confusion it made no attempt to attack her. Instead, it moved toward the man and slowly lowered its head to his. Horrified, she thought then that the beast meant to rip the man's throat out, and she jerked her morning star from her belt, poised to lunge to his defense. But then, much to her surprise, she heard the creature whine anxiously, and as she watched, stunned, it nuzzled the man tenderly, licking his face and wagging its tail.

Rhiannon realized then that incredibly the timber wolf was tame and that it sought only to protect its oblivious master. She tucked her morning star back into her belt. Then, empty hands spread wide, she took a hesitant step toward the animal.

"I intend him no harm," she uttered softly in the language of the Boreals. "Can ye understand me? I want only to help him. There are plants in that basket there that may be of use"—she indicated the wooden trug—"and I have some things in the rucksack I wear upon my back as well. But I must touch him to learn how he suffers. Will ye permit me to do that?"

The beast only stared at her, baring its teeth, another low, menacing snarl issuing from its throat before it turned its attention back to its master. In desperation Rhiannon repeated her words. This time she spoke the Common Tongue, Tintagelese. At that the creature pricked its ears forward alertly; and then, moments later, shocking her to the very marrow of her bones, she heard its voice in her mind.

"Approach, then, khatun," said Anuk (for it *was* he), addressing her by a title she did not understand, the Iglacian word for *lady*. *"But be warned: I shall watch ye closely, and if ye seek to harm the khan, ye shall regret it."*

"It is as I told ye: I want only to help him, so be at ease, timber wolf," Rhiannon replied.

"Timber wolf!" Anuk snapped, indignant. *"Do not number me among the ranks of such commoners as those, khatun! What place is this, then, that ye do not know a lupine when ye see one?"*

"Borealis—where we have no such animal, if such ye be," Rhiannon explained contritely. "Nor have I seen your master's ilk before, either. I apologize if I gave offense. It was not intended, I assure ye. Now, please, allow me to tend to your master, lest he catch his death of cold in those wet clothes."

"Very well. Proceed, then—but remember my warning."

Rhiannon bent once more to her task of caring for the man, peeling away his garments as best she could to inspect him more closely. She was surprised, as she did so, to discover a solid-gold torque about his neck, for despite his godlike appearance, he had not the look of a rich man about him. Perhaps he was a brigand, she thought uneasily, for that might also explain the peculiar tattoo upon his brow. But as he was injured and hardly in a position to harm her, she pressed on with her examination. Some of his ribs were cracked, she surmised, for there was a large, ugly bruise upon his side, to say nothing of the other purplish blue marks that shadowed his body. It was apparent that the ocean had battered him badly. He bore several assorted scrapes and cuts, also. But of most concern to Rhiannon was a deep gash upon his head. It was this blow by whatever had struck him—a piece of driftwood, perhaps—that she felt had rendered him unconscious.

Taking a cloth from her rucksack, she cleansed the wound carefully, then treated it with some healing balm and covered it with a special mountain moss from her basket. After that she bundled the man back up and threw her fur-lined hreinnskin mantle over him in an effort to warm him.

By then her brother had arrived. At Yael's appearance the hackles of the lupine rose again, and it sprang from where it had been sitting to position itself aggressively between the man, Rhiannon, and her brother. Yael drew up short, startled, as his eyes took in the scene before him. Swiftly, fearing that Rhiannon was endangered, he reached for the huge broadsword at his back.

"Nay, Yael, don't!" she cried. "The beast is tame and belongs to the man. It seeks only to protect him." She turned to the lupine. "That is Yael, my brother," she elucidated. "He will hurt neither ye nor your master, I promise. If ye will permit it, we will take your master to Torcrag, the dwelling place of our tribe, where our healer can care for him. He needs warmth, else he will become frostbitten; perhaps he will even die. Little as it was, I have done all I can for him here."

"All right," Anuk agreed, though reluctantly. He was not sure he trusted the unknown woman, but she *had* treated the *khan;* and besides, the lupine saw no other practical options at this point in time for him or his master. It was as the woman had said: If the *khan* did not have warmth, and soon, he might die. *"Tell your brother he may join us. But tell him also that I shall watch him as closely as I watch ye. With my very life will I guard the* khan, *if need be."*

"I understand," Rhiannon rejoined. "We are strangers to ye, and therefore, ye are naturally suspicious of us. So would I be, too, were I in your place. But I give ye my word of honor that ye shall not be ill treated among our tribe."

With that she beckoned to Yael, and he circumspectly approached, keeping a prudent distance from the lupine.

"Ye talk to the—to the beast," he observed uneasily, frowning.

"Yea"—she nodded—"and somehow I understand it when it talks back, though its voice is silent and I hear its words only in my mind. Such a thing has never happened before. But though I suppose that it must have something to do with the strange Power I possess, I must confess I am glad of it in this instance, for the beast would not have allowed me to touch the man otherwise; and as ye can see, he is near death. Yael, do ye think ye can carry him to the sled? We must get him to Torcrag as quickly as possible."

"No problem," her brother grunted. "From the look of him, he's scarcely half a foot taller than ye and probably weighs but half a stone more. Washed up from the sea, did he? I wonder who he is and whence he came. Did the—did the beast . . . say?" he asked awkwardly, loath to refer even indirectly to her Power, which remained a difficult subject between them.

"Nay"—Rhiannon shook her head—"though it calls him the *khan,* a word in some strange language I have never before heard, but that from the context I presume must be a title of some sort. Perhaps it means chieftain," she conjectured, "for the man bears an odd mark upon him, and though 'tis true 'tis no outlaw's brand I have ever seen, he may be a reiver, even so. The beast refers to its own self as a lupine. It does not comprehend Borealish, but speaks the Common Tongue—after a fashion."

"Well, perhaps Ulthor, who has traveled far and wide, will know the language and thus the man's origin and caste, if the beast cannot or will not reveal them. Still, scoundrel or nay, he's no threat to us in his condition. Come. Let us go. Twilight falls, and we have lingered overlong as it is."

So saying, Yael lifted the unconscious man up easily in his arms and carried him to the sled, which was some distance away, at the foot of the mountains. Rhiannon and Anuk followed in her brother's wake.

When they reached the sled, Rhiannon saw that while she had searched for wildflowers and herbs, Yael had slain four fat mountain goats; and the woolly carcasses made a comfortable pallet for the man to lie upon. Her brother, too, sensing the man's greater need, parted with his own fur-lined cape, which he tossed over the man, who had begun now to shiver. Then, to prevent him from falling off, she and Yael lashed the man to the stout vehicle.

After that, gathering up its long ropes, her brother hauled the sled toward Torcrag, Rhiannon striding alongside him, while Anuk padded silently, watchfully, behind.

Chapter 7

As might be expected, I was highly confused and disoriented when first I awoke. I did not know where I was or what had happened to me; and for a moment I did naught but lie quietly and try to assemble some order from the chaos in my mind.

I was hurt—badly. That much was evident, for my head pounded excruciatingly, and as I gingerly examined it, I discovered a tender place that caused me to wince fiercely with pain when I probed it. Vaguely, then, I remembered the massive wave that had slammed down upon the skiff, washing both me and Anuk overboard. Struck with sudden concern for my faithful companion, I attempted to rise, glancing around wildly to determine if he had survived and was at hand. But he was nowhere to be seen.

Still, I grasped abruptly that this meant little, for it was clear to me as I surveyed my unfamiliar surroundings that somehow not only my memory, but also my vision had been affected by the blow to my head. I seemed to view things through a vignette, hazily—and distortedly, I thought—for all appeared almost frighteningly out of proportion to what I was accustomed. The simple room that contained me towered above me endlessly, its rafters soaring to the height of five men or more.

107

The rough pallet that served as my bed was huge—it dwarfed me utterly—and the crude table and chairs that sat nearby were the largest I had ever before beheld, as though fashioned for a tribe of titans. I rubbed my eyes and tried hard again to focus them. But still, the room did not change. Groaning at this realization, to say nothing of the painful throbbing in my skull, I fell back upon the pallet, believing I must be delirious with fever—or dead and lying in the great hall of some Keeper.

As I moaned and thrashed upon the pallet, a slight movement in the room attracted my attention; and from the corners of my eyes, I observed then what had previously escaped my notice: Upon one of the enormous chairs was perched what I initially perceived as a child, her piquant face lost amid a glorious mane of hair that blazed like tongues of fire in the sunlight streaming in through an unshuttered window.

Startled from her reverie by the sounds of my stirring, she slid from the chair and walked toward me, and it was with such an otherworldly grace that she approached that I thought: Yea, I am dead, and Ceridwen, the Keeper of the Earth, has come to guide me to the Light. . . .

—Thus it is Written—
in
The Private Journals
of the Lord Iskander sin Tovaritch

SHE WAS NEITHER A CHILD NOR A KEEPER. THIS ISKANDER recognized as she drew near and bent over him to press her hand to his brow. Her fingers were as long and slender as a wraith's; her palm was as soft and smooth as the petal of a flower, and her touch was as gentle as the brush of butterfly wings against his skin.

Yet despite all this, her hand was reassuringly tangible —real and kind and womanly—no matter that she herself appeared as out of place as he in the oddly disproportionate room. As he stared up at her, Iskander saw she was both young and beautiful, although her features were marred by the frown on her face as she examined him. Unmistakable concern for him shone in her golden eyes, lessening his momentary uneasiness that she might intend him some harm.

"Who—who are ye?" he croaked in the Common Tongue, wondering if she would understand him, and clumsily he clasped her wrist, as though despite her apparent corporealness, she might somehow evanesce.

He was shocked to hear how faint his voice sounded, to feel how weak his body was, as though both had been drained of their strength during his ordeal. Clearly the unknown woman was startled by his speech, his action. Softly she gasped.

"I—I thought ye still feverish," she stammered, in strangely accented but fair Tintagelese. Then she flushed and tried to pull away from him. "But ye are conscious at last. I must fetch Hjalmer, our healer, at once."

"Nay, wait," Iskander rasped. "I beg of ye: Don't go—at least, not just yet. Please. Tell me who ye are, where I am, how long I have been here. . . . Please. Ye cannot know what it means to suddenly awake and find yourself an alien in an alien land."

To his surprise his words had a curious effect upon the young woman. She ceased her struggle to free herself, and a painful expression crossed her pale countenance. Averting her gaze, she slowly sank down upon the edge of the pallet, her long, fiery tresses falling about her in such a way that he could no longer view her face, did not see how she bit her lower lip as she fought to hold at bay the sudden, unexpected tears that stung her eyes. A sweet fragrance he did not recognize wafted from her hair, as though it had been recently washed and scented with the essence of herbs and wildflowers; and for an impulsive moment, Iskander longed to reach out and touch it. But he did not, fearing to frighten her away.

"Very well, then." She spoke again, quietly. "I will answer your questions as best I can. I am Rhiannon Olafursdaughter. 'Twas I who found ye washed up on the far western shore of this land, which is called Borealis. From your appearance and the wreckage that strewed the ocean, it seemed evident that you were asea when your vessel was caught in a bad storm and capsized. Ye were injured and feverish, so my brother, Yael, and I brought ye here, to Torcrag, which is the dwelling place of our people. Ye have been here a fortnight, during which time I and our healer, Hjalmer, have cared for ye. Nay, do not strain yourself by trying to talk further. There will be time enough later for the remainder of your questions, I promise ye. Now I must fetch Hjalmer. He will be most upset if he learns how I delayed in summoning him upon your awakening."

"Nay, wait," Iskander insisted again. "I had a lupine with me—"

"Anuk?" Rhiannon smiled gently, her face lighting up at the thought of the animal she had come to know and grow fond of the past two weeks. "Yea, I know. A most loyal companion. Please. Do not fret about him. He is here and well and has scarcely left your side since your arrival. However, today I managed to persuade him that your life no longer hung in the balance and that he had been cooped up inside Hjalmer's lodge for far too long. Although most reluctant to leave you, he finally agreed to go hunting with my brother. They should return before sundown, and I will send Anuk to ye then. Now truly I must go."

So saying, Rhiannon slipped from Iskander's grasp and swiftly left the lodge, afraid that if she did not escape from it right then, she would break down before the stranger, unable to maintain any longer the composed facade she had struggled to present to him. Her breath came quickly, her heart pounded, and her knees trembled so that she feared she might fall. Once outside, she leaned for support against one wall of Hjalmer's timber abode, her eyes closed as she tried to collect herself.

Her emotions were in such a turmoil that she could scarcely comprehend or contain them. Ever since she had found the stranger, it had been so. He was the first man who was not a giant to whom she had been exposed for any length of time. It was therefore only natural that she should be drawn to him, she thought. But deep down inside, Rhiannon sensed that there was more to it than that. The stranger fascinated her. She wanted to know everything about him—whence he came, who he was, what he had been doing asea in the boat caught in the squall—everything.

Despite the tentative friendship that had developed between her and Anuk the past weeks, she still had learned little of the lupine's master, not even his name, for the beast had continued to refer to him only as the *khan.* But occasionally the chary Anuk had let slip bits and pieces of information that had led Rhiannon to conclude that both the lupine and its master had their origins in the East. The possibility had excited her no end, for she had realized that here at last was an opportunity for her to discover more about her own antecedents, the tribe whence she had sprung. Her desperate yearning to truly belong somewhere had even caused her to seize on the slim chance that the stranger might be able to take her to Vikanglia, her real home; for if he had come from the East, he surely meant to return. That he was quite possibly a brigand she had conveniently thrust from her mind. When she and Yael had arrived home with the stranger, they had learned that Ulthor, who might have known the man's status, had left Torcrag to journey south to Port Avalanche, the coastal stronghold of the giants, where he planned to trade for goods the furs they had trapped that winter. He and those who had accompanied him had yet to return.

The stranger's first words to her had wrenched Rhiannon's heart, for she *did* understand what it meant to be an alien in an alien land. That she shared this bond with him had led her to believe that he would not prove insensitive to her plight were she to voice her innermost feelings to him. Despite the small warning voice at the back of her mind, it was all she had been able to do to restrain herself from blurting out her wistful dreams to him.

That the stranger was both handsome and different from every other man she had ever known only added to his attraction. While he had lain unconscious and she had cared for him, Rhiannon had unabashedly studied him and touched him when tending his hurts. Doing so, she had in some dim corner of her mind become aware that he had unwittingly stirred to life within her some hitherto unknown emotion that both thrilled and frightened her with its scope and intensity.

Today, when she had looked into the stranger's lucid grey eyes, crystalline as the icicles that encrusted the boughs of the pine trees during winter, Rhiannon had suddenly felt a strange warmth, an inexplicable shiver, like nothing she had ever felt before, pervade her body. And when he had taken hold of her, she had been acutely conscious of both his masculinity and how his hand was just the right size to encircle her wrist. She had nearly burst into tears at the poignant realization that at long last here was a man whose being did not diminish hers or make her feel as physically small and fragile as a child and, as a result, incapable of fulfilling his wants and needs.

It had been all she could do to answer the stranger's questions when what she had really wanted was to run away to her hiding place, where she could savor and contemplate in privacy the electrifying emotions that assailed her.

Now, instead, cognizant of her duty as the healer's assistant, Rhiannon forced herself to breathe deeply to steady her erratic pulse. Then, with a calmness she did not feel, she went in search of Hjalmer to tell him the stranger was conscious at last.

Much to my frustration, the woman, Rhiannon Olafursdaughter, had raised many more questions in my mind than she had answered. In some ways I felt more bewildered than ever. Borealis, I recalled from Cain and Ileana's tale of their three-year journey, was a land of giants, which would explain the immensity of all that surrounded me, meaning, to my great relief, that there was nothing wrong with my vision after all.

Yet Rhiannon herself, though a tall woman, could hardly, I thought, be classified as a giant. Indeed, she was no more suited to the massive environs that currently encompassed me than I was. So I was puzzled by the apparent anomaly of her being. Was it possible there was such a being as a dwarf giant? I wondered skeptically. Or had I, because of the severe blow I had suffered to my head, somehow misremembered Cain and Ileana's story? I did not know.

Given my state of mind, it is perhaps understandable that because this paradox was so obvious, it first captured my attention, and that it was not until later, much later, that I thought to ponder what was even more perplexing—Rhiannon's inexplicable knowledge of Anuk's name.

—Thus it is Written—
in
The Private Journals
of the Lord Iskander sin Tovaritch

"She hears me, khan, in her mind, just as ye do," Anuk explained that evening as he lay beside Iskander's pallet, relieved to see his master on the mend. The lupine made the equivalent of a Kind shrug. *"Such communication is not, after all, so uncommon a thing."*

"Not among the Chosen, nay," Iskander slowly agreed. "But according to Cain and Ileana, the West has little, if any, knowledge of the Power. Ileana herself informed me she was frequently looked upon as a witch here; and Cain, of course, because of the beast inside him, was especially feared. I do not understand, then, Anuk, why Rhiannon Olafursdaughter is able to speak with ye."

"No more do I, khan," the lupine said. *"Sometimes a thing simply is."*

Knowing that this was so yet still not satisfied, Iskander questioned Anuk further. But if the lupine had been friendly but reticent toward Rhiannon, she had been equally unconfiding. He could tell his master little more about her, other than that she was not a giant, but a foundling who had been adopted by the Boreals. This explained her physical appearance but nothing else, and so Iskander's curiosity about her remained unsated. He had hoped she would return to the lodge, but she had not. Only Hjalmer, the healer, had come, shaking his head and *tsk*ing his disapproval at spying Iskander attempting—and, to his frustration, failing—to rise from the pallet.

"Here, here, lad!" Hjalmer had harrumphed in his booming voice. "You're not well enough to be up and about! 'Twill be some days yet before ye regain your strength. However, a good, thick stew will go a long way toward that end, and fortunately Yael and your pet there"—he had indicated Anuk—"enjoyed good hunting this day."

Hjalmer's skill with herbs was not just medicinal, Iskander had soon learned. For shortly later an enticing aroma had begun to rise from the stewpot the kindly healer had set to simmering on the hearth and into which he had tossed chunks of fresh meat from Yael and Anuk's kill, along with several vegetables from those stored in the giants' winter larders. Iskander had not realized how hungry he was until the tempting odor had wafted to his nostrils.

Now, with a thick crust of hard bread, he sopped up the last of the gravy in his wooden bowl and popped the morsel into his mouth, chewing contentedly. Then, his stomach filled to bursting from the three helpings of stew he had consumed, he set the bowl aside and continued his conversation with Anuk, wanting to learn as much as possible about their situation before Hjalmer, who was tending another patient, returned to the lodge. It was not that Iskander did not trust the giants, for clearly they meant him no harm. It was simply that he, like Anuk, wisely preferred to exercise caution when faced with the unknown.

They had lost nearly everything they possessed, Iskander discovered, when the skiff had broken apart in the storm. All that remained to them now was the Sword of Ishtar, which had been strapped to Iskander's back, and his heavy pouch of coins, which had been belted to his waist. Though he regretted the loss of what little they had had, Iskander was nevertheless deeply relieved to hear that the two belongings he considered of utmost importance and necessity to his mission were safe. The magic sword was irreplaceable. With the coins he could buy more supplies, which he would have had to do in any event. Even the loss of his crude maps Iskander could not count a real tragedy, as he felt he could re-create them from memory.

Though he chafed at his weakness, at the delaying of his expedition, and at the realization that he and Anuk had not washed ashore upon the continent of Montano as he had hoped, Iskander could only be glad they had been found and cared for by the giants rather than captured by some unheard-of tribe that might have held them prisoner—or worse. He was forced to admit, too, that the urgency that had driven him to reach Persephone before the spring thaw had lessened now that he had left the northern polar cap behind him. Despite his fretting, he knew that the sensible course of action was to stay a while in Borealis, to recoup his strength, replace his provisions, and reconnoiter the land.

This would give him a chance, also, Iskander thought, to learn more about the enigma that was Rhiannon Olafursdaughter. Now that his head had begun to clear and he had learned she was not a giant, he belatedly realized she resembled physically the Vikanglians of the East; and he wondered, both intrigued and excited by the prospect, if it was possible that she was the offspring of a member of a lost expedition dispatched to the West years ago from the East.

In Time Past, in the hope of finding other tribes that had survived the Wars of the Kind and the Apocalypse, both the planetary and the continental governments of the East had sent various ships to the West, about which little had been known. With the exception of the elfin-built *Spice of the Seas* Cain and Ileana had commissioned in the western land of Potpourri to replace their own lost vessel, the *Moon Raker,* none of these ships had ever returned; nor had but a single trace of them or their crews ever been discovered.

If Rhiannon Olafursdaughter should prove to be the child of two members of such an expedition, she would, in a sense, be a missing link who perhaps could provide the East valuable information about the unknown fates of so many. Iskander would be derelict in his duty if he did not make some attempt to solve the riddle of Rhiannon's being, he felt.

Further, he mused, if she were indeed of the East, it was highly conceivable she was one of the Chosen. This would explain her ability to communicate with Anuk and raised the likelihood that she possessed other talents as well. This, too, was food for thought. That Rhiannon was both beautiful and had saved his life were only additional incentives prodding Iskander into wanting to learn everything he could about her; and he firmly resolved to do so at the earliest opportunity.

That his decision was not motivated solely and strictly by professional interest, he determinedly thrust to the back of his mind as unworthy of a twelfth-ranked priest charged with a crucial mission.

Chapter 8

Once, long ago, in the library of Mont Saint Christopher, I read of another world far away and of an ancient fable told by one of its tribes. According to this fable, there were three white-robed Fates who fashioned the threads of life. It was said that the smallest, the most terrible, of the three was Atropos, for it was she who, with her shears, finally cut each Kind's thread and so, to each in time, brought death.

I never understood why this Fate was the most feared, for why should one be afraid of what is but a door, a gate to a higher dimension of existence on the path that leads to the Immortal Guardian?

Nay, had I been of that faraway world, it is the other two Fates of the fable, Clotho and Lachesis, of whom I should have been frightened: Clotho, who, with her spindle, it was said, drew out and twisted the fibers of all the Kind into the threads of life; and Lachesis, who, with her rod, measured them. For between the two was wound a tangled skein, each Kind's destiny foreordained, the right of Free Will nonexistent.

Though I knew that the fable was but a tale, that each Kind was the master of his own fate, yet how often in the days that were to come was I to remember this old story, and wonder. . . .

Was it really naught save chance that had brought me to Borealis—and to Rhiannon Olafursdaughter—or was my destiny, like Cain's, written in the stars before my time and I merely fulfilling the predetermined course of my LifePath? Or had the Light truly given each Kind a choice, as Cain had eventually, despite all that had afflicted him, come to believe; and was all that happened in those days yet ahead because I chose it and so, like Cain, changed what was written for me?

In truth, sometimes, I wonder yet.

—Thus it is Written—
in
The Private Journals
of the Lord Iskander sin Tovaritch

IT WAS A FEW DAYS LATER WHEN ISKANDER FINALLY FELT strong enough to rise from the pallet. To his exasperation, however, he soon discovered he could barely stand and needed Hjalmer's assistance to walk outside and to settle himself on the pelt the healer considerately spread for him upon the rich earth damp from melting snow. Still, despite his continued weakness, it was good to be out of bed at last, Iskander thought. His back braced for support against the wall of the timber abode, he surveyed his surroundings interestedly as he reveled in the feel of the warming spring sun shining through the branches of the pine trees, soaking into his bones.

Torcrag, the dwelling place of the giants, could not really be called a city, he reflected, for it more closely resembled a village, being composed principally of the large timber lodges that were the giants' homes and a single building that, from observation, Iskander correctly deduced served as inn, tavern, and trading post combined. Still, the village was pleasing in design, set harmoniously amid the towering trees of the Piney Woods, with every effort clearly having been made to preserve the natural environs.

This won Iskander's wholehearted approval, for one of the most important lessons every child of the East was taught from birth was of the havoc wreaked upon Tintagel in the Time Before by the Old Ones' callous disregard of the planet's ecological balance. Eventually the Old Ones had so polluted the atmosphere and indiscriminately felled so many forests that treated-glass domes had had to be erected over Tintagel's inconceivably immense cities to protect their populace from the deadly rays of radiation that had streamed to the planet's surface; and in order to breathe, the Kind themselves had been forced to resort to wearing filter masks over their faces.

Now, as he studied his pleasant, peaceful milieu, Iskander could scarcely credit the Records of the Time Before, carefully collected in the Archives that had eventually been established by the Survivors after the Wars of the Kind and the Apocalypse. Still, even so, he knew that the terrible tales contained in the Records were true.

He had read *The Book of Dämmerung* in the Holy Book, *The Word and The Way,* wherein the Time Before was described in great detail: the vast, sprawling cities of the land, with their tall skyscrapers set side by side—so close that not one single tree, not one single flower, not one single blade of grass born of the Light Eternal and guarded by Ceridwen, the Keeper of the Earth, might grow from the ground covered by these concrete monstrosities, these steel affronts to all of nature. He had read of the diabolical factories wherein the materials for these unnatural structures had been made, of the evil computers and robots that had replaced skilled journeyworkers, whose arts and crafts had thus been lost over the ages. He had read of the littered asphalt highways, great six-lane, many-tiered roads over which gasoline-fueled automobiles had traveled, and of the grimy railroad tracks, along which steam-driven trains had journeyed, that had crisscrossed the countryside, boring through mountains, uprooting forests, and besmirching plains to join these cities; and of the huge iron tankers that had sailed the seas between these cities, trailing in their wake large pools of oil that had floated on the water to kill fish, fowl, and fauna alike; and of the winged metal crafts, the jumbo-jet airplanes, that had flown like birds through the sky to these cities, spewing fire and smoke into the firmament. He had read of the satellites, the rockets, and finally the spaceships that had pierced the heavens above these cities, strewing nuclear waste and debris amid the stars, the planets, and the moons. And he had read of to what all this had led: the Wars of the Kind and the Apocalypse.

This was the reason the wicked Technology that had fostered the horrors and destruction of the Time Before was now forbidden. In Time Present to even think of creating an infernal machine was to risk solitary confinement, during which time one was benignly but resolutely shown the error of one's ways and one's misguided spirit was redirected into the orderly channels that guarded against chaos. In Time Present it was the inherent but too-long-suppressed talents of the Kind that were exalted.

Foremost among these inborn traits were those of the Chosen, whose senses were so highly attuned to the forces of the universe as to be considered sublime. Yet even the Chosen could be brought low, Iskander mused ruefully as he contemplated his sad state.

He realized now that in addition to the blow to his head, he was suffering from the lingering effects of exposure on the tundra and in the bitterly cold arctic sea, and of hunger, too, due to his stringent rationing of his provisions during his travels. Indeed, now that he pondered all he had endured, he could only conclude that his survival was miraculous. He knew that by rights he ought to have died; and he thought that it was no wonder that out of all the expeditions previously dispatched from the East to the West, only Cain and Ileana had ever returned.

This made Iskander more eager than ever to delve into the mystery that was Rhiannon Olafursdaughter; and so it was with a good deal of anticipation that sometime later he spied her coming toward him, accompanied by her brother, Yael, another Boreal whom Iskander did not recognize, and, surprisingly, a woman who was clearly no more a giant than Rhiannon herself. Turning to Anuk, who sat beside him, Iskander absently stroked the animal's thick, silky black fur.

"It appears we are about to be formally welcomed to Borealis, Anuk," he noted, his voice low. "Speak not, but, rather, continue to shield your thoughts as much as possible, as ye have done since our arrival here. We have been well treated by the Boreals, 'tis true. But until we know for certain where we stand in this place, I do not want Rhiannon Olafursdaughter privy to any more knowledge than necessary about us."

"As always, your wish is my command, khan," Anuk replied softly.

Within moments the approaching group reached Hjalmer's lodge and came to a halt before Iskander and Anuk. Then Rhiannon, who had evidently been appointed spokeswoman, stepped forward. Suppressing his groan at the effort, Iskander struggled to rise, but with an upraised hand, Rhiannon forestalled him, addressing him by the lupine's title for him, since, for all that he had been at Torcrag for more than a fortnight, she did not yet know his name.

"Good day to ye, *khan*," she greeted him in the Common Tongue, wondering if his unknown rank was such that she ought properly to acknowledge it in some fashion. At last, undecided, she contented herself with a nod in his direction, hoping that this would serve to avoid any unintentional offense. "Nay, please do not attempt to stand," she told him. "We do not expect it, I assure ye. We know that ye have been ill."

Somewhat relieved, Iskander sank back onto the pelt, resettling himself as comfortably as possible.

As she gazed at the stranger, Rhiannon's heart pounded so loudly in her breast that she thought he must hear it. Her mouth tasted dry as an old aurochs bone, while perversely her palms sweated so profusely that she unconsciously wiped them along the sides of her leather leggings. Since his awakening, Rhiannon had purposefully avoided the stranger, all too cognizant of his effect upon her and also of the fact that, because of her longing to truly belong somewhere, she was vesting too much hope and faith in her supposition about his origin. For even if the stranger *did* come from the East, there was no particular reason to assume he meant to return to his homeland or that he would take her with him if he did. If he were a reiver, banished by his tribe, it might be fatal for him to go home; and even if he were not, the more she had thought about it, the more Rhiannon had despondently come to believe that the stranger would have no desire whatsoever to saddle himself with her during what must certainly be a very long and difficult journey—especially once he discovered she was a witch. But still, the secret dreams in her heart would not be banished; and as a result, she viewed this day, when she would surely learn for certain whence the stranger had sprung, as the most pivotal moment of her life.

In fact, Rhiannon was so wrought up that it was

some time before she realized she was staring quite rudely at the stranger—and that he and the others were waiting expectantly for her to continue. Blushing crimson, she quickly averted her eyes and cleared her throat.

Then she said, "'Tis good to see ye so improved, *khan*. I trust ye are feeling better?"

"Yea," Iskander rejoined, "well enough to have remembered I never thanked ye and your brother for saving my life. I do so now. I am most grateful for what ye both did for me."

"'Twas naught but what anyone would have done, *khan*, surely," Rhiannon pointed out, "though naturally Yael and I were glad to do it." Then, feeling she had adequately dealt with the amenities, she turned to introduce those at her side. "Yael, of course, ye already know." She indicated her brother, whom Iskander had met briefly when, after their hunt, the giant had brought Anuk back to Hjalmer's lodge. "And this is Ulthor and his wife, Syeira. Among our tribe Ulthor is the most widely traveled—indeed, he just returned from a journey. And so, since he speaks the most fluent Tintagelese, we felt he was best suited to answer the many questions I know that ye still must have. I apologize for the delay in satisfying further your quite natural curiosity, but unfortunately Ulthor only arrived home this morn. Nor would Hjalmer hear of your being disturbed until today."

"That I can believe," Iskander admitted, smiling, for though the healer was most congenial, he was also quite firm about the care of his patients, brooking no disregard of his orders. "Indeed, 'twas my fear he would carry out his threat to tie me to the pallet that has kept me abed until this morning!"

Iskander went on to relate a few further anecdotes about Hjalmer's strict instructions to him, while the wheels of his mind churned so furiously that he thought Rhiannon must surely sense it. He could barely repress his sudden excitement, for he had recognized the names Ulthor and Syeira, and he felt certain they must be the giant and the gypsy whom Cain and Ileana had spoken of as having accompanied them on their quest for the Sword of Ishtar. Iskander could hardly believe his good fortune, for if this were indeed the case, he knew for sure that he was not only among friends, but could count on receiving help.

Abruptly, having reached a decision, he broke off his narrative about the healer, saying, "But enough of Hjalmer's bedside manner, for in truth, he is a fine healer. It is I who am a poor patient, I'm afraid, unused, as I am, to being confined to bed. Come. Unroll your furs and sit." He motioned toward the pelts they all carried, obviously for this purpose. "I fear I have been guilty of rudeness in keeping ye standing, and for that I apologize." Politely protesting that Iskander had been ill and was unfamiliar with their customs (and they with his, which had discouraged them from sitting, uninvited), the Boreals arrayed themselves in a half circle around him, after which he turned to Anuk. *"Do ye go inside and fetch my blade from Hjalmer's lodge,"* he mentally commanded the startled lupine. *"I would do so myself, but I am afraid I must plead my recent illness and ask your indulgence."*

"I understand, khan," Anuk responded. Though curious about his master's request, he asked no questions, but obediently trotted inside to retrieve the weapon.

Once the lupine had entered the healer's lodge, Iskander returned his attention to the Boreals, surreptitiously glancing at Rhiannon to see if she had overheard his communication with Anuk. She looked puzzled, as though she had sensed but not grasped what had passed between man and beast. And in that moment Iskander realized that though she might possess the Power, she was most likely unskilled in its use—Chosen but lacking Druswidic knowledge. He felt a stab of pity for her then, for he remembered the fear and bewilderment his own gifts had caused him in his childhood, before he had been sent to Mont Saint Christopher for training. He thought that the burden of her talents must weigh heavily upon her.

She sat upon the fringe of those around him, as though, having completed the introductions, she deemed her initial role as spokeswoman fulfilled; and so it was to Ulthor that he directed his next words.

"As Rhiannon Olafursdaughter said, I have many questions," Iskander declared. "But I also know that ye must be curious about me, the stranger ye have so kindly taken into your midst and cared for these past few weeks. It must be clear to ye I am not of these parts. Yet ye have not pressed me, despite your not knowing even so much as my name. So perhaps 'twill be best if we begin by my telling ye a little something about myself."

"That sounds most agreeable, indeed," Ulthor averred, "for I confess ye are something of a rarity among us, stranger. 'Tis not often an inlander ventures so far north as Torcrag. Yet for all that you're Kind, you've not the look of a Finisterrean or a Gallowish about ye, and plainly ye are not of the other tribes that we know inhabit these two continents of Aerie and Verdante, of which Borealis is a part. Only once before in my life have I seen a man wearing that particular gold torque that hangs about your neck"— Ulthor indicated the heavy piece of jewelry Rhiannon had noticed when tending the stranger—"or who bore the mark of a sunburst upon his brow. So, say on, stranger, if ye be so inclined, and we will listen and learn what we will."

"Very well, then," Iskander said. "I am Iskander sin

Tovaritch. I've not the look of a familiar tribe about me because I come not from the West, but from the East, as perhaps ye have already guessed—from the continent of Iglacia, which is a place of trees and tundra much like your own Borealis. I left my homeland some months ago, intent upon reaching the western continent of Montano. To do this I traveled by sled across Persephone, the northern polar cap; and then, when I came to the Sea of Clouds, I continued my long journey by means of a small skiff I carried with me. Unfortunately Anuk and I were but a few days upon the ocean when a strong southerly current caught us in its grip and swiftly bore us off course. Shortly afterward the storm that destroyed our boat struck, and I knew nothing more until I awoke and found myself here.

"Now, ye may think that such a thing would be upsetting to a man, and so at first it was to me, for I did not know whether I had fallen prey to a tribe of rogues who would hold me prisoner—or worse. But I am happy to say that once I learned where I was, my fears were eased and many of my questions were answered; for contrary to what ye may have supposed, I am not ignorant of the land of Boreal or of the tribe of the giants." Iskander smiled as Ulthor's eyebrows flew up in surprise, then lowered in bafflement.

"I see I have taken ye unaware, Ulthor set Torcrag, as ye are known to me," Iskander continued, startling the giant, who would have spoken had not Iskander's upraised hand deterred him. "A moment, please, friend giant," Iskander insisted softly, "and then I hope that much will be known to ye, also." At that Ulthor was clearly more confused than ever, but apparently good manners prevented him from arguing with a guest. He clamped his mouth shut, his terse nod indicating his concession. Iskander turned to Anuk, who had reappeared at his side. Between its traplike jaws the lupine held its master's sheathed sword. Taking the scabbard, Iskander handed it to the giant. "Withdraw the weapon inside, Ulthor set Torcrag, and tell me if ye recognize it," he instructed the Boreal.

Ulthor eyed Iskander speculatively for a long moment. Then at last he glanced down at the leather sheath in his hands and slowly pulled the blade free.

"By the Light!" the giant swore, astounded, as he gazed at the weapon. "On my honor, I would know it anywhere—though I be blind as a newborn! 'Tis the Sword of Ishtar!" Then suddenly, his eyes narrowing, he glared at Iskander suspiciously. "How came ye by this, stranger?" he growled. "'Tis a magic blade and belongs by right to her who drew it from the crystal flames of Truth!"

"Would ye believe me, friend giant," Iskander inquired gently, "if I told ye the Lady Ileana herself laid it in my hands and bade me use as I would to battle the Darkness that would devour all Tintagel if It could?"

"Nay!" Ulthor cried—and then, despite himself, his heart filled with hope, he asked, "Is it so? Is it really so? Do ye speak the truth, then, Iskander sin Tovaritch? Did they make it safe home—those two wondrous souls braver than any I have ever known or shall ever know again upon this earth?"

"They did . . . and told a tale of the giant Ulthor—and of a thousand warriors strong and true who marched from the mist one morning onto the Strathmore Plains, shouting, *'Uig-biorne, märz ana! Uig-biorne, märz ana!'* and, to the last intrepid man and woman, held back the Darkness, in the Name of the Light."

Hearing this, Ulthor was visibly moved. He recalled his slain brethren, and his eyes filled unashamedly with tears, causing his wife, Syeira, to reach comfortingly for his hand while she blinked back her own tears at her grim memories of the Strathmore Plains. Yael, whose familiarity with the Common Tongue was less than that of the rest, sat in silent confusion, attempting to fathom the meaning of what he had heard. Beside him, having both a better grasp of Tintagelese and a quicker mind than her brother, Rhiannon, though saddened by the reminder of how so many heroic giants had perished, nevertheless trembled all over with excitement.

The stranger—this Iskander sin Tovaritch—was not only from the East (which alone had elated her immeasurably), but he apparently had some connection to the Lord Cain and the Lady Ileana, both of whom, according to Ulthor, had possessed Power. This meant that Iskander himself must know of the Power, Rhiannon reasoned, and that perhaps he could enlighten her about her own! Scarcely able to contain herself at the thought, she waited impatiently for the conversation to continue, unconsciously drawing nearer to the rest.

Although he did not glance in her direction, Iskander was vividly aware of how she leaned toward him, of how her body quivered ever so slightly, like that of a graceful hreinn poised for flight. He alone sensed the eagerness, the excitement that filled her—though he found himself puzzled by her emotions—in sharp contrast to those of the other Boreals. For a moment Iskander considered probing her thoughts. Then reluctantly he dismissed the notion, suspecting that however untrained she might be, Rhiannon was nevertheless sentient enough to be cognizant of his mind touching hers.

His nostrils flared as the sweet fragrance of her long, unbound hair wafted on the gentle wind to him, reminding him of how she had bent over him when he had regained consciousness, her tresses like tongues of flame enveloping her, her hand smooth as silk against his brow.

Despite how he tried to quell the disturbing, inexplicable feeling, Iskander knew that deep down inside, he was drawn to her in a way that had little to do with his curiosity about her; and a part of his mind dwelled on her even as he listened to Ulthor's next words.

"Ye tell me that the Lord Cain and the Lady Ileana returned safe home," the giant said slowly, "and as proof of your words, ye offer the Sword of Ishtar, given unto ye by the Lady Ileana herself to use as ye see fit against the Darkness. That can only mean that the Druswids do not feel that the Darkness has been conquered," Ulthor observed, his face grave, "and that ye have some mission, which is the reason for your long and dangerous journey. Is that so?"

"Yea," Iskander stated soberly, then went on to explain at length the purpose of his travels, while the others listened silently, their faces reflecting their understanding of and growing apprehension at his words.

When at last Iskander had finished speaking, Ulthor sighed heavily and shook his head, much depressed by what he had heard.

"'Tis true that since the battle of the Strathmore Plains, we have spied a few UnKind now and then," the giant announced, "but we thought them isolated cases, SoulEaters who somehow escaped the carnage of the Strathmore Plains or who were never there to begin with. Now ye say they must spring not from these two continents, but from those two yet farther west, and ye would find the heart of the Darkness and strike at It before it is too late." Ulthor paused, then continued. "Truly, my friend, the Light guided ye to the shores of Borealis when your boat sank. What can we do to help ye in your quest? Name it and 'tis yours—for no more than the Lord Cain and the Lady

Ileana have we Boreals forgotten the battle of the Strathmore Plains and those who gave their lives to save our world. On my honor, *that* is a sacrifice we will not allow to become in vain," the giant insisted fiercely.

"I was hoping that ye would say that," Iskander confessed. "I shall need another boat, of course, and provisions, plus parchment, quill, and ink to re-create my lost maps, along with whatever knowledge ye may have about the lands through which I will most likely pass during my journey. For these things I shall be more than happy to pay. I have coins—"

"Yea—and ye may keep them, also, Iskander sin Tovaritch!" Ulthor averred stoutly, offended by the offer. "Ye will have far greater need of them later on, no doubt. What we Boreals give, we give freely—for the Light and for Tintagel!" He turned to the others beside him. "Syeira, Yael, Rhiannon, go and spread the word among the rest of our tribe about the Lord Iskander's identity, his quest, and his requirements—and give fair warning to all that any who should prove slow or slack in responding shall answer to me! The welfare of our very world may be at stake—and that is not a thing to be treated lightly!" After barking these orders, Ulthor once more directed his attention to Iskander.

"And now, my friend," the giant continued, his voice choked with emotion, "if ye are not too tired, I should like very much to hear of those two who held back the Darkness one long winter solstice past—and who shall always hold a special place in my heart. Please. Tell me of the Lord Cain and the Lady Ileana, for they have oft haunted my thoughts since that dread night, and I would know how they fare and if they prosper. . . ."

Chapter 9

I was beside myself. The Lord Iskander sin Tovaritch, as I had discovered he was so titled and named, had proved far more than even I had hoped for—for not only was he not a brigand, but of the Royal Blood of the East, and so high in standing among the six Eastern Tribes that he was well acquainted with the Lord Cain and the Lady Ileana, personages so mystical and far removed from me as to seem like legendary heroes in a bard's tale.

Because of this, in my mind the Lord Iskander loomed more than ever like some ancient pagan god, larger than life, no mere man at all. I had never before known another like him. He seemed in all respects far beyond my ken. In truth, I stood in such awe of him that, perversely, I now heartily wished he were less than what he was. For having learned of the both difficult and dangerous quest he had undertaken against the UnKind, I could not help but think how small and, yea, even petty my own problems seemed in comparison. That he, a lone man, should risk his life in pursuit of the source of the SoulEaters was so sterling and unself-ish an act that I, surrounded by a loving family and in no real peril, despite the covert fear and suspicion the giants had had of me ever since learning of my strange Power, could only despise myself for being so ignoble and self-centered.

As a result, I could not even bring myself to approach the Lord Iskander, much less to trouble him with even so much as asking if he could read the scroll contained in the small casket my blood mother had left behind at her death.

So depressed was I by all I had gleaned of him, in fact, that I did naught but mope about alone for days afterward. It was as though I had reached for a star only to realize at the very last moment that I was unworthy of even a single shaft of its heavenly light.

I could not recall when I had ever before felt so wretched—and worse, I knew I had only myself to blame for my misery.

This last was the bitterest pill of all to swallow.

—Thus it is Written—
in
The Private Journals
of the Lady Rhiannon sin Lothian

HE MOVED SO SILENTLY, LIKE A MAN BORN OF CERIDWEN, the Keeper of the Earth, and so one with all her domain that Rhiannon did not hear him approach, was not even aware of him until the shadow he cast in the daily lengthening rays of the spring sun fell across her, abruptly jolting her from her woebegone reverie.

Instinctively her hand slid to the morning star belted at her waist, then halted in mid-action as she glanced up into the silvery eyes of the man who had penetrated the sylvan glade, intruding upon her solitude.

"Forgive me"—Iskander spoke softly—"I did not

mean to startle ye. I did not realize that ye were so deep in thought as not to have heard my footsteps."

"Even had I not been, 'twould have taken a keener ear than mine indeed to have discerned your approach, for ye walk with the stealth of a snow-tiger," Rhiannon rejoined, her voice low, her heart beginning to hammer slow and hard in her breast at his nearness, at the realization that he must have especially sought her out to have discovered her favorite place of seclusion. "Do ye always tread so lightly?"

"I suppose I must—though I confess I have never really thought about it before," Iskander said. He paused for a moment, then continued. "Yael told me where I might find ye. May I sit down?" He indicated the ground beside her. "I would like to talk to ye, and I have seen ye so little since my recovery that there has been no opportunity for conversation between us."

At that, thinking guiltily that perhaps he had somehow sensed she had been deliberately avoiding him, Rhiannon bit her lower lip and looked away. How rude he must believe she was if he knew the truth, she thought, feeling more dejected than ever.

"I—I would be honored to have ye join me," she managed to choke out, edging over to make room for him on her pelt.

With the fluidity of movement that came so naturally to him, Iskander sank down beside her, so close that Rhiannon was acutely conscious of his proximity, of the heat that seemed to emanate in waves from his lithe, muscular body, and of the fresh, clean scent of soap that wafted from his smooth bronze skin. From beneath her lashes she peeked at him, much surprised that he had shaved off his mustache and beard. He looked younger, she thought, and more handsome than ever. The nakedness of his face emphasized his thick, gleaming black hair that contrasted sharply with the unusual wings of silver at his temples, so he appeared even more foreign and godlike, of a tribe far older than that of the giants, an otherworldly being.

The presence he possessed puzzled her, for he was neither as tall nor as broad as a Boreal. Yet somehow he seemed an imposing figure, one who commanded and received respect. He was, she felt, accustomed to giving orders—and to having them obeyed. No doubt, this was because he was of the Royal Blood, of which Rhiannon knew little, though she rightly equated it to the long line of chieftains who had ruled Borealis since before she could remember.

Surreptitiously she continued to study him, wondering what he wanted of her and waiting expectantly for him to speak again. Beside her, as usual, in her rucksack, lay the small casket that had belonged to her blood mother. Rhiannon's fingers itched to open it, to draw forth the scroll within, for she yearned to ask the Lord Iskander if he could read it. Then she remembered his quest—and she once more chided herself sternly for even thinking of bothering him with her trivial troubles. Yet to her surprise, when finally he spoke, it seemed he was not ignorant of these.

"Khatun," he began slowly, as though weighing his words, "I hope that ye will not think I am trying to pry, but for a number of reasons—not the least of which is that ye saved my life—I am most curious about ye. I know a little of your story already—for clearly ye are not a Boreal, but were adopted by the tribe—but if ye are not averse to telling me, I should like to hear more. If ye are reluctant to enlighten me, however, I will understand. But before ye decide, please rest assured I do not ask merely and only for curiosity's sake. Let me explain." Again Iskander paused, collecting his thoughts. Then he went on.

"I know that ye can communicate with Anuk, *khatun,*" he announced, much startling Rhiannon. She gazed up at him sharply, her amber eyes narrowing as she considered how he might have learned this, for she did not think Yael would have told him such a thing. Before she could ask Iskander about it, however, he pressed on. "That is a talent that, so far as I know, only the Chosen possess. Because such Power is little grasped or even known here in the West, and also because I have gradually realized that ye very much resemble physically one of the six Eastern Tribes, I have come to believe that perhaps your blood parents were part of one of the several expeditions we in the East dispatched over the years to the West but that never returned home. Nay, please. Wait. Let me finish."

With an upraised hand Iskander stilled Rhiannon as she started to interrupt him, but he did not miss the sudden glittering of her eyes or the way her hands fluttered in her lap and her body tensed and trembled. Hurriedly he plunged on, fearing that he had somehow offended her, that she intended to refuse to answer his questions or, worse, to run away from him.

"If what I believe should prove to be true," he said, his eyes holding hers intently, "it might help me to discover the unknown fates of so many who, in Time Past, have been so mysteriously and dishearteningly lost to us. This, in turn, would probably give me a much better understanding of the dangers that lie ahead in my quest.

"So, ye see, if ye could help me, *khatun,* not only would I be most grateful, but ye might at long last be able to set to rest the minds of the families of those from the missing expeditions. It is hard not knowing what has befallen a loved one. It will be even more difficult now that the Lord Cain and the Lady Ileana have managed to return home safely to tell of this vile Darkness that has beset our world—these UnKind that will destroy us all, if they can."

Involuntarily Rhiannon shuddered, recalling the SoulEaters she had glimpsed in the Piney Woods. Truly they were the spawn of the Foul Enslaver, she reflected. Surely she could not now be thought of as imposing on the Lord Iskander if she told him of her past and showed him her blood mother's scroll.

"It may be that we can help each other, *khan*," she said at last, to Iskander's gladness. "Indeed, I must confess I had hoped, once I discovered that ye were from the East, that ye could translate for me a scroll that belonged to my blood mother. But when I learned of your quest, I felt I could not bother ye with what seemed so trifling a matter. Now, however, it appears from your words that ye think I may be some kind of missing link between the East and the West; and perhaps ye are right, for this much I know: My blood parents *did* come from the East, just as ye surmised. They were of a tribe called the Vikanglians. But I know little more than this; and since I, too, would give much to know who and what I truly am, I can only hope that between us we can somehow fit together the pieces to make a whole."

After that Rhiannon described to him what her giant mother, Freya, had told her about her blood parents. Then, with an eagerness she could not conceal, she opened the small casket that had belonged to her blood mother and handed him the scroll inside. As excited now as Rhiannon, Iskander quickly unrolled the parchment and scanned its contents.

"Can ye—can ye read it, *khan?*" Rhiannon asked nervously, sick to her stomach at the thought that perhaps he could tell her nothing further after all. But finally, much to her relief, Iskander nodded.

"Yea," he declared. "'Tis written in Vikanglian, but fortunately I am not unfamiliar with the language. 'Tis a legal document, what is known in the East as a

Progignere. It is, to put it simply, a history of your bloodlines. By the moons!" he swore softly as he read on. "Anuk was right to address ye as *khatun,* which is the Iglacian word for *lady,* for not only are ye indeed a Vikanglian, but ye are of the Royal House of Lothian, no less!"

"I—I am?" Rhiannon queried, much startled as she considered this wholly unexpected revelation; for of all she had ever envisioned, she had never dared to dream she was of Royal Blood. "Does—does that mean I have—have kin in the East . . . blood kin?"

"Yea," Iskander replied. "The Royal House of Lothian numbers many. It is a very old and respected House that has ruled Vikanglia for centuries. Ye can be proud to call it yours, *khatun.*"

It was too much to take in all at once. Rhiannon was overwhelmed. She did not know what to say. To think that in the blink of an eye, she had gone from being nothing more than a mere foundling to a lady with an extended family, the Royal House of Lothian, the Royal Blood of the East. To think that at long last she knew who she was, what she was, where she belonged . . .

"I—I just can't believe it," she stammered, still trying to absorb what she had learned, not quite daring yet to accept Iskander's words.

"Believe," he urged, smiling, "for I assure ye that 'tis true, that there is no mistake."

"This scroll, this—this . . . *Progignere* is proof of that?" Rhiannon inquired suspiciously, still fearing in some dim corner of her mind that his disclosure was simply too good to be true.

"'Tis, indeed. For that is the crest of the Royal House of Lothian"—he pointed to the broken seal affixed to the parchment—"and that is your blood mother's signature, attesting to your birth"—he indicated some writing that Rhiannon could not read and so eyed skeptically.

But . . . what reason would the Lord Iskander have to lie to her? she asked herself logically. After all, he had nothing to gain by it. Nay, he *must* have spoken truly.

At the realization Rhiannon pinched herself covertly. She was secretly afraid that perhaps she was only dreaming. But to her growing elation, she was conscious; the Lord Iskander's words were real.

"They would claim me, then, this Royal House of Lothian?" she continued to probe, wanting to make certain of the facts this time before allowing her hopes to soar.

"Yea, of course," he replied, slightly surprised. "If one is of the Royal Blood, one is of the Royal Blood. That is all that matters."

"Is it?"

"Yea. The blood is all, the blood is absolute."

Although this was what Rhiannon had longed intensely to hear, still, a knife of doubt stabbed her, tainting her excitement and happiness at all he had divulged. Would her Royal Blood be enough once it was learned she was also a witch?

She could communicate with Ánuk, and that, the Lord Iskander had contended, was a talent only the Chosen possessed. But he had said little more than that; and now Rhiannon could not help but wonder if this was because he shared the giants' superstitions regarding the Power. Yet clearly he did not fear his friends the Lord Cain and the Lady Ileana, whose Power Ulthor had witnessed and of which he had told the Boreals. At the thought confusion burgeoned in Rhiannon's mind and, coupled with her churning emotions, proved too much stimulation for her to cope with. To her horror she was abruptly beset by the signs she had come to recognize always preceded her metamorphosis into something other than what she was.

"Nay . . ." The low moan burst from her lips as without any warning her body swayed violently, imbalanced by a sudden onslaught of dizziness. "Nay . . ."

She was only vaguely aware of Iskander's concern, of his hand shooting out to grip her arm, steadying her as she rocked uncontrollably from side to side, pressing her palms hard against her temples in an attempt to hold at bay the tumultuous sensations that savagely assailed her. But though she struggled with all her might to regain command of herself, her battle was futile. Moments later her vision clouded as though obscured by a veil of mist and the horizon tilted sickeningly before her eyes before she squeezed them closed to shut out the giddying sight. Then at last, terrifyingly, the world spun away, and she seemed to hear Iskander's voice coming at her from a great distance.

"Rhiannon, what is it?" he asked sharply. "Are ye all right?" Yet even as he spoke, he saw what was happening to her, knew she was ill . . . ill in a way only one such as himself would have recognized—and understood.

ShapeShifter.

The revelation stunned him. He had known that Rhiannon must be one of the Chosen—it was the only explanation for her ability to communicate with Anuk. But even Iskander had not guessed the extent of her Power—raw and inexpert, as he had supposed, but far more potent, he realized now, than he had ever imagined.

Her voice rang in his ears—a wail of anguish that frantically implored him not to look at her, to leave her—but he paid it no heed. Though she did not know it, she had need of him.

"Breathe!" he ordered tersely as she groaned and gasped for air, her chest heaving, her body shaking. "Breathe! Don't fight it! *Don't fight it!* Let it happen. Let . . . it . . . happen. . . ."

And then it did. Her shape began to blur, to change color, to distort—coarsely, erratically, wavering back and forth until finally the transmutation was complete and Rhiannon was gone.

In her place sat a wolfish beast not unlike Anuk, but primitive in appearance, the edges of its body ragged, as though it were not quite fully formed, its russet fur tinted with a bluish cast that made it glow faintly, eerily, like the stalactites and stalagmites of a grotto. The creature's eyes gleamed yellow-orange as citrine; its tongue lolled, crimson as blood, before it lifted its head and howled—a tormented cry. Then, abruptly, like the flame of a candle being snuffed out, the animal vanished and Rhiannon sat again upon the pelt, her head flung back, a sob issuing from her throat before she suddenly fell forward in a dead faint, collapsing in a heap upon the ground.

She would regain consciousness in a few minutes, Iskander knew, and would be momentarily bewildered before, horrified, she would recall her wrenching metamorphosis and wonder bitterly why she should be afflicted by such an accursed Power. In the meanwhile there was naught he could do for her but make her as comfortable as possible. This he did, shifting her body so she lay full-length upon the pelt, her head cradled in his lap.

As he gazed down at her, he saw that her hair was drenched with sweat and that a trickle of blood oozed from her lip where she had bitten it in her panic. Tenderly he wiped away both the perspiration and the blood, his heart aching for her. Though the Boreals had cared enough to adopt her, still, her life could not have been easy among those who were largely ignorant of, and so feared, the Power.

For the first time Iskander thought to wonder if there were others like Rhiannon in the West. It was assumed in the East that all the members of the lost expeditions dispatched to the West over the years had perished. Now there was good reason to doubt this supposition—and to wonder as well if other children had been born to those expedition members who might have survived. It was a disquieting notion, to think that perhaps there existed those whose homelands had been lost to them forever and those, like Rhiannon, who would never see the East to which they rightly belonged. Remembering how, following the storm at sea, he had awakened to find himself an alien in an alien land, Iskander felt he had some inkling of what it must be like to know oneself displaced, dispossessed; and more than ever he sympathized with Rhiannon, a victim of circumstances beyond her control.

She was slowly returning to awareness now, her eyelids fluttering open to reveal eyes blank and dazed until at last comprehension dawned. Wildly then she struggled to sit up, her face averted and scarlet with mortification that Iskander should have witnessed what he had.

Rhiannon wanted to die a thousand deaths. She wished fervently that the earth would somehow open up and swallow her, and it was all she could do to keep from leaping to her feet and running away. But that would accomplish nothing. The damage had already been done. In the Lord Iskander's eyes, she must now be a thing of untold loathing, she thought. She could not understand why he continued to sit beside her as though nothing untoward had happened—a curious action, in light of what had just occurred. But perhaps he was too shocked to move—or even to speak. She longed intensely to look at him, to try to discern his thoughts. But she could not bring herself to meet his gaze, to see the revulsion she felt certain must now mar his dark visage at the sight of her.

"Why—why did ye stay?" she asked, her voice low and trembling with emotion. "Why didn't ye leave me, as I begged? Are ye not afraid now to be alone here with me—a witch?"

"Is that how ye think of yourself, *khatun?*" Iskander inquired, his voice curiously gentle, as though he spoke to a wounded child. "As a witch?"

"Do ye doubt it?" Rhiannon cried, stung by what she perceived as his lack of understanding and, worse, his pity. "What are ye—blind that ye did not see what happened?"

"Nay, I saw," Iskander rejoined. "I saw a rare gift of the Power, childish, crude, untrained, but a gift all the same. Why should I fear it? More to the point, why should ye despise yourself as a witch for possessing it?"

"Because 'tis unnatural, a curse—"

"Nay, 'tis an exceptional Power much to be admired, for only a handful of the Chosen are ever so blessed. Had ye been reared in the East, ye would know the truth of what I say."

"Are ye telling me that—that ye know others such as I am?" Rhiannon queried hesitantly, wanting desperately to credit his words but nevertheless finding them hard to swallow. "Nay! I—I don't believe ye."

"This is the second time today that ye have doubted me, *khatun,*" he pointed out somewhat ruefully. "I must confess I am unaccustomed to being so maligned, and as a result, I am beginning to wonder what ye must think of me. Nevertheless, since ye *do* doubt me, let me convince ye of my veracity."

So saying, Iskander rose and, much to Rhiannon's bewilderment, strode away to stand some feet beyond her.

"Now, watch, *khatun*," he demanded softly, "and I will show ye how it ought to be done."

With that he closed his eyes and ears to shut out his surroundings and, taking a deep breath, brought his palms together in front of his chest as slowly, deliberately, he summoned his Power. Like a sleeping beast, it awoke within him and, as strong and steady as his heartbeat, started to pulse through his blood, gradually spreading throughout his entire being. As his Power flowed through him, Iskander began to move, his body bending forward with a grace and a suppleness Rhiannon would not have thought possible, his back arching effortlessly into a convex curve, his arms coming down, half reaching before him, his hands open, his fingers curled, his knees flexing limberly until he stood in a half crouch, looking uncannily like some fierce predator poised to spring upon its prey.

Startled by the eerie, extraordinary resemblance, Rhiannon continued to watch, mesmerized, as after taking shape his entire body started to glow with a diffuse blue light that sinuously stretched and molded itself about him, defining and refining the animalistic form he had assumed, until every line, every curve, every infinitesimal detail was as clear and precise as though chiseled by a master stonecutter. Then slowly the encompassing aura began to alter color, melting into a kaleidoscope of light and shadow that eventually separated, stabilized, solidified, so that incredibly, moments later, had she herself not witnessed Iskander's electrifying transformation, Rhiannon would have staked her life on the fact that it was Anuk who stood before her, silver-eyed, black-furred—real as she.

She was so stunned by the sight of the man-become-beast that for an interminable minute, she doubted what she had seen, the truth her own eyes beheld even now. Then suddenly, like a hard, physical blow knocking the wind from her, the actuality of what Iskander had shown her hit her; and she grasped his point and held on to it like a lifeline.

She was not a witch. She was not even a freak of nature. *She was not alone.* Rhiannon was so overcome by the realization that she was unable to hold at bay the quick, hot tears that brimmed without warning in her eyes, then slid down her cheeks. There were others like her—and the Lord Iskander was such a one. She was not accursed, but blessed. "A rare gift," he had called her Power, and so it now seemed. Then she remembered that he had also termed her use of it "childish, crude, untrained"; and as she dwelled on his expert metamorphosis, she knew that in this, too, he had spoken truly: She was not even remarkable. Indeed, compared to him, she was a bungling novice. At this understanding Rhiannon cried all the harder —silently, miserably, gulping for air. In all honesty, she thought dejectedly, she was nothing more than an ignorant, inept, foolish girl. No wonder the Lord Iskander had not run away from her. The idea that anyone had ever found her frightening was laughable. If her family and friends knew the truth about her, they would pity, not fear, her.

Having forgotten in her anguish that Iskander was witness to her tears, she dashed them away angrily, embarrassed, as at last, having resumed his natural state, he rejoined her on the pelt. Much to her relief, guessing her feelings and respectful of her need to master her emotions, he did not look at her, but gazed off into the distance, as though unaware that she wept, giving her the time and privacy she needed to recover herself. After a moment he spoke.

"We Druswids call it ShapeShifting," he explained

quietly as she struggled to compose herself. "'Tis born of the Power Terrestrial, the Power of the Earth; and as I told ye, 'tis a relatively uncommon ability among us. 'Tis therefore highly esteemed." Iskander paused, allowing this to penetrate. Then he continued.

"There was a time, however, when I was a small boy, that I did not know what a singular gift my Power was. I could not comprehend what was happening to me when the ShapeShift came upon me—uncontrollably and with so little warning. As a result, I was so terrified by it that I dared not tell even my parents about it. I was afraid they would shrink from me in horror, convinced they had whelped a monster.

"But then, of course, inevitably there came the day when I could no longer hide the way in which I would be so suddenly and violently transformed, and my parents saw what I was. I was fortunate, *khatun*, that I was born in the East, where the Chosen are known and revered. Contrary to my fears, my parents not only understood my talent, but valued it; and though, having known only six years at the time, I bitterly protested being sent away, they wisely, despite their pain at losing me, made arrangements for me to leave home and enter the monastery of Mont Saint Christopher, to be trained in the Art of ShapeShifting.

"The journey from my homeland of Iglacia to the main island of the Isles of Cinnamon, Bark Island, where Mont Saint Christopher stands, was the longest I had ever made in my short life; and at first I was not only scared and lonely, but dreadfully homesick. I missed my parents terribly and cried myself to sleep at night, thinking that perhaps they had lied to me and sent me away because, having learned I was a monster, they no longer loved or wanted me. The kindly priest who accompanied me on my trip did his best to assure me this was not so. But of course, being only a child, I was suspicious and mistrustful of him, whom I viewed as my jailor, and I didn't believe him.

"It was only when we finally arrived at the monastery that I discovered he was an honest man who had spoken truly; for, from the beginning, all save two of the other novices were in awe of me, and of my Power. I realized then that though I *was* different, I was indeed special, as my parents and the priest had told me. No longer alone, I ranked among the elite of the novices at Mont Saint Christopher; and consequently I am quite ashamed to confess that within a few days of my arrival, I forgot all about being homesick and developed instead a very large chip on my shoulder." Iskander smiled sheepishly at the memory; and despite herself, Rhiannon found her tears dissipating, her curiosity piqued by his tale, as he had intended. Pretending not to notice her interest, he went on. "I swaggered about most boastfully and bullied the other novices disgracefully because their Power was not so strong or unusual as mine. Only they who were to become the Lord Cain and the Lord Jahil did I spare, for even then their Power, though disparate, rivaled mine.

"But then, all too quickly, there came the morning when my training began and I met my mentor, Brother Yucel, for the first time. How well I recall it, even now. Like the rest of the monastery, Brother Yucel had heard my shameless bragging, but still, he spoke no word of censure to me. Instead, he merely stood there, his eyes piercing mine. Then, after a very long and, for me, uncomfortable minute, he said sagely, ''Tis the way of the wise to look and learn, sirrah. So, let us see if there is hope for you or if you are, in truth, foolish as your behavior within these hallowed walls has made it appear.' And then, while I watched, he began to ShapeShift—so smoothly and facilely that, despite my youth, I needed no one to tell me that all my crowing was that of a fledgling's in the face of a hawk's mighty cry." Iskander shook his head ruefully at the recollection. "I had been gifted with a rare Power, yea. But I was not its master; it was mine." Iskander was silent for a moment, remembering.

Then he stated gravely, "Ye see, *khatun,* it is not enough simply to possess the Power. One must also know how to use it—and judiciously—lest one will be forever its slave or, worse, corrupted and turned to the left hand of the Darkness. In time I came to understand this, and so I learned to will the Power to come at my command, in the Name of the Light. So now, too, is that choice yours, *khatun.* May ye choose wisely and well."

Then, silently as he had come, Iskander rose and slipped away, so subtly and unexpectedly that before Rhiannon even had time to grasp that he was leaving her, he was gone, the green boughs of the pines closing light and feathery as mist behind him. She called after him, but the sound that emanated from her throat was but a soft, broken sob—and he did not return.

Chapter 10

I know that the Lord Iskander meant well with his words to me that day in the glade, and 'tis true that afterward my mind and heart were much gladdened by the knowledge, understanding, and insight he had displayed toward me. But still, like a two-edged sword, his kindness cut me deeply, for although the choice of whether to use my Power to serve the Light or the Darkness was easy, how I was to become skilled in commanding it when I had no mentor to teach me posed a quandary to which there was only one answer: The Lord Iskander himself must instruct me. Yet how could he?

His quest, though perilous, was vital, and he was not the sort of man who would fail if there were the slightest chance of his succeeding instead. So I knew that he would not, for me, set aside his mission—nor was I selfish or unperceptive enough to ask that of him. Already he had done more for me than he, a stranger, had needed to do. I had no right to expect anything more.

But still, I dared to hope, to dream. Somehow I would *learn* how to use my Power, and wisely and well, I vowed. To that end, then, I began to lay my plans; and in doing so, I took the first step upon the torturous road that was to be my LifePath, for *there was no turning back for me after that—not then, not later, not ever.*

—Thus it is Written—
in
The Private Journals
of the Lady Rhiannon sin Lothian

IT WAS A PALE SUN THAT BRUSHED THE CANVAS OF THE horizon, painting the grey dawn sky in shades of orchid and indigo and dusky rose that filtered through the trees and low-lying mist, reflecting off the melting snow beneath to cast a thousand rainbows in the slowly growing light. Whorls and slants of colors shimmered in every crystal droplet of water, and with these the thawing earth abounded. Forceful streams rushed down from the lower reaches of the Shivering and Hailstone Mountain ranges, flooding the Rivers Snowy and Sleet, turning them into dangerous rapids and currents. Slowly diminishing icicles dripped from the branches of the evergreens, and the ground was dotted with pools and puddles as the frozen land gave way before the ever-strengthening onslaught of spring.

Never did the earth smell so clean and fresh and rich as it did now. Fragrant pine needles and cones carpeted the forest floor, where the aroma of winter's decaying leaves mingled with the scents of moss and mold and fertile black loam, soft and spongy from the humus and the dampness. Iskander's boots sank gently into the seldom-used track that wended its way south and westward, toward the Groaning Gorge that marked the boundary between Borealis and Finisterre. The Sword of Ishtar rode his shoulders, and Anuk padded quietly at his side.

They had left Torcrag shortly before daybreak, having said their goodbyes last evening. Welcome as the giants had made them, he and Anuk had lingered overlong, Iskander knew. Yet he did not admit to himself, even now, that it had been more than just his need to fully recover that had caused him to remain. He had done what he could for Rhiannon Olafursdaughter; he could do nothing more. But still, unbidden, flaying him, the thought came: *She was sin Lothian, of the Royal Blood—far more even than that, for she was a ShapeShifter.* She had saved his life. She had deserved better at his hands than what he had given her. For it had come to Iskander that in his kindness and pity, he had been cruel, declaring she must master her Power, when he had known there was none save him to teach her how.

I could do nothing more for her! he reiterated in his mind, so vehemently that he felt certain Anuk had heard. But the lupine made no response, and that in itself was damning.

The realization that Anuk thought his master had behaved badly shamed Iskander, and that, in turn, made him angry. But it was an anger that ought to be directed at himself, he knew, and so he said nothing in the face of the lupine's silent rebuke. Instead, he hoisted more securely upon his shoulders the well-provisioned rucksack the giants had given him, and he strode on through the woods, the muscle that flexed in his set jaw the only visible sign of his inner ferment. He must concentrate on his quest, he told himself sternly. He must not permit himself to forget what it was that he had traveled to the West to accomplish. What was one woman in the face of that? Nothing. Less than nothing. Yet she haunted him. The rising sun was the color of her eyes; each fiery ray was a tress of her flaming hair. She had needed him. Iskander forced himself to thrust from his mind the thought that no one had ever needed him before.

Determinedly he fixed his attention on the trail snaking through the thick timber. Both were unfamil-

iar to him. The mist billowed and drifted so across the
path, and the pines stood so close together, that he
could not see the twists and turns ahead; it occurred to
him that not only the UnKind, but also brigands
might roam the Piney Woods, and the notion of being
ambushed nipped at the back of his brain, disquieting
him, then gnawed at him more fiercely as he thought
of dying in this strange land, so far from home. He
recalled then the tale of Rhiannon's blood parents,
dispossessed and then dead, with no loving hands to
lay them out for burial, no loving voices to repeat for
them the Prayer of Passing, no loving hearts to mourn
them; and he suddenly felt more alone than he had
even in the arctic wasteland of the East. He felt the
weight of the blade he carried and remembered the
foulness he had unwittingly loosed in the weapon
when he had battled the snow-tiger; and briefly he
longed for a plain, unmagicked sword, one on which
he could depend in a fight, and rued the loss of his
targe, lying now at the bottom of the sea. He feared,
too, to lose his way, for now and then a fork branched
off from the narrow road and he had only a rough map
Ulthor had drawn to guide him to Finisterre, to the
Strathmore Plains, at whose edge the keep of Ashton
Wells stood. There, he hoped to obtain aid from the
Prince Lord Gerard, the boon companion of Ulthor's
traveling days.

Iskander needed a boat; without one all was lost. He
would have no means of reaching the continents of
Montano and Botanica, and his long, hazardous journey would be for naught. The knowledge was bitter as
gall in his mouth, its acid edge sharpened still further
by what lay coiled like a beast in a dark corner of his
mind: Without a boat there was no way home for him,
either.

"The Prince will help ye," Ulthor had assured him.
"He fought at the Lady Ileana's and the Lord Cain's

sides that winter upon the Strathmore Plains. Before that his brother, the Lord Parrish, was taken captive by the SoulEaters. Gerard knows what that means. Do not despair, Lord. He will not turn ye away."

On these words did all Iskander's hopes hinge. It was both more and less than what he could have wished for.

He broke his fast as he walked—Boreal food still strange to his tongue, though no less palatable for that, a mixture of dried meat and meal subtly flavored with herbs. Their scent reminded him of Rhiannon, and he finished the small repast quickly, willing thoughts of her not to intrude yet again upon his senses. He quenched his thirst at a clear rill that broke the track, shallow enough that he was able to slog across it to the far side, narrow enough that the leap was an easy one for Anuk. From the bough of a fir, a snowbird, startled by their passing, took flight, fluttering through the branches of the trees until at last it broke free of them to wing its way across the lightening sky.

The sight made Iskander's heart ache, for there were snowbirds in the forests of Iglacia, too, and for a bittersweet moment, he could almost imagine himself home, in the woods surrounding Tovaritch Fortress; and once more he wondered if he would ever see it again. But presently, knowing that, thanks to Cain's determination and insistence, he had been warned beforehand of the risks his quest would entail, Iskander shrugged off his melancholy mood and set himself the task of carefully observing his environs so he would not be unprepared if anything out of the ordinary occurred.

Dusk was just falling when he halted for the night, but the early darkness that was winter's dying gasp came swiftly in the timber, and with it the thin mist thickened so, that he could no longer be sure of the trail. It was better to set a cautious pace than to waste time traveling in circles, he decided wisely. He built a fire of dead branches he gathered from the forest floor. The wood was damp, but he placed pine boughs among the branches, igniting them with the blue flame that sprang from his fingertips when he summoned his Power. He fed them with brittle, dried leaves and twigs he fortuitously discovered in a nearby hollow log, sheltered from the worst of the wind and the wet; and soon the fire burned brightly, if a trifle smokily, taking the chill from the twilight air. After that Iskander stripped from the lupine's back the packs it carried, one of which was a little tent that he hurriedly erected. Then, from his own rucksack, he drew forth a small pot and pan and set about boiling tea and cooking something to eat, while Anuk bounded away into the darkness to hunt, returning sometime later with some unknown nightbird dangling from his jaws.

By then Iskander sat cross-legged before the fire, huddled deep in the warmth of his cloak as he consumed his scanty meal, his eyes averted from the blaze itself—for a man who gazed long and deep into the flames would be temporarily blind once he looked away, and he was not such a fool as that. He ate hungrily; the miles he had traveled had quickened his appetite, and after the cold rations of this morn and noon, the hot food was welcome in his belly. But his motions were mechanical, even so; the forest that had seemed so homelike during the day had taken on a faintly sinister cast with the coming of the dark. He dared not slacken his vigilance, but listened intently to the stillness of the night, the silence that was broken only by the snap of the fire as it danced in the wind, the crack of the bird's fragile bones between the lupine's sharp teeth, the steady dripping of water from the branches of the trees, and the hoot of a snowy owl somewhere in the distance.

And then suddenly there came a sound that did not belong—the snap of a twig beneath a booted heel, followed by the soft swish of pine boughs falling into place after being brushed aside.

"Khan, *beware!*" Anuk uttered, his hackles rising even as, for an instant, Iskander tensed and inhaled sharply, the hair standing up on the back of his neck as a frisson crept down his spine.

Then deliberately he forced himself to breathe, to relax, and to scoop up with his fingers the last of his supper and chew it slowly, as though he had not heard that menacing noise, before setting his wooden bowl aside, the gesture as leisurely and casual as though he were unaware that someone—or some*thing*—lurked in the woods. He yawned and stretched, seeming to toss back naturally the hood of his cloak as he did so, so the hilt of the sword that rode his shoulders lay bare, within easy reach. Briefly he thought again of the bane he had previously unleashed in the blade, and he wondered whether it had indeed spent itself in the snow-tiger, as, at the time, it had appeared. He hoped fervently that it had, but he had no way of knowing for certain until he once more drew the sword from its sheath and called forth the Power at his command. Still, tainted or nay, the blade was the only weapon he had; it must serve against whomever or whatever skulked in the shadows—though Iskander thought grimly that *skulked* was hardly the right word, for now the sounds of approach issuing from the thicket were unmistakable. Clearly the intruder was making no attempt at stealth.

The realization lessened some of Iskander's apprehension, yet every nerve in his body was stretched tight as thong. Then at last the shadowy figure stepped into sight, her long, unbound hair a cascade of flame in the moonlight, her fur mantle white as the mist that swirled about her hem, so she seemed to glide toward him, ethereal as a Weeping Wraith, embodiment of Ceridwen, Keeper of the Earth. *Rhiannon* . . .

A short distance away she came to a halt, facing him across the fire, looking, in its flaring incandescence, all golden, glowing eyes in a face pale as death. Though she gave no sign of it, he thought she must be hungry, and tired; and though he knew he should have despaired of it, he was instead suddenly fiercely glad he had set an easy pace and made camp at dusk. He did not acknowledge to himself, even now, that deep down inside, a part of him had hoped she would come.

She spoke no word of greeting, no explanation of how she had come to be in the woods—though it was plain she must have followed him—but said only, passionately, her voice throbbing, "Ye must teach me," flinging the words at him defiantly, like a gauntlet. But her eyes entreated all the same, and she trembled a little, though it might have been from the cold, Iskander knew.

Pity wrung his heart even as a wild, irrepressible surge of joy welled within him at her words. But then reality set in—unrelenting, uncompassionate—and in the wake of his first emotions came wrath and distress, a sense of his own helplessness against the quest that bound him, taking precedence over all else.

"I cannot, Rhiannon," he told her earnestly. "Ye know I cannot."

"But ye must!" she cried; and then suddenly she was kneeling at his feet, her head bowed, her control broken as she sobbed out her loneliness, her yearning to belong, her need to understand who and what she was, her need—the Light spare him—of *him,* and made one rash promise after another—promises Iskander knew that she could not keep, that he could not let her keep—if only he would take her with him and teach her how to master her Power.

"Do ye get up, *khatun*," he exhorted as he tried awkwardly and without success to raise her to her feet. "Ye do but shame yourself with such words, and me, also. Do ye think I would take ye on such terms as ye have proffered? Do ye truly think me so cold, so callous as that, that ye must offer even yourself— By the moons! Have ye so little sense, then, of your own worth as a woman, and one of the Chosen, besides? Do ye get up, *khatun,* I say! Rise, and let me hear no more of such foolish talk. I am a priest and a Lord and an honorable man; and though that may mean nothing to ye, it means something to me. I would not take a common concubine in such a manner—much less a high-born maid. Ye insult us both with even the suggestion."

At that she slowly stood and lifted her head, her chin quivering, color staining the face she turned from him so he would not see her shame, her tears as she struggled to compose herself.

After a moment, softly, she beseeched, "Pray, forgive me, Lord, for my outburst. I did not plan it; it just . . . happened. I meant no disrespect. 'Tis only that I—I do not know what is to become of me. . . ." Her voice trailed away as again she strove to control her emotions. She bit her lower lip, then said contritely, "I'm sorry. 'Tis plain I have trespassed where I'm not wanted. I should not have burdened ye with my troubles, especially when you've those of your own far greater than mine. I do not know what made me so bold, so wanton, except that—except that . . . I wanted so badly to learn what ye alone could teach me, and I had nothing but myself to offer in return. I see now that 'twas indeed foolish of me, as ye said—a bad bargain."

"Only for ye, *khatun,* had I proved a brutal master. There are evil men in this world, all too willing to use a maid however they will, with no caring or tenderness. Did ye never think of that?" Iskander asked gently.

"Nay, Lord, only that ye were fair of face, strong of limb, and treated me kindly. It was enough. It was far more than for what I, a beggar, had any right to ask."

"Then ye do, indeed, hold yourself too cheap."

She turned to him then, and he noticed for the first time the morning star belted at her waist. It was a favored weapon of the Vikanglians. He wondered if that was the reason she had chosen it, to try to honor what little she knew of her heritage, to try to gain a little of her own identity, however meager; and it was all he could do to harden his heart against her. It would be the height of folly to take her with him, worse yet to take that with which she had so desperately and pathetically endeavored to bribe him. He was a twelfth-ranked priest—no fool, no rogue. And still, Iskander's heart warred within his breast. Was he due nothing for all he had risked? he asked himself— then hated himself for asking.

"I'm sorry, *khatun,*" he insisted. "But 'tis for your own sake that I must refuse what ye ask of me. I do not know where I go or into what dark peril or at what cost—only that I must do what must be done, no matter what. For this I would give my own life—and yours as well, if such ever became necessary. Do ye understand me? The whole of Tintagel is at stake, and I cannot afford to be merciful if ruthlessness is all that will serve me. Better a life here among all ye know than to die alone in a place where naught is familiar. 'Tis no easy thing . . . what I face—and I would spare ye that."

"Then ye should have no difficulty carrying out your duty, Lord," she rejoined, a flash of pride and disdain now in her eyes, "for though ye have meant well, every kindness ye have shown me has held a small but painful barb, as now, born of your devotion to your quest. None could doubt that where ye are concerned, *that* is supreme, so unshakable that ye would spare me a dubious death for a life whose unhappiness is only too certain. But I say unto ye that no matter how well intentioned your aim, my choices are not yours to make, Lord. Free Will is Light-given, and no Kind has the right to take it away from another. Do ye dare to do that and still call yourself a True Defender of the Light?"

The point hit home. Yet still, Iskander protested.

"For all your Power, ye are untrained, *khatun*," he contended. "Ye will be a hindrance to me. Ye will slow me down. I will not be able to depend upon ye. Always at the back of my mind will be the thought that perhaps when I need ye most, ye will fail me because of your ignorance and your lack of skill."

"For all that it is crude, it is still Power I possess, Lord," Rhiannon shot back smoothly, her tone persuading now, for she sensed that she had a chance yet to win him over with logic where tears had failed. "And that may be a claim that here in the West, I alone can make, save for yourself. I learn quickly. If I can keep up with Yael, I can keep up with ye. I will neither ask for nor expect any quarter from ye. I will do my share of what needs doing, and more; and I will bend my Power to my will or die trying. For always at the back of my mind will be the thought that when ye need me most, I must be there without fail, come what may—for your sake, and all Tintagel's."

Softly Iskander swore.

"May the Blue Moon weep if even had I not seen your *Progignere*, I would not know ye for a Vikanglian, *khatun*," he averred, "for they are all accursed, silver-tongued devils, each and every last one of them, yea—and ye one of the worst I have seen in many a long day. In truth, have ye no shame to speak so boldly, to twist my words will ye, nill ye and cast them back at me in such an untoward manner?"

"None at all—if it means I am to become what I would, Lord," she replied, her eyes once more meekly downcast so he would not see, he felt sure, the triumph within them at suspecting she had at last prevailed.

And she had, for he no longer had the heart now to turn her away, not when she had spoken so bravely and eloquently, despite his own words to the contrary.

"Kneel, then," he bid her finally, in his voice a note of despair and resignation; for against all his better judgment did he concede to her, his only balm at his decision the Lady Ileana's words to him when he had departed from Mont Saint Christopher.

Turn away no one and nothing that might in some way serve ye, Iskander, she had advocated, *however doubtfully, for 'tis a hard lot we have given ye—and the only heroes are dead ones. Nor, no matter how agonizing it proves, count the cost of your quest to friend or foe. For Tintagel no price is too high.*

That she who had herself paid so dearly should have so counseled him had rent him, like a sword cleaving him, and he had vowed to himself that despite her advice, no innocent should suffer on his behalf. Even now, at the sight of Rhiannon kneeling before him, her bright head expectantly bowed, he could not help but think of her lying dead or, worse, taken prisoner by the SoulEaters; and for a long moment, he nearly reneged and withdrew his sanction.

But her words rang in his head—*Free Will is Light-given, and no Kind has the right to take it away from another. Do ye dare to do that and still call yourself a True Defender of the Light?*—and in the end Iskander knew that if he denied her, he would, in truth, be little better than the UnKind he hunted; for did not the greater sin lie in the condemnation not of the flesh, but of the spirit?

"I am no knave. I will take ye as my vassal—but no more than that," he said to ease her mind—and rid his own of unworthy thoughts.

Then at last he drew from its sheath the Sword of Ishtar, and he lightly but firmly brought it to bear upon Rhiannon's shoulders, in the time-honored accolade of the East, telling her the traditional words to speak that obligated her as vassal to his liege, forcing himself to ignore the small shiver of foreboding that touched him, like a grue, as she pronounced her fiat and kissed the sword to seal her oath.

"The Lady Rhiannon sin Lothian," he intoned solemnly, "heretofore known as Rhiannon Olafursdaughter, I, the Lord Iskander sin Tovaritch, do accept your pledge and your service, and ask naught but that ye, as my vassal, serve me faithfully and well in all things for so long as ye are bound to me, as I, as your liege, shall treat ye honestly and fairly in all things for so long as ye are mine to command. That being sworn by us both, do ye rise, Lady, and receive the Kiss of Peace."

At that Rhiannon stood; and placing his hands on her arms, Iskander kissed first her right cheek, and then her left, his mouth soft as the brush of a butterfly's wings against her skin. As man and woman touched, something warm and electric leaped between them, so fleetingly that it might have been born of their imagination, though each felt it and knew it to be real. Iskander's nostrils flared, and a blush rose hotly to Rhiannon's cheeks. Quickly each stepped back from the other, as though to say, "We are only liege and vassal, vassal and liege, nothing more, *nothing more.*" But in the awkwardness and confusion of the moment, Iskander's breathing was long and deep and harsh, Rhiannon's short and shallow and delicate, as though they had run a long way and now hovered before the edge of some precipice, while behind, a pack of hellhounds bayed. Above, lightning split the black sky, and thunder rumbled ominously.

It was done; the vow was made. Regardless of whatever second thoughts assailed them, they were committed to each other now. It was a realization at once sobering and yet welcome as the sun that marked the end of the long, dark winter of the tundra. Despite themselves, in their secret hearts each rejoiced at the twining of their LifePaths.

"Hold!" a voice bellowed, shattering suddenly the spell that had seemed to come upon them. "Hold, I say!"

At the shout Iskander and Rhiannon started, reaching instinctively for their weapons, for lost in reverie, neither had heard the interloper's approach; nor had Anuk, silent witness to their exchange of promises, seen fit to cry warning.

"Be at ease, khan," the lupine stated in answer to its master's sharp glance. *"There is no danger to ye—at least, not this time. But next time ye might not be so fortunate, and so, with my silence, have I shown ye, in the hope that the lesson will be better remembered. Befriend the Lady, yea, since it seems ye must. But heed my words, and take care that ye do not let your feelings for her blind ye to all else, jeopardizing your quest and imperiling your very life."*

A hot, defensive retort rose to Iskander's lips; with difficulty he compelled himself to bite it back, knowing that Anuk was right—for had he not himself considered these very things? And still, just now, because of Rhiannon, he had permitted his sound reasoning to be swayed, his mind to wander—mistakes that might easily prove fatal. He could not even fault the lupine for not warning him of the interloper's presence, for now Iskander realized that sometime while Rhiannon had knelt before him, the wind had shifted. Anuk had smelled the interloper's familiar scent and known there was no cause for alarm. It was Yael striding from the mist and the shadows of the trees into the firelight.

"Yael!" Rhiannon cried, stricken, as she recognized her brother. "What are ye doing here?"

"I might ask ye the same question," he retorted grimly, on his face a conflict of emotions, not the least of which was pain, Iskander thought, "though I think I need not look far to find my answer." Yael's crystal-blue eyes glittered with anguish and anger, slid challengingly to the tall, dark man at Rhiannon's side. Seeing the two of them standing there so close together, it crossed the giant's mind that they made a fitting pair, different yet equal, neither dwarfing the other. The unwitting thought was like a knife in his heart.

"Does the Lord mean so much to ye then that ye needs must sneak like a thief in the night from our parents' lodge, with never a word as to your leaving or why?" he demanded, his voice rasp-edged with feeling. "Did ye not think they deserved better than that, Rhiannon Olafursdaughter, our parents who loved ye as though ye were their own blood child and who will likewise grieve at your loss? Did ye not think ye owed them at least some explanation, some word of solace and love to ease their hearts and minds in the wake of your absence—or were ye so callous and cruel and ungrateful as not to care that they would be sick with fear in their ignorance of what had become of ye?" The Boreal reproached his sister pitilessly, driven as much by his own hurt as the thought of his parents' heartache. "For shame, Rhiannon Olafursdaughter! For shame!"

Tears of remorse streamed down Rhiannon's cheeks at her brother's stern admonishment, for she knew she was all too deserving of the accusations, and her guilt was surpassing.

"I—I never wanted to wound them—or ye, either, Yael," she choked out softly. "'Tis just that I was—I was afraid they might forbid me to go, and then I would have been forced to add insult to their injury by disobeying them; for I could not bear to throw away the chance to master my Power, to become what I would. I could not! The Lord Iskander has Power—Power such as my own. He can teach me of mine. . . . Oh, Yael, do ye not know what that means to me? Do ye indeed wonder that I acted as I did?"

"Nay," he replied more gently, "for Ulthor told me of the Lord's sunburst tattoo and the dodecagon torque, the marks of a Druswid, a twelfth-ranked priest of the East, and what that meant; and so this morn, when I saw ye gather your belongings and slip away, I guessed what ye were about, what ye sought, and I understood. I explained all to our parents, and then I followed ye. I hoped to turn ye from this path ye have chosen, but it seems I have come too late—" Yael broke off, pausing for a moment, as though collecting his thoughts. Then he continued, directing his next words to Iskander.

"Do ye take Rhiannon as your vassal, ye must take me as well, Lord," he declared, so his sister realized he had witnessed at least a part of what had passed between her and her liege, and she flushed with agony to think Yael knew of her disgrace, the bargain she had put forth to woo the Lord Iskander to her will. "Ye may have need of a strong right arm at your side," the giant pointed out, "and ye will find no man better than I to serve ye."

"Nay, Yael, do not ask this of my liege," Rhiannon implored, "not on my account, I beg of ye. There is no need—"

"The choice is mine to make. I did not decide for

ye, Rhiannon. Do ye not decide for me," her brother adjured, a stubborn thrust to his jaw that she recognized all too well and that made her heart sink.

Though she could not be certain Yael had heard them, to have her own irrefutable argument to her liege so paraphrased and sullenly tossed back at her stung severely. She knew now the helplessness Iskander had felt when she had harried him, her words as keen and on target as a blade, and she understood, too, the despair and resignation in his voice when at last he had bade her kneel before him and take oath as his vassal. Now she also was forced to give way, and she said no more, though her heart was sore beset at the thought that his love for her was such that she had unintentionally brought Yael to this—and thus dealt their parents a doubly bitter blow.

"Do ye know what ye are asking of me?" Iskander queried gravely of the Boreal. "'Tis doubtless to your death I will lead ye, as I have so warned Rhiannon."

"There are many kinds of dying, Lord," Yael returned with quiet dignity; and in his eyes when they looked again upon Rhiannon was love deep and abiding, though not that of a brother for his sister.

This, Iskander saw and, to his dismay, comprehended; and his guilt and sorrow for the giant were increased a thousandfold by the like desire harbored deep in his own heart, the memory of the Kiss of Peace he had bestowed upon Rhiannon and that had proved anything but peaceful. Perhaps that, too, Yael had seen. Perhaps it was what drove him now . . . the thought that Rhiannon might be lost to him in more ways than one. It was a thought Iskander understood.

"There is that, also, which is worse than dying," he observed, in his voice a note of wistfulness and ache he had not expected; and he knew, even as he spoke the words, that he had heedlessly laid himself bare as the Boreal.

For a long, hard moment, Yael gazed at him steadily, then said, "Yea, there is that, Lord. There is that," and thus, both with great respect and genuine regret, did each man learn the other's measure.

"Would you call me liege, even so?" Iskander asked curiously and not without admiration.

"I would." The response was unhesitant, unafraid.

"Then kneel, Yael Olafursson, and do me homage —and pray that neither of us lives to wish this night's work undone."

And so Yael knelt and bowed his head and swore fealty to Iskander. Such was the giant's mighty fiat that it rang long and loud, the oath torn from his mouth by a sudden and fierce rising of the wind, which did not abate. *Let it be done!* The words still echoed faintly, lost amid the now-wild rustling and swaying of the forest, when, without further warning, the rain came hard and fast.

DAY STAR

ShapeShifter

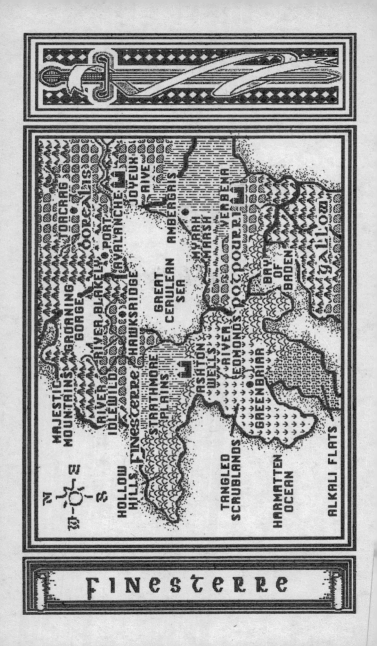

FINESTERRE

Chapter 11

The Light help me, in truth, for although I knew I ought to have sent them both back to Torcrag, I was glad of Rhiannon's and Yael's company. It was only when night fell and I lay alone in my small tent that an icy fist of fear clutched my heart when I thought that they must surely follow me to their doom, that I would surely bring upon them what I myself most dreaded: a death far from home and all known and beloved.

Yet even this they would endure for what little I could offer them. It was a faith of which I could not feel myself deserving, but which I nevertheless set about as best I could to earn—for how could I do any less?

Rhiannon, I taught the teachings of the Druswids, as my mentor, Brother Yucel, had taught me, as though she were a child; for how else does one begin except at the beginning? Daily she learned, for her mind was indeed quick and bright, and her eagerness to please me was such that sometimes I hardly knew how to respond so she would not read into my words of praise more than I intended. We were liege and vassal, adept and novice; more than that would prove a complication I knew was best avoided.

Yet even so, I must confess I was not loath to sit silently in the shadows of a firelit evening and watch the way in which the flames played across her pale countenance so her eyes shone like burnished gold and the heat brought a roseate glow to her skin, softening planes and angles that grew sharp-edged as the days passed; for once we crossed the River Snowy and entered the Shivering Mountains, the miles we traveled were hard and the hunting was too often lean. The fat, woolly goats that inhabited the crags were swift and agile, as were the occasional deer, smaller cousins of the dëor, mounts favored by the Vikanglians. Though Yael carried his stout longbow, his arrows were numbered, and there was little time for the stealthy tracking of either goats or deer, besides. Good fortune was seldom with us in slaying either. We were luckier with the snares we laid, likely to entrap at least a few rabbits or birds. But a brace of either did not go far when there were four mouths to feed—and one of those belonging to a ravenous lupine and one to a giant, though Yael frequently stinted himself so there would be food enough for the rest of us, and Rhiannon likewise picked at her share, claiming she was not hungry.

Yet her unaccustomed manipulation of her Power drained her, and I fretted for her health, as did Yael; for she was both what drew us together and perversely, on a deeper level, distanced us, though we never spoke of this last to her—or even to each other. But it was there all the same—in the glint of Yael's eyes when my approval brought a smile to Rhiannon's face, and in the frown that would darken my own visage when I saw how he coveted her.

His love for her was nothing to me, I told myself firmly, nor were her feelings for him. Yet of a *sudden would my heart lurch a little when I saw the mauve smudges that ringed her eyes, how her battle to command her Power sapped her strength, and how, regardless, she ate less than she should— and pressed on Yael what remained of her portion. More often than not I went to bed famished to ensure she did not and hunted even farther afield the next morn so there should be no lack at our fire that evening.*

—Thus it is Written—
in
The Private Journals
of the Lord Iskander sin Tovaritch

The Groaning Gorge, Borealis, 7275.5.47

IT WAS STEADY BUT SLOW PROGRESS THE QUESTERS MADE, knowing but little of the trail they followed and hindered still further by the rain that continued to fall, if not hard, at least persistently and which there was no eluding. It soaked through fur cloaks and leather garments to the skin, aided and abetted by the mist and the wind that whipped up the mountain heights and chilled even Anuk to the bone, despite that spring was by this time well and truly upon them. Every pine bough was a source of dripping water, too, and there were swift mountain streams to be forded, also. It seemed to Iskander that he could not remember a time when he had been warm and dry. Almost, he thought they should have gone the long way around the mountains, toward Port Avalanche, where at least there would have been a warm welcome and food aplenty for them, decent shelter for a night or two, a respite, however brief, from the wet. But he had chosen instead to journey through the mountain passes, a harder but more direct route—one he had reckoned, for the former reason, would be less traveled and therefore less dangerous. The first had certainly proved true—they had met no one on the poor winding path they followed—but the second was debatable. Of either the UnKind or reivers, they had seen no sign. But game was scarce, and the steep, narrow road was slippery and treacherous from the rain and the mist, often with crumbling edges that fell away into nothingness, dizzying drops that held sure death far below. More than once, boulders and smaller rocks dislodged by sluicing waters blocked the track, and these the companions were forced either to climb or to find other means around. Iskander realized now why the Boreals kept no herds for riding; they had no use for them. The thick forests and mountainous terrain that covered much of the land were easier and safer to navigate afoot.

But finally, much to their relief, there came the day when the travelers reached the Groaning Gorge. There, the going was not so difficult as before, all downhill into the gorge itself, which was not truly a gorge at all, but, rather, a ragged-edged but otherwise distinctly bowl-shaped plain, ringed by the towering Shivering Mountains of Borealis and the equally lofty Majestic Mountains of Finisterre. The border between the two lands lay halfway across the expanse, according to the crude map Ulthor had drawn, and to Rhiannon's and Yael's own knowledge—limited and uncertain, since, for the most part, the giants kept to themselves—of what was beyond the boundaries of Borealis.

Northernmost region of the whole of Aerie, Borealis was entirely surrounded by water and mountains, effectively isolated from the rest of the continent.

North and east and west, Iskander knew from his lost maps and own experience, were oceans, the Tempest whence he had come, and the Zephyr and the Harmattan. To the southeast was the fairyland of Valcoeur, which men avoided if they could, for few, if any, were ever seen again who trespassed there, and those few like to be mad of the experience—though Cain and Ileana had escaped that unhappy fate. At Borealis's southern shore lapped the waves of the Great Cerulean Sea, vast and unpredictable of temperament, as though some massive, unknown force pulsed at its submerged heart, disrupting and distorting its fathomless depths. And lastly, to the southwest, lay Finisterre, of which Ulthor had voiced most knowledge and which was the questers' destination.

At the summit on the Borealis side of the Groaning Gorge, they paused to rest and draw breath, for their torturous ascent had taken its toll. Nor, for all that they had sought it eagerly, was what awaited below as heartening as they had hoped.

Far and away the gorge stretched, so far that the Majestic Mountains—barely discernible through the rain and the mist as a dark, jagged oblique against the horizon—looked like anthills in the distance. What was between here and there, none could guess, the gorge being blanketed by a swirling white fog so thick that it was scarcely affected by the drizzle, so it seemed a colossal cloud floated at the sunken hub of the encircling peaks, with nothing below it but emptiness, a great bottomless hole in the earth. For a moment, crazily, Iskander wondered if he leaped off into it, if he would come out on the other side of Tintagel, perhaps popping up somewhere in the Gloriana Mountains of Cygnus, whence it would be but a short voyage across the Mistral Ocean to Tovaritch Fortress and home. Then he chided himself sternly for the foolish thought, realizing he was sodden and cold, hungry and tired—no fit state for anyone and one to which he did not willingly acquiesce, though he bore it as the others did, uncomplainingly.

He had little inclination at the moment for the downward trek into that churning, uncompromising whiteness, along a precipitous, serpentine trail that was slick and muddy from the dismal weather and across which stones lay scattered and swollen creeks flooded. But the day was less than half gone, and there was still, if the companions were lucky, game and a shelter to be found before dark. So at last, wearily, Iskander stood and pulled on his rucksack, as did Rhiannon and Yael, despite that they, too, were exhausted. Then the small party stumbled forward, Iskander leading the way, Anuk bringing up the rear.

Down and down, they wended, and down still farther, until it seemed they must descend unto the very Gate of the Darkness, slipping and sliding as they went, grabbing for whatever purchase they could find, precarious handholds amid loose rocks, saplings, and bushes sleek and glistening with mizzle and mist, and more likely than not to be uprooted from the muck to which they cleaved than to bear the weight that scrabbled and tore at them, sometimes frantically. And still, incredibly, it was a less arduous trip than what the travelers had faced going up—and would face again once the gorge lay behind them.

It was toward dusk that they broached the seemingly impenetrable white fog and found it not so dense as they had at first supposed, though, still, it proved an impediment. It flowed and eddied like a sea, occluding the path; and the trees that previously had thinned with the heights now began once more to thicken, bristly branches hanging low, with the rain seeping through them.

Of game the questers had spied none. But just as the

First Moon rose, the color of silver frost and ringed eerily with moondust and mist in the darkening sky, they came upon an outcrop of stone. Beneath the low overhang, in the face of the mountain, was carved a crescent niche, not large, but with room enough for the four of them, who welcomed the shared warmth of body heat in the chill of the night. They sought the refuge gladly, unmindful of the thorny brush that grew about and within it, the lichen and cobwebs that clung to the ceiling and walls, the animal bones, withered leaves, and other decay that littered its floor. It was better protection than their small tents would offer against both the rain and the wind—guarded by the overhang and set deep into the mountain face.

Iskander and Yael gathered wet wood and pine boughs, which Rhiannon, after a few tries, set afire with the blue flame she was slowly but surely learning to call from her fingertips. Hunkered beside her, Iskander watched, patiently correcting her mistakes, while Yael retrieved pots and pans and provisions from the rucksacks, his eyes averted from this witchery that he still secretly feared and loathed, that brought painfully home to him how different from him Rhiannon was—and how like the Lord. She was gradually becoming a stranger to him, the giant thought, then determinedly thrust the unwelcome notion from his mind. They had grown up together, he reassured himself; he knew her as well as he knew himself. But still, he kept his distance as she ignited that unnatural fire of wood too damp to have burned otherwise, and he forced himself to concentrate on preparing both mulled wine and tea, which he then gingerly set to boil upon the blaze. Surreptitiously, after he turned away, he made the ancient pagan sign against evil and prayed to both the Boreals' old gods and the Light to ward him against all Power. As though in response, the fire crackled and hissed and smoked, and despite the welcome heat of it, Yael shuddered.

This Iskander saw—and did not know whether to laugh or to cry at the Boreal's fear and ignorance, both stemming, as ever those two demons did, from lack of knowledge and understanding. The mind was like a child; it must be taught, trained, and disciplined, lest it grow wild as a savage beast, knowing only surviving, never living. For it was only among the civilized that peace and tolerance and order could flourish instead of war and bigotry and chaos; and like weeds in a garden, the latter threatened ever to encroach upon the former and must be continually, ruthlessly, uprooted.

In silence the companions ate their meager meal, savoring the mulled wine that Rhiannon had brought and that was nearly gone, though they had hoarded it carefully, knowing there would be no more until they reached Ashton Wells. Beyond their cramped shelter, lightning flashed through the trees, thunder rumbled, rain cascaded like a waterfall over the edges of the outcrop, and mist drifted and billowed. Within, the fire spat and sizzled, and the travelers huddled inside cloaks drying too slowly for real comfort in the warmth of the flames, and chafed themselves against the cold night air that crept in despite the blaze.

It was as though they were utterly alone, cut off from the rest of the world, sealed in a cocoon. It was a sensation they had known before, for the mountains were riddled with nooks and crannies and this was not the first time the questers had sheltered in such a place. But still, the howl of the elements beyond, in sharp contrast to the hush within, weighed heavily upon them; and finally, in an effort to lighten the gloom that enveloped them, Iskander smoothed a little space of earth before him and, picking up a nearby twig, began to scratch a series of runes upon the floor, so Rhiannon knew that it was time for her lesson.

Eagerly she drew close to the Lord, a pride pervading her as she realized how many of the symbols she had come to know, she, who had had scant knowledge of reading and writing ere now. And deep down inside, despite the pain she had brought both her parents and Yael, she was glad she had followed her heart—and the Lord. Though she did not as yet command it, she grasped the essence of her Power now, understood why it was so rare and revered, this gift she had been given. For the Art of ShapeShifting was like no other. It required a delicate balance of the senses that was not only difficult to master, but dangerous to command.

"One does not actually *become* the shape one takes," Iskander had explained to her one evening. "That is, one's body does not literally dissolve and re-form during the shift, which would be an unnatural thing. What *does* happen is this: The ethereal essence that is the pure and elemental substance of one is, during the change, channeled from one's body into one's aura, giving it color, texture, shape, and matter, so what appears to the beholder is a paradox—both real and illusion. The metamorphosis is tangible, in that it is perceived by all the beholder's senses; but it is not *true*. Few of the Chosen are ever blessed with the ability to alter their auras in this fashion, and the art is not without peril. For during the transformation, the body is, on a physical plane, virtually an empty shell, highly exposed and vulnerable to the ethereal essences of others—BodySnatchers, we Druswids call them. And unlike a simple TelePath, which is only a Sending and no more, the energy required to maintain a ShapeShift is such that one may lack the well of Power, the reserve of strength necessary to fend off the invader. Thus, each time one ShapeShifts, one risks being forever displaced from one's own body and becoming a lost soul. That is not a thing to be taken lightly, *khatun,* and it has happened . . . it has happened to some I have known. Such was the price they paid for their carelessness, their foolhardiness. So, do ye heed my words, and learn your limitations, and stay within them; for those who do not practice prudence and wisdom in this art do not long possess it—or aught else in this dimension."

Now, recalling Iskander's words, Rhiannon shivered and bent to apply herself diligently to this night's lesson, while, scowling, Yael removed himself to the farthest corner of the shelter, his body rigid with disapproval, despite that he knew that it gave his sister pleasure to learn what the Lord taught. That Ulthor, who knew both of the world and of Power, had trusted and believed in Iskander, Yael conveniently forgot; and covertly, as the lesson progressed, he eyed his liege suspiciously and thought uncharitable thoughts.

Almost, he wished he had not sworn fealty to Iskander, for it had been born not of any real desire to serve him, but for Rhiannon's sake. Yet deep down inside, Yael knew, too, even so, that he had not been averse to this adventure, that he had often envied Ulthor's travels and longed to know more than just what lay within the boundaries of Borealis. More than once he had chafed at the inherent clannishness of his tribe, which stemmed from the fact that too often in Time Past, the young warriors, the lifeblood of the giants, had ventured beyond Borealis—and had never been seen again. Ulthor was one of the few who had lived to return and tell of what was now legend, too long past to belong to the memories of even the elders of the tribe. For there had been a great war once, or so the bards sang, a war to end all wars; and afterward Tintagel as the Kind had known it had been no more, and those who had valued their lives had kept to their own hearths, lest the Darkness that had lain upon the world claim them and theirs. This was the lesson the giants had learned and remembered.

And yet when, in her darkest hour of need, Tintagel had called upon them, not only the young warriors, but the old of Borealis had marched down from the north to answer the world's cry. For of this, also, did the bards sing: Never again must the Darkness be permitted to wreak Its will upon Tintagel, because in that will lay madness—and the end of all. And perhaps, if he were honest with himself, that, even more than Rhiannon, was why Yael had knelt before the Lord and taken the oath to serve him. And if he were more truthful still, Yael knew he must admit his respect for Iskander, no matter how grudging, his admiration for the Lord, who alone had dared to undertake this quest to brave the heart of the Darkness, who had accepted as vassals both him and Rhiannon, despite their ignorance, and taught them both, in his own fashion, and asked naught in return save their loyalty.

On such things as these did Yael Olafursson think long and hard as he stared out into the oppressive night and watched the rain pour from the overhang, while Iskander scrawled his glyphs in the dirt and Rhiannon learned what she would learn.

As for Anuk, he dozed by the fire, a simpler creature than the Kind—and glad of it.

Chapter 12

To whosoever may readeth this record, let it be knowne that, once, we were a peaceful and prosperous tribe who dwelt here upon this faire and hallowed plain, Grünen Gorst, rulen by our pale and beauteous Morgen-Stern, she who, being not only of the stars, but also from them, was bothe our Goddess and our Queene, and in whose honour we did raiseth these Standing Stones; and here, we did worshippeth her, and payeth her much homage, and bringeth her giftes of golden and other sich riches and offerings as might findeth favour with her, for though she was bothe kinde and bountiful, she was also prideful, and her wrathe was terrible to behold.

Thus, to be further assured of her Blessing, we did also, without fail, each Mittespringan, MitteSumor, Mitteautumpne, and Mittewintar— the holy times—cometh here and maketh much feasting and musicks and dancings to pleasen her, for she did ever luveth the harpe, especially, and was much taken with the notes that did issueth forth from its silver strings. This was because here, amidst these Standing Stones, did her Power haveth its source on this gude earthe, and its song was the song of the harpe, also, and echoed the voice of her own harpe most sweetly whensoever she did playeth it, which was not oft, for her own harpe was a wondrous thing, possessed of an awesome magick not meant for mortal eyes to witness.

And so we dwelt here on this faire and hallowed plain and did revereth she who was bothe our Goddess and our Queene, and all was well.

But then in the Year of Our Goddess-Queene 1459, by the Common Reckoning, Men did cometh to the Grünen Gorst, Southron heatheners, to maken War upon us; for the King of these Southron savages did abideth by no law or order save his own, and he did desireth our Goddess-Queene, of whom all Men spake most gude and faire, and her Power, of which tales were told and bards sang far and wide, and of which wicked and ambitious Men did groweth ever more greedy and jealous as time did passeth.

By that called horsen did these Southron barbarians cometh, armoured and armed, and they did bringeth much fear and panick amongst us, who knew naught of sich eviel and pagan weapons as they did looseth upon us, that spake lightning and thunder, and that did slaughtereth us without leaving any marke; and so did these Southron philistines breacheth the Standing Stones to prisen open the door of our Goddess-Queene's Great Halle and to layen rude and violent hands upon her.

Then did our Goddess-Queene Morgen-Stern, upon seeing how these ungoddessly enemies were come upon her, riseth up whence she dwelt in her Great Halle; and in her fright and fury, she did taketh up her magick harpe of golden and silver, which few Men save our own had gazed upon ere that dreadful day and which ever no Man did toucheth save her, and she did striketh harsh and discordant notes upon it and thereby did unleasheth her direful Power on the Southron swine.

Then did a tremendous and most fearsome boreal beginneth and, shrieking and groaning, did swirleth up horribly from the Great Halle, across Grünen Gorst. None could stand against that chill wind. With mine own eyes, this I saw and do sweareth: All in its path were taken and swept up and hurtled unto the stars, which place was the True and Rightful Demesne of our Goddess-Queene, though she had deigned to live and walk amongst us; and there, the Southron King and his Warriors, being so carried, did trembleth and boweth at her feet and crieth out most piteously for mercy, for there did our Goddess-Queene goeth, also, to sit upon her great throne, in stern Judgement of them.

Alas and alack, never did our Goddess-Queene Morgen-Stern returneth to Grünen Gorst after that calamitous day; and I, Rutghar the Scribe, who do serveth her still by carving this Record upon this Standing Stone, am the last and onliest survivor of what befell our tribe at the hands of the Southron beasts and brought sich sad and bitter ruine upon us.

On the twelfth day of the seventh month of the Year of Our Goddess-Queene 1459, by the Common Reckoning, did I affixeth my name hereto.

—Thus it is Written—
on
A Menhir of the RingStones
in the Groaning Gorge of Borealis

THE RAIN HAD NOT CEASED DURING THE NIGHT. IT WAS still drizzling drearily when Rhiannon, who had taken the last watch, moved to wake the others. Gingerly easing themselves from their cramped positions upon the floor, groaning at their aching joints and muscles, Iskander and Yael rose. Anuk was already up; he hunted early when he could, sometimes managing to bring down small prey he shared with the rest. Providence had been with him this morn; two snowshoe rabbits were roasting tantalizingly on the fire. Within sight of the shelter, Rhiannon had found several handfuls of ripe early berries, as well as some small but abundant mushrooms, now simmering in a pot. It was unexpected and tasty fare, and eagerly the questers broke their fast, washing their meal down with hot tea, which soon took the worst of the chill from them. Then, warmer, their bellies full, and as a result, their mood much improved, they repacked their supplies and headed out, thankful that this morn, at least, they were starting off with cloaks that were dry.

It was toward noon when they finally reached the foothills of the mountains, the edge of the Groaning Gorge, and saw what they had not been able to see before through the mist: What had looked to be a plain was instead a marshland, vast and flooded knee-deep or more by melting snow and rain and runoff from the swollen mountain streams. Tall grasses, spiky weeds, and hollow reeds, all nearly waist high, grew here, tangled amid a profusion of budding heather, slender bracken and, most of all, thick, greening gorse, weirdly twisted and bent sideways by the lash of the wind, spindly branches looking like witches' long, straggling hair. Here and there, odd hummocks rose, spongy with moss and decay, and gnarled, stunted trees sprouted, branches deformly outstretched. In the very center of the whole stood a towering mound, crowned by ancient RingStones that had an eerie cast beneath the leaden sky. Of dark grey rock, they seemed a ruin built by pagans to the old gods. Massive dolmens eroded by the unrelenting elements leaned into one another, as though pushed over by some titanic hand; others, the menhirs, having fallen to the ground, lay about like sacrificial altars waiting for blood to be spilled upon them. Between the megaliths the mist floated and whirled, as though wraiths danced upon the distant tor. In the wind the verdure stirred and swayed like the waves of a sea; the rain dripped steadily into the standing water that filled the marsh. Now and again sounded a splash made by some creature snaking through the slough, and a solitary bird piped a lonely cry. It was a cheerless scene. Clearly Ulthor had not known the state of the Groaning Gorge in the spring.

Softly Iskander swore.

"Well, I'm damned if I've a mind to wade through that morass," he declared, "not knowing the lay of the land, how low it may be in places, how deep the water is—or what inhabits it. Yael, do ye cut us some stout limbs from those trees yonder, from which we can construct a raft—one that will carry us all. Rhiannon, search the shore for strong vines with which we can bind the branches together. I will look about for something we can use as poles. Anuk, there are bound to be marsh fowl here; see if ye can catch some for our supper."

These commands were no sooner given than they were acted upon. The *thwack* of Yael's mighty battle-ax echoed loudly in the hush as he industriously chopped wood, quickly piling up logs, while Rhiannon gathered long ropes of some fibrous, kelplike plant she spied drifting in coils upon the surface of the water, easily pulling the shallow roots from the mire. With his dagger Iskander cut down several slim saplings that stood at the edge of the marsh, and he efficiently stripped them of their suckers and leaves. Anuk flushed out a speckled brown bird crouched amid the golden-green reeds; but much to his disgust, it proved too quick for him and, crying a warning, took flight, alarming an entire flock of its kind, which rose up suddenly from the foliage, like a quiver of arrows loosed in the sky.

Presently the companions managed to assemble a crude but serviceable raft. Carefully they climbed aboard and, once they were certain the makeshift vessel would bear their weight, pushed away from the shore, using their long poles not only to guide and propel the raft across the water, but to drive off the occasional slimy shape—be it beast or plant—that lurked below, an unknown threat. Beyond the shore there was a current of sorts that helped to carry the vessel along, and silently the travelers moved fleetly forward.

An uneasiness lay upon them all, and Iskander had no need to caution them to be on guard. At the prow of the raft, Anuk sat watchfully, his ears pricked forward, his nose sniffing the wind. Now and then he growled low in his throat at the furtive things that skulked beneath the surface; and once, Rhiannon cried out softly at a sudden, sharp tug upon her pole, but it was only snarled in a mass of the kelplike plant with which she and the others had fashioned the vessel. She wrenched the pole free, and the raft swept on.

The wind was stronger upon the water, and colder. The spray cast up from the waves lapping against the sides of the raft was even chillier than the mist, which now, like a shroud, enveloped the questers so they could scarcely see their way. Rhiannon half feared they would become turned about in it, wandering aimlessly in circles; and she was much relieved when now and then the wind lifted the veil and she spied the mound where the RingStones stood—the only point of reference in the marsh. By this she knew that the vessel was still on course, and she marveled at Iskander's uncanny ability to guide it unerringly.

It was almost dusk when, in the distance, lightning began to flare and thunder to roll across the heavens. The companions glanced worriedly at the rapidly darkening firmament, at the bloated black clouds massing menacingly on the horizon; for there was no shelter here in the marsh, and the only high ground was the remote tor, a bleak refuge at best. Still, it was all that was offered, and the small party strove toward it as swiftly as they could, knowing that a storm was about to break upon them. But the grim sky lay beyond, not behind, them and with each hard thrust of their poles against the bottom of the marsh, they drew perilously closer to the ominous clouds. As they did so, the air thickened until it was almost tangible, suffocating, and increasingly charged with a force that perceptibly strengthened as the raft approached the dominant mound that now, like a forbidding keep, loomed just ahead.

A grue crept up Rhiannon's spine at the sight; the fine hairs on her nape stood on end. This had once been a sacred place; she felt in her bones that it was so. There was Power here—long dormant, but Power all the same. Iskander felt it, too, she thought; for his visage was dark and troubled, and a shudder racked his body, though this might have been due to the wind, which was steadily rising. Strands of Rhiannon's hair, which she had neatly plaited this morn, tore free of her sodden braids and whisked across her face, momentarily blinding her before, with one hand, she pushed them back, only to have them lash her again and yet again. The current intensified, snatching the hapless raft along at an increasingly alarming speed; and for a horrible moment, it appeared as though the vessel would be overturned. But Yael drove his pole hard into the mud, and though the raft rocked and spun frighteningly, it steadied at last and somehow held the course.

One by one, huge drops of rain started to spatter from the sky. And then suddenly, much to Rhiannon's dread, an eerie phosphorescent light began to glow erratically amid the RingStones atop the tor, a macabre green flame that sparked and pranced and whorled as though possessed by a demon. Moments later it seemed as though the megaliths themselves had come to life, shimmering and vibrating with a Power that clashed on the wind, like cacophonous notes struck upon a harp. And she knew, abruptly, that she did not want to climb that mound, to take whatever small comfort might be found at its heart.

In Iskander a like emotion warred with common sense. The waves swelled higher and higher as the rain sheeted down. He did not know how far the water would rise, only that he and the rest could not continue upon it. Their improvised vessel could not be counted on to bear them safely on. The shore was beyond reach. Only the tor offered any hope of protection, however slight. But there was Power here, strong and old, Power he had never before felt and so did not understand. It made him wary of the mound and of the RingStones, which he would not normally have feared. There were RingStones at Mont Saint Christopher and Mont Saint Mikhaela both. Yet somehow these of the Groaning Gorge disturbed him in a way the others never had.

But Iskander knew there was no choice but to ascend the tor. The rest realized this, also, and their faces were apprehensive at the prospect. Still, none rebelled against the orders he gave them, shouting to be heard above the roar of the elements. Within moments they had disembarked and were laboriously hauling the raft up the mound so the vessel would not be washed away.

Heads bent against the rain and the wind, they staggered up the bemired tor. Though the incline was gentle and in fairer weather would have posed no difficulty, they slipped and slid precariously in the muck, using their poles not only to brace themselves, but also to fend off a horde of some foul, caimanlike creatures that, in search of a secure place to ride out the storm, had slithered from the marsh and now waddled from amid a scattering of half-buried rocks, long tails swishing, and hissed and spat at the companions threateningly, baring sharp, jagged teeth. The reptiles were not as fierce as they appeared, however, and scuttled away after a few of the bolder ones among them had been jabbed and struck on their snouts by the travelers' poles.

Finally the small party reached the crest, where they discovered a large, flat, rectangular stone set in the center of the earth. With relief they stumbled toward it, dragging the raft behind them. Here, at least, was a place that, while wet, was less likely than the remainder of the summit to be muddy. At one end, in an effort to shield them all as much as possible from the tempest, Yael and Iskander struggled mightily against the wind to heave the vessel up at an angle, while Rhiannon solidly wedged their poles beneath on either side, interweaving as best she could the supple tips of the saplings through the vines on the raft to hold it canted and firm.

Then, glad of respite, however scant, from the elements, the questers huddled under the hastily contrived retreat, too miserable and exhausted for the moment even to unpack their rucksacks. The torrent of rain pelted down, streaming through the cracks between the knobby branches of the upturned vessel; and at last, spurred by the wet and the cold, the companions unrolled their small tents, draping them about the exiguous shelter to further protect them from the worst of the rain and the wind. After that Iskander dashed outside to fetch one of the smaller rocks strewn upon the ground, his face drawn in the green fox fire that continued to flicker among the RingStones. The rock was not a true hearthstone—as his own, now lying at the bottom of the ocean, had been—but it would serve his purpose, he thought, though he hesitated to use his Power in this place, which keened like a *bain sidhe* with Power of its own, a Power far more ancient, he sensed, than his.

It puzzled him, this unknown Power; for like his own, it seemed to be of the earth in origin—yet somehow it was not the same. What would happen if he summoned his own Power here, he could not guess. Still, it was a risk he must take, for he feared he and the rest might grow ill or even die of cold and exposure otherwise.

Returning with the rock to their dubious haven, Iskander settled himself on the pelts Yael and Rhiannon had spread upon the floor in his absence. Then, slowly, controlling it ever so carefully, he called up his Power. Little by little, to his fingertips came the blue fire of the Druswids, small and pale but enough to heat the rock, which, to his relief, proved strong enough not to crack or shatter from the stress. The warmth was insubstantial, unevenly distributed, and would not last as long as that of a true hearthstone, he knew. But it was better than nothing at all; and even Yael, in his wretchedness, cast off his dread of such things and crept close and held his hands out to the blue glimmer. But the faint heat did not come without a price, for the wailing of the RingStones intensified, as though their Power had been somehow roweled by Iskander's own, and the fox fire quickened and leaped high, thin green fingers stretching between the menhirs and the dolmens, half joining them; and he knew, suddenly, instinctively, that the circle must not be completed, that if it were, something not easily contained would be unleashed, though its results he could not guess. As though she, too, surmised this, Rhiannon shivered, her teeth chattering as she wrapped her soaked mantle more closely about her, in an effort to ward off more than just the elements, perhaps.

Her eyes met his, frightened but filled with understanding now as to why he had not asked her to make the preternatural fire that warmed them. She was still ignorant of much. She had seen the restraint he had needed to exercise in summoning his Power, how it had taxed him, so sweat had beaded his brow and his face had set tensely, a muscle working in his jaw. She could not have been so prudent, so precise. She would have loosed more Power than was needed. Perhaps then the ululating of the RingStones would have risen uncontrollably, the fox fire would have completed the circle, and some hideous, unknown thing would have befallen her and the others. The notion chilled her more than the weather, and she shook with fear and dismay that despite all she had thus far learned, she was still so benighted when it came to her Power. She thanked the Light for the Lord, for the fateful squall that had brought him to the shore of Borealis and her to his side. Surely without him her Power would have mastered her, and she would have evolved into the abomination she had once believed herself to be.

The silver lightning, the green fox fire, the blue flame of his own Power illuminated Iskander's face fitfully in the darkness; but still, Rhiannon saw the weariness there and ached for him. That he alone had shouldered the burden of the quest that weighed so heavily upon him astounded her. Had there ever been a man such as he? She had never known one. She longed to stretch out her hand to him, to smooth the damp black locks from his knitted brow, the frown of worry from his face; her fingertips yearned to trace the curve of his mouth gently, to bring a smile to his lips. But there was little about the unstable tor to lighten the hearts of the travelers, including Rhiannon's; and finally, sighing deeply, she turned her attention from Iskander to her rucksack, whence she took her flask that held the last of the mulled wine. Pouring it into a pot, she heated it upon the blue-glowing rock and then filled their cups. In silence they drank the potent spirit, and cooked and consumed what remained of the rabbits from this morn, though it was little enough and barely tepid, so tenuous was the rock's warmth.

Too edgy to sleep, despite his being utterly drained, Iskander took the first watch, armed with a leftover pole and his dagger, for he feared more than anything the thought of drawing the Sword of Ishtar in this place, not knowing what harm its magic might wreak. As slowly the long night passed, the storm spent its rage and the wind lessened, the fox fire dwindled, as did the dissonant song of the RingStones. But he dared not trust this apparent reprieve. The Power here was too strong, too old, too unpredictable for him to feel safe within its sphere—especially when Rhiannon had yet to gain complete control of her own Power. If a ShapeShift should suddenly come upon her . . . Iskander cut off the thought in mid-formation. Fear was a demon, and doubt was fatal—had not this been drilled into him at Mont Saint Christopher all his life?

But still, his eyes were anxious as they fell upon her sleeping figure, lying close between Yael and Anuk, one hand wrapped in the lupine's thick black fur. Her face was pale and pinched in the dim light, though no less beautiful for that, he thought, knowing the hardships she had endured. Shadows curved like crescent moons beneath her closed eyelids, folds of skin so delicate that he could see the gossamer webbing of veins within, and edged with lashes so long and thick as to look like smudges against her cheeks. Her lips were parted slightly, and now and then she moaned softly, as though her rest were disquieted by more than just the inhospitable weather, the cold, hard stone upon which she had spread her pelt. Iskander wondered if she dreamed, and of what? Of him, perhaps?

The Light forgive him for hoping that it was so.

Chapter 13

It was Iskander who lay beside me. This I knew—even before I opened my eyes and saw that it was so—for his body was of a length to fit mine, and the close quarters of the passing weeks had given me a familiarity of him that I would otherwise have lacked. For a long moment I did not move, but stayed still and mute, scarcely daring even to breathe, loath to wake him when he needed so badly to sleep.

All night long he had kept watch over Yael and me, rousing Yael only toward dawn, when the storm had finally blown itself out and, in its wake, thankfully, the eerie fox fire and the unnerving singing of the RingStones had died. Yael had been on guard ever since, not disturbing me at all, a kindness for which I could only be grateful, despite my guilt at the knowledge that between them he and Iskander had covered my turn at watch.

Iskander's arm was flung heedlessly across my body; his sable cloak half blanketed me as well. Under other circumstances this would not have been proper. But on a journey such as ours, modesty and privacy were luxuries ill afforded, and indeed, one was only too glad to share mantles and body heat, lest one freeze to death in the cold

193

and the dark. Such things as this, I had also learned.

Yet it was more than gratitude I felt as his body pressed near to mine, more than mere warmth that flared within me as he unwittingly tightened his arm around me, pulling me closer, snuggling himself against me. I know that it was wrong of me; but much as it shames me to admit it, I must confess I did not resist, but shut my eyes and feigned sleep—and hoped that Yael could not hear the hammering of my heart in my breast and so know that I was awake and aware as Iskander wrapped himself about me, his breath like the first, quickening breath of a khamsin against my cheek.

Presently I slept again—and dreamed of the man who held me.

—Thus it is Written—
in
The Private Journals
of the Lady Rhiannon sin Lothian

IT WAS THE SUN PIERCING FIRST THE SCUDDING CLOUDS AND then, more brightly, the windows of the dolmens that woke her—that, and the silence. For a while Rhiannon lay still, knowing that something about the morning was different but puzzled as to what it was. And then she knew. The rain had stopped; the wind had diminished to a breeze, light and cool against her skin where she lay beneath the shelter of the tilted raft. She had slept again, she realized; and as she abruptly remembered her earlier pretense of slumber when Iskander had unconsciously enfolded her in his arms, her gaze flew to his face, and she observed, suddenly flustered, that he was now awake, watching her. Involuntarily color stained her cheeks, and casting her eyes down in some confusion, she sat up, careful that no part of her should touch him.

"Good morning," he said after a moment, his voice like a caress to her ears.

"Yea, 'tis indeed that, Lord," she rejoined, not looking at him as she began to undo the skein of her braids, so her hair fell free, like a curtain, hiding her face from him. "Sorcha has broken through the clouds at last."

She wondered if he knew how she had let him clasp her to him, as though they were lovers. He was so sentient, so perceptive. Sometimes he seemed even to know her innermost thoughts. Recalling his words to her the night she had so desperately offered herself to him—that he was a priest, a lord, and an honorable man—she blushed with shame that perhaps he knew she had not opposed his oblivious embrace. Still, if he did, he said naught of it.

Instead, after a time he rose and tactfully stepped from beneath the heeled vessel to give her a modicum of privacy in which to complete her toilette. With a sharp, unexpected pang of homesickness, Rhiannon took from her rucksack the comb her giant father, Olafur, had carved for her of pine wood. Such a small, simple thing, it was—yet its every curve and edge had been born of love for her. It came to her then that perhaps she would never see her giant parents again, and she sorrowed for that, though in her heart she knew she had done them the most loving kindness she could by sparing them the burden of her Power. They had understood it even less than Yael; secretly they had feared her as much as the rest of the giants had, and in time perhaps they, too, would have wished her gone. Yea, it was best this way. But still, tears stung her eyes as slowly she drew the comb through her long, unbound hair, easing it gently but deftly through the snarls and tangles begat by the storm.

As Rhiannon worked, she stared out over the massive mound upon which she and the others had sought refuge last night. This was her first clear glimpse of the tor, and she thought that oddly the RingStones did not seem nearly so frightening now in the early morning light, but, rather, merely old and timeworn, eroded and tumbling down. Seeing them so, she could almost believe she had only imagined their Power, and she thought that it was no wonder Ulthor had referred to them simply as an ancient ruin upon a hill, a cairn of little significance except as a landmark. For some reason the sight of them now—as Ulthor must have beheld them—saddened her, as though something valuable and sacred were being lost with the years. Silent, the RingStones stood—but perhaps not utterly mute, Rhiannon realized as, of a sudden she observed that one of the menhirs bore a series of runes upon its weathered face. Iskander had noticed this, too, she saw; for now he strode toward the megalith, halting before it to study its inscription. Hurriedly she finished replaiting her hair. Then she got to her feet and left the shelter to stand beside him, curious as to what was written upon the mammoth stone.

"What does it say?" she asked, awed at the size of the menhir, which dwarfed her utterly as tentatively she stretched out one hand to trace the fading symbols there, as though in this manner she might unlock the secret they held.

"I don't know," he replied, frowning. "'Tis written in the Old Tongue, of which I know but certain words—and those being only of rites I learned by rote. It appears to tell of a queen named Morgen-Stern and of a Southron king and of a great battle between them. It speaks of the Power and a wind and the stars; but the words are cryptic, and they make no sense to me."

"Did ye see the date, Lord?" she inquired, stunned as she recognized the numbers amid the indistinct glyphs. "Fourteen fifty-nine, C.R. These stones have stood for nigh on six thousand years. How is that possible?"

"Where there is Power, all things are possible, *khatun*. Remember that," Iskander urged. He paused, scrutinizing the megalith intently. Then at last, shaking his head at his inability to decipher the runes, he spoke abruptly. "Come. Let us break our fast and gather our belongings. I want us to leave this place as soon as we can. I mislike this strange tor, these RingStones so like and yet unlike those of the East. There is something here that both troubles and eludes me, and I would have us gone from this place before we inadvertently loose whatever it is that bides among these ancient stones."

So saying, he turned on his heel and left her, making his way to where Yael had laid bunches of reeds he had gathered at daybreak and, with ordinary means and doubtless no small measure of satisfaction, lighted a fire. Upon this the giant had set tea to boil and was roasting strips of meat from one of the caimanlike creatures he had managed to trap and kill. Anuk had discovered a bird's nest, and the eggs from this were cooking in a pan, along with the tender shoots of some edible marsh plant Yael had found. The questers would not go hungry this morn.

After they had finished eating, they broke camp, Iskander and Yael bundling up supplies and carrying these and the raft down to the bottom of the tor, while Rhiannon smoked what remained of the meat, stowed it in leather pouches, and extinguished the fire. She would have liked to bathe and wash her hair; it seemed a long time since she had felt truly clean. But this she knew she could do once they had reached the southern shore of the marsh; and she agreed with Iskander that they would be well away from this peculiar place and its unknown hazards.

She was startled, once she had descended to the bottom of the mound, to see how far the water had risen in the night. It was more than waist high. Nearly a third of the tor was submerged. She shuddered at the sight and thanked the Light for Iskander's shrewd forethought in insisting upon building their crude vessel. Afoot, fighting the swelling waves and the ever-strengthening current in the rain and the wind, they surely would not have attained high ground before the storm had unleashed its full fury upon them. Inevitably they must have been stranded in the marsh and drowned.

Perhaps the others had grasped this, too; for despite this morning's promising weather, both Iskander and Yael were silent as they finished loading the raft and, after all had climbed aboard, took up their poles and shoved off. Gradually, however, once they had left the RingStones behind, the grim mood of both men lifted, and now and then a lighthearted word or two was spoken, brightening the journey. Anuk's stance at the prow was more relaxed as well—occasionally his tongue lolled, his tail wagged, and he batted playfully at some small creature in the water—and this, also, eased the minds of the companions, though wisely they did not entirely abandon their vigilance.

The current was still fairly swift, and the vessel moved forward briskly. As the day wore on, the wind picked up, gusting across the marsh. Once or twice, a filmy grey cloud passed across the face of the sun. But the weather held, and by late afternoon the small party had achieved the southern shore, where the scattered foothills of the Majestic Mountains of Finisterre began. Here, the travelers discarded the raft, and Iskander called a halt.

"Let us make camp early," he said. "This looks a good place to rest and refresh ourselves, and in truth, after yesterday's ordeal, I think we are deserving of that. We would do well, also, to hunt and replenish our stores before our mountain trek, in case the elements should choose once more to set themselves against us."

It seemed strange not to be pressing on while the sun was yet in the sky; nevertheless, all were glad of the respite. Their small tents were quickly erected, their pots and pans and provisions unpacked; a proper fire was built at the heart of the camp. Iskander set off in search of game, Anuk at his heels. Yael stood guard, while, among the screen of the tall grasses and reeds that edged the shore, Rhiannon sloughed off her garments and, taking a deep breath, plunged into the chilly marsh water. Remembering the murky shapes and shadows that had glided beneath the waves, she did not venture far; nor did she linger. With soapberry that to her delight she fortuitously discovered growing amid the verdure, she lathered her body and hair, scrubbing herself hard. Then, teeth chattering, she hurriedly rinsed herself off and, emerging, wrapped herself tightly in her cloak. Inside her tent she dressed herself in her only change of clothes, a soft leather shirt and breeches, which, though sadly crushed, were at least clean. After that, while Yael bathed, she washed their dirty raiment and, after wringing it out, spread it near the fire to dry. Then, perched upon a small rock, she took up her dagger and set about scraping the mud from their boots. Himself now clean and garbed, Yael came to sit beside her, and they worked in companionable silence for several minutes. But at last her brother spoke.

"'Tis a hard path ye have chosen to follow, Rhiannon Olafursdaughter," he observed, his voice husky with emotion, "and who knows where it may lead? Likely to your death, as the Lord warned, for his quest is indeed fraught with many perils." He paused, then continued. "There is still time to turn back. Within weeks we could be home in Torcrag, safe in the lodge of our parents."

"Would ye see us both foresworn, Yael?" his sister asked quietly, stricken by the thought. "We took oaths to serve the Lord—or have ye forgotten? Break yours and go home if ye would; in truth, though 'tis no doubt wrong of me, I counsel ye most strongly to do so, for there is naught for ye in this journey but danger and mayhap death, indeed. But as for me, I shall stay. I cannot do aught else and hope to learn to command this Power with which the Immortal Guardian, in Its wisdom, saw fit to vest me. For if I am not its master, Yael, then I must become its slave; and I think that even ye would fear me then. Ye do already, a little."

Her brother did not answer that, for he knew it to be true. Oh, if only she were an ordinary woman— But she was not, nor ever would be. Almost, he hated her for that, despite that it was no fault of her own. Then, ashamed of his bitter, resentful feelings, he said, "'Tis only that I am afraid of losing ye, Rhiannon. Each day, ye grow a little farther apart from me. Soon I fear we will be nothing more than strangers to each other."

"I do what I must," she reiterated, troubled but unyielding. "I grow as I must to become what I would. For all that they loved me, and I them, your parents were not mine, Yael. I am not Rhiannon Olafursdaughter, but Rhiannon sin Lothian. I am not a Boreal, but a Vikanglian."

"By the moons! 'Tis a place ye have never even seen!" the giant protested.

"And perhaps I never shall. But its Royal Blood flows through my veins, and with it this Power of mine. Would ye have me cast off my birthright, deny my heritage? Nay, for deep down inside, ye know that

that would not be right, as do I, for no more would I ask such a thing of ye, whom I love as a sister loves her brother. More than that I cannot give, Yael, nor have I ever said I would. This ye well know, for I have tried to spare ye pain. I am not yours to lose. If we are becoming strangers to each other, 'tis because *ye* wish it so, not I. In my heart ye hold the place ye have ever held, dear and beloved. More plainly than that I cannot speak—except to say only this: If ye swore fealty to the Lord for my sake, in the hope of somehow wresting me from his side, ye did a foolish, futile thing—and him a great wrong. I will not be swayed from my purpose, not even by ye, Yael. If ye love me as ye profess, ye will not ask me this again—and there is an end to it."

Rhiannon's face was so earnest, so resolute that the giant knew she meant what she said. Inside him his heart broke, and for a moment he could scarcely breathe, such was the pain of the blow she had dealt him. He had expected it, had steeled himself against it, and still, it hurt so badly that he wanted to cry out in anguish and refusal. But he saw that this would avail him nothing—indeed, would only wound them both further—and turning away so she would not see, he swiped at his stinging eyes and, sighing heavily, went to gather more wood for the fire.

By now the sun had set and the gloaming was upon them, threads of lilac and sapphire blue and damask woven through the greying fabric of the sky. On the far horizon the First Moon had begun its slow ascent into the heavens. The wind stirred, rustling the foliage of the marsh and the branches of the trees that dotted the mountains beyond. Rippling waves lapped against the shore; in the distance the cry of some bird sounded, sweet and forlorn. At Rhiannon's feet the fire snapped. Nearby, a twig broke underfoot as Iskander materialized from the lengthening shadows, the carcass of a deer—throat torn open by the lupine's powerful jaws—slung about his shoulders, Anuk trotting behind.

The size of the deer was such that the resulting meat would be more than they could carry on the morrow, Rhiannon knew. There would be no stinting of food tonight. Her mouth watered at the thought. Swiftly she stood and, fashioning a rough torch from a branch she ignited in the flames of the fire, moved to search along the shore for greens, tubers, and roots to supplement the evening meal, as she ought to have done ere now. Still, Iskander said naught of her unwonted dilatoriness but heaved the deer to the earth and, with his dagger, started expertly to skin and carve the dead animal, tossing various of the internal organs to the lupine as he worked. These Anuk wolfed down hungrily until finally, belly replete, he crept away to doze by the blaze, one ear warily cocked, in case of threat. Yael returned with an armload of wood, which he dumped on the ground. Lost in reverie, he fed the fire, stirring and poking at it with a stick until it burned bright and high. Then he turned to lend a hand to Iskander.

Between them the butchering was soon completed. By then Rhiannon had a potful of vegetation stewing and had set the tea to boil. With small sticks denuded of leaves, she skewered plentiful chunks of the sweet, stringy meat and put them to roast in the fire. While the supper cooked, Yael busied himself by constructing a crude rack upon which to smoke and dry the remainder of the deer, and Iskander walked down to the water to perform his own cold but welcome ablutions, which included ridding himself of the unaccustomed stubble that again bearded his face.

That evening the questers gorged themselves almost until they were sick, so long had it been since they had eaten until they could eat no more. Afterward

Rhiannon carried their pots and pans down to the shore to wash them thoroughly, and scrubbed Iskander's garments, too, spreading them near the fire to dry, while he and Yael cut what was left of the deer meat into strips, which they hung upon the improvised rack to smoke and dry slowly over the flames during the night. After that Iskander gave Rhiannon her evening lesson. Then both men sought their tents and sleep, leaving her to take the first watch. She did not mind; indeed, she felt that this was only fair considering that neither man had wakened her at all last night.

The ink-black firmament was clear, strewn with a thousand glittering stars. Beneath, the forest and the marsh were hushed; the wind was but a whisper across the land. Tranquilly water rippled and splashed. A snowy owl hooted far away. Drawing the folds of her cloak more securely about her, Rhiannon settled herself comfortably against the trunk of a tree and reflected on the thoughts that, ever since she had left Torcrag, had been uppermost in her mind.

And as she kept hers, so did the RingStones in the distance keep their own silent vigil—and the secrets of the heart.

Chapter 14

There was murder done in the keep of Ashton Wells—fratricide, a heinous crime. For the land of Finisterre did follow the ways of the Old Ones, its throne descending, according to the law of primogeniture, from one male heir to the next. It is important to remember this, for of this was the dire deed born that came to pass in the reign of the King Lord Arundel.

Though in the end it proved an ill blessing, the King Lord Arundel was productive, and his Queen, the Lady Bryony, was fruitful, and she bore him three fine sons—the Prince Lord Niles, the Prince Lord Gerard, and the Prince Lord Parrish, in that order. And all in the kingdom rejoiced that the throne should be so secured. Its heir was in good health, a sage and bonny lad, and much beloved by the people.

But alas and alack, there was one who did not love the heir and so who sought to take his throne. That malignant one was the youngest of the three brothers, the Prince Lord Parrish. In secret, deep in the bowels of the castle, he did study the Art of Necromancy and did take from others their Free Will, so they would do his bidding; and thus did he give birth to and nurture his monstrous plot. He would kill the Prince Lord Niles, and blame his middle brother, the Prince Lord Gerard, for the terrible act, leaving himself the sole heir to the throne.

In the Year of Our King 7260, by the Common Reckoning, was this great evil wrought. Then were the unsuspecting bodyguards of the Prince Lord Niles drugged by some foul potion given unto them by the minions of the Prince Lord Parrish; and then did the Prince Lord Parrish himself enter into his oldest brother's chamber and, there, did cast upon him some unknown spell that robbed him of wits and left him helpless while the Prince Lord Parrish brutally garroted him to death.

Pausing only to disarrange the chamber and to lay the badge of his middle brother, the Prince Lord Gerard, upon the floor, as though he and the Prince Lord Niles had struggled and, during this mortal combat, the badge had been ripped from the middle brother's surcoat, the Prince Lord Parrish then quit the chamber, unseen by any.

Sometime later was the body of the Prince Lord Niles discovered and a great hue and cry raised. Now, the King Lord Arundel loved all his sons, and he could not bear to hang any one of them, be that one ever so guilty of fratricide. So, as punishment for his abominable crime, the Prince Lord Gerard was named an Outcast and was banished forever from the land of Finisterre. Thus did the Prince Lord Parrish achieve his wicked end, for then was he left the sole heir to the throne.

As Garrote the Dispossessed—a name he took to remind him of both that of which he was unjustly accused and his unhappy fate—the Prince Lord Gerard roamed far and wide, in the company of his friend the giant Ulthor of Boreal. While they traveled, the Wheel of Time turned thirteen years, and it came to pass that, in the gypsy land of

Nomad, the Prince Lord Gerard and Ulthor met a band of questers in search of the fabled Sword of Ishtar. They did join these same questers, and in the course of events it happened that they journeyed to the elfin land of Potpourri, whose the Princess Lady Rosemary had once been betrothed to the Prince Lord Gerard.

From her, who loved him still, he learned the truth of his youngest brother's guilt in the murder of the Prince Lord Niles—and of the dread fate that had befallen the Prince Lord Parrish, also. Having, in a drunken stupor, unwittingly babbled of his vile deed, he had, fearing his father the King Lord Arundel's wrath and the combined forces against him of the court's magicians, run away from Ashton Wells and had been taken prisoner by the hideous UnKind, the SoulEaters, who had invaded these two continents of Aerie and Verdante, of which Finisterre is a part.

And so was the Prince Lord Gerard restored to his rightful place as heir to the throne; and from that day hence, never has the Prince Lord Parrish been heard of again.

—Thus it is Written—
in
The Annals of Finisterre
recorded by the Historian Tremayne
set Ashton Wells

FOR MANY WEARISOME DAYS THE QUESTERS WENDED THEIR way through the Majestic Mountains of Finisterre until at last, meeting nothing untoward, be it weather or mishap, they came to the Strathmore Plains, that place of battle now legendary. Here had Cain and Ileana stood fast against the UnKind, as had the brave Boreals.

As far as the eye could see, the plains stretched—from the Majestic Mountains to the Tangled Scrublands, from the Hollow Hills to the Great Cerulean Sea—and must have been beautiful once, before the blight that had come upon them. For it was clear that great Power had once been wielded here, in phenomenal force. As though the sun sinking slowly into the Harmattan Ocean on the far western horizon had set it aflame, the land seemed an inferno, an incarnation of what the Old Ones had called Hell, though no such place had ever existed in the Darkness that was the nothingness. Hideously the deepening colors of the sundown—vermilion, umber, citrine, and ocher—delineated all that grew here, bloodily limning and shadowing the verdure that was stunted and twisted, gnarled and deformed, as though lashed by a savage, unrelenting wind. For life here was unnatural, unwholesome, warped beyond imagining and perhaps forever by the beast within Cain.

Cain would be sick to see this despoilation, Iskander thought, and inwardly grieved for what his friend had suffered. Truly he had not known until this very moment, Iskander realized, the horrendous weight of the terrible burden Cain bore. How had he ever managed to carry its ponderous load? Iskander did not know. He knew only that Cain, in his honesty and compassion, had done all he could to spare him a like fate. He wept then, silently. The hot tears that squeezed painfully from his eyes trickled down his cheeks, faint tracks scarcely discernible in the sunset; for he was not a man given to weeping. Still, he was not ashamed of his tears and made no attempt to dash them away.

Beside him, Rhiannon and Yael stood quietly, throats choked with emotion, also. A thousand of their friends had died here upon these darkling plains. Ulthor alone had survived. Somehow that had not seemed real until now. The Boreal warriors had marched away—and had never returned. But when one does not see the bodies of the dead, one never quite believes that those whose Time of Passing has come are truly gone forever; one still hopes somehow that death has been cheated; one still listens for a beloved voice, a welcome footstep. . . . But looking now at the Strathmore Plains, Rhiannon and Yael knew with certainty that death had indeed reaped its grim harvest here, and brother and sister bowed their heads and prayed and lamented those departed souls cut down by the blade of death's equitable and inescapable scythe.

Yet all was not desolate. At the heart of the fiery, misshapen heaths was a place untouched by the aberration that surrounded it—a small place, to be sure, but a patch of earth that was like a spark of hope amid the ravagement. Instinctively the companions were drawn to it. Here, valiant and victorious in their battle to save their world, Cain and Ileana had once stood and sworn their undying love to each other. Here, every winter solstice since, a strange and beautiful flower bloomed for a single long night—a moonflower, some called it, for it was lilac as the Passion Moon that had risen in the night sky as the two lovers had embraced. It was this flower, some claimed, that had created the enchanting fairy ring upon the plains, the tiny piece of heaven that flourished despite the hell that ever threatened to encroach upon it. The spirit and beauty of it was such that it took the breath away, made the heart ache; and yet, too, somehow it made the Strathmore Plains more bearable—like a light in the darkness.

At the southern edge of the moors, Ashton Wells rose, dominating the sweeping expanse before it; for it was a tall and massive fortress built of grey stones hewn from the Majestic Mountains and fashioned with soaring towers, flying buttresses, and ornate battlements. Banners waved from its ramparts, and the portcullis stood open, a welcome sight. Beyond lay the town itself, a picture of peaceful domestic activity —shopkeepers shuttering their stores for the evening, marketplace vendors loading their carts with the day's unsold goods, everyone on his way home for supper. From the distant hills and scrublands came the mournful mooing of cattle, the plaintive bleating of sheep as they were herded toward pens for the evening, and now and then a bellwether rang on the wind.

It was a scene in stark contrast to the scourge of the plains, and for this the companions could only be grateful. In truth, despite Ulthor's tales of Finisterre, they had not known what to expect. But it seemed that for all that the plains were laid to waste, life went on here and, outwardly at least, appeared normal. Seeing this, the small party made their way toward the castle, Rhiannon and Yael speechless with awe at the sight of it. For though Ulthor and Iskander both had told them tales of such places, neither sister nor brother, in their wildest dreams, had imagined anything like Ashton Wells, which to them seemed so fantastical as to be an otherworldly dwelling in a bard's song. They could only stare at the grey stone walls that rose higher than those of any lodge in Torcrag, appearing to pierce the very clouds. They could only gape at the turrets and parapets and machicolations that adorned the keep, not quite able to believe that Kind had built such a structure or lived within it. Yet Iskander strode toward it confidently, as though it were nothing out of the ordinary; and with a pang Rhiannon recognized that to him it was not. From his descriptions of it, his own home, Tovaritch Fortress, must be just such a place, she thought. For the first time it occurred to her just how backward and benighted he must, in truth, think her—and not just where her Power was con-

cerned, either. She knew naught of Tintagel beyond
the boundaries of Borealis, while he had journeyed
halfway around the world. Even Ulthor had not been
so far.

Rhiannon's heart sank at the realization. So eager
had she been to learn from Iskander all he could teach
her that she had not really considered, until now, how
she must appear to him. How pitiful her bold words to
him when she had followed him from Torcrag must
have seemed. Despair pervaded her. For the first time
she contemplated turning back to Borealis, so Iskander would no longer be burdened by her—or Yael,
either, who would accompany her, she knew. Still, the
fact remained that they had sworn fealty to Iskander
—and an oath was not something to be lightly broken.
And they *had* been of help to him, Rhiannon told
herself fiercely; for all that they might not be worldly-
wise, she and Yael knew how to live off the land and
how to use the weapons they carried. Surely that must
count for something. Nay, she would not go home.
She would stay and prove her worth to Iskander,
somehow. For some strange reason it was vitally
important to her that she should—though she did not
care to probe her heart too deeply to discover why this
should be so. She did not like to admit even to herself
how often Iskander filled her thoughts, her dreams—
and how, sometimes, shockingly, she wished he were
not a priest, a Lord, and, most of all, an honorable
man.

The travelers reached Ashton Wells just shortly
after twilight had fallen and, to their dismay, just as
the stalwart iron gate was being lowered for the night.
Still, Iskander was not to be deterred. Stepping forward, undaunted, he explained to the watch at the
gatehouse that he and those with him had come all the
way from Borealis and beyond, seeking an audience
with the Prince Lord Gerard, and he demanded to be

admitted to the castle forthwith. At this a heated quarrel sprang up among the guards. Some of them, doubting the tale and not liking the looks of the questers, were all for refusing them entrance to the fortress. Others, not so sure, argued that the Prince was certain to be wroth if they turned away personages such as these claimed to be. At last one man cleverer than his fellows suggested they admit the companions and let the warders at the donjon decide whether or not to send them packing. Thus agreed, a few grumbling under their breath at the extra work, the sentries slowly winched the portcullis back up far enough so the small party could pass beneath, then pointed them toward the imposing keep preeminent amid a large square courtyard formed by the castle walls. After climbing the steps of the hold to the heavy doors at its fore, the travelers were indeed challenged by a pair of more rigorous guards, who, taking great exception to Anuk, crossed their pikes before the portal, barring the questers' way. Finally, however, Iskander managed to persuade the two warders to allow him and the others to pass, and the companions were escorted into a huge hall, where they were met by what was evidently a courtier of some importance and authority; for the sentries instantly ceased their muttering and, snapping to attention, saluted him smartly before abruptly pivoting and striding back outside, firmly pulling closed behind them the stout doors of the donjon.

"Good Masters and Mistress, I am afraid you've arrived too late for an audience with the King today," the courtier, the Lord Perceival, announced, hurrying forward and eyeing the small party askance, for they looked a disreputable lot, he thought, like a band of brigands or barbarians, bristling with weapons, bedecked in fur and leather, a giant in their midst, a wild beast at their heels, and dirty—yea, certainly, above all, dirty. From the bell-like sleeve of his long tunic, Perceival withdrew a small, clove-studded pomander and discreetly held it to his nose. "Did no one inform ye? Nay? Oh, dear," he sniffed, silently cursing the derelict watch who had permitted these dubitable intruders ingress to the fortress. "I'm so sorry, but ye needs must return with your petition—whatever 'tis —tomorrow. My Lord's reception hours are over for the day."

"We are not here to see the King Lord Arundel, though we would, indeed, hope to pay our respects to him," Iskander rejoined smoothly, repressing—for he had no status here—his sudden desire to speak sharply to the disdainful courtier. "'Tis the Prince Lord Gerard with whom we seek audience. Please be good enough to inform him—*at once*—that the Lord Iskander sin Tovaritch, Iglacian emissary from the six Eastern Tribes, is here, and with him the Lady Rhiannon sin Lothian and the giant Yael set Torcrag, both from Borealis. Inform your Lord, also, that we have come at the recommendation of his boon companion Ulthor set Torcrag, on a matter of utmost urgency and concern to all Tintagel, and that we beg to see him without delay. That is all."

Hearing this news, Perceival's eyes grew round with astonishment even as his mouth turned down sourly at Iskander's peremptory instructions and high-handed dismissal. Perceival was not accustomed to being the recipient of either. Still, it was clear to him now why the guards had not refused the travelers entrance to the keep. Friends of Ulthor—and one of these a Lord and an Iglacian emissary of the six Eastern Tribes! No wonder his demeanor was so imperious! The Prince Lord Gerard would indeed wish to know of this immediately! Indicating that the questers should make themselves comfortable upon the chairs that lined the hall, Perceival hastened away, his breast swelling pompously at the thought that he should be the bearer of such tidings.

Presently he reappeared, trailing in the wake of a tall, dark man with a scarred face and a black patch over his left eye, and a slender, fair-haired, blue-eyed woman with delicate pointed ears. The companions recognized the couple at once from Ulthor's stories of them; they were the Prince Lord Gerard and his elfin wife, the Princess Lady Rosemary.

Because—unjustly, as it was later learned—he had once been banished from Finisterre, the Prince had for many years lived the hard life of an Outcast and so was unaccustomed to standing on ceremony. He greeted the travelers genially, with what was, to Perceival, an unwonted lack of restraint and decorum on the part of both a prince and the heir to the throne of Finisterre. Nor did his wife, the Princess Lady Rosemary, prove any less reticent, a failing Perceival could only attribute to her husband's wayward influence, for her own tribe, the Potpourrians, tended to be a more reserved lot. He hoped that the visitors comprehended the honor done them that the Prince and the Princess had risen from their evening meal in the great hall and come to meet and welcome them. But still, he suspected that with the exception of the Iglacian Lord, they did not; and sighing heavily, he shook his head again at their bedraggled state, once more covertly pressed his pomander to his nose.

"Percy!" Rosemary's sweet, musical voice startled him from his reverie. "Do ye go and see that chambers are prepared straightaway for our guests, and have a substantial supper brought to them there and baths drawn for them as well. I am sure they are both hungry and tired after their long journey."

"Yea," Gerard confirmed, glancing at his wife as he turned from Iskander, with whom he had been deep in conversation. "But there is much I would hear, and I would delay that no longer than I needs must. Send word to me immediately, Percy, once our guests have dined and refreshed themselves." Again directing his attention to Iskander, he continued. "We shall talk more later this evening, if that is convenient, Lord. In the meanwhile do ye and the others be welcome at Ashton Wells. If there is aught ye require, ye need only to ask, and Percy shall see that it is done."

"My thanks, Lord," Iskander replied with heartfelt sincerity. "Already I am assured that our friend Ulthor counseled wisely in advising me to seek ye out. I shall look forward to our meeting this night."

After that the Prince and the Princess returned to the meal that awaited them in the great hall, while Iskander and the rest followed Perceival up a long, curving flight of stone steps that led to the keep's upper floors, Rhiannon and Yael peering about surreptitiously, awed by the hold's sumptuous interior. Within minutes the questers were installed in a large private chamber with two smaller adjoining rooms on either side. In the midst of all stood Perceival, clapping his hands and barking orders to the manservants and handmaidens who scurried to and fro, bearing tapers, linens, platters laden with food, buckets brimming with steaming-hot bathwater, and other assorted odds and ends. Presently candles were lighted in the sconces and fires were ignited in the hearths; the beds were made up with fresh sheets and turned down for the night; the table was set as though for a feast, and the bathtubs were filled, beside which were arrayed cakes of fragrant soap, flacons of scent, clean towels, and silken garments the haughty but highly efficient Perceival had produced from the castle's coffers.

Finally the whirlwind of activity ceased; the manservants and handmaidens departed, and Perceival, assuring himself that all was satisfactory, took his leave—devoutly praying that when next he saw them, the brutish visitors would somehow have been miraculously transformed into civilized beings. He had offered the assistance of some of the servants, but sensing that Rhiannon and Yael would be uncomfortable in their presence, Iskander had dismissed them and, with a devilishly raised eyebrow, had effectively silenced Perceival's protests against this.

Now, alone in the small room that had been assigned to her, Rhiannon could only stare. She had never before seen such finery as this. Precious candles instead of rushlights—and so many of them that she was aghast just imagining what they must have cost. Licking her thumb and forefinger to avoid being burned, she pinched the wicks of all but the few needed to sufficiently illuminate the chamber. Then, suddenly doubtful, remembering the number of torches blazing in the corridors and fearing that perhaps she had committed some unknown breach of conduct, she quickly lighted all the tapers again. After that, with the poker that leaned against the stone hearth, she tentatively prodded the strange fire— generated by hard black lumps of some unfamiliar rock. The flames were real enough, but she did not understand what made the rocks burn; for the effect was not at all the same as when Iskander had heated the stone upon the tor in the Groaning Gorge. At last, unable to solve the mystery, she laid aside the poker and approached the bed, a huge, canopied affair hung with curtains and having a pallet so high off the floor that to lie down it was necessary to climb a little set of wooden steps placed alongside the bed frame. This Rhiannon did, instantly sinking into the pallet plumper and softer than any she had ever known. It was not stuffed with pine boughs; of that she felt certain. Hesitantly she bounced upon it once or twice, smiling at the luxurious feel of it. Then finally, realizing that her bathwater was getting cold, she stripped off her clothes and gingerly stepped into the hammered-brass bathtub.

The water was sheer heaven, warmer than any in which she had ever bathed in her life, being accustomed, as she was, to performing her ablutions in cold mountain streams. The tub itself was large enough that she was able to immerse her entire body, leaving only her head above the surface, and this she did, grateful beyond words for the heat that soaked into her aching joints and muscles, gradually soothing the pain of them.

One by one, Rhiannon unstoppered the crystal flacons that sat on a bench close at hand and sniffed their contents curiously, finding one—a mixture of herbs and wildflowers—similar to the favored essence she had distilled in the past. This she poured into the water. Then, puzzled, she inspected the cakes of soap, at last discovering that they served the same purpose as soapberry. Lathering herself generously, she scrubbed her body vigorously with a rough, porous object that, when she accidentally dropped it into the water, turned soft as fine leather and seemed intended to be used as a washcloth. She laved her hair, too, then rinsed herself off with buckets of clean water that sat nearby.

After that she dried off and, after some minutes of trial and error, managed to dress herself in the foreign garments that lay to one side. They were so delicate and airy that at first Rhiannon felt uncomfortably naked; and she glanced around for her own clothes, only to find that they had apparently been taken away by the horde of servants, doubtless to be washed. Catching a glimpse of herself in the cheval mirror that stood in one corner, she gaped at her reflection, not quite able to believe that the image that stared back at her was her own. She looked so strange and different, she thought; and for a moment she was actually frightened by the changes taking place in her. No wonder Yael had feared she was becoming a stranger to him. But then she reminded herself that this was what she had wanted, what she had left Borealis to obtain; and her uneasiness receded. Even in Torcrag, she would not have remained the same forever, she told herself.

Then, noticing how the candles had burned down, she recognized that the hour had grown late; and gently she knocked upon the door that adjoined her room to Iskander's. At his terse "Come," she opened the door and, somewhat shyly, went in, still feeling nervous and awkward in her unaccustomed garments and environs. This was not helped by the sight of Iskander, confidently and elegantly arrayed in a black silk kurta and chalwar, a wide hizaam at his waist. He had never looked more lordly, she thought. The shirt, with its onyx studs set in gold, clung to his broad shoulders and chest and his lean, hard belly, emphasizing his musculature, the litheness of his body. At his throat, laid bare as she had seldom ever seen it, gleamed his gold torque, the symbol of his Druswidic rank. The pantaloons, trimmed with black braid, were pleated and exquisitely draped about his thick, corded thighs and narrowed at the knees to fit tightly around his calves and ankles, encased in high black leather boots. In addition to the sash at his waist, he wore a black leather belt with a scabbard in which reposed the Sword of Ishtar, which never left him. His entire costume melded with the jet of his hair—in striking contrast to the unusual wings of silver at his temples, the steely grey of his eyes—and underscored the self-assurance of his bearing, the fluidity of his movements.

This was the real Iskander, Rhiannon realized, and in that moment she grasped how little she knew of him, in truth, how barbarous she must seem to him in comparison. Something cruel and sharp pierced her at the understanding, and wounded, sick inside, she whispered, "Lord," and impulsively knelt before him and bowed her head so he would not see the sudden tears that glittered in her eyes.

"Do ye get up, *khatun*," Iskander commanded, startled. "Kneeling is something one does during a ritual, or a courtesy one extends only to those of the highest rank—and your own is the equal of mine. As my vassal, you should stand and salute me, right hand closed and placed over your heart. However, in a purely social setting such as this, 'tis more proper for a Lady merely to offer her hand to a Lord, palm down, like so," he instructed, slowly drawing her to her feet and taking her hand in his, "and for him to kiss it lightly, like this"—he demonstrated, brushing his lips across the back of her hand, his breath warm against her skin, making her shiver a little with some emotion she could not name. "Nay, do not snatch your hand away like that; 'twould be considered most rude. Only if a Lord holds it overlong may ye gently insist upon its release."

"I-I see," Rhiannon stammered, blushing. "I'm— I'm sorry, Lord. I meant no offense. 'Tis just that I am—I am ignorant of such things—"

"Which is the point of my teaching ye, I thought," Iskander observed.

And in that moment, as he looked at her, he was glad it should be so. Her green satin abayeh, edged with gold, shimmered in the firelight, making her long, unbound hair seem aflame, her eyes like pools of liquid amber, her skin pale as the palest white rose of summer. She was, he thought, half woman, half child, under his tutelage awakening to the world—in all its aspects. Her hand trembled in his; her full red lower lip quivered until she caught it between her white teeth. Color deepened in her cheeks, like peaches in bloom, and her soft, round breasts rose and fell shallowly, straining against the thin fabric of her caftan, making Iskander all too aware of her lissome body, normally wrapped in fur and leather.

He inhaled sharply as desire for her quickened without warning inside him. Almost, he pulled her to him. His bed stood but a scant few feet away. But abruptly, shattering the spell that seemed to have held them both frozen in time, there came a stout rap upon the door; and after a moment, her voice husky with emotion, Rhiannon said quietly, "I think ye have held my hand overlong, Lord," and gently but insistently drew away from him, her eyes downcast so he could not see the thoughts within them.

Inwardly Iskander swore, and his tone was curt when he bade the intruder to enter, both he and Rhiannon cognizant of the fact that it must be Yael— as, indeed, was shortly proved when the giant appeared, garbed in his only change of clothes; for the castle coffers had yielded no raiment big enough to fit him. At the sight of Rhiannon and Iskander standing a little apart from each other, his sister's face flushed, his liege's dark with some unreadable emotion, Yael's eyes narrowed and he drew up short. A tense silence reigned in the chamber, and Rhiannon could not bring herself to look at either man, certain she would see anger and hurt upon Yael's face, and not at all sure what she would see upon Iskander's.

With effort the Boreal bit back the hot words of suspicion and confrontation that sprang to his lips, for he had no right to speak them, he knew—Rhiannon had told him as much—and in his furs and leathers, he felt more alienated than ever from his sister, now clothed in a way he had never seen her. For a long painful moment, Yael yearned to be other than what he was, to be a man such as his liege, dressed as his liege . . . because then mayhap Rhiannon would spare him more than a passing glance. But then the giant thought of his tribe, and he was ashamed that he should have longed to disavow his birthright and heritage. He should be proud of who and what he was; he could be nothing else. And in the end, wasn't that all Rhiannon sought—a chance to be herself?

At the realization, forcing himself to smile, Yael remarked, "Why, Rhiannon, ye look so like a fairy princess that I hardly recognized ye," and the taut stillness of the room was broken.

To Yael's gladness his sister flashed him a grateful look. Clearing his throat, Iskander suggested they should be seated at the table to partake of their supper before it got any colder. From the sideboard he himself poured wine and ale for them, while Rhiannon and Yael uncovered the platters before them and began to dish up the abundant meal. The questers ate with gusto; even Anuk had a trencher heaped high with raw meat—the capable Lord Perceival having surmised the lupine's preferences and, however distastefully, provided for them.

Once the companions had finished dining, Iskander rose from the table and, by means of the young page posted outside the chamber door, sent word notifying the Prince Lord Gerard that his guests were now at his disposal. Not long afterward, the Lord Perceival himself arrived to escort the travelers to the Prince's private chamber.

Chapter 15

There was much knowledge in Finisterre, more than I ever dreamed possible, as though all that had ever happened in the world were recorded in the donjon at Ashton Wells—though, unbelievably, what was kept there was nothing compared to what was contained in the libraries at the Druswidic cloisters of the East, or so Iskander told me, and I had no reason to doubt his word. Still, I was awed by the Records of the hold. There were shelves and shelves of parchment bound as I had never before seen—"books," Iskander called them, and said they had belonged to the Old Ones and so dated from the Time Before, which meant that they were even more ancient than the great war that had nearly destroyed Tintagel—the Wars of the Kind and the Apocalypse, Iskander named it.

The rooms in which the Records were stored were known as the Archives, and here, I whiled away many an hour, reading what little I could. For much was written in languages I could not understand, let alone read or write: Finisterrean, Potpourrian (scribes in the Princess Lady Rosemary's homeland were kept busy making exact duplicates of the manuscripts in the libraries of

*Potpourri, which copies were then delivered to the
Princess, so, it was hoped, no record, however
small, would ever be lost in Time Future),
Gallowish, Nomad, Cornucopian, and even Val-
coeurish, as well as the Old Tongue, this last of
which even Iskander knew but little. But what was
put down in Borealish and the Common Tongue I
could read tolerably well; and so I learned that
many of the tales told by the bards of Boreal had
their origins in fact and that once, on Tintagel,
there had existed things beyond my wildest
imaginings: ships that flew—and, incredibly, to
the moons and the stars; great cities, with build-
ings tall as mountains; and myriad machines
capable of performing tasks that, to me, seemed
fantastical. Yet Iskander assured me that the Records spoke truly. Indeed, he claimed they did not
even begin to tell the whole of Tintagel's history,
because the Old Ones had stored most of their
knowledge on things they had called "disks,"
which no one in Time Present knew how to
transcribe; so much had been lost over the ages.*

*This was why, he explained to me, it was the
bounden duty of everyone in the East to write a
private journal, which, once one's Time of Passing
had come, was placed into the Archives of one's
homeland, so, it was hoped, those of Time Future
would always know what had gone before and be
able to learn from Time Past. Thus do I now record
as best I can my thoughts and the pattern of my
LifePath.*

—Thus it is Written—
in
The Private Journals
of the Lady Rhiannon sin Lothian

IT WAS FROM THE ARCHIVES MAINTAINED AT ASHTON Wells that knowledge of how to construct the ship was gained, an easily understood Record, for it was a recent entry, dating only as far back in Time Past as Cain's and Ileana's departure from the West to return to the East. One member of their expedition had been the Mistress ShipBuilder Halcyone set Astra, she who had designed the mighty windjammer *Moon Raker,* in which Cain, Ileana, and their companions had sailed from Cygnus nearly to the shores of Cornucopia before the vessel had been attacked and sunk by a gargantuan octopus, only a handful of those aboard escaping in the lifeboats. Having survived the quest for the Sword of Ishtar, it had been Mistress Halcyone who had instructed the elfin Potpourrians of the town of Bergamot how to build the small but sturdy ship, *Spice of the Seas,* that had carried her, Cain, Ileana, and the rest of their party home. At Cain's and Ileana's behest, Mistress Halcyone had left behind a set of these plans, in case the elves should ever have need of them; and as a safeguard against their loss, a copy of these had been duly made and dispatched to the Princess Lady Rosemary to enter into the Records in the Archives at Ashton Wells.

Now, as Iskander gazed at the vessel, christened the *Frostflower,* that bobbed gently on the waves of the Harmattan Ocean just beyond the Hollow Hills of Finisterre, he thanked the Light for both the Potpourrians' and the Finisterreans' thirst for knowledge and their propensity for such meticulous record-keeping; for without both, the ship could not have been fashioned. He and the others would have been forced to attempt in a coracle or skiff to cross the sea that separated the continents of Aerie and Verdante from those of Montano and Botanica. In the *Frost-*

flower he and the rest at least stood a fair chance of safely navigating the ocean. He could not ask for more than that.

Indeed, as he glanced around the massive camp that had been erected on this far western shore of Finisterre, Iskander thought that the Prince Lord Gerard's promise of assistance had been more than kept. A profusion of pavilions sprawled along the coast, in which were housed journeyworkers of every kind, from metalsmiths to woodcrafters to weavers, all of whose combined efforts had been required to construct the vessel moored to the long wharf that had not some weeks ago existed, but that now, like a finger, pointed out into the ocean. Marveling at what had been wrought in so comparatively short a time, Iskander turned to the Prince Lord Gerard at his side.

"I do not know how I can ever express my deep gratitude or repay ye and your people for all ye have done for us, Gerard," he said simply.

"Burn the boat, Iskander," the Prince replied gravely, knowing what he asked of the man who, in the time they had spent together, had come to be his friend. "If ye are fortunate enough to reach the western side of the sea, burn the boat so the UnKind cannot somehow obtain possession of it and use it to invade these lands again. For if, as ye believe, the heart of the Darkness lies in Montano or Botanica, the number of Soul-Eaters there must be beyond counting, and they will stop at nothing to spread their evil however far they can, as I, who survived the Battle of the Strathmore Plains, can attest.

"The Light knows, I would not see ye stranded over there, Iskander. But if ye must travel inland to find what ye seek, ye will be compelled to abandon the boat—and even if ye somehow managed to hide it, ye could never be wholly certain of its security during your absence. For all that they are diseased—and, as a result, mad—the UnKind are both intelligent and cunning, and driven by a rabidity that is terrifying. They comprehend how vessels can be made to serve them; and much as I wish I could, I dare not grasp at any straw to help save the lives of ye and your companions at the risk of exposing Aerie and Verdante to another plague of the SoulEaters. For if ever they were to gain an unassailable foothold here, they would surely eventually overrun the entire world, and we would all be doomed. 'Tis that certain knowledge I must weigh against only the possibility that they have already conquered the whole of Montano and Botanica."

"I understand," Iskander rejoined soberly, "and I do not blame ye for what ye ask, Gerard. Were I in your place, I should request the same. Rest assured, my friend, that your wish shall be carried out. With my own hands, if need be, will I torch the boat if I discover we must leave it behind us. I give ye my word."

"Then I wish ye good luck on your journey, my friend, wherever it may lead ye. Here." The Prince thrust a packet of scrolls into Iskander's hand. "Rosemary herself made this copy of the Mistress Halcyone's designs of the ship. Take it. It may be that some tribe in Montano or Botanica can and will help ye as the Potpourrians of Bergamot once assisted Cain and Ileana. 'Tis the only hope I can offer ye, Iskander."

"Once more my thanks, Gerard," Iskander reiterated, tucking the scrolls into the leather pouch belted at his waist. "Rest assured that with my life will I guard these plans. And now, I and the others must prepare to board the *Frostflower*. If the calculations of your astronomers are correct, the moons will be at their most distant points from Tintagel this night. I should like to sail as far as we can before they draw nigh again to wreak their havoc upon the seas. Goodbye, my friend. Fare well."

"Go with the Light, Iskander," the Prince returned, his face solemn and filled with a great sadness at their parting, at the knowledge that it was doubtless to his death that Iskander went, "and know that, come what may, as Cain and Ileana are remembered here in Finisterre, so shall ye be—for so long as Ashton Wells stands, and beyond. This I swear by all that is holy."

They were seven who, after the moons had risen and the tide had turned, cast off the mooring lines, embarked upon the *Frostflower,* and unfurled the ship's sails against the night wind. For as Cain and Ileana had attracted partisans in the West, so, too, did Iskander; and three from Ashton Wells had elected to join the questers. These three were Sir Weythe, an older Finisterrean soldier who had, during the Battle of the Strathmore Plains, lost his left arm but who still wielded a sword better than many two-handed men; and two Potpourrian warriors, Chervil and Anise, of the Princess Lady Rosemary's personal guard.

Sir Weythe was a big man, grizzled and weathered from years of exposure to the elements; for he was the son of a simple fisherman, and before he had gone for a soldier, he had spent his boyhood helping his father fish the shallow waters of the bay whence the *Frostflower* now departed. Because of this, he knew something of boats, and of the Harmattan Ocean, also; and so, although Iskander had done all he could to discourage the swordsman from accompanying them, he was nevertheless glad of his presence. Though he was aged, Weythe's rheumy eyes were still keen, his shrewd mind was still alert; and there was no better teacher than experience, Iskander knew. The old soldier had seen much in his day; and having lost not only his arm but his family to the UnKind, he had his reasons for volunteering for the perilous mission and would not be dissuaded.

Nor had the Potpourrians paid any heed to Iskander's warnings. Husband and wife, Chervil and Anise had seen more than a few friends slain in the Battle of the Strathmore Plains; and it was they who had escorted Cain's and Ileana's homeward-bound entourage to the elfin town of Bergamot and overseen the arrangements for the building and the launching of the *Spice of the Seas*. After talking it over at some length, the elves had announced that they, too, would join the companions. No doubt, the expedition would have need of two more good warriors, they had declared, and with their crossbows they were both marksmen of the highest order; and though not journeyworkers, they had some understanding of ships, besides. Further, their hearing was acute, they were excellent trackers, and their knowledge of lore was extensive. It was not only their duty but their privilege, they had insisted, to serve however they could the friend of Cain and Ileana, who had prevented the continents of Aerie and Verdante from falling prey to the SoulEaters.

Now, as he stood at the stern of the modest but stalwart vessel carrying them farther and farther away from shore, Iskander could only hope and pray that his followers' faith in him was not misplaced. He had done naught to deserve it, he knew; and as he had been from the very beginning, he was troubled by the thought that he was surely leading them all to their doom. Lost in reverie, he stared at the slowly diminishing coast of Finisterre. The fires of the camp blazed brightly, like beacons in the darkness, a final, farewell gesture to those aboard the *Frostflower*. At the sight he thought of last evening, when all had gathered around the campfires and Rhiannon and Yael had stood and sung the Borealish requiem to honor their dead heroes of the Battle of the Strathmore Plains, the Finisterrean bards adding their own voices and tales to the epic that was now legend. It had been a deeply moving moment. It was after that that Sir Weythe, Chervil, and Anise had sought Iskander out to tell him they wanted to join him in the search for the heart of the Darkness.

Sighing heavily at the memory, he turned away from the stern, glad that the nature of his expedition was such that he was spared the necessity of acquiring an army for a pitched battle against the UnKind, like what had been waged on the Strathmore Plains. He did not want to be responsible for that; and he pitied Cain and Ileana for the scars they would carry forever.

Moving to the ship's prow, Iskander spoke to Sir Weythe, who stood at the helm, steering the vessel forward into the night.

"How are we coming?" he asked the swordsman. "Any problems?"

"Nay, Lord. 'Tis good fortune we've had thus far," Weythe responded. "The *Frostflower* may not be much, but what there is of her is solid, thank the Light and the Prince Lord Gerard. Barring some unforeseen catastrophe, she'll bear us safely enough, I'm thinking. The wind and the tide both be with us as well this eve, and these be waters I know from my youth, before my soldiering days. 'Tis once we're beyond Wickmere Pass, on the far western tip of Finisterre, that we'll be on our own, with none of us knowing the way. 'Tis then we must turn to our maps, Lord, and hope that they're more right than wrong. If the weather holds and the skies remain clear, we'll have the polestar at night to guide us, too; and so long as it's to the north of us, we'll know we're heading due west, and I reckon that, in that case, we're bound to reach Montano or

Botanica eventually, else they've been swallowed up by the sea."

And that, Iskander reflected dismally, was always a distinct possibility—and one he did not like to contemplate. Such things had happened before on Tintagel, or so the bards sang, telling tales of ancient lands that had either fallen into the oceans or been swept away by their fearsome storms and tides: Mu, Pan, Lumania, Lemuria, Atlantis, Lyonnesse, and Ys. Once, it was said, the world had abounded with these great civilizations whose knowledge had been so vast that it had enabled them to colonize many planets. Now, all that was left of them were the sunken castles the pearl and sponge divers of Lorelei swore they sometimes spied fathoms deep beneath the seas. Others claimed that such sightings were only stories, that such "fortresses" were naught but mountains, cliffs, and boulders that had crumbled into the oceans, which continually eroded the land, changing and reshaping it. Whatever the veracity of the accounts, it was true that the earth had altered over the years; this was what made so unreliable so many of the precious few maps and sea charts that had survived the Wars of the Kind and the Apocalypse. In fact, the Wars of the Kind and the Apocalypse themselves had been responsible for fire and ice such as had never before been seen, devastating the land, in places destroying it. For both during and afterward, chunks of shorelines had been ripped away from mainlands, sea floors had upheaved, mountains had walked, fissures had cracked wide apart, and islands had disappeared. This, Iskander knew from the Records kept in the Archives of Mont Saint Christopher and elsewhere in the East.

It must have been horrifying, he thought, what the Old Ones had wrought upon themselves and their worlds. He shuddered a little in the night wind and drew his cloak more closely about him to ward off the chill of the sea air and the spindrift that sprayed up from the prow. Overhead, the moons gleamed like three jewels cast against the black-velvet firmament; the stars glittered like diamonds, reflecting off the waves, so it seemed a thousand spangles strewed the ocean. The wind blew, and the two white sails of the *Frostflower* billowed and flogged in the breeze. Far off in the distance, the coastal birds of Finisterre piped their shrill, lonely cries, in harmonious counterpoint to the gentle lap of the waves against the bow of the ship as it swept steadily westward, a solitary silhouette against the horizon.

For a wild moment Iskander imagined the *Frostflower* sailing onward forever, like the doomed vessel of another planet far away, about which he had read in the library at Mont Saint Christopher. If Montano and Botanica no longer existed . . . But one or the other at least must, he reassured himself. Otherwise, whence had the UnKind come? From the stars? From the seas? He could not believe that. The vile disease must, as Cain had hypothesized, be some wartime creation of the Old Ones that had lain dormant for centuries before at last—hideously—rearing its foul head and infecting the Kind. The Immortal Guardian only knew how it had come into being. The knowledge of the Old Ones had been vast but, aided and abetted by the Demons Fear and Greed, was corrupted by their evil Technology. With such as this, in places of perversion—"laboratories," they had called them— they had worked much that was ill—depraved experiments, genetic tamperings, unnatural couplings—the dire results of which had been both unwittingly and deliberately loosed during the Wars of the Kind and the Apocalypse. It was not right, Iskander thought, what the Old Ones had done in the name of their almighty gods Research and Development, the terrible legacy they had left to untold generations of their blameless and unsuspecting progeny. As one of these, Iskander cursed them.

"Lord?"

He had been so deep in rumination that he had not heard her approach, though he would have known the sound of her voice anywhere, he thought. *Rhiannon* . . . From the rail of the ship he turned to face her, struck anew, as he often was, by her beauty. She was wrapped in her white fur mantle, but its hood had blown back in the wind and her long, unbound hair streamed about her piquant face so it seemed pale and lost amid a halo of fire in the moonlight. Her amber eyes glowed; her full red lips were dewy with the kiss of the ocean's spray—cast up by the wind and the bow of the vessel—and parted slightly, as though in expectation.

"Lord," she said again quietly, contrite, "I'm sorry. I did not mean to disturb ye at your meditation. . . ."

"Nay, 'tis quite all right. I have done, and in truth, my thoughts were so brooding that I welcome your interruption. So, tell me, *khatun:* What is it that brings ye from below deck and the warmth of the brazier on this cool spring night?"

"'Tis only that 'tis past time for our evening lesson, Lord. Are we to have none tonight? I know that the boat is cramped, but I thought . . . that is, I would be happy even to practice my reading and writing, Lord, if ye are so minded to teach me. I would my tongue would grow well accustomed to the Vikanglian language ere I first set foot upon my homeland."

"Is your faith in me so great, then, Rhiannon, that ye never doubt the success of this quest or our survival?" he queried gently.

"Yea," she replied, her eyes holding his steadily, "for ever since I first beheld ye, I have sensed that ye are favored by the Light, Lord. I do not think that ye will fail us—or Tintagel, either."

Once more Iskander sighed.

"I wish I could be so sure of that," he admitted.

"Do ye then doubt yourself, Lord—or is it that ye feel responsible for the rest of us that weighs upon ye? But that burden is not yours to carry, as once I told ye. We are not children; and we each, for our own reasons, decided to join ye, Lord. It was our choice, not yours. Ye did not ask us; ye did not order us. In truth, ye warned us all repeatedly against accompanying ye, making clear the risks we would face. What more could ye have done than that?"

"Refused to accept fealty from any of ye, I suppose—"

"And, by so doing, have set yourself above us? Nay, Lord, ye could not have done that. 'Tis our world as much as yours, and we have an equal right to defend it. Feeling as we all do, no doubt we would each of us have followed ye anyway. Are ye to blame for that? Is it not better this way, with all of us helping and protecting one another? I do not believe that any Kind should have to face alone this horrifying Darkness that has come among us. 'Twas unconscionable of your people to send one man on such a quest, I think."

"Nay, *khatun,* ye are wrong about that, and had ye grown up in Vikanglia, as was your birthright, ye would grasp the truth of what I say when I tell ye that, in the East, we have learned from Time Past, and we try above all not to repeat the mistakes of history. War is a terrible thing—and the imperilment of the spirit even worse; for to be one with the Light is all. Why, then, condemn thousands of lives and souls if one will serve? In that way lies the madness of the Old Ones, who forgot that the greater needs of the whole must always prevail over the lesser needs of its parts. Look ye there at the helm, at Sir Weythe, *khatun.* Do ye think he would have back his left arm at the cost of his life?" Iskander demanded, his voice earnest.

"Nay, Lord," Rhiannon uttered softly. "Nay, I think he would not."

"Then ye understand whereof I speak." He paused for a moment, then continued. "But enough of this. 'Tis a mood that suits us ill when we've an unpredictable sea and an unknown road ahead of us—a dampening enough prospect as 'tis. Come. Let us walk as far as we may on this small deck, and I shall give ye a lesson of another kind, *khatun,* one I hope will be more to your liking. Come."

In silence, then, they strolled the length of the ship until they reached its stern, where the deck ran the width of the vessel and there was some room for maneuvering, however limited. Here, Iskander spoke again.

"Ye have learned well, *khatun,* what I have taught ye thus far, but our confined space makes it difficult to continue your studies along the same lines as before. So, though this is far from the ideal stage of your progress in which to introduce such a lesson, I have decided nevertheless to begin to instruct ye in what are the hardest ShapeShifts of all to master—the creatures of the heavens.

"These involve a highly complex use of the Power because obviously one cannot oneself actually fly. Thus, unlike with the animals of the land or even of the seas, one cannot in true conjunction move with the shape of a heavenly creature one is projecting . . . that is to say, when you assume the form of a lupine, for example, and you start to run, it appears to the beholder that 'tis a lupine running, because the shape does whatever ye yourself do, just as though ye had literally *become* a lupine. Is that not so?"

"Yea," Rhiannon agreed, listening intently.

"But ye are Kind and therefore—unless borne

upon the back of some flying beast—earthbound. So if ye ran and flapped your arms to mimick the movements of a bird in flight, for instance, and your aura, in the proper shape of that bird, moved with ye in the usual way, ye would appear as a bird blithely winging its way along only a scant few feet off the ground, which, for any length of time, would be unnatural and thus open to doubt, to question in the mind of the beholder. Do ye understand what I am telling ye, *khatun?*"

"Yea, but . . . how is it that the ShapeShift is accomplished, then, Lord?" she probed, puzzled.

"In this way: by dividing and coloring your aura so what is earthbound is made invisible and only the heavenly creature is seen. As you might suspect, this takes tremendous control of one's Power and self, *khatun,* for one's aura is a part of oneself, not easily split away. Now, do ye watch, and I will show ye how 'tis done."

So saying, Iskander stepped a little away from her, carefully scrutinizing his surroundings for several moments before summoning his Power. Then, ever so slowly, he began the ShapeShift, his aura glowing bright blue until, like a kaleidoscope, hues and form permeated its nebulousness and he evanesced, a black hawk materializing in his place, hovering waist high above the deck. Briefly the bird fluttered there before, with a piercing cry, it rose, wings beating steadily as it soared into the night, moonlight glinting off its feathers, giving them a sheeny cast.

Aboard ship, Iskander had vanished as surely as though he had faded into his environs, though Rhiannon knew that this was not so. As he had on previous occasions taught her, she stretched out her hands and moved forward, this time, however, forced to search the air as though blind until at last her sensitive fingers detected the subtle heat of his aura and she realized he was standing beside her. Quickly she drew her hands back, knowing from past experience the faint electric tingle that would pass through her if she touched him. The ignorant would dismiss the fleeting sensation as a minor atmospheric shock. But to one versed in the Art of ShapeShifting, it was a sure—and the only—indicator that a beast, for all its apparent tangibility, was illusion, unreal, the creation of a ShapeShifter.

But there was no animal on deck. Rhiannon marveled that it should be so, that Iskander's mastery of his Power was such that with his aura he was able to mask his entire body and blend into his milieu as surely as though he were not there at all, while above the vessel, the hawk screamed and swooped across the melanotic welkin—so perfectly that she could discern not even a trace of the slender silver ethereal thread that joined his essence to his body.

After a while the bird came to rest upon the rail of the stern, then flitted to where Iskander stood, and gradually merged with him until he himself reappeared, in his grey eyes an expression Rhiannon had never before seen: exhilaration and triumph beyond the wildest imagining. His dark visage was flushed, his breath came hard and fast; and in that moment she thought that so would he look poised above her in the throes of lovemaking. Suddenly her heart jerked so painfully in her breast that she inhaled sharply and glanced away, unable to bear any longer the intensity of his gaze.

For an instant the night air crackled with a tension honed to a keen edge. Then finally, his eyes shuttered to veil his thoughts, Iskander spoke.

"Now, do ye attempt the ShapeShift yourself, *khatun,*" he directed. "Ye need not cloak yourself as I did, for ye are yet a novice and 'twould pose too great a strain upon your Power, I fear. But the separation of your aura, the metamorphosis into a bird . . . that ye can safely try, I think, provided, however, that ye do not seek to sustain the transformation any longer than a few minutes at most this first time. 'Twill be enough if ye simply manage to do it."

Rhiannon nodded, needing no further admonition, for she was well aware now of the dangers to herself if she pushed the limits of her Power. Iskander's caution and counsel were wise; his wrath if she unnecessarily placed herself at risk was merciless as the cruel lash of a whip, as she had come to know. In this above all she must obey if she wished to continue her lessons.

Taking a deep breath and closing her eyes and ears to shut out her surroundings, she called up her Power, only half conscious—such was her concentration—of her deep inner pleasure at its response to her will. Slowly it wakened at her command, surging through her veins, and with it came the emanation of her aura. At first it was only a swirl of purple mist. But little by little, as her Power grew in magnitude, the halo lightened until it was the true blue fire of the Druswids; and it was then that Rhiannon started to color and fashion it as though it were wet clay and she were the most proficient of potters. Gradually a white bird, a sea dove, took hue and form amid the blue aura, its every detail so delicately wrought that Iskander, watching, swelled with pride at what she had learned in so comparatively short a time. So must his own mentor, Brother Yucel, have felt at seeing him grow and develop, he thought. Now Rhiannon was sheer, raw talent being disciplined and molded at his hands. But in truth, someday, her skill would rival his own, Iskander sensed, and that was a claim few on earth could make.

The bird was whole, finished. Now, bit by bit, Rhiannon began to compel it away from the rest of her aura, startled by the pain and resistance of it, as though she were trying to wrest her hand from her body. For a moment the sea dove lunged and flapped its wings wildly, as though caught in a trap; and then all at once, as she poured her ethereal essence into it, it tore away without warning from the halo—free.

Never before had she known such a feeling as she knew then, unfettered by her body, flying, soaring, climbing higher and higher into the firmament. Her wings beat in unison, the world spun away, and she cried aloud at the pure, overwhelming joy of knowing no boundaries, no limits, just the infinite heavens, realm of the Light. This must be what it was to die, she thought, and knew she would never again fear that rite of passage, the closing of that physical door for the opening of this incorporeal one.

Far below, on the deck of the *Frostflower,* empathic tears of gladness stung Iskander's eyes as he heard on the wind the echo of her trilling; for he knew what she was feeling, all the sweeter and more poignant for its being her first time. Briefly he watched her as she giddily flew and dipped and rose, and as once, long ago, Brother Yucel had not him, so had he not the heart to restrain her. Instead, reassuming the shape of the black bird, he joined her in the clouds, and together hawk and dove swept across the star-strewn night sky, while at the helm of the vessel, Sir Weythe, bemused, tracked their flight and marveled at the sight of them so far from land.

But at last, noting how Rhiannon's chimerical white wings fluttered ever more slowly, Iskander indicated to her that they must return to their bodies, still standing as though petrified on the deck of the ship, neither veiled, but visible, their auras swirling like blue mist about them; for the meshing of herself with her environs Rhiannon had yet to attempt, and in his haste to join her, Iskander had foregone it, knowing there was no danger to either of them on the *Frostflower*.

Down—

Down—

Down . . . they swooped to become whole and Kind once more, hearts overflowing with emotion, hers with the incredible experience that had left her breathless and weeping with joy, his with the knowledge that here at long last was a woman who could share with him every part of his life, with whom he needed no words to explain who and what he was. Rhiannon's face glowed in the moonlight; the tears that coursed down her cheeks glistened like dew upon roses. Her lips parted.

"Oh, *khan,*" she whispered, reverting to the more personal title Anuk favored, "oh, *khan,* I never knew . . . I never dreamed that my Power could be like that, so wonderful. I would it had gone on forever. . . ." Her voice trailed away, and in her eyes was a look that beseeched him more eloquently than words to show her how to recapture that glorious interlude when they had been one with the stars.

There was between them then a moment highly charged as a storm; and then, suddenly, Rhiannon was crushed in Iskander's arms and his mouth was on hers, hard and hungry as all the primeval passion of their emotions came spilling out in a wild, desperate torrent born of their mutual want and need. It was a questing of a different sort, old as time, known to him, whose years outnumbered hers by one more than a decade; and so of this too did he teach her and did she eagerly learn. Sweeter than sweet was the taste of the night wind and the spindrift that clung to them as they clung to each other, lips and tongues and hands unstill, Iskander's fingers wrapped in Rhiannon's streaming hair, his mouth swallowing her breath again and yet again, while all about them the waves swelled and surged, and on the far horizon, the moons began their slow, inevitable slide into the dark, engulfing sea.

EVENING STAR

Shadows of the
Blue Moon

Labyrinth

Chapter 16

We did not speak of that night, of that sudden passion that had flared between us, born of so much, also, of which we rarely spoke, though that night had been different. Then had I known Iskander's thoughts as surely as I knew my own. Even now I guessed what gnawed at him, because I knew what gnawed at me; and I thought that perhaps it would have been better had we not stolen so little as those few fierce kisses out of time. They had wakened within us things that had been best left sleeping, things that, given our uncertain destiny, could be naught save bittersweet.

The Light help me—I dare not let myself come to care for ye, he had told me, in his eyes such pain that I had wanted to weep for him, and for myself. His quest was all. If naught else would serve him but to send me to my death, so would he have done once—and perhaps still would, however much it grieved him to do it. This I knew and understood. Of the greater whole of Tintagel, we were but lesser parts. In the scheme of the world, what did we matter?

Yet he did seek me out, if for nothing more than to stand quietly at my side while we watched the whales that called the Harmattan Ocean home, and that sometimes swam so near to the ship that we could feel the cold spray when they surfaced and spouted, though they never harmed us, being, for all their enormous size, of a peaceful nature.

And once when a storm blew up and our little vessel was rocked so violently that I thought we must surely sink, Iskander grabbed me as I slid perilously across the deck and, for a moment, clutched me to him tightly, uncaring how the wind and the rain lashed us, so great was his relief that I had not washed overboard and drowned.

On such things as this, then, did we live. It was all we had. It was all we dared between us, not knowing what the future held—or even if we would have one at all.

—Thus it is Written—
in
The Private Journals
of the Lady Rhiannon sin Lothian

The Eastern Shore of Labyrinth, *7275.9.6*

LIKE THE SPINES OF A SEA-DRAGON'S BACKBONE, THE steep, craggy black mountains rose suddenly from the frothy waves of the ocean—mountains both forbidding and foreboding, eerily limned and shadowed as they were by the Blue Moon that hung in the night sky above them, as though it were a glinting sickle poised to strike, a portent of what awaited the questers in this unknown and unwelcoming land.

At the bow of the *Frostflower* they stood, staring silently at what loomed before them, awed and daunted by the grimness of the monstrous peaks. Even the thin line of shore was a mass of jutting boulders and shards of black shingle ungentled by the inrushing waves of the ocean. It seemed a pall lay over the expanse, filling the companions with a sense of uneasiness.

"Perhaps 'twill not seem so bleak in the morning," Iskander said at last—though it was plain from the tone of his voice that even he did not believe these words. Indeed, he confirmed this by continuing, "But I confess I mislike the look of it now, even though its appearance may be due only to some trick of the moonlight. So let us take no chances, but bide here a while and venture no closer to the coast until dawn. Chervil"—he turned to the elfin warrior—"do ye and Anise take the first watch."

"By your command, Lord," the Potpourrian responded gravely, his eyes scanning the horizon intently.

With the exception of the waves breaking against the shore, he could discern not even the slightest movement, a circumstance about which he did not know whether to feel glad or anxious. Gripping their crossbows, he and his wife took up their positions on deck, while the rest went below to the small communal room where their sleeping hammocks were stretched. But if the travelers slept, it was only in snatches, and they were all relieved when the night ended and the first faint streaks of morning greyed the sky. But still, the sun did not break through the clouds or the veil of mist that shrouded the sea, the dawn revealing instead a firmament that promised rain and so did little to raise their spirits as they gathered on deck and worriedly began their preparations to get under way.

Almost, they wished that they had not spied the land, that it had disappeared into the depths of the ocean after all. But they had come so far that even if they wanted to do so, they dared not turn back now.

Their supplies were nearly exhausted and would run out long before the ship could complete the return voyage to Finisterre. They must take their chances in those ominous black mountains instead.

Cautiously the *Frostflower* edged toward the austere shore, those aboard trusting to luck, their ancient navigational chart of the Harmattan Ocean, and what little sailing skill they possessed that the vessel would not run aground in the shallows, where the outlying rocks protruded like sharks' teeth from the foamy waves. But the drifting mist occluded the coast, the sea's backwash was treacherous, and fortune did not smile upon the questers. Despite their best efforts, they were suddenly caught up in the rough trough of the ocean, dashed violently by the sluicing waters against the jagged boulders. Without warning, the ship lurched and groaned and heaved, pitching the companions helter-skelter across the deck as, with a terrible splintering, the hull was ruptured and the waves flooded into the hold. For a moment the vessel was impaled like a fish by a spear, struggling wildly to escape, Iskander frantically shouting orders, the others scurrying to obey as the sails billowed and fluttered crazily, the timbers creaked and strained, and the *Frostflower* heeled horribly to one side. Then, with a racking shudder, the hapless ship managed to wrench free, only to be ruthlessly tossed and driven into the rocks again. This time the bow was sickeningly shattered, and the travelers realized they must without delay abandon the vessel. What little provisions that remained were now lost to them; they could hope only to save their lives.

It was Iskander who took the first plunge into the shallows, while Rhiannon, hands clenched tightly about the rail of the canted ship to maintain her balance, watched helplessly, her heart in her throat, as he vanished beneath the tumultuous waves, then, much to her relief, bobbed again to the surface, slinging water from his eyes and panting for air. Striving mightily against the churning backwash, he struck out toward the shore, grabbing desperately at the slick, rugged boulders to keep from being swept away. At last he was able to touch bottom, and seeing this, the rest, too, leaped from the vessel.

Rhiannon gasped at the shock of the frigid water, gulped instinctively for air before the waves closed over her head, rendering her unable to breathe. Her heart felt as though it would burst in her breast as, feeling the savage undertow, she blindly clawed her way to the surface. She battled it to reach the coast, thankful now for the deadly rocks amid which she found precarious handholds. She could hear Iskander yelling her name hoarsely but could not see him for the mist until suddenly he appeared before her, his strong fingers closing about her wrist, tugging her forward. After what seemed an eternity, her feet found the ocean floor, and she staggered after him, both of them battered and knocked down repeatedly by the waves.

Choking, fighting for breath, the two pressed on together until finally somehow they managed to gain the coast, stumbling, crawling onto the hard black shingle, uncaring how the sharp stones cut into their hands and knees. Falling facedown upon the beach, Rhiannon coughed and gagged, retching up seawater until she emptied her belly of all she had swallowed, while beside her Iskander did the same. After a long while, they sat up, he hugging her close.

"Rhiannon, are ye hurt?" he demanded roughly, tilting her face up to his, his eyes naked with emotion. "Are ye hurt?"

"Nay, I don't think so, not really. Just badly scraped and bruised, I fear. Oh, Iskander! I was so scared— If ye had not come . . ." Her voice trailed away as she bit her lower lip, weeping silently, clutching him, and shaking from cold and fright.

Her respect for him as her liege was such that she seldom spoke his name, and so, despite everything, his heart was gladdened a little as, afraid she would catch a chill, he disentangled himself from the sea-weed wrapped about them both and stood. Hurriedly casting off his own cloak, he draped it about her, hoping that it would help to warm her, though it was sodden as her own. Then he gazed out to sea, searching for signs of the rest between the folds of the blanketing mist. Moments later, to Iskander's great relief, Chervil and Anise dragged themselves up on the shingle and wearily dropped to their knees, followed by Yael and Anuk, who, between them, had managed to save the disadvantaged Sir Weythe and now hauled him onto the beach.

It was a long time before the questers moved—or even spoke. Then they could only thank the Light that they had all survived. It seemed a miracle somehow. But inevitably there came the time when they realized they must get up or freeze to death not only from the wind that felt like ice against their skin as they huddled miserably in their seeping mantles, but also from the waves that crested and broke upon the shingle, soaking them where they sat. Above the intimidating mountains, forks of lightning flared erratically, thunder rumbled, and scudding black clouds massed in the lowering sky. Drops of threatening rain spattered from the heavens.

Though the *Frostflower* was, he knew with certainty, done for and would never sail again, Iskander, remembering he had given his word to the Prince Lord Gerard, rose and waded a little way into the sea, where, beyond, the doomed ship, keeled to one side, quavered and rasped amid the fatal boulders. Through the mist he could see that its sails were now tattered, one of its masts was snapped in two, and the hull was ripped open wide. Summoning the blue fire of the Druswids, he somberly set the vessel ablaze, while the others watched, their hearts filled with despair but knowing that it must be destroyed and why. For a moment the wet wood and rope of the wreckage sizzled and smoked; but then the ragged sails caught and erupted into flame, burning the rest until it sputtered and charred and collapsed into the ocean, a blackened, broken ruin.

Truly there was no way home now. The travelers had known there would not be, but still, they were unprepared for the brutal reality that weighed heavily upon them as, one by one, they turned away from the dismal sight and wordlessly scrutinized their inhospitable surroundings.

The shore upon which they stood was narrow and barbarous, a thin, wending strip of beach composed only of the coarse, unrelenting black shingle strewn with seaweed but otherwise depressingly void of anything green and growing. To the west lay the edge of the Harmattan Ocean. To the east the hulking mountains hove up sternly, unbelievably high, seemingly impossible to climb. As he stared up at them, it occurred to Iskander that if at points both north and south the crags stretched to the sea, he and the rest might be trapped on the strand; and he quickly began issuing orders to search the coast, to see if this appeared likely.

The questers had managed to save their weapons, which had been strapped to their backs when they had jumped into the ocean. Now, as they spread out to explore their environs, they fortuitously discovered that, contrary to what they had initially feared and believed, all else was not lost to them after all. Washing up onto the beach, along with the debris of the *Frostflower,* were supplies from the ship. Eagerly the companions waded into the surf to salvage what they could, brightening beyond measure at the retrieval of two of their tents, several of their rucksacks, some casks of staples, and, more important, flasks of fresh water. Relieved, the small party knew they would at least have shelter, food, and water, and the means to transport it all as they learned the lay of this alien land.

Prying open the barrels, they evenly distributed the provisions among themselves, carefully tucking everything into their rucksacks. Then, gathering up these and the tents, they proceeded with their investigation of their milieu.

From the black clouds looming over the mountains now fell a steady drizzle, and so the shingle was not only scabrous, but slippery as well, which made the going difficult. But the travelers persisted, and eventually they came upon a narrow track that led up from the shore to the mountains. Observing no other egress from the strand, they started in single file up the steep, rugged trail.

With the exception of a few lone sea gulls nesting in the peaks, nothing stirred. But as she stumbled along, Rhiannon was unable to shake the unnerving feeling that she and the others were being watched; and now and again she glanced furtively over her shoulder, as though she might spy someone or some*thing*. Apparently, the rest felt it, too, for they hurried on as best they could, their eyes darting this way and that.

"I do not like this," Iskander observed, drawing to a halt, his dark visage set grimly. "These twists, these turns . . . we cannot see what is ahead, what is behind, and we are hemmed in on both sides. 'Tis a likely track on which to be ambushed, I'm thinking. Do ye all keep your eyes open, your wits about ye, and your weapons close at hand. We do not know what may lurk or live in these mountains, be it brigands or aught else, and I sense that unfriendly eyes are upon us and have been ever since we first set foot upon this trail."

"Yea, I have sensed it, also, Lord," Rhiannon admitted, troubled.

The others chimed in quietly to voice their own concerns, at which Iskander's frown deepened. Perhaps it was this foreign land, these formidable mountains, the unfavorable weather that had them all on edge, and nothing more. But he did not think so.

"Let us look for a place to shelter, Lord," Yael pleaded on behalf of them all, "and build a fire and boil some tea to warm ourselves. We have had a harrowing morning. We are hungry and tired, drenched from the sea and the rain, and chilled to the bone. We cannot go on like this, Lord. Ye cannot ask that of us. We must rest and catch our breath. We must get out of this wind and this wet ere we are frozen. We can find someplace—a nook, a cranny; it need be nothing more than that—a place where we can shield ourselves from the elements and defend ourselves against attack."

"We will lose time by stopping," Iskander insisted, "and may later find ourselves with no refuge and darkness nipping at our heels. The night may fall swiftly in these mountains—and likely will do so this eve because of the rain. What then? Would ye have us camp on this accursed path, exposed to assault? Or, worse, become lost wandering on, not knowing where we are going, not able even to hazard a guess, since what poor maps we possessed now lie at the bottom of the sea? Nay, we must press on while there is still light enough to see."

"Lord, we are making little progress as 'tis," Yael persisted stubbornly. "Rhiannon and Anise are nigh dead on their feet. We will all of us do better fed and rested. We will make up the time lost as a result of the delay, I swear."

Noting Rhiannon's face, drawn with exhaustion, and knowing in his heart that the giant was right, Iskander allowed himself to be persuaded.

"Very well," he said tersely, his voice sharper than was its wont. "If we happen upon someplace, we will make use of it awhile. But more than that I do not promise. The mist thickens, and the rain comes harder. I will not waste the whole of this dreary day, seeking respite, when 'tis likely 'twill grow no better."

He turned away and began once more to clamber up the slope, leaving the others to follow as they would— or not. For a moment they stood staring after him, downcast by his ill mood. Then Rhiannon spoke.

"'Tis the responsibility he feels for our well-being," she explained. "It preys upon him. He would not have aught befall us, and this baleful place has worked on his nerves. That is all."

After a time the rest nodded in understanding, and Rhiannon at their fore, they resumed their upward climb. Farther ahead she could see Iskander, and slipping and sliding on the track, she hastened to catch up with him so he would not think himself deserted. His eyes held hers intently for a long moment before he stretched out his hand to help her over a particularly rough patch of earth. Then, in silence, they walked on.

To Rhiannon's relief, as the trail grew more winding, its incline moderated, sometimes actually dipping in places where broken by small ravines or streambeds. Vegetation, too, appeared—moss and lichen and other green plants that sprouted from cracks and crevices in the rock; and in the gorges where the creeks flowed were tangles of trees and gorse and vines that must have harbored animals of some kind, for now and then came the sound of tiny creatures skittering through the undergrowth, though, with the exception of the disturbed foliage, Rhiannon never really saw anything move. Whatever caused the rustling noises was quick, nothing more than fleeting shapes at the corners of her eyes, gone before she could even turn her head. It unsettled her, for more than once it crossed her mind that the amorphous figures were not without cunning—and intelligence of a sort—to so neatly elude her detection.

The same thought occurred to Iskander.

"Anuk," he called silently, mentally, *"do ye go and investigate whatever 'tis that seems to be stalking us."*

"As ye wish, khan," the lupine replied and, breaking away from the others, bounded off down the side of the nearest gulch, vanishing into a snarl of brush.

For a moment Anuk stood motionless, sniffing the wind, and then the earth. But the rain made it difficult to nose out any unfamiliar scent, and finally he crept forward stealthily, grey eyes glinting. He glanced about charily, suddenly startled when an unexpected screech rang out just above him. Then, moving swiftly, something dropped out of the trees. He caught only a vague glimpse of whatever it was that struck him such a stunning blow that it would no doubt have crushed the skull of a lesser beast and killed it. Pain exploded in his brain. Howling, he staggered back, blood spurting from the wound on his head. The shape came at him again. Dazed, head reeling, blood dripping into his eyes, Anuk saw it as no more than a rapidly advancing blur. Instinctively he bared his teeth, growling threateningly, and whatever it was apparently thought better of assailing him again and scurried off instead.

Hearing the lupine's wail, Iskander scrambled down the ravine, yelling hoarsely for Anuk and crashing like a madman through the undergrowth, in search of him. The others, taken unaware, were slower to react, and by the time they moved to act, Iskander had disappeared.

"Anuk!" he shouted. "Anuk!"

"Here, khan."

The answer was so faint that it barely penetrated Iskander's brain. He knew that the lupine must be badly injured and skidded down the slope, slapping heedlessly at the branches that tore at him, scratching his face and hands. The rain beat down, a steady tattoo, nearly blinding him; and at the bottom of the gorge, he at last spied Anuk crouched beneath a skein of trees and bushes. The lupine whimpered. Quickly Iskander knelt down.

"By the moons!" he swore, ripping off his rucksack and tossing it aside. "What has happened to ye, my friend? Nay, do not try to tell me now," he protested as a confusion of images, words, and pain poured into his mind from Anuk's. "Just rest, while I see how badly ye are hurt."

Weakly but gratefully the lupine licked Iskander's hands as gently he probed the injury. Blood welled from the ugly gash. The cut was not deep, but already there was a tremendous amount of swelling. Iskander worried that the lupine was concussed, that its skull might even be fractured. Although he knew full well that there was naught in his rucksack in the way of medical stores, he nevertheless grabbed it and rifled its contents frenziedly, as though it might contain something he had forgotten. But it did not, and he did not know what to do. Yanking the dagger from the sheath at his waist, he hacked away a strip of his leather shirt and with it bound Anuk's wound—not knowing whether to be glad or horrified that the lupine had now slipped into a coma. Then, tenderly gathering Anuk up in his arms, Iskander made his way to where the rest waited anxiously, backs to one another in a tight-knit circle, weapons drawn and ready.

Seeing Anuk's limp figure, Rhiannon gasped and hurried forward to assist Iskander up the acclivity to the path. Anise also moved speedily to lend a helping hand, while the other three spread out warily to cover the vulnerable four.

"Blessed Immortal Guardian!" Rhiannon cried. "Is he dead? Is he dead?" she sobbed, even as, her hands trembling, she frantically but gently examined Anuk's furry body to reassure herself that he still breathed, still lived.

"Nay, but like to be," Iskander replied grimly. "He's a gash on his head—not deep, but serious enough—and a knot there the size of a goose egg. The Light only knows what else—and us with no medical supplies, much less an apothecary at hand—"

"What happened? By the Light! What happened?" she asked.

He shook his head.

"I don't know. All I got from him was a jumble. A creature of some sort set upon him from the trees. Whatever 'twas, it must have been both shrewd and strong to have brought down Anuk. We had best beware."

"Lord"—Yael spoke, joining them—"I have found a shelter a little way up the track. 'Tis not much, but 'twill serve well enough in this instance. Do ye let me carry the beast; his weight will be nothing to me. . . ." His voice died away as suddenly all around them, materializing as though from nowhere, there appeared a horde of small, dark beings of which he had never before seen the like. "Lord," he choked out softly. "Lord."

Iskander did not need ask what ailed the giant. He, too, could see they were totally surrounded, cut off from any avenue of escape. There must have been

255

fifty, a hundred, of the gnomish beings standing on the rocks above, blocking the trail, and poised just below the edge of the gulch. Not a single one of them was more than two feet tall, but they were unmistakably Kind; nor did their diminutive size detract from their threatening appearance. Even the seemingly youngest among them was wizened as a prune, with leathery, barklike bronze skin. All had a mass of wild, shoulder-length hair ranging in color from brown to black to grey, from which their round eyes, set in simian faces, stared hostilely, suspiciously, at the questers. Each of the gnomes was garbed in an outlandish mishmash of raiment; several were adorned with feathers and the teeth and claws of various creatures as well. All were filthy. Bristling with arms, each carried a short-handled, vicious-looking pick and hammer, and all gave the impression of being highly proficient in the weapons' use. Indeed, Iskander now correctly surmised that it was with one of the tiny but heavy mallets that Anuk had been struck.

"Do *nothing*," he warned the others in the tense silence that had fallen upon them. "Make *no* sudden moves. In the eyes of this tribe, *we* are the invaders here—and we are grossly outnumbered, besides."

"Wise advice and observations both, stranger," an older and evidently authoritative gnome announced suddenly in oddly accented Tintagelese. "Who are ye—we've not seen the like of any of your ilk before—and why do ye trespass in our land of Labyrinth?"

Relieved that at least this leader of the gnomes knew the Common Tongue, Iskander responded, "I am the Lord Iskander sin Tovaritch, of Iglacia, emissary of the six Eastern Tribes, and these are my vassals, the Lady Rhiannon sin Lothian, of Vikanglia; Yael set Torcrag, of Borealis; Sir Weythe set Greenbriar, of Finisterre; and Chervil and Anise set Verbena, of Potpourri. This animal"—he indicated

Anuk, whom he still cradled in his arms—"is my lupine, Anuk, whom one among your tribe did without provocation set upon and injure, perhaps mortally." His tone, though even, was nevertheless accusing. "Is this the way of your tribe . . . to assault innocent travelers who have offered ye no harm?"

"The beast frightened us. When it broke away from ye, we did not know what it intended. So we sought to defend ourselves," the gnome declared, though without apologizing. "I do not know these places of which ye speak, and which must be far distant, for ye came from the sea. Our Watchers spied your boat and saw it flounder on the reef. They also reported a most peculiar thing—that with some unknown weapon that shot blue flames, ye burned your wrecked vessel. Why would ye do that unless ye wished to conceal your arrival here? And why would ye want to do *that* unless ye have some nefarious purpose here? Ye have yet to answer my question, stranger. Why do ye trespass in our land of Labyrinth?"

"We are questers," Iskander explained, "in search of the heart of a great and terrible Darkness that has come upon our world, creatures we call the UnKind or SoulEaters. They are diseased, reptilian in appearance, though they were once Kind, and they seek to infect us all so we will become as they are—lost souls, forever condemned to the Foul Enslaver. Have ye seen these dread creatures of which I speak?"

To the companions' surprise, at Iskander's words a murmur ran through the Labyrinthians. Then several started to chatter excitedly in what must have been their native language. With an upraised hand and a sharp command, the leader hushed the outburst. But this, in turn, gave rise to an apparently heated exchange between him and a handful of his bolder followers, for they all began gesturing wildly and talking so rapidly that even had they been speaking

Tintagelese, Iskander doubted he could have comprehended them. He wondered uneasily what the discussion portended, even as he pondered the odds of their escaping. His arms hurt from bearing Anuk, and he longed to lay the lupine down and tend to it before its condition worsened. But he would not risk leaving Anuk behind should an opportunity to flee present itself; nor, given the Labyrinthians' fear of the lupine, was Iskander at all certain they would permit him to care for Anuk.

Finally the quarrel ended, and the leader turned back to the questers.

"We are divided as to what course of action to take where ye are concerned," he stated flatly. "Therefore, 'tis our decision that ye shall accompany us back to our village, Imbroglio, where we will hear more of ye and your quest before resolving our difference of opinion. Be warned: Make no attempt to attack us or to escape. If ye do, we shall not hesitate to use our weapons against ye, and though we have not your stature, we make up for our small size with our sheer numbers and our ferocity in battle."

"Very well," Iskander agreed, knowing that just one of the Labyrinthians had managed to fell Anuk; he shuddered slightly at the thought of what a hundred of them might accomplish. He turned to Yael. "Do ye carry Anuk," he instructed the giant, "as gently as ye may. I would no further harm would come to him."

"Be at ease, Lord," the giant rejoined soberly. "I will bear him as tenderly as I would a child and call out if there is any change for the worse in his condition."

"Thank ye, Yael," Iskander said simply.

Anuk cradled in the Boreal's arms, the companions started down the path, herded along by the gnomes, who marched both before and aft and, deft as mountain goats, scampered alongside, over the rocks above and through the ravine below. They must have made a comical procession, Iskander thought—he and the others towering above the Labyrinthians and yet their captives. But he did not feel like laughing. Anxiety about Anuk gnawed at him, and more than once he considered using the blue fire of the Druswids to blast the gnomes. But he knew that not only would this be an abuse of his Power when they had proved willing to give him the benefit of the doubt, but also that he could not possibly hope to slay them all before they turned on him and the rest. He did not know how hard and fast and far the Labyrinthians could hurl their picks and hammers, but he felt quite sure he did not want to find out, especially if it meant placing his friends at risk.

Briefly Iskander wished Rhiannon were further along in her training. If she had better command of her Power, she could throw up a protective aura around herself and the others while he attacked the gnomes. But he felt she was not yet strong enough to sustain her Power in the face of a concerted assault, and so reluctantly he discarded this plan. Besides, from the manner in which they had reacted to his questions, Iskander suspected that the Labyrinthians had some knowledge of the UnKind; and this he could not possibly hope to learn unless he convinced them to trust him.

So he drew his cloak more closely about him, hoping that he and the rest were not following the gnomes into a trap from which there would be no escape.

Chapter 17

*We are the last survivors of the holocaust. If there
are others, we do not know of them. As predicted by
our scientists, the multitude of bombs detonated in
space, in the air, and on our planet's surface
during the final days of the Intergalactic Wars have
resulted in a worldwide nuclear winter. Latest
studies estimate that it will be at least several years
before the stratosphere clears of dust, smoke, and
chemicals, and the sun will be able to sufficiently
penetrate the atmosphere to end this age of coldness and darkness that has come upon us.*

*The effect of the pollutants upon Tintagel's
ozone layer, already partially destroyed by fluoro-
carbons and other noxious emissions, is currently
indeterminate. But it appears likely that as a result
of the bombing, at least some further portion of the
remaining layer of ozone has been destroyed, and
that once the sun is finally able to penetrate the
atmosphere, our planet will be bombarded by even
more numerous and stronger ultraviolet rays than
before. Prior reports had placed the time span for
ozone-layer regeneration at one hundred years.
Now it is not known when, if ever, the ozone layer
will recover. In the long run, widespread cases of
skin cancer are projected—to say nothing of the*

additional malignancies expected due to the known long-term effects of radiation and chemical exposure.

The majority of Tintagel's natural resources not previously exhausted were ignited and burned during the holocaust. What fuel we had stored in our fallout shelter is nearly depleted. As a result, without solar rays all power and communications systems have been disrupted or have failed utterly. Windmills have proved incapable of withstanding the 150+ mile-per-hour windstorms that have resulted from the cataclysmic changes in both Tintagel's atmosphere and climate, rendering even wind-driven generators useless. As anticipated, black rain has fallen; and recent measurements of the radiation, chemical, and bacterial levels on the planet's surface indicate they are still dangerously elevated.

Despite this, there are those who have dared to venture above. None have returned. We do not know what has happened to them and can only assume they are now dead. Despite all our precautions, many of us below are exhibiting the symptoms of radiation sickness and chemical poisoning, and bacterial and other diseases among us are epidemic. We are overrun by rats and roaches, which, unchecked by sanitation controls and extermination procedures, have multiplied at an alarming rate. It is terribly clear that the protection of our fallout shelter is inadequate; it is rumored that faulty construction and substandard materials due to the skimming of funds by contractors and kickbacks to government officials are to blame. Among our newborns, puniness and birth defects are common. I fear that if any of us survive at all, it will be as a breed of mutants.

*Our stores of fresh water and food and medical
supplies are almost gone. I do not know how much
longer we can hold out before we are all of us dead
or forced to the planet's surface to take our chances
with whatever we may find there*—(Note: Here,
the Record breaks off.)

—Thus it is Written—
in
A Time-Management System
of an Unknown Old One of Labyrinth

IT WAS THE STENCH THAT STRUCK THE QUESTERS FIRST—OF
a thousand unwashed bodies, privies, and rot. And
then the heat—an unrelenting blast of hot air that at
first was so welcome that Rhiannon thought she would
never get enough of it. But after its initial warmth had
seeped into her bones, making her soaked garments
steam, it became almost intolerable and combined
with the fetor was enough to make her head spin, her
stomach roil so badly that she thought she would pass
out or retch. She had never in her life seen anything
like Imbroglio.

The entire village was contained in a catacomb of
caverns, tunnels, shafts, and pits deep inside the black
mountains. Within were hundreds upon hundreds of
gnomes, living virtually like animals, all of them dirty
beyond belief. The stink of sweat permeated the
infernal atmosphere born of the forges that blazed day
and night, night and day, spewing sparks, sulfurous
fumes, and soot into the air. For the Labyrinthians
were miners and metalsmiths, diggers and workers of
ore.

Here and there, a hearth fire burned, upon which
stewpots simmered and around which the floor was
littered with morsels of decaying food and old bones.

On every rock ledge in sight were spread mangy sleeping pelts. As she stared around the huge, central cave, Rhiannon detected few other signs of civilization; and she thought that if she were appalled, how much more so must Iskander be, to whom the Boreals had seemed primitive. Nevertheless, he did not remark on their rude surroundings as he and the rest of the companions followed Fagin Flint, as they had learned the gnome leader was called, across the large, subterranean chamber.

"Do ye sit there," Fagin ordered, pointing to some hides scattered like rugs on the floor. Then he turned and called loudly, "Gunda! Gunda Granite!"

At his words an incredibly wrinkled old gnome stepped forward from a group of frightened, whispering women who had hastily gathered up their babies and, shooing other children before them, had fled to one corner at the approach of the small party. The old gnome herself, however, did not appear in the least cowed by the travelers, but appraised them boldly, her dark eyes snapping with interest and speculation.

"This is Gunda Granite," Fagin introduced the woman, "one of the Elders of our tribe. She also speaks the Common Tongue and will see to your needs while ye are among us. Ye will be summoned when we are ready to hear more of your tale. Meanwhile, because we are not yet agreed that ye pose a threat to us, do ye eat and rest and be welcome in Imbroglio. But know this: Ye will be treated as guests only so long as ye behave as such. Should ye make any hostile moves toward us or attempt to escape, ye will be chained as prisoners until your fate has been decided."

With those parting words Fagin left them, whereupon Gunda edged nearer to study them more closely.

By this time Yael had carefully laid Anuk on one of the pelts, and Iskander was bent over the lupine, gingerly peeling away the blood-encrusted, makeshift bandage wrapped about its head, while the others watched worriedly.

"What's the matter with the beast?" Gunda croaked, startling them, for in their concern for Anuk, they had nearly forgotten her presence.

"One of your tribe struck him on the head—with a mallet," Rhiannon replied coldly, glaring down at the gnome.

"Oh." Gunda considered this for a moment, then observed, "Well, it must have been one of the youngsters, then, else the beast would be dead. We Labyrinthians might be small, but we're strong from working the mines and forges. Lucky for ye that I'm one of the best healers in the tribe, besides. Let me fetch my herbs, and I'll see what I can do for the beast."

Rhiannon wanted to utter some protest, seriously doubting that the gnomes knew anything about medicine, unclean as they all were. But then she realized she dared not throw away any chance, however slim, to save Anuk's life. If Gunda Granite really was an herbalist, a healer, she would have knowledge about the plant lore of Labyrinth and medicinal stores that Rhiannon and the other questers lacked.

After several minutes Gunda returned, hauling a large, bulky leather sack behind her. Squatting beside Iskander, she peered with interest at the lupine's wound, stretching out one tiny, grimy hand to probe the injury.

"Nay, wait!" Rhiannon commanded sharply. "First, ye must wash your hands with some soapberry and hot water."

"Soapberry? What's that?" Gunda inquired tartly.

"And just how do ye think that's going to help the beast? 'Tisn't *I* who needs treatment! Are ye sure ye weren't the one hit on the head by a hammer, girl—putting forth such a heathenish notion? Now, do ye want me to tend the beast or not? If so, then cease your yammering and let me get on with my work!"

"Not until ye wash your hands," Rhiannon insisted stubbornly. "Otherwise, dirt will get into the wound, which might then fester and putrefy."

"Nonsense!" Gunda expostulated, eyeing Rhiannon askance. "Why, everyone knows there's nothing harmful about the earth's good black dirt. 'Tis washing it away that is likely to cause one to take cold and die. Think ye I'm such a fool that I don't know that?" Gunda's eyes narrowed suspiciously. "Or is that what ye hoped, that I'd be so ignorant that I'd do as ye wished and catch my death of a chill? *Faugh!* I didn't live to be so old by being a dunce, girl! And here I was trying to help ye!" Gunda's tone was hurt.

"The Lady told ye the truth, Gunda Granite," Iskander said gravely. "Dirt spreads germs and disease. This is why 'tis the way of our tribes to cleanse themselves, especially before treating a wound. The Lady meant ye no harm. However, if ye are afraid, do ye at least the kindness of bringing us a bowl of hot water, and we will wash and tend Anuk ourselves."

At last, shaking her head and muttering under her breath, Gunda did as Iskander bade, from her bag even managing to produce, after Rhiannon had described it, what passed for soapberry in Labyrinth. Iskander and Rhiannon both laved their hands vigorously, then rinsed them in the clay bowl brimming with steaming water that Gunda had brought, while she looked on, astonished and unhappy, and made the ancient pagan sign against evil. Neither Iskander nor Rhiannon paid her any heed. They tenderly lathered and cleaned Anuk's injury, then rubbed into it a mixture of crushed herbs and healing balm Gunda grudgingly offered, though she mumbled dire predictions all the while, expressing her doubts about the medicine's effectiveness since Iskander and Rhiannon had got rid of the dirt. In a singsong voice the gnome repeated some obscure chant as a precaution against their having offended the Labyrinthians' Earth Goddess, then licked her right thumb and slapped her right fist against her left palm, something that was evidently supposed to ensure good fortune.

After that, shoving her medicinal supplies back into her sack, she trundled off, only to return a short while later with what were presumably a few of the braver gnome women trailing in her wake. They carried mugs of beer and bowls of stew for the companions, who, despite their hunger, viewed the fare skeptically, wondering if the Labyrinthians' apparent reverence of dirt extended to their eating it. Finally Yael tasted both the beer and the stew, pronouncing the beer robust and flavorful and the stew, if not tasty, at least edible—though none of the small party cared to examine too closely the strange meats and vegetables lumped in their bowls. The beer was especially welcome, for it was so hot in the cavern that in just the short time the travelers had been there, their clothes had dried and they had been forced to discard their cloaks. Yet beyond the wide mouth of the cave, they could see that, outside, the rain was still falling, quite heavily now, while the wind swept the mist hither and yon.

Inside, now that the initial fear and excitement generated by the questers' arrival had passed, the gnomes went busily about their work, watching the companions both furtively and curiously, as though not quite daring to believe that the small party made no attempt at either attack or escape, but instead sat talking quietly among themselves before at last stretching out upon their cloaks to doze, the giant alone remaining awake; for Yael, knowing that the rest were exhausted, had volunteered to take the first watch. So far the Labyrinthians, reserving judgment, had proved hospitable enough, not even trying to take the travelers' weapons away from them. But still Iskander preferred to be safe instead of sorry and so had insisted on one of their number standing guard— just in case.

What was in Yael's mind the gnomes did not know, though more than once they spied him gazing at Rhiannon's sleeping figure, his face sad, and wondered at the cause of his grief. Now and then he checked on Anuk, who, the Boreal was glad to note, breathed easier and seemed to have fallen into a more natural slumber. This gave him hope that the lupine would after all survive, and he was glad for Iskander's and Rhiannon's sake, who, he knew, loved the beast. Even he had come to admire the steadfast lupine, Yael admitted to himself, and stroked Anuk's silky black fur and wished him well—even as his own heart ached at the sight of Iskander and Rhiannon lying so close together, their hands unwittingly intertwined, as though, if only in their dreams, each drew strength and comfort from the other.

> *The Sky God minded the sun,*
> *The moons, the stars, and the clouds.*
> *But still, this was not enough for him,*
> *For he was a jealous and greedy god.*
> *And so he sought to steal*

His sister the Earth Goddess's domain
And cast down from the heavens
Terrible fire and ice upon the land.
In fear for their lives
The Earth Goddess gathered up her children
And hid them in the bowels of the mountains,
The very heart of her realm,
While on the land far above,
She battled her brother the Sky God.
For many long years their war raged.
But at long last the Earth Goddess prevailed,
And from their Shelter her children came,
And the Earth Goddess wept to see them,
For somehow, unbeknown to her,
They had been discovered by the Sky God,
And he had flown on the back
Of his brother the Wind God
Into the Shelter of the children
And cursed them so they were forever changed.
But the Earth Goddess's power was great,
And despite her own grievous wounds,
She sustained her children in their darkest hour,
And so they survived and flourished
To honor and worship her always.

—Thus it is Written—
in
A Song of Labyrinth
by the Bard Ruthven Riverrock set Imbroglio

It was not until after supper that the questers were
summoned before the Elders of the Labyrinthians to
tell their tale. In some ways the companions were
grateful for this, for having eaten and rested, they felt
much more likely to keep their wits about them during
the forthcoming interrogation, much less apt to say or

do something that would inadvertently turn the gnomes against them—perhaps at the cost of lives on both sides. This Iskander hoped to avoid above all else, even if he failed at persuading the Labyrinthians to befriend them—a prospect that to him seemed a real possibility.

The gnomes were seated several rows deep in a large niche of the main chamber, around a hearth fire, behind which rose a large rock on which Fagin Flint stood, so he could be seen and heard by all. Their faces, as they listened to him, were grave. Some were openly suspicious, hostile; others were timid, scared. All were wary, watchful. So the dwarfs of Cornucopia had been, Cain had said, having been terrorized by the UnKind. This might account for the Labyrinthians' attitude also, Iskander thought, then directed his attention to the gnome leader.

"Elders," Fagin Flint was saying, "ye have heard the report of how the Watchers spied the strangers approach our land, Labyrinth, in a boat that was driven against the reef and of how the leader of these strangers, the Lord Iskander sin Tovaritch, of Iglacia, which is a place unknown to us, then used some strange weapon that shot blue flames to destroy the remains of the wrecked vessel. Why would the strangers do that unless they wished to hide their presence here? many of us have asked ourselves. And further, why would they wish to hide their presence here unless their purpose in our land is evil? This seemed plain to us until the leader of these strangers mentioned the UnEarth Ones, and this gave us pause, for we are not unfamiliar with these creatures. We decided we would hear more from the strangers before making up our minds about them. So now I call upon the Lord Iskander sin Tovaritch, of Iglacia, to speak and let us hear his defense, if such he can offer."

At that Fagin turned and motioned for Iskander to step forth. Seeing he would tower over the gnomes if he stood upon the huge rock at their fore, Iskander strode forward and slowly sat down upon it instead, thinking that this would make him appear less intimidating. He had already marshaled his thoughts, considered what he would say; and now, as he spoke, his voice was low but confident.

"Hail, the Tribe of the Labyrinthians," he began respectfully, in Tintagelese, hoping that the Elders who knew the language were also aware of his formality. "I bring ye greetings from the six Eastern Tribes, of which my own, the Iglacians, is one. I, and those who accompany me, come in peace. We mean ye no harm, despite what ye may believe. 'Tis true, as Head Elder Fagin Flint has told ye, that I destroyed the boat in which we journeyed here. But this was not done, as some of ye think, to conceal our arrival in your land, but, rather, to prevent the . . . UnEarth Ones as ye call them, from seizing possession of our vessel and using it to reach the lands whence we came." He paused, then continued.

"I do not know how much ye know of our world, Tintagel, for 'tis much changed since the Wars of the Kind and the Apocalypse, and much knowledge has been lost over the ages—especially here in the West, which apparently, for reasons unknown to us, was much harder hit than the East. But Iglacia, the land whence I come, is on the other side of the world, and for many years we in the East have been sending emissaries to the West, to try to learn what we could of it, to discover if any of its tribes survived the Wars of the Kind and the Apocalypse. None of these emissaries ever returned—until last year, when one expedition did come back.

"Before this the Druswids, the . . . spiritual leaders

of the East, had sensed a great wrongness in the land. We feared that the Time of the Prophecy, which had long been foretold by the Druswids, was upon us. We feared that a terrible Darkness such as was loosed during the Time Before was again upon us. And It was . . . It *is,* or so our expedition reported. But there are those who can tell this part of the story much better than I—and who *should* tell it, because they were there, and I was not, and so it is their right." Iskander turned to his faithful followers. "Tell them of Cain and Ileana," he directed softly. "Tell them of the Strathmore Plains."

And so it was that as they had done the night before the departure of the *Frostflower* from Finisterre, Rhiannon, Yael, and the rest solemnly stood and sang of their dead heroes, of what had become legend in their lands, their voices rising, falling, entwining strongly and beautifully in the cave. Such were their emotions—passionate, heartfelt—that it seemed the questers wove not only their tale, but magic in the firelight, while beyond, outside, the rain kept time with its steady tattoo and the wind keened in harmony. On and on, they sang—and the gnomes listened, many so moved that tears glistened in their dark eyes and upon their wizened cheeks; for even those who did not understand the Common Tongue somehow grasped the essence of the story, felt the pain and the pride of the companions in those who had defended their world. The appeal of the epic was universal; the Labyrinthians were not without their own bards, their own such tales—and they knew, too, of the UnEarth Ones, the UnKind.

At last the final notes of the song died away, and for a long while, all were silent, lost in reverie, the hush of the chamber broken only by the sparking and snapping of the hearth fires. Even the incessant forges were still, the gnomish metalsmiths having for once laid their hammers aside out of reverence and respect. Iskander's next words dropped gently into the silence.

"Now ye know why I burned our boat and why we have dared to trespass here, in your land. We seek the heart of the Darkness, the UnEarth Ones, the UnKind. We must strike at them before they destroy us all. So, what say ye? Will ye count us as friends—or foes?"

Iskander waited tensely for the answer. He had taken a big gamble—and he knew it. If the Labyrinthians somehow turned out to be allies of the SoulEaters, he would have made a hideous mistake. Still, given the nature of the UnKind, he did not think that this was likely; nor could he believe he had misjudged the gnomes, the expressions he had seen upon their faces during the ballad, the requiem of the Strathmore Plains. Nor was he proved wrong.

"I think I speak for us all when I tell ye that we have a saying here in Labyrinth," Fagin announced. "'The enemies of our enemies are our friends.' Lord, the UnEarth Ones are our enemies—a dread plague that has come upon us."

"Yea, a plague!" the other Elders chimed in. "A plague!"

Fagin raised his hand for silence, then went on soberly.

"The Earth Goddess help us, we did not know—we did not know what they were at first. We thought they were simply another tribe who wished to trade for our metalwork. But then, once they had lulled us into a false sense of security, they turned on us, revealing their true and gruesome nature; and many of our tribe—many of our tribe fell prey to them." He paused for a long moment, remembering, grieving, then continued.

"The Earth Goddess protected us from their wickedness in that those among us upon whom they cast their evil eye died instead of becoming as they are, as they had intended with their black arts. When they saw this, the UnEarth Ones took to hunting and killing us for food, as the depraved Frigidians, who are also our enemies, have been known to do. Soon it became clear to us that the UnEarth Ones meant to slaughter us all if they could.

"But the twists and turns of our mines are unknown to them, and we led several to their deaths in our deep pits, which, once the UnEarth Ones had fallen into, we set afire, burning the horrible creatures. At night we close the steel doors to the mountains, the legacy of our ancestors. In this way have we survived." Fagin shook his head sadly.

"'Tis not much of a life, perhaps, but 'tis better than none. Still, we would welcome more than what we now have, Lord. I do not know how ye and a handful of warriors can possibly hope to prevail over the UnEarth Ones. Indeed, I fear that your quest is surely doomed. But whatever we can do to help, we will do. Just tell us what ye need, Lord."

The remainder of the evening was spent with the questers making plans for the journey that lay ahead of them. According to the gnomes, to the north of Labyrinth was the land of Frigidia, a terrible place, cold, inhospitable, and peopled by a tribe that was barely Kind; for though they could speak, their vocabulary was rudimentary, and they were known occasionally to practice cannibalism. Other than sporadic raiding forays, they tended to keep to themselves but were vicious in battle. The Frigidians had, the gnomes claimed, staved off several attacks by the SoulEaters. Because of this, it seemed unlikely that this was the direction in which the companions must travel to find the heart of the Darkness. That left only west, for to the east and south were the Harmattan Ocean and the Gulf of Uland. This Iskander carefully noted on the rough map he was drawing, based on the Labyrinthians' limited knowledge of what lay beyond the boundaries of their land.

Much to his disappointment, they had no Records, no Archives—though, from the tales told by their bards, it appeared that the black crags of Labyrinth, the Jigsaw Mountains, as they were known, had once sheltered the Old Ones. This supposition was further strengthened by the fact that there were, indeed, huge steel doors that sealed off the entrances to the network of caverns, tunnels, shafts, and pits. Evidently the barriers had once been operated by some powerful mechanism, now long defunct. In its place the enterprising gnomes had devised a system of weights, pulleys, fulcrums, and levers, which they deftly manipulated to open and close the doors. But if the Old Ones had left behind anything else, it was not known to the Labyrinthians. So Iskander must make do with what little they could tell him.

To the west of their land was Bezel, and it was with the Bezels that the gnomes did most of their trading.

"Many others used to journey here from the southern lands, Lord," Gunda Granite explained to Iskander. "But gradually, over the years, their numbers grew smaller and smaller, and now few come at all. We do not know for certain why, but we surmise that they have almost all been captured and transformed or eaten by the UnEarth Ones."

This, to Iskander, seemed a fearsome but, under the circumstances, all-too-likely possibility. If the whole of Botanica, the southern continent, was in the hands of the UnKind, he did not know how he and the rest stood even a chance at getting through. Still, there was no point in borrowing trouble and no way of accurately assessing the situation until he addressed it face to face. So, for the time being, he forced himself to set aside his doubts and to concentrate on the preparations at hand, reminding himself that however long or short, hard or easy a journey, it could still be made only one step at a time.

Chapter 18

To our profound relief, within the next few days
Anuk recovered fully, only to find himself infested
with fleas from the mangy hides upon which he
had lain, a discovery that nearly caused him to
suffer a relapse, he was so incensed. With a great
show of pitifulness he rebuked both Iskander and
me, sniffing and declaring that his faith in us had
been proved grossly misplaced that we had allowed
such an indignity to befall him; and he spent much
of his time afterward licking and biting his fur
diligently to rid himself of the tiny pests, casting
injured glances at us all the while.

Iskander only laughed, teasing Anuk that if he
had not been so foolish as to allow himself to be hit
on the head with a mallet, he would not be in such
a miserable state. But I myself felt badly and went
to some lengths to soothe Anuk's ruffled pride,
crushing into a fine powder several herbs I ob-
tained from Gunda Granite and that I applied to
Anuk's fur, in the hope of driving away the fleas. As
a result, for several days afterward Anuk talked
only to me, ignoring Iskander until, as a peace
offering, Iskander presented him with a beautiful
silver collar fashioned by Lido Lodestone, the
gnome who had struck Anuk with the hammer.

Lido was young and much mortified that he had

hurt Anuk, who had scared him deeply in the ravine; and he had created the collar in the hope of making amends, he explained. I'm afraid that Anuk was something of a vain beast, and being flattered, he took a perverse liking to the young gnome, so much so that he sometimes permitted Lido to ride upon his back, something that amused Iskander no end and made Lido the envy of all his friends.

Eventually, in the days that passed, all the gnomes overcame their fear of Anuk, and he became a great favorite among them. Indeed, the children soon grew so bold as to sneak up behind him and pull his tail, only to shriek with laughter and scamper off when he pretended to growl and gamboled after them. Their antics lightened the mood of us all; and it was in much better spirits that we in search of the heart of the Darkness finally took our leave of Imbroglio to resume our perilous journey.

—Thus it is Written—
in
The Private Journals
of the Lady Rhiannon sin Lothian

AS IT HAD BEEN FOR MANY DAYS NOW, RAIN WAS FALLING steadily when the questers set out through the Jigsaw Mountains toward the Twisted Forest and Baffle, another of the gnomes' mountainous villages. Baffle lay at the far western border of Labyrinth, which was separated from the land of Bezel by the River Knotted, a long, wide waterway that stretched from the northern Dangle Bay to the southern Gulf of Uland, so that Labyrinth was, in effect, an extremely large island. This was, in part, what had helped to protect the gnomes from the UnKind.

The companions now numbered nine, having been joined by Gunda Granite and Lido Lodestone. Despite her age, Gunda had volunteered to act as guide and healer, claiming that the small party was sorely in need of both—though it was Rhiannon's opinion that the feisty old woman thought to learn as much from them as they did her, and was eager for adventure, besides. For when Iskander had warned her of the dangers they would face, she had cackled and declared dryly, "Lord, at my age, you're entitled to take a few risks. I'm thinking that maybe I've been cooped up in these mountains for far too long. 'Twill do me good to get out and about. Why, I might even get a new lease on life and live to be a hundred!"

Lido was another story, however. He felt he owed the travelers a debt, and he had become greatly attached to Anuk. The young gnome being only fourteen, however, Iskander had ordered him to remain behind. But they had not gone far when they discovered him secretly tagging along. Fearing he was too stubborn to return to Imbroglio and would continue to dog their path, they had seen little choice but to take him with them, lest some mishap befall him.

The days passed, with the weather growing no better. It seemed that Rhiannon could not recall a time when she had not been trekking through mountains and rain. But at least now, thanks to the generosity of the Labyrinthians, the questers were adequately outfitted, each carrying a small tent and a rucksack filled with provisions. Although—not certain what lay ahead—Iskander did impose rationing, this was limited due to the abundance of game. Because of their small size, the gnomes' needs were modest; a large buck or doe would feed several of their number for days. So in the woods that forested much of Labyrinth, nature was permitted, more or less, to take its course, and the animals indigenous to the land proliferated. Herds of mountain goats and other woolly beasts capered in the crags. Elk and deer grazed in the copses below. Smaller creatures such as rabbits, squirrels, and birds were plentiful. It was seldom that the companions must go hungry. As they journeyed westward, Gunda taught Rhiannon and Anise both about the plants of the land, and together they gathered edible berries, greens, and roots with which to supplement the travelers' otherwise largely meat diet. Now and then there would be a little stand of wild grain, which Gunda ground between stones to make a flat but filling bread.

Iskander was glad to see that because there was enough to eat, the planes and angles of Rhiannon's face softened, and she no longer ate less than she needed or pressed her portion on Yael. She smiled more often, too, plainly delighting in the company of Anise and Gunda both; and he realized that it must have been hard for her before, having no other women with whom to share her burdens. Yet she had not complained, but had borne her lot stoically and doggedly continued her attempts to master her Power, even though her lessons were an additional strain and drain upon her strength.

Iskander never ceased to marvel at her rapid progress. Her spontaneous metamorphoses had become a thing of the past, for in this regard she had achieved full command of her Power, so it flowed and ebbed as she willed. Now it was a matter of her attaining precise control of it, so every shape she assumed was real as though it actually existed, without flaw in form or color, movement or sound. This alone required years of training, Iskander knew, for every creature a ShapeShifter would portray must be carefully observed and studied. Its every habit and peculiarity must be assimilated and capable of being mimicked down to the very last detail if one wished to become a true master of the art. So, in essence, the learning process of a ShapeShifter was never-ending, a constant expansion of one's repertoire. A highly developed ShapeShifter such as Iskander could skillfully transform into over a hundred creatures. There was also the need to continually stretch the limits of one's Power in order to sustain a shape for longer and longer periods of time. Iskander could project the image of a lupine, his favorite form, for three days.

Still, he was not displeased with Rhiannon's level of proficiency. She had got down the rudiments of the art. The rest was merely a matter of trial and error— and endless practice.

Because of Anuk's proximity and his own familiarity with the shape, Iskander chose the lupine as the primary form on which Rhiannon should concentrate, and each night, they worked on refining her technique at accurately producing and maintaining this image. Despite their exposure to Cain and Ileana, Sir Weythe, Chervil, and Anise were fascinated by this manifestation of Power and, when not on guard duty, sat quietly watching the evening's lesson, amazed. Gunda and Lido, however, were initially shocked and horrified at the sight of Iskander and Rhiannon metamorphosing into duplicates of Anuk.

"Lido, we've been tricked!" Gunda shrieked, ripping her hammer from the belt at her waist and taking a stance for battle. "They're the UnEarth Ones in new guise, come to turn us into such as they are!"

"Oh, for heaven's sake, Gunda!" Rhiannon exclaimed, abruptly melting back into her Kind shape. "Now, see what ye made me go and do—and just when I was doing so well, too!" She glared hard at the gnome, inquiring sharply, "In the days before we left

Imbroglio, did ye not listen to the tale of the Strathmore Plains and hear of the Light and of the Power? Did ye not learn that 'twas not with a strange weapon that Iskander burned our boat but with the blue fire of the Druswids? And did ye not grasp that the Power manifests itself in many ways in the Chosen?"

"Well . . . yea," Gunda admitted reluctantly. Then her eyes narrowed. "But I didn't know that ye and the Lord could turn into beasts, like the UnEarth Ones!"

"The Art of ShapeShifting has nothing at all in common with those unnatural creatures, Gunda!" Rhiannon rejoined stoutly. "They are diseased, we told ye, infected with some vile pestilence from the Time Before and all-too-hideously real—not simply projecting an image, as Iskander and I are. Have ye ever seen the UnKind as other than reptilian creatures? Nay, ye have not, for they are not Shape-Shifters. Their saurian attributes derive solely from the dread sickness with which they are afflicted, and the only way in which they can turn ye into one of their own is to contaminate ye with the awful malady they carry. 'Tis like a plague, Gunda, as Fagin Flint said."

"Ye mean—ye mean 'tisn't done with the black arts? 'Tisn't magic?" The gnome persisted. "'Tisn't because they put the evil eye on ye?"

"Nay." Rhiannon shook her head. "The SoulEaters have no Power, Gunda—only germs such as Iskander tried to tell ye about our first night in Imbroglio. 'Tis germs that make people ill—and have caused the UnKind to become as they are."

"And all this washing ye do . . . this is to get rid of these . . . germs?" Gunda asked, wavering.

"Yea," Rhiannon replied. Then she ordered crossly, "Now, do ye put down that mallet so I can get on with my lesson. We are no friends of the UnKind or anything like them. The Art of ShapeShifting is a rare gift, bestowed only upon a handful of the Chosen. 'Tis why of all those in the East, the Lord alone was picked for this quest. Besides, as you've already seen, with the Power we possess, if we'd wanted to harm ye, we could easily have done so by now. But we have not—and I am deeply hurt that ye should think we would. That is not the Way. We serve the Light, Gunda, not the Darkness. Ye have naught to fear from us. But of course, if ye feel that ye do, ye and Lido both are perfectly free to return to Imbroglio. We will not try to stop ye, I swear."

At last convinced, knowing in her heart that all Rhiannon had said was true, the gnome slowly lowered her hammer, sliding its handle through its sturdy leather loop on her belt. Everyone breathed a sigh of relief. Their journey was fraught with enough difficulties without their quarreling among themselves and turning on one another. Mumbling an apology, Gunda resumed her place before the fire and, along with Anise, applied herself to the task of plucking the feathers from the brace of birds Yael and Chervil had killed for supper.

After a moment Iskander and Rhiannon continued the lesson, he slowly, for the first time, touching her mind with his own, tentatively, gently, so as not to startle her.

"That was well done of ye, khatun," he told her silently, mentally. *"I do not think I could have handled it better myself."*

It was not the echo of the voice inside her head that took Rhiannon unaware, for she was by now well accustomed to conversing with Anuk in such a manner. It was the timbre of the voice that stunned her. Her golden eyes widened, and she gazed with astonishment at her liege.

"Is-Iskander?" she stammered the telepathic word.

"Yea, 'tis I, Rhiannon," he answered lightly. *"Ye seem surprised. But ye know that such communication is possible. I myself have explained to ye the principles of both a Sending and a mutual TelePath, and how such are accomplished. And ye talk to Anuk after all."*

"Yea, but still, ye yourself have never before spoken to me in this way."

"Nay, that is true," he conceded.

"But . . . why haven't ye?"

"Because . . . between a man and a woman, it can become . . . a very intimate form of communication," he explained, faltering over the words as, unbidden, the image of that night upon the *Frostflower* rose between them, filling their thoughts. *"Thus do ye see for yourself the dangers inherent in this, where each has no secrets from the other,"* he said softly, his tone husky. Delicately tracing a hand in her mind, he brushed the potent image away, like a sea rushing in upon the sand. *"Do not think of it, Rhiannon. It must not be. This was a mistake. I knew that it would be— But I wanted . . . I wanted to thank ye for your words to Gunda, and we are so seldom alone these days that I dared to trespass without invitation in your thoughts."*

"I do not consider it trespassing, Iskander." Rhiannon's voice was earnest. *"Ye are always welcome, however ye may seek me out. Is it so very wrong, then, whatever 'tis that lies between us? Do we not deserve to snatch whatever little happiness we may find together?"*

"At what price, Rhiannon? At what price? The whole of Tintagel? Ye do not know this Darkness, how cruel and deceitful 'tis, how it takes your feelings and twists them inside out to use them against ye. Do ye think we dare to take the chance that each of us might unwittingly be turned against the other—and be helpless to

prevent it, to act against it, because of our feelings for each other? Nay, we cannot risk that. We must not risk that."

Tears stung her eyes, for she knew he was right. But it did not make the pain any easier to bear.

"*Then do ye leave me now,* khan," she uttered formally, though there was a tremor in her voice, "*for I would that this lesson this night were ended.*"

"*Yea, as ye wish,* khatun," he agreed, then wrenched himself so abruptly and swiftly from her mind that she nearly cried out.

Turning on his heel, Iskander left her. But Rhiannon knew how difficult it was for him to walk away from her. Of its own volition her hand reached out, as though to catch hold of him, to bring him back to her. But in her heart she knew the futility of that, and after a moment she lamely dropped her hand to her side. Quickly, so the others would not see her anguish, she bent her head and busied herself with her chores, swallowing hard to choke back the sobs that threatened to erupt. She must be strong, she told herself harshly. She must not allow herself to become a millstone around Iskander's neck. Squaring her shoulders, she forced herself to get on with her work.

But there were two who were not fooled by her sudden industry. Watching her quietly from among the trees, Yael observed that her eyes were haunted by shadows that owed nothing to the flickering flames of the fire and that her mouth trembled a little, soft and vulnerable. At the sight he longed fiercely to do his liege some violence; and this, hunkered inside his tent, staring out moodily through the open flaps into the darkness beyond, Iskander sensed as strongly as he felt the depth of Rhiannon's pain, mirroring his own.

Chapter 19

For the first time since I had had the Tyrian-crimson sunburst tattooed between my brows and received the Druswidic collar of rank, I wished I had not been Chosen. Those who are not blessed with the gift of the Power do not understand that sometimes it weighs so heavily upon one that it seems like a curse.

There is such a thing as being too sentient.

I was painfully aware of Rhiannon, of her thoughts, of her emotions, of the knowledge that I had hurt her—and of the unspoken accusation in Yael's eyes, he who loved her even as I did. Yea, I do confess it. I loved her, perhaps had loved her from the start, when I had first opened my eyes in Torcrag and beheld her as Ceridwen, Keeper of the Earth, whence my Power comes. For is not like ever drawn to like? And we were so like that we were as halves of a whole.

This I knew in my heart, and despaired of; and I cursed the quest that had brought her into my life—only to perversely keep us apart.

—Thus it is Written—
in
The Private Journals
of the Lord Iskander sin Tovaritch

THE JIGSAW MOUNTAINS LONG BEHIND THEM NOW, IT WAS deep in the heart of the Twisted Forest that the questers heard the screams. Shrieks of fear and pain echoed hideously through the woods, sending a grue up Rhiannon's spine, for the chilling sounds were unmistakably Kind. With an upraised hand Iskander stilled the companions, and all listened, horrified, to the din.

"This way!" Iskander shouted, and began to zigzag through the trees, yanking the Sword of Ishtar from its sheath upon his back.

The rest of the companions followed hard on Iskander's heels, Yael pausing only to scoop up Gunda, who could not keep up, and settle her securely upon his shoulders before rushing on, his strides eating up the ground. Lido had already grabbed a fistful of Anuk's fur and hauled himself onto the lupine's broad back, his face pressed into Anuk's neck to avoid being knocked off by the low-hanging branches of the woods. Sir Weythe's sword was in hand; Chervil and Anise held their crossbows at the ready, arrows nocked. Rhiannon's fingers were curled tightly around the handle and chain of her morning star; her heart pounded.

The unrelenting drizzle had turned the earth spongy, so the leather boots of the companions made little sound as they wove rapidly in and out of the towering trees of the aptly named forest, contorted and knotted, its warped branches interlaced like a canopy, green leaves shivering and dripping in the rain. The leaden light came mottled through the limbs. Wisps of mist twined themselves like snakes around tree trunks. The whole forest seemed to shudder as the terrified screams continued, unabated.

At last, breathing hard, the small party reached the edge of a clearing, whence the shrieks emanated, and here, all drew up short at the grisly scene that met their eyes.

To one side of the glade stood a little, brightly painted caravan perched on two high wheels and harnessed to a team of horses tethered to a tall black tree stump that some time ago had apparently been struck by lightning. White-eyed, whinnying with fear, the horses were rearing and prancing furiously, struggling violently to break free of the strong hemp straps that held them captive. The wagon tottered precariously on its huge wheels, tilting crazily from side to side, its shutters and single door banging against its wooden sides, pots and pans within clattering. Some of its contents had spilled out onto the ground; shards of glass and other debris littered the area around it.

But this was not what petrified the travelers. It was the sight of what was plainly the owner of the cart. The poor young man cringed at the center of the clearing, crying and screaming piteously, his silken garments in tatters and soaked with blood from the wicked gouges that crisscrossed his entire, shaking body. All around him prowled beings enormous as giants. But there, the similarity ended; for save for the UnKind, the pathetic man's persecutors were the ugliest, most repulsive creatures Rhiannon had ever before beheld.

They were stoop-shouldered, almost hunchbacked in appearance, their massive arms seeming too large for their bodies, hands hanging below their knees and tipped with talonlike nails, to which clung bits of their hapless victim's flesh. Their chunky, oversized heads sat upon short, squat necks. Beneath their low foreheads and wild, beetlelike brows were tiny, squinty black eyes and noses so broad and flat that they appeared to have been squashed by some gargantuan hand. Their jaws were powerful, as though meant to crush, the lower thrust out disproportionate to the upper, so their thick, drooling lips revealed a line of big bottom teeth with prominent canines. The beings were so hirsute that from a distance they might have been mistaken for apes. All carried stout, spiked clubs, though it seemed likely that these had not yet been put to use on the cowering young man, for he was so slight that one blow would surely have killed him.

This was not the worst of it, however. Clearly the troll-like creatures had at some point come into contact with and been infected by the SoulEaters, for all were in various stages of the abominable transformation engendered by the UnKind disease. Clumps of their long, matted hair had fallen out, and patches of black, scaly hide had appeared on their misshapen bodies.

Anxiously Rhiannon glanced at Iskander, wondering what he would do, if he would take action to save the life of the young man, who would most certainly otherwise be tortured to death by his grotesque tormentors. Before Iskander could voice his thoughts and orders to the others, however, the matter was decided for him.

"Frigidians!" Gunda hissed, and before anyone realized what she intended, she jerked her mallet from her belt and hurled it straight at the nearest troll.

Perched on Yael's shoulders, Gunda had an unobscured view of the glade, and her aim was strong and true. Her hammer struck the Frigidian right square between the eyes, and with a yowl, he toppled like a poleaxed steer, landing so heavily that the very ground seemed to quake from the impact.

Plainly the trolls were not too intelligent, for it took a long moment for it to sink in that they were under attack. Then, grunting angrily, they lumbered forward to meet the assault that ensued when Iskander yelled the Tovaritch battle cry and sprang from the trees to lead the questers' charge. Surprise was on their side.

Yael's mighty battle-ax sheered one of the Frigidians' torsos clean in two before the troll could even blink, and Iskander's blade took the head off another. Scrambling from Anuk's back, Lido sent his pick flying, while the lupine lunged for a Frigidian's throat. The elves' crossbows thrummed as their arrows arced through the air. Sir Weythe's weapon glinted as he parried a blow from the mace wielded by a troll quicker than his fellows. The muscles in Rhiannon's right arm flexed as she swung her morning star around and around, finally smashing it against the head of the closest Frigidian.

The sickening collision jarred her to the bone, staggering her. Gasping, she fell back, feeling as though she would retch as segments of skin, spurts of blood, and splinters of bone spewed from the troll's caved-in skull. He lurched on his feet, stumbling sideways, then collapsed, dead.

She had killed a Kind. For an instant that fact registered sharply in her brain, piercing her to the core, revolting her. Then it receded to some dark corner of her mind as she was assailed by another Frigidian. Swiftly Rhiannon dodged to narrowly escape being crushed by his club as he brought it crashing toward her. Her foe, though slow and clumsy, was both formidable and persistent; and unlike the troll she had just slain, this one would not be taken unaware. She sensed she was but a heartbeat from death. Instinctively, only dimly cognizant that she did so, she summoned her Power.

Like a sudden burst of fox fire, it exploded from her being, an aura of blue flame that changed in a flash to a white-hot glow fueled by her heightened emotions. The Frigidian bearing down on her was sent reeling from the force of the blast. The nauseating smell of singed hair and flesh permeated the air as he was scorched by her aura. She raised her morning star, only to discover that it could not penetrate the wall of warding she had flung up about herself. Frantic, she strove to think, to remember her lessons. . . .

Concentrating with all her might, she compelled the barrier to shift, to split, even as she maintained its protection around her vital parts. The morning star whipped free, slamming into the troll's belly. He groaned with pain, doubling over, and blindly, panic-stricken, Rhiannon hit him again, this time on the nape. The blow broke his neck instantly. Yet mingled with her relief was the appalling realization that she had killed again. Somehow the knowledge that she would be dead herself otherwise did not make it any easier.

She turned to see that Iskander, also, was enshrouded by the blue fire of the Druswids, with which he was attempting to shield Sir Weythe, Gunda, and Lido as well, who doubtless would otherwise by now have fallen victim to the Frigidians, for neither the one-armed swordsman nor the two gnomes were a match for the monstrous trolls. Wisely Chervil and Anise had each climbed a tree, from which safe distance their arrows rained punishingly upon their targets. Yael was laying about him savagely with his massive battle-ax, while Anuk harried the Frigidians however he could, his muscular jaws and razor-sharp teeth inflicting considerable damage to the enemy. Dead trolls strewed the ground, but still more remained standing, fighting on with a ferocity that was terrifying.

Grimly Rhiannon fended off yet another brutal attack, her morning star again striking true. Stepping over the body of the fallen Frigidian, she glanced about wildly, expecting a further assault. But for her, at least, there was a momentary lull in the heated battle, the rest of the trolls being otherwise engaged. She paused, her breath coming in rasps, grateful for the brief respite. Her head swam, and she had a painful stitch in her side. Drizzle and sweat streamed down her face. Vaguely, her stomach churning biliously at the recognition, she became aware that she was spattered with blood from head to toe. Feeling faint and ill, she choked down with difficulty the vomit that rose in her throat.

It was only gradually that she realized there was something wrong with Iskander's aura. It was shot through with jagged tridents of a sickly yellow-green color that appeared to be originating from the Sword of Ishtar. His visage was drawn and harsh in the rain, as she had never before seen it, and in his eyes was a bleak light of apprehension and determination. The wall of warding he had cast up around himself and the others wavered erratically, evanescing bit by bit, while the dreadful forks of celadon issuing from the blade grew ever stronger. It was clear to Rhiannon that not only was Iskander expending too much energy, draining his reserves of Power, but he was striving desperately for control of the weapon. As she watched, stricken, Gunda and Lido were thrown without warning from the barrier's interior, as though pitched out by some monumental force. They sprawled headlong upon the wet earth, dazed and shivering. An instant later Sir Weythe was sent flying from the protective realm of the blue fire.

Suddenly Rhiannon recalled Iskander's telling her how Cain had bent the sword's magic to his will, warping it so it served the left hand of the Darkness, and some primal instinct warning her, she screamed, "Get down! All of ye! Get down!" and began to run. Yael and Anuk looked up, startled, taking in at a glance the wild, unstable charge of Iskander's aura, the malignant chartreuse luminescence that poured from the blade in his hand. They spied the old soldier and the gnomes lying stunned upon the ground.

Rhiannon's words rang in their ears. Her figure was a white-hot blur racing across the glade. With the alertness born of their elfin reflexes, Chervil and Anise had already dropped from their trees to flatten themselves upon the muddy floor of the forest. Now Yael and Anuk also threw themselves down, the lupine shielding with his own body those of the gnomes. The unknown young man whose plight had been the cause of all the conflict huddled at the center of the clearing, wailing, quivering with terror, the hem of his ragged, bloodstained gallibiya ridiculously pulled up over his head, as though the garment might somehow save him from harm.

Caught off-guard by this abrupt halting of the battle, the undefeated Frigidians stood dumbly, muttering and glaring suspiciously about the glade, not understanding what was happening. After a moment, noticing Iskander, they started and suddenly galumphed back, intuitively frightened, guttural sounds of alarm issuing from their throats, their hairy hands gesticulating wildly.

By then Rhiannon had reached Iskander's side. The heat of his aura was such that she could feel it through her own. Yet she did not hesitate, did not question whether her command of her Power was such that she could withstand the potency of his, did not even consider the danger to herself as, flinging away her morning star, she plunged through his wall of warding, merging her aura with his.

The impact of the two barriers colliding made it appear that a conflagration had erupted. Man and woman were engulfed in a blaze of multicolored fire. Sparks showered in every direction. Rhiannon could hear the sounds of her aura and Iskander's own roaring like a tempest in her ears as without warning a blast of pure evil rocked her so violently that she stumbled and would have fallen had she not clutched

Iskander's arm. It was as though a vast storm of wind and light and color swirled around them, nearly blinding her. Strands of her hair, loosed during battle from her braid, whipped across her face. She pushed them back, trying desperately to orient herself in the chaos created by the clashing auras. She had not known that this would happen. She could tell from Iskander's grim expression that he was powerless to help her. Tentacles of yellow-green ichor crept from the Sword of Ishtar to curl around her body, sucking at her greedily, as though to consume her. With all her might she fought to hold them at bay, unwittingly providing Iskander with a brief respite. Frantically he did what little he could to stabilize their roiling auras, woven together by the warped threads of glowing celadon that unspooled from the blade.

He was shocked and appalled by Rhiannon's unexpected presence at his side. But he no longer had the strength to cast her beyond the boundaries of his aura, as he had Sir Weythe, Gunda, and Lido.

"Run, Rhiannon! Run! I cannot hold the sword much longer! I cannot contain what is within it! Run! Run, do ye hear? Get away as fast as ye can!" Iskander's voice reverberated urgently in the chasms of her mind.

"Nay, Iskander. I came to help ye."

"Nay, nay, do not—" But before he could finish the protest, she had clasped her hands around his on the hilt of the weapon.

The touch of her hands against his and the metal of the sword itself jolted Rhiannon to the very marrow of her bones. She wanted to weep as she felt the full force of the bane that befouled the blade, for she did not know how Iskander had withstood it as long as he had. It was twisted, unnatural, and threatened to devour her utterly. A wave of hideous images rose in her brain, scenes of what must have been the Battle of the Strathmore Plains, somehow imprinted on the weapon by Cain's Power and now unleashed by her own and Iskander's. He saw them, too, she sensed, fumbling to reestablish through her dread the fragile link with his own equally besieged mind. And then suddenly, just when Rhiannon believed that the two of them were surely doomed, there appeared a vision of goodness and light, a child of winter wrapped in a cloak of flurrying snow, her love a staff that pointed the way.

For Ileana, too, had left her mark upon the Sword of Ishtar.

"Breathe, Rhiannon!" Iskander commanded silently. *"Breathe—and think of the Light. Think only of the Light. . . ."*

Slowly, deeply, she breathed, remembering that night upon the *Frostflower* when Iskander had kissed her, taking her breath away, giving her his own. The thought filled her mind, spilled over into his until they breathed as one, and the Light grew within them as together they struggled against the venomous rays emitting from the sword. Little by little, they compelled the baleful incandescence from the hilt, up the length of the blade, to its tip, where the malevolent yellow-green flames exploded in a wild, uncontrollable burst of energy that enveloped the whole of the clearing. The trolls watching, petrified, were roasted where they stood, seared to cinders in the blink of an eye as the huge celadon fireball whizzed from one to the other, before consuming them, at last whatever had propelled it burned itself out and it floated to the forest floor, a dying puff of smoke. Simultaneously the auras of Iskander and Rhiannon both winked out, the Power that had sustained them totally exhausted. The Sword of Ishtar hung lamely at Iskander's right side, as cold and dark as though it had never glowed. With his left arm he embraced Rhiannon's trembling body tightly, gazing down at her lovingly; and in that moment, slowly getting to his feet, Yael knew, finally, as he looked at her face, naked with emotion, her heart in her eyes, that he had lost her, utterly and forever. For he sensed that whatever had passed between her and Iskander when their auras had melded had forged between them a bond that would never be broken so long as they lived. A lump rose in the giant's throat, choking him. Passing his hand across his stinging eyes, he averted his glance so as not to intrude upon the intensely private moment he had had the misfortune to witness.

One by one, the rest shakily stood, silent in the aftermath of what had befallen them, none of them truly grasping what had occurred to destroy the trolls, the questers knowing only that they themselves were alive and safe. Before any could speak, however, daring at last to peek from beneath the hem of his gallibiya, the young man persecuted by the Frigidians began to babble hysterically in some language no one could understand. He was on his knees, his hands outstretched before him, and every time he gasped for breath, he bowed, pressing his forehead to the ground. He appeared to be even more terrified of them than he had been of the trolls, and after a moment the companions correctly deduced that he was pleading for his life.

"Do ye get up, stranger," Iskander insisted gruffly in the Common Tongue. "Ye have naught to fear from us. We won't hurt ye, and the trolls who sought to do so are dead."

"Oh, thank the Gods!" the young man cried in the same language, his overwhelming relief plain. "Ye are an educated man who speaks Tintagelese!" At that, weeping profusely, he crawled forward on his knees and flung himself at Iskander's feet. "Oh, dear sir, dear sir!" he sobbed. "Never have I witnessed such a stupendous display of magic! 'Tis clear ye are a mage of the highest order, and I am humbled, grateful beyond belief that ye and your friends should have put yourselves to the trouble of rescuing me from those barbarians of Frigidia! How can I ever repay ye? Oh, let me serve ye! I should count myself fortunate to be your devoted slave for life!"

Mortified by the young man's impassioned behavior and quite offended by the ill-advised suggestion he had put forth, Iskander frowned darkly and growled, "Slavery is an evil practiced only by those who would serve the Darkness! Are ye of that ilk, then?"

"Oh, nay, sir! Nay!" the young man hastened to assure him. "I worship the Gods, not the Demons, I swear! Permit me to introduce myself. I am Moolah san Eippuy by name, late of Bezel, and a merchant by trade—and once a prosperous one at that. But alas, I fear I have fallen upon hard times recently, and now all I have left in the world is the shambles ye see over there." He pointed sadly to his little caravan, which had in the end toppled over on one side, its contents scattered helter-skelter, its horses torn free of both tethers and harness, and run off. "Oh, woe is me! Woe is me!" Moolah wailed abruptly, wringing his hands at the sight. "I have lost everything. *Everything!* What am I to do? What am I to do? What is to become of me now?"

"For the Light's sake!" Iskander snapped. "Do ye get up and stop that sniveling at once—before I am sore tempted to do ye some mischief we shall both regret! Chervil . . . Anise . . . go and see if ye can find Master Moolah's horses. Take care. There may be more trolls lurking in these woods. Yael . . . Weythe . . . lend me a hand, and let us try to get that wagon righted if we can. Rhiannon, do ye and Gunda do what ye can to tend Master Moolah's wounds. They appear numerous but not serious, for in truth, he acts more rattled than hurt." Iskander's tone was dry. "Lido, start picking up all those pots and pans and that broken crockery. Anuk, stand guard. I want nothing sneaking up on us, be it man or beast. We have endured enough for one day!"

These orders were no sooner given than they were carried out, the elves, weapons in hand, melting soundlessly into the woods to search for the missing horses, Anuk diligently prowling the perimeter of the glade. While Iskander, Yael, and Weythe set about attempting to heave up the cart, Gunda fetched her sack of herbs and other medicines, and she and Rhiannon began carefully to cut away the worst of Moolah's blood-soaked raiment. Contrary to Iskander's supposition, several of the Bezel's gashes were, in truth, quite deep. Rhiannon guessed he was actually in severe shock, running on nervous energy bordering on hysteria, and that he had not yet realized the extent of his injuries. Indeed, this soon proved to be the case as, when he spied the damage done to himself, Moolah promptly passed out. It was just as well, Rhiannon thought, for she felt that the cleaning and treating of his wounds would have been most painful for him otherwise. The ugliest of the gouges required stitches, and both she and Gunda worried about putrefaction setting in. The trolls had been infected by the UnKind's disease, and neither woman knew at what stage the sickness became contagious or even if it could be spread by the type of contact the Bezel had endured. Indeed, for all that both she and Lido had grudgingly taken to washing themselves, Gunda still harbored doubts about the existence of germs, and she continued secretly, albeit now halfheartedly, to suspect that the SoulEaters' affliction was brought about by black magic wrought through the evil eye.

Rhiannon, more enlightened, fretted over the state of Moolah's health. If by some chance the Bezel chose to remain with them for any length of time, he would have to be closely watched for signs of the illness, she insisted as she confided her fears to Iskander. He nodded gravely, comprehending at once the danger to them all if Moolah was now on his way to becoming one of the UnKind.

Iskander, Yael, and Weythe had succeeded in righting the caravan. Now they carried the unconscious Moolah inside and laid him on the narrow bunk within so he would be sheltered from the rain. There was no question of the travelers moving on. They could not leave the injured Bezel, alone and unprotected, to fend for himself, and the elves had yet to return with the missing horses, besides.

"We'll camp here tonight," Iskander stated flatly, for he did not like the idea of lingering in the clearing any more than the rest did. "'Twill be dark soon, and this is as good a place as any—no matter how little any of us thinks so. Let's get the tents erected and a fire started."

This the questers did, but even the fact that, just after dusk, the drizzle at long last ceased did not lighten either their glum mood or their uneasiness. The moons rose in the night sky, the Blue Moon closer at this point in its orbit than its sisters and seeming to stare down through the trees straight at the companions—like Gunda's proverbial evil eye, Rhiannon fancied, shivering. For the Blue Moon was fabled as a harbinger of doom; when it waxed full, upon its pale, eerie face could be seen the figure of a leaping hellhound, a legendary beast said to herald the approach of death and to guard the Gates of the Darkness. It was from this animal that those such as

Anuk were said to have descended, but Rhiannon could not credit this and thought the tale only a fable, the creature itself but a myth.

Still, drawing her cloak more closely about her, she starred herself for protection—and wished that the dawn would come quickly.

NIGHT STAR

The Darkness

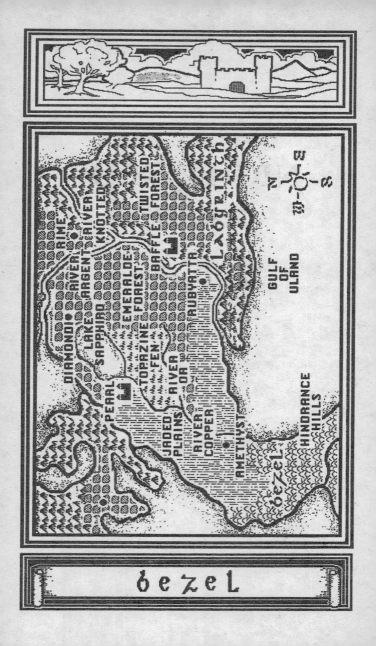

bezel

Chapter 20

Moolah lay ill—feverish and delirious—for many days, and we had no choice but to take him with us, for we had to move on. During the course of our journey, summer had come and gone, autumn was now well upon us, and winter nipped at our heels. Beyond the Twisted Forest lay the Windchill Mountains, which stretched from the north of Frigidia to the south of Labyrinth, and we must be through their passes before the first snowfall, else we would be stranded in Baffle, unable to travel on until spring. This Iskander did not want, for time worked against us—and for the UnKind.

Chervil and Anise had recovered Moolah's horses, and these and the caravan made our journey swifter—though I did wonder what Moolah would have to say upon discovering our appropriation of his horses and wagon, and the fact that we had whisked him away in the opposite direction from which he had been traveling. I suspected he would not be too happy about the matter.

"Too bad. Tintagel's need is the greater," Iskander said tersely when I mentioned to him my qualms. "The merchant is lucky to be alive—and

fortunate that we did not abandon him in the forest."

After that I did not bring up the subject again. Iskander had changed since our slaying of the trolls. In many respects, though we were closer than we had been before, there was perversely a distance between us, too. He had grown harder, more determined, as though he were driven by the images we had beheld in the flames of the Sword of Ishtar. So clear and real had the scenes been that we might actually have been there upon the Strathmore Plains that winter solstice of the battle—and the horror of it stayed with us both.

Sometimes late at night I awoke in a cold sweat, the images haunting my dreams, and I guessed that Iskander did the same, for he was like a man obsessed, his quest paramount. He spared none of us, himself least of all, as we pushed on toward Baffle, and many were the times we who followed him felt like a whip the sting of his dark moods, the lash of his sharp words.

Often in the evenings he would sit within his tent, staring out at the fire; and now and then he would pull from its scabbard the Sword of Ishtar, running his hands slowly along its length, like a blind man, as though he could feel the bane it harbored and sought some means of displacing it. His Power was different from Cain's, he had told me. That was why he could not seem to overcome the curse of the blade. Yet somehow he must, else he dared not draw it again—and how, then, would we be able to defend ourselves against the heart of Darkness?

Like spurs, the thought roweled him. I could see the pain and despair in his eyes, and my heart ached for him—in all the ways a woman's heart *could ache for a man. Such I have come to learn is love, the greatest joy on earth—and the deepest anguish.*

—Thus it is Written—
in
The Private Journals
of the Lady Rhiannon sin Lothian

The River Knotted, Labyrinth, 7275.10.43

ONCE, LONG WOODEN BRIDGES HAD SPANNED THE RIVER Knotted, joining Labyrinth and Bezel. But in the wake of the SoulEaters, the gnomes, out of self-preservation, had destroyed the bridges that had linked them to the world beyond their boundaries. Now there was only a single ferry that was kept hidden upon the eastern shore and that must be uncovered and carried down to the water's edge when needed—though even these precautions did not prevent the crossing of the river by those who possessed boats. The raft was large and ponderous enough that the Labyrinthians must move it by means of log rollers. But this operation, directed by Sarn Shale, the Head Elder of Baffle, was smoothly, though warily, accomplished, under heavy guard. For in the tall grasses, reeds, and weeds that lined the shore of the River Knotted had been discovered a small coracle and the bodies of several of the UnKind and Frigidians. Clearly a vicious skirmish had recently taken place between the opposing forces, with the SoulEaters, greatly outnumbered, being slain by the trolls. It was these UnKind, the questers theorized, who had infected the Frigidians they had encountered in the Twisted Forest.

Iskander was appalled by the sight of the decaying corpses of the SoulEaters. But still, he forced himself to kneel and study them closely, even to the point of running his hands over one of the bodies searchingly, much as he did the Sword of Ishtar, of late. Watching, Rhiannon choked down with difficulty the bile that rose in her throat.

"Come away, Lord! Come away!" she begged softly, urgently. "None of us understands how ye can bear to touch that thing—or why ye feel ye needs must."

"Do ye not, truly, Rhiannon—or is it just that ye don't want to face the knowledge of what I must do when we find the heart of the Darkness?" he queried, his voice low, harsh. "Tell me the truth, damn ye! Have ye not once during our journey asked yourself how I plan to infiltrate the ranks of the UnKind, to spy upon them at close quarters? Have ye really not yet grasped the reason why I, a ShapeShifter, was chosen for this quest?"

"Nay, Iskander, nay—"

"Do not lie to me!" he grated. "Do not try to spare my feelings—or yours. There is too much between us for that. Ye know the answers to your questions," he said grimly. "I can see in your eyes that ye do. I do what I must, what is necessary, as I've told ye before —and that, ye of all people should understand. Do ye fear me now for that, Rhiannon? If I were to take ye in my arms this moment, would ye tremble with passion —or loathing? Ye cannot answer me, can ye? By the moons! Do ye know now why I have fought so hard to hold at bay what lies between us?" He paused, nostrils flaring with emotion, then continued roughly. "Go! Tell Sarn Shale that I have seen all I need to see here, that he is to burn these corpses, that even the buzzards will have naught to do with them, else the presence of the bodies would have been known to us long before we stumbled upon them. Go, I say! Unless ye wish me to release ye from your pledge—"

"Nay, I do not ask that of ye, Lord," Rhiannon rejoined quietly, hurt. "I will do as ye have bidden, as I have ever done."

Biting her lip to stem the tears that threatened to spill from her eyes, she turned and left him, lifting her chin and squaring her shoulders. Silently, knowing how he had wounded her, Iskander watched her go. Then, spitting a foul curse, he stood, giving the UnKind corpse at his feet a savage kick that, though it provided an outlet for the violent emotions pent up inside him, did little to make him feel any better. As he stared down at the vile, dead creature, Iskander knew that if he were honest with himself, he must admit he was afraid. Having at long last come face to face with the SoulEaters, he had learned that the reality of them was much worse than anything he had, even with his extensive knowledge of them, ever imagined—and his visions of them had been horrifying, indeed. Unjustly he had taken his fear out on Rhiannon, unable to bring himself to tell her that the evil with which the Sword of Ishtar was imprinted was the same evil he felt emanating from the bodies of the UnKind, only magnified tenfold. And if he could not conquer the blade, how then could he possibly hope to successfully strike at the heart of the Darkness? Iskander did not know. Doubt consumed him. Had he come so far, only to fail now? Nay, he could not, *would* not admit defeat. He made his way to the raft bobbing gently on the waves of the River Knotted.

The companions had reached Baffle three days ago. The village was much the same as Imbroglio, except that due to their more frequent trade with the Bezels, particularly, in the past, before the SoulEaters had encroached upon both lands, the gnomes of Baffle were cleaner and more advanced than those of Imbroglio—though they were no less terrified of the UnKind. Baffle, too, possessed huge steel doors to seal off its entrances, relics of the use of the mountains by the Old Ones as a shelter in the Time Before; and as their counterparts in Imbroglio did, the gnomes of Baffle closed these stout barriers at night and, during the day, no longer ventured abroad any more than was necessary to forage for food.

It was Gunda and Lido who had spoken to Sarn Shale, telling him of the vital quest and convincing him to assist the travelers. Now, soberly, the Head Elder bade them farewell, wishing them good luck as they boarded the waiting ferry. Then he turned to begin issuing the necessary orders for the burning of the corpses of the UnKind and Frigidians, as well as the coracle that must have been the SoulEaters' means of reaching Labyrinth. Minutes later the flames blazed high, the smoke billowing into the air to be carried away on the wings of the wind. For a moment the questers watched the fire from the raft as the gnomes of Baffle, by means of a stout rope stretched across the river, slowly hauled the ferry across to the western side. The cremation of the bodies and boat reminded the companions of the destruction of the *Frostflower,* and they understood the sense of desolation Gunda and Lido must be feeling at seeing their homeland grow farther and farther distant, at knowing that once the raft deposited them on the far shore, they would be stranded until it returned for them—because for them there was that hope, at least. The rest could only go forward.

Even Moolah, lucid now, his fever down, raised no protest at accompanying the travelers, fervently insisting he owed them his life and must pay his debt.

His was a story typical of Bezel, he had told them. He had come from a poor family and had struggled to make his way in the world, determined to better his station in his life. He had started off with a tiny pushcart, from which he had sold myriad cheap trinkets in the town bazaars of his homeland. Gradually he had managed to purchase a caravan, and then finally a shop in Pearl, on the banks of Lake Sapphiro. In time he had expanded his store. Eventually he had opened a second shop in Diamondi, and then a third in Rubyatta and a fourth in Amethyst. For the flood of foreigners who had come from the south, fleeing for their lives, had proved a boon to his business. But as the relentless war against the marauding UnKind continued to drag on and on, the towns of Bezel were repeatedly overrun, besieged. During such perilous battles, trade was frequently cut off, food supplies dwindled, and plagues spread. Panic ensued, and with a loaf of bread selling for a golden, the terrified moneylenders demanded repayment of their loans. Moolah, who had relied heavily on credit to finance his stores, had been caught up in one such invasion and could not pay. In lieu of what he had owed, the moneylenders had seized his shops. He had felt himself fortunate to have escaped not only with his life, but with his small caravan.

In the hope of recouping his losses, he had decided to brave the risky journey to Imbroglio and also to the even more distant Maze, the easternmost village of Labyrinth, thinking to bargain at each for wares. For all the Labyrinthian villages had their own distinctive styles of metalwork, and unlike those of Baffle, the gnomish goods of Imbroglio and Maze were now a rarity in the town bazaars of Bezel, because few merchants and traders cared to travel so far in these uncertain times. After his experience at the hands of the trolls, however, Moolah was not eager to retrace his steps; and believing that Iskander was possessed of a potent magic that would protect them all, the Bezel had offered his horses, wagon, and services to the questers, paying little heed to Iskander's warnings of the perils ahead.

Shaking his head in dismay at yet another addition

to his entourage, Iskander had stridden away, swearing hotly under his breath and vowing to leave Moolah behind at the first Bezel town they reached. At the time Rhiannon had thought this an empty threat. But now, standing beside Iskander on the ferry, surreptitiously studying his stern profile, she was not so sure. Perhaps his mind frame was now such that he meant to be rid of them all; for had he not just offered to release her from the oath that bound her to him? Silently, though she knew it to be an admirable trait, she cursed his concern for the welfare of those who followed him. He needed them, she thought. Whether he admitted it or not, he needed them. For twelfth-ranked priest or not, what was one man alone in the face of the SoulEaters—especially when he dared not even draw the only weapon that might prove his salvation?

No matter what Iskander said or did, she, at least, would not be driven away, Rhiannon promised herself fiercely. She would stick by him to the end, come what may. Thus determined, she turned her face to the wind, her heart constricting in her breast as the ferry approached the eastern shore of Bezel. For now, from where she stood upon the raft, gazing at the land in the distance, she could see the terrible devastation wrought upon it.

Once, it must have been vastly foreseted, like Labyrinth. But clearly ages of war had taken their toll here, for massive portions of the woods had been burned, creating an endless expanse of blighted plain, the charred tree stumps not yet fully decayed telling their bleak story.

"'Twas done to destroy the Scalies, the UnKind, as ye call them," Moolah said sadly as he limped forward to stand beside Rhiannon and Iskander. "We knew what they were, ye see, from the southern foreigners who fled here from Botanica. Many times has the land been set ablaze since that first time so long ago. What ye see before ye is all that remains of what was once a forest that stretched to the southernmost hills of Bezel. We call it the Jaded Plains now, for since the woods were first burned, no tree has been permitted to grow in the whole of the south, so the SoulEaters cannot march upon us and take us unaware. In this way have we defended ourselves."

"But what of attacks during the winter, when the snow lies thick upon the ground?" Rhiannon asked, knowing that this was what had prevented the same technique from being employed upon the Strathmore Plains.

"We have dug large moats around our towns," Moolah explained, "and when the first snow falls, these are filled with the dry grass cut from the plains, which we harvest each autumn and store for the winter. During an UnKind assault, the trenches are ignited, and they blaze day and night, so the SoulEaters cannot scale our high walls and gain entrance to our towns. And like ye, we, too, have our fiery weapons, though their flames are not born of magic, but of a black powder that was known to our ancestors and with which, in celebration, they made the heavens glitter with a thousand colored lights. For this bright legacy we have found a new and darker purpose—but one that has served us well."

"How many other forests have been burned in this manner, Moolah?" Iskander queried, his tone grim with a worry that neither Rhiannon nor the Bezel comprehended.

"I do not know, Lord," Moolah replied, "though 'tis said that much of the southern lands of Botanica have been despoiled. Why do ye ask?"

"Because of what is written in the Holy Book, *The Word and The Way* . . . that no tree is to be taken from the earth without another's being planted in its place, for from the forests come life-giving moisture and the very air we breathe, and each of us needs fifteen trees apiece to sustain us during our LifePath. 'Tis written that in the Time Before, in the name of their almighty god Progress, the Old Ones slashed and burned the woods until the land was sucked dry and the air was nearly gone. The Time of Passing came for many then."

"I—I did not know this, Lord," Moolah stammered. "I swear I did not! I do not know this Holy Book of which ye speak. Is it—is it a book of great magic, Lord?"

"Nay," Iskander rejoined quietly. "It is a book of great truth."

No more was said. The ferry had reached the end of its crossing.

Chapter 21

For the first time since we had begun our long journey, we were totally exposed on the land, without mountain or ravine, forest or brush to conceal our presence, naked and vulnerable to attack. Even when the first of the snows came, we dared not light a fire, lest we draw attention to ourselves, but took turns huddling around the brazier in Moolah's caravan, cold and miserable. We feared that raiding parties of the UnKind or even the Frigidians might swoop down upon us; and all of us did double guard duty, half of us keeping watch, while the other half snatched what little sleep they could in the tension-fraught nights.

It was during this time that Iskander began to speak to us of the Holy Book, The Word and The Way, which all those in the East knew by heart, such was its importance to them. Long into the evenings, like a storyteller, he quoted its passages to us, his low voice as beautiful and musical as a bard's as he unfolded its tales one by one.

I was never without fear and heartache those nights, for it seemed to me, who saw him through the eyes of love, that his demeanor was that of a

313

man about to die and desperate to leave some worthwhile legacy behind him.

And so it was that I came to understand what had driven Ileana to teach Ulthor as Iskander taught us: of Tintagel as it had been in the Time Before, of the Wars of the Kind and the Apocalypse, and of the Time of the Rebirth and the Enlightenment, when Faith, the Keeper of the Flame, had appeared to the Survivors and spoken again of the Way to the Being, the Immortal Guardian of all things that ever were or ever shall be, the Light Eternal that forever holds the Darkness at bay so long as even one of the Kind believes that the Being is. And though I knew her not, I felt a bond even so with Ileana, that child of winter whose image I had seen in the fires of the Sword of Ishtar and whose love had brought Cain back from the depths of the Darkness.

Somehow, almost as though she were there beside me, hers was the light that guided me, also, that helped me to understand what Iskander sought to accomplish with his words: that if we who followed him survived, we should bear witness to the truth, so his quest should not have been in vain, so Tintagel should never again be cast into the realm of the Darkness.

"Ye are each a ray of the Light," he said one evening. "Remember that. Remember all I have told ye; for a lesson forgotten is a lesson unlearned, and ignorance is the breeding ground of all evil. That is why we must all of us—always—be seekers of knowledge, speakers of truth, with the will and the courage to stand up and do ever what is right."

So simply and quietly spoken, those words were —and yet in my heart, I knew that of all Iskander

*had ever taught me, this last was the greatest truth
of all.*

—Thus it is Written—
in
The Private Journals
of the Lady Rhiannon sin Lothian

SOMETIMES IT SEEMED TO THE QUESTERS THAT THEY MUST
be all alone in the world, for despite their fears,
neither Kind nor UnKind stirred upon the Jaded
Plains. Even the few small creatures that abided there
were furtive and frightened, as though even they
sensed the wrongness in the land. Except for the
keening of the wind and the flurrying of the mist and
snow, the crunch of the horses' hooves and the wagon
wheels upon the frozen ground, all was utterly, eerily,
still, as though the earth had been smothered.

So in silence, for the most part, did the companions
wend their way southward along the banks of the
River Knotted, toward the town of Rubyatta. Within
days its stout, high walls rose before them, a welcome
sight, though, glimpsed from a distance, by the light of
the First Moon beginning its slow ascent into the
night sky, the town appeared hushed, even deserted,
scarcely inviting. Still, it was a place to shelter unex-
posed on the plains, and for that alone it was eagerly
sought, greeted with gratitude.

"'Tis almost the hour of curfew!" Moolah exclaimed, dismayed, glancing anxiously at the firmament. "We must hurry, Lord! For when the Passion
Moon rises, the gates will close for the evening, and
not even for ye will they open again until dawn. This is
the law of the land since the coming of the UnKind."

"Let us press on quickly, then," Iskander ordered.
This the travelers did, relieved when, drawing

nearer, they spied through the snow the first of the torches being ignited on the ramparts of Rubyatta's encircling walls. Now, too, as they approached what Moolah said was the Dragon Gate, could the questers see the figures of patrolling guards and hear the noises indigenous to town life.

"Halt! Who goes there?" a voice barked in the language of the Bezels as two armed sentries stepped forward to block the path of the caravan upon the wooden drawbridge that spanned the dry moat surrounding the town.

"I am Moolah san Eippuy, a merchant of Pearl," Moolah responded in the same tongue, "and my companions are foreigners from Labyrinth and the lands beyond the seas. We seek provisions and a few nights' lodging in Rubyatta."

"Foreigners!" the guard who had spoken now bellowed, snapping to attention. Motioning with his spear, he demanded, "Move into the light so I can see ye—all of ye!" Then, turning to his fellow, he growled, "Istu, search the caravan!"

At Moolah's direction the travelers climbed from the wagon so the first sentry could inspect them, while the second one examined the cart, even thrusting his spear sharply through the pallet on the bunk to make certain no one was hiding within or beneath it.

"The caravan's empty, Vazir," Istu announced, rejoining his fellow.

Vazir grunted, still eyeing the questers suspiciously, walking all around them, paying particular heed to Chervil and Anise, whose appearance was clearly strange to him. Anuk he peered at especially closely as well, rubbing the top of the lupine's head intently, his brow knitted.

"What kind of an animal is this?" he finally asked Moolah sharply. "It looks like a hellhound, but it doesn't have any horns, and near as I can tell, they haven't been sawed off—which is a trick I'm wise to, let me warn ye, Master Moolah. Say"—Vazir's eyes narrowed—"come to think of it, that name sounds familiar. A merchant, ye said. Yea, I remember now: Didn't ye used to have a shop in the bazaar here, the Brass . . . ?"

"Ring"—Moolah supplied the word obligingly. "Yea, I did. But, alas, like so many others, I'm afraid, I had . . . er . . . overextended myself and was wiped out during an invasion."

"Yea, well, that's happened to a lot of people," Vazir observed, his tone a shade friendlier and tinged with sympathy. "Too bad. I recollect that my wife traded in your store, claimed ye had the best Labyrinthian silver in all Bezel."

"Plainly a woman of excellent taste, Sir Vazir," Moolah declared warmly, venturing a small smile. "I am indeed flattered. In fact, I was on my way to Imbroglio, in the hope of obtaining some more of that quite exquisite metalwork, when I was unfortunately set upon by a raiding party of Frigidians. If not for my companions, I doubt very much that I should be standing here right now. Now . . . about Anuk, Sir Vazir . . . I know he resembles a hellhound—I'll admit I thought so myself, at first—but he is *not,* I assure ye, one of those fiendish creatures. He is a lupine, which I understand to be some kind of sledding beast used in the tundra of Iglacia, the Lord Iskander's homeland."

"Yea, well, since 'tis ye vouching for the animal, Master Moolah, I guess that it's all right, then," Vazir stated at last. "You're all free to pass, and I'm sure that ye at least, Master Moolah, know the laws. See Sir Dothan inside the watchtower. He'll assign ye to a quarantine officer and tell ye where to report if ye remain in Rubyatta longer than three days. Please instruct your companions accordingly, and inform them that if for any reason they fail to check in weekly with their quarantine officer, they will be arrested and executed. Please also inform them that if any among them are discovered to exhibit symptoms of the Scalies' disease, they will be killed at once, without exception."

"Yea, I shall. Thank ye, Sir Vazir," Moolah said.

Once inside the town's walls, the travelers were issued the necessary papers to show that they had properly entered Rubyatta, Iskander remarking with interest how smoothly and efficiently everything was run and making mental notes to propose a similar system to the cities of the East. Better to be prepared, to have such safeguards in place *before* they become vital to survival, he thought.

Iskander had plenty of coins in the leather pouch that never left the belt at his waist, and Moolah knew of good lodgings, where the questers were less likely to be overcharged or robbed. So, the rest following, he led the way through the winding streets of town to what was a clean but obviously poorer quarter; and presently the companions were ensconced at the Copper Kettle Inn. They got two small adjoining chambers, one for the men, the other for the women; and once they were comfortably settled in, they went downstairs to the common room, where they ordered wine, ale, and a late supper. The drink was potent, the food plain but filling fare, and the travelers, when it shortly arrived, fell upon the meal hungrily, paying little heed to the curious stares occasionally directed at them by the other customers.

The inn was packed—plainly this was a busy night —and filled with the talk, laughter, and music usual in such a place. Clouds of tobacco smoke and the aromas of savory stew and hot bread hung in the air. In the bright lantern light, Rhiannon could see that the crowd of men and women gathered in the common room represented an assortment of tribes, and she correctly deduced that many of these had been displaced from the southern lands, whence it now seemed clear the UnKind must have originated. The customers were a coarse but merry lot, evidently undisturbed by thoughts of the SoulEaters; and for the first time since she and the others had reached the continents of Montano and Botanica, Rhiannon felt they could sleep easily.

A short while after she and the rest had finished eating, the door of the inn opened, and in strode a rough-and-ready group, at their fore a man nearly big as a giant, though Rhiannon knew he was not a Boreal. He was brawny and muscular of build, his skin swarthy as that of a Nomad gypsy, and none too clean, his dark brown hair oily and flowing like a mane. Thick, unruly brows arced above his glittering black eyes. A hooked nose jutted over his bushy mustache, generous lips, and full beard. A silver hoop earring gleamed at one lobe. He was dressed all in black—kurta, hizaam, and chalwar—with a vest of silver chain metal over his shirt. On his hands were finger-less black leather gloves studded with sharp silver spikes. High black leather jackboots adorned with silver spurs encased his corded legs. Like Iskander, he wore his sword sheathed at his back and boasted an impressive array of daggers and chains at his belt, besides. The hilts of two more knives protruded from his boots. The rest of his motley crew, including the women, were similarly attired; all bristled equally with myriad weapons.

At the band's appearance a hush fell over the common room as everyone present keenly assessed the newcomers, those in the know marking them for what they were.

"Scalie Scalpers!" Moolah hissed excitedly to the questers. "By the moons! They're Scalie Scalpers, Lord!"

"And just what *are* Scalie Scalpers, Moolah?" Iskander inquired.

"They are the most respected and feared men and women of the land, for they hunt the Scalies—the UnKind, Lord. They kill them and scalp them for the bounty money the King Lord Hakim has offered for each set of horns . . . two whole platinas for those of the Scalies themselves, a mere fifty goldens for those of their hellhounds—which, of course, is nothing to sneer at, for after all, a man might live very well indeed on fifty goldens a year."

For a long, taut moment the Scalie Scalpers stood in the doorway, surveying the inn intently. Then they moved to take seats at two empty tables, whose benches had been hastily vacated by their previous occupants and whose surfaces were now being speedily cleared of dirty mugs and dishes by several barmaids. The brief lull was ended as the conversation in the common room resumed, though it seemed to Rhiannon that it was more subdued than before, as though the presence of the fierce Scalie Scalpers had somehow strained the otherwise jovial atmosphere, reminding everyone that the land was at war and that no one was truly safe in these uncertain times.

It was some minutes later when the Scalie Scalpers noticed the questers and, provoked, pointed out to their bearded leader the lupine that lay at Iskander's feet and that he and the rest of the companions had grown uneasily aware resembled the ferocious hellhound they had until recently thought no more than a legend.

"Would ye look at that, Kaliq," one of the men drawled in Bezel, an edge to his voice, which was loud enough that another tense silence gradually spread through the inn as, one by one, its customers became cognizant of the disturbance. "The town guards must have been asleep at their posts to have let that bloody hellhound slip past them," he sneered, "or else some damned idiot was fool enough to be taken in by that horn-sawing ruse of the Poxed. Either way, I reckon that makes everybody sitting at that table over yonder suspect, don't ye?"

"Yea, Hordib, I reckon it does," the leader, Kaliq, agreed, the unpleasant smile that twisted his lips not quite reaching his eyes, which glinted hard as nails in the lantern light.

"Ye know, Kaliq, fifty goldens would more than pay for our supper," Hordib continued, his tone goading; clearly he eagerly anticipated a fight.

"Yea, it would," Kaliq acknowledged, slowly rising and sauntering toward the travelers' table, Hordib and three other men right behind him.

"Oh, dear," Moolah squeaked, alarmed. "Oh, dear. Lord, I'm very much afraid that there's going to be trouble. The Scalie Scalpers . . . Lord, they think that Anuk's a hellhound, that we're all Poxed. . . . Oh, dear—" The frightened Bezel broke off abruptly as the brutal bunch came to a halt before Iskander, their leader gesturing rudely at the lupine at Iskander's feet and making some taunting remark that caused Hordib and the other three men to exchange sly glances and wicked smirks.

Then, rocking back on his heels, nonchalantly hooking his thumbs in his belt, Kaliq stared challengingly at Iskander, plainly expecting him to respond.

Instead, his eyes flicking toward Moolah, Iskander directed softly, "Inform this . . . barbarian that I do not speak Bezel, and ask him if he knows the Common Tongue."

"Yea, I know it," Kaliq answered in Tintagelese before Moolah could undertake the necessary translation, "at least, well enough to understand when I've been insulted, stranger."

"Then perhaps ye are not as . . . lacking as ye appear," Iskander commented. "Master Moolah has told me that ye believe my lupine, Anuk, to be a hellhound—which he is not—and that ye consider my friends and me to be 'Poxed,' from which word's context I take it to mean that ye think we have all been infected by the Scalies, as ye Bezels call them—which we have not. None of us, therefore, being any of your business whatsoever, I suggest that ye and your men return to your own tables, without further dispute."

"Oh, ye do, do ye?" Kaliq rejoined, scowling.

"Please, oh, please, good sir!" Moolah interjected anxiously. "Do as the Lord Iskander has bidden ye. He has told ye the truth about both the lupine and ourselves. Sir Vazir, at the Dragon Gate, inspected us all most closely, I assure ye, and we have the proper passage papers to prove it." Seeing the skepticism on Kaliq's face, Moolah babbled on hurriedly, wishing to avoid a quarrel. "Good sir, the Lord Iskander is a powerful mage—in truth, the most powerful mage I have ever beheld. His sword possesses a great and terrible magic, with which he burned a dozen Frigidians to cinders in the Twisted Forest of Labyrinth. I, who had been set upon and badly beaten by these same trolls, was witness to this incredible feat. He is from the eastern land of Iglacia, good sir, and is an emissary of the six Eastern Tribes. He is here on a crucial quest—to strike at the very heart of the Scalies!"

"Why, what nonsense is all this, man?" Kaliq sputtered, indignant. "Do ye take me for a simpleton —to be cozened by such drivel? A magic sword . . . Eastern Tribes . . . a dozen trolls . . . a crucial quest. *Faugh!* What would such a powerful mage be doing here at the Copper Kettle, eh? And who among us knows of aught to the east save for Labyrinth, home of the gnomes? As for the Frigidians, they are slow and stupid, and to kill a dozen of them is an easy task indeed—as we Scalie Scalpers know. But even we who hunt the horns do not venture beyond Epitaph Pass, for that would be the act of a maniac or a fool! Do ye say, then, that this man ye claim to be a wondrous wizard is also deranged or dim-witted?"

At Kaliq's last words Hordib and the other three men, who apparently spoke the Common Tongue as well, began to hoot and howl with laughter and to caper about wildly, striking ridiculous poses and making droll faces at one another as each attempted to best the others at imitating a mad or muddled mage.

It was at this point that Iskander slowly stood, saying in a low but purposeful voice, "I should be very careful, if I were ye, whom I mocked and offended; for I am a stranger in your land, and ye know nothing about me save what Master Moolah has told ye. I am one of the Chosen—and a twelfth-ranked Druswidic priest, if that means anything to ye. If it does not, then I daresay ye would find the extent of my Power most . . . illuminating—should ye care to cross swords with me, that is . . . "

"Why, Kaliq, I do believe we've just had the proverbial gauntlet flung in our faces!" Hordib cried triumphantly, while the rest crowed, "A duel! A duel!" and started to argue among themselves as to who would have the privilege of putting the upstart in his proper place.

"Do ye think to choose, then, but one man from your ranks to meet me?" Iskander needled scornfully. "Why, that would hardly be worth the energy 'twould take for me to draw my blade from its scabbard! Good sirs, I am an honorable man. If I fight, it must be fairly. I shall stand all five of ye at once. That should make the odds square!"

A great outcry of cheers and jeers both rose at this, with the remainder of Kaliq's band leaping from their benches to shove back the tables in the common room, clearing a space for the forthcoming fray.

Evidently such was not an unusual occurrence, or else the innkeeper feared to intervene; for to Rhiannon's shock, though he began nervously to yank several glass bottles off the bar, lest they should be broken, he made no protest against the imminent duel. Her hope that the confrontation would be stopped was dashed. She did not know what had got into Iskander, why he had not sought to placate the Scalie Scalpers, except that they were rude and had affronted his dignity and pride. Still, that he would dare to pull the unpredictable Sword of Ishtar and loose it amid innocent people appalled her. For the first time she thought to wonder, horrified, if the beast in Cain was also within Iskander, if somehow, some way, she and he were reliving the nightmare Ileana and Cain had endured.

As though he sensed her worry, Iskander's eyes met hers, holding her gaze steadily for an instant before he turned away to prepare for the duel, shrugging off the leather harness that secured the Sword of Ishtar at his back. The Scalie Scalpers, quaffing ale, had grown boisterous, shouting boasts about their prowess and crude gibes about Iskander's lack. Wagers were being laid, with most of the money being placed against Iskander. Moolah, though he had admittedly done his best to try to stem the unfortunate tide of events, was now shamelessly covering all bets, having staked his horses and caravan, with little thought of his penury, so certain was he of the fight's outcome.

"Sir Weythe"—Iskander spoke, laying his sheathed sword on the table before Rhiannon—"your weapon, if ye please."

"Lord?" The old soldier's brow knitted with puzzlement.

"Your weapon, Weythe," Iskander reiterated. "Surely ye did not think I would unleash the Sword of Ishtar upon these arrogant but otherwise admirable mercenaries. They may be a hard and mannerless lot, but they are not without courage beyond surpassing if they 'hunt the horns,' as they call it. Your weapon, Weythe."

So great was Rhiannon's relief at this that she trembled and nearly buried her head in her hands and wept; and as Iskander reached for the swordsman's blade, she swiftly unknotted the thong that bound the long braid hanging over her shoulder. Unwinding the thin leather strip, she stood and tied it about Iskander's arm.

"A favor from a Lady, for luck," she murmured, blushing, as he looked down at her, his grey eyes unfathomable in the lantern light. "Is this—is this not what is done in the East, Lord, at such a time?"

"Yea. For luck and for . . . other things." His eyes searched her face for a long moment, as though memorizing every detail of it. Then, hefting Weythe's weapon, he turned to Kaliq, Hordib, and the other three men. "Come," he urged, "if you're still of a mind to do so."

Of a sudden it seemed Kaliq hesitated, some instinct warning him, perhaps, or Iskander's quiet confidence unsettling him at last. But then rash Hordib grinned and declared, "Why, man, we would not miss it!" and the battle was on.

The common room held its collective breath as the Scalie Scalpers spread out to form a ring around Iskander and began to circle him charily. From the onlookers there was a hiss of indrawn breath as he summoned his Power and an aura of blue fire enveloped him, like a shroud, wispy as mist, the barest of protective shields. Startled, the Scalie Scalpers retreated a little. But then, seeing that this was all he intended, they grew bold once more, Kaliq growling, "Man, if that pathetic display of magic is the best ye can offer, I would call ye no adept, but a mere conjurer, a trickster, a charlatan, in truth!"

Another appreciative burst of ribald remarks and contemptuous laughter erupted in the inn but died abruptly when Iskander started to move. He was like the wind, everywhere, nowhere, savage as a storm, subtle as a sigh, attacking, parrying, feinting, lunging, a dervish of blue flame. His blade flashed and streaked like lightning. One man went down, wounded, effectively disabled, and then a second and a third until only Kaliq and Hordib remained, breathing hard, the smiles wiped from their faces at what had befallen their fellows. The rest of the band were silent now, all their jollity gone. They were the bravest and best fighters in the land. To see three of their number so easily defeated and Iskander still standing, without even so much as a mark on him, shocked them to the core. An angry, frightened mutter ran through their ranks; what manner of deviltry was this?

His pride pricked, Hordib grew reckless—when a cooler head would have served him far better—and Rhiannon grasped then why Kaliq and not he had risen to become the group's leader. Kaliq hung back, watching, learning, testing, discovering finally that there were chinks in Iskander's aura, that he was not invulnerable to assault. Deftly Iskander's weapon slashed and stabbed. Crying out, Hordib staggered back, his blade clattering upon the floor, blood spurting from his sword arm, laid open to the bone. His eyes were shadowed with pain and surprise. He had thought himself a match for any man. Now he knew different.

Only Kaliq and Iskander were left; and it was as though all that had gone before had been but a prelude to this moment when they came together. Both men were tired, it was obvious. Each rasped for breath. Now, to conserve his strength, Iskander let his Power recede into its deep, dark, inner well; his aura vanished. A great cheer roared from the onlookers as they realized that he would meet Kaliq on equal terms.

"Now . . . *now* we duel, man." Iskander flung the words harshly, mockingly, at Kaliq; then ruthlessly he advanced to press his attack.

Their weapons clashed, spitting sparks. This, Rhiannon knew instinctively, was swordplay at its finest. For if Iskander were a master of the art, then so, too, was Kaliq, clever, calculating, not giving an inch. Their blades scraped against each other furiously as the two who wielded them danced and whirled and sprang, quick and graceful and deadly, their booted feet light as the paws of a smilodon. Sweat beaded the brows of both men; the muscles in their forearms strained and rippled as their weapons flew, cutting wide swaths in the air.

Rhiannon sat so still now that she might have been a statue, holding her breath, her heart in her throat as Kaliq's sword at last slipped past Iskander's guard— to her horror, drawing blood. For the first time she feared for his life, for she thought that Kaliq, his men humiliated, would kill Iskander if he could. Yet Iskander only smiled grimly and returned the scratch in kind. The Scalie Scalpers gasped, stricken, to see the blood that welled from Kaliq's shoulder. They had thought him unscathable, invincible, favored above all by their gods. But it seemed there was one more esteemed than he.

The conflict continued, Rhiannon's face pale as death as she watched, mesmerized, one hand clenched unwittingly about the hilt of the Sword of Ishtar, as though she meant to pull it from its scabbard. It occurred to her suddenly that this was what Iskander had intended, that if he were slain, she must use the blade to defend herself and the others. For she alone had the Power to key the weapon, and without it to protect them, she and the rest would surely be killed by the Scalie Scalpers. Still, she cringed at the thought of drawing the terrible sword, of loosing its foul bane, of trying to conquer it without Iskander.

The rafters of the inn seemed to shake with each blow of the blades. *Clang! Clang!* They twisted and twined, shoved and yielded, the tips of each smeared with blood, their silver lengths glittering. Then suddenly Kaliq's weapon was sent sailing through the air and Iskander's sword was at the mercenary's throat. In the dread hush all eyes were locked on the scene. All waited breathlessly, expectantly, for Iskander's blade to ram home.

But instead, quietly, he said to Kaliq, "For all that ye are prideful, I think that ye are a man of honor. My lupine, Anuk, is no hellhound. My friends and I are not Poxed. 'Tis all ye need to know. Whatever and whoever else we are is not important. In three days we shall be gone from Rubyatta, I swear."

Then slowly he withdrew his weapon and, wiping it against his leather chalwar to rid it of bloodstains, returned it to Sir Weythe. A startled murmur hissed through the ranks of the Scalie Scalpers. Grateful though they were, they did not understand why Iskander had spared their leader's life. Only Kaliq knew, recognized now how shrewdly he, Hordib, and the others had been manipulated. By challenging them as he had, Iskander had prevented a bloodbath that would have ended in death for many—perhaps even innocents among them. This a man Poxed would not have done, Kaliq knew; nor would such a one have wounded instead of killing his five foes.

"The Lord has fought well and fair—and spoken truly," Kaliq uttered. "Let all in Rubyatta know that he and those who follow him are to be left in peace, that I, Kaliq the Hornhunter, stand as surety for the Lord's words and oath."

Then he bowed to Iskander and, turning on his heel, gathered his band and departed from the Copper Kettle to be swallowed up by the night and a flurry of wind and snow. In the Scalie Scalpers' wake, the winter outside swirled into the inn, and Rhiannon became aware of her hands wrapped tightly around the Sword of Ishtar, of the way her palms tingled from the imprint of another's. *Ileana*. Child of Winter. Daughter of the Light. Now, more than ever, Rhiannon felt the sorceress's presence, her mark upon the blade. What did it mean?

Rhiannon did not know, and as Iskander slid the weapon from her grasp, the fleeting impression slipped like mist through her fingers and was gone. There was only Iskander, then—and the love that flowed between them as his eyes kissed hers.

Chapter 22

In the taverns and shops of Rubyatta, I learned, chillingly, that the whole of the southern lands, the continent of Botanica, was in the hands of the UnKind, and that if not for the resistance of the Bezels, the Labyrinthians, and, to the west of Bezel, the Craghes, as well as the inherent warlike nature of the Frigidians, the continent of Montano would be overrun by the SoulEaters, also.

They periodically attempted a mass invasion of Montano, as, from the Strathmore Plains, they had tried to conquer the continents of Aerie and Verdante. But each time, they had been repelled by the Bezels' setting the land ablaze. For if there was one thing the UnKind feared, it was fire; and the Bezels did indeed, as Moolah had said, possess weapons that shot flames. These were long, thick, hollow tubes with a central wick, around which was carefully packed layers of a strange black powder that erupted in burning balls. The Bezels called the weapons "Boomers," because of the sound they made when ignited. It took courage to use them, for they occasionally exploded in one's hand and, like as not, maimed it for life or, even worse, blew it clean off at the wrist.

I confess I did not know what to think of the Boomers. They were a legacy of the Old Ones, *perhaps even in some fashion small replicas of the horrendous weapons of destruction, the great bombs that the Old Ones had loosed upon the land and that had caused the Apocalypse to come to pass.*

Yet even so, I did not see how I could condemn the Bezels for using the Boomers when they were all that held the Darkness at bay; for deep down inside, whenever I gazed at Rhiannon, I knew with grim and terrible certainty—and contrary to all I had ever been taught—that I myself would use whatever means necessary to keep her safe rather than permit her to fall prey to the UnKind.

Thus, because of what was in my heart, did I, a twelfth-ranked Druswidic priest, imperil not only my crucial quest, but perhaps even my very soul.

For that the Light must judge me as It will.

—Thus it is Written—
in
The Private Journals
of the Lord Iskander sin Tovaritch

ONE FINAL TIME BEFORE LEAVING RUBYATTA, ISKANDER sought to warn the others that they no doubt followed him to their deaths, and he pleaded with them to return home however they could, while they still could, rather than accompany him any farther. But to the last one, the questers adamantly refused, declaring that they would ride with him to the very Gates of the Darkness if need be. He was so deeply moved by their bravery and loyalty that there were tears in his eyes when he turned away to mount up.

Moolah had sold his caravan, and with this money and that won from the wagers placed on Iskander's duel with Kaliq, Hordib, and the rest, there had been funds enough to purchase horses for all the companions. This, Iskander had felt, was a necessity; for he had learned in Rubyatta that the UnKind possessed steeds and were known to ride them, though most of the SoulEaters traveled afoot.

Now, Iskander in the lead, the horses' hooves clattering on the cobblestone streets of town, the questers galloped through the southern gate, the Griffin Gate, of Rubyatta just as dawn broke on the eastern horizon. Much to their surprise, beyond the high walls waited the Scalie Scalpers, a hundred warriors strong, all mounted, armed, and provisioned, Kaliq at their head.

"Good morning, Lord," he greeted Iskander pleasantly, with no sign at all that he bore him any grudge; Iskander had, it seemed, proved himself a worthy rival. "I see that ye are a man of your word, for 'tis the third day, and here ye are, departing from Rubyatta, just as ye said ye would."

"Did ye doubt me?" Iskander asked dryly. "Is that why ye are come?"

"Nay, Lord," Kaliq replied, shaking his head. "Nay . . . we are come to join ye."

"Join me!" Iskander exclaimed, startled. "Why, have ye lost your wits, man? Did ye yourself not say that a man would have to be a maniac or a fool to venture beyond Epitaph Pass?"

"Yea, but since it appears from the inquiries ye have been making in town and the supplies ye have purchased that ye are indeed determined to do so, we Scalie Scalpers thought we would ride along with ye. Many of their horns having fallen victim to our blades, the Scalies have grown wary of us, their raiding parties fewer, so the hunting has been lean of late. But ye are bound to draw them out, Lord, and we would have our share of the spoils."

"As I have already warned my own followers, ye

and your band would do well to have naught to do with me," Iskander stated flatly. "I do what I must for Tintagel and the Light. But I ask no other to ride the road I travel."

"For all that ye are a man of honor, Lord, I think that ye are prideful," Kaliq remarked, grinning, as he reversed Iskander's own words to him that night at the inn and returned them. "To say nothing of stubborn —and foolishly so, methinks. It may be that ye are indeed a powerful mage, and none having seen the duel at the Copper Kettle would dispute your prowess with a blade. But ye are still one man, your followers but a handful; and with all due respect, for all that they are obviously devoted to ye, most of them are not seasoned warriors like my own. Admit it: Ye could use our help—and ye don't have a monopoly on defending the world, either. So, quit trying to hog all the glory by playing the martyr, and let's get going. Whether ye like it or not, you're stuck with us, man. We know this land better than ye do, so you'll not give us the slip; and we'll not have it said that a smattering of foreigners dared what we Scalie Scalpers would not!"

There was no arguing with Kaliq, Iskander saw, and so he gave up the attempt, thinking that perhaps Kaliq was right. Perhaps, in his concern for the lives of others, he *was* being foolishly stubborn. After all, what if when he reached the heart of the Darkness, he found that he *did* need assistance to carry out his mission successfully, that because of his refusal to accept aid freely offered, he had himself jeopardized his quest?

"Perhaps ye are right," Iskander agreed at last, though not without reluctance, for he still doubted the wisdom of his decision. "Ye will do as ye please in any event, I feel certain. But do ye ride with me, ye ride under my command."

"Done!" Kaliq said. "'Tis your quest after all, Lord."

Nodding, Iskander set his spurs to his horse's sides, heading south toward the Hindrance Hills, toward Epitaph Pass, the questers and the Scalie Scalpers hard on his heels.

After the many difficulties the companions had encountered on their long journey, it now seemed amazing to them how swiftly the miles passed. The horses made it possible to ride like the wind, so despite their vastly increased numbers, the travelers covered in hours ground that would previously have taken them days to trek across. Even the occasional snowfall did little to slow them down and was quickly outdistanced, the air growing warmer the closer they got to the equator and the southern lands of the continent of Botanica.

After some weeks hard riding, the questers reached the Bezel town of Amethyst, the last haven they would know before entering the Hindrance Hills and making their way through Epitaph Pass. In Amethyst they learned that while UnKind raiding parties had been sporadically sighted, the land was, for the most part, quiet, its inhabitants dug in for the winter, with little sign that the SoulEaters were planning yet another attempt at mass invasion—though the sentries who patrolled the ramparts were always on the watch, never letting down their guard. Amethyst lay too close to the southern border for that. More than once, in the past, it had nearly fallen victim to the UnKind.

The companions remained in town for two days, taking stock and replenishing their supplies—the last chance they would have to do so before moving on. Then, departing, they came at last to the Hindrance Hills, where they drew to a halt at the sight that met their eyes.

The towering hills were aptly named, for they were

almost mountainous in appearance, though they did not rise quite so high as their taller cousins, and their pinnacles were mounded rather than peaked. Still, they were bleak and forbidding, standing so close together that passage through them was limited to a single, winding track—what had come, since the time of the SoulEaters, to be known as Epitaph Pass. For this reason the knolls would, Iskander suspected, readily lend themselves to an ambush, and for the first time, he was glad of the presence of the Scalie Scalpers, who would, he knew, be fierce warriors in battle.

"Do ye see now why no one ventures south, Lord?" Kaliq asked, his bearded face grim with apprehension as, reining his horse up beside Iskander's, he stared at the hills that loomed before them. "Rest assured that the Scalies will have lookouts posted along the pass and will know of our coming long ere we cross the border into what was once the land of Sylvania. We must proceed carefully, Lord, for there are many places along the trail where an ambush would be possible," he stated, confirming Iskander's fears.

"'Tis still not too late for ye—all of ye—to turn back," Iskander declared, his voice rising, echoing down the ranks, so everyone would hear him, "and I would strongly urge ye to do so." But no one budged, and silently he prayed he would prove himself worthy of their trust. "Then let us ride," he said.

Snow they had left behind them. But now, as the travelers approached the hills, it began to sleet, the icy rain gradually becoming a steady drizzle the farther south they rode. The wind was cool, tinged with the briny scent of the seas that lay to the east and west of the hills, and now and then the gusts brought wisps of ghostlike mist in their wake, which did little to improve the restive mood of the questers as they trotted onto the narrow road that snaked through the knolls. Previously, on the Jaded Plains, the companions had ridden ten abreast, or more. But now they must go in quartets, sometimes even in pairs; and acutely conscious of the vulnerable target they presented, they bunched up as closely as possible to limit their exposure.

A few days into the hills, Iskander started to feel uneasily that, as in Labyrinth, eyes watched their every move, and he kept Rhiannon at his right side, knowing he alone had the best chance of defending her. To her right rode Yael, so she was effectively shielded between them, with Kaliq on Iskander's left. Anuk, acting as scout, ran ahead, returning every so often to report his findings. So far the lupine had spied nothing. But still, Iskander was troubled. More and more densely as the travelers progressed along the wending path were the hills beginning to be populated with trees that would provide good cover for any UnKind sentries. Kaliq thought so, too, and dispatched several warriors afoot to learn what they could. But they, also, saw nothing untoward.

At night the questers pitched their tents wherever they could, glad for any respite, however meager, from the dismal rain, which continued unabated. Cold and miserable, they huddled in their shelters, with only the smallest of campfires over which to boil tea and heat their supper, and to take the chill from the night air. For despite the inclement weather, Iskander feared that the smoke or flames would be spotted by the SoulEaters, who tended toward nocturnal activity, sleeping by day. But the miles passed, and still no sign of the UnKind was sighted.

No one knew what to make of this, and perversely, instead of relieving their anxiety, it increased it. They feared that the guards of the SoulEaters had somehow escaped their detection and were even now dispatching warnings to the strongholds of the UnKind, where an army would be raised to march against them. For it seemed impossible to the companions that despite all their precautions, from the muffling of their horses' bridles to the lighting of but scant and few campfires, the advancement of a party the size of theirs through the hills had not been noticed by the SoulEaters.

"I like it not, Lord," Kaliq insisted the day they came at last to Epitaph Pass. "The Scalies are exceedingly cunning. It could be that they are waiting for us to egress the hills, after which time they plan to send troops here to cut off our escape route, trapping and crushing us between two overwhelming forces."

"Yea, that thought had crossed my own mind as well, Kaliq," Iskander confessed, "a most unpleasant prospect and one that we must guard against happening. For that reason I think it best if we leave the bulk of your warriors here, to hold the pass, proceeding with only a small, mobile detachment whose movements can be more easily concealed and that can strike swiftly at the heart of the Darkness, then retreat rather than engaging in a pitched battle against a massive deployment of UnKind forces." He glanced about intently at the narrow pass that marked the border between the northern and the southern lands. "A large army would not necessarily prove an advantage here, where there is so little room to maneuver. Thus I believe that, even outnumbered, your warriors could successfully defend this pass."

"Yea, Lord," Kaliq agreed as he, too, thoughtfully scrutinized the pass. "Ye are right. It could be done. Shall I give the order, then?"

"Yea." Iskander nodded.

And so it was that eighty-five of the Scalie Scalpers remained behind, while the rest of the travelers—now twenty-five in number—continued on through Epitaph Pass. Iskander made one last attempt to persuade his own followers, particularly Rhiannon, to stay with the bulk of the Scalie Scalpers, but once more all adamantly refused. They had not come so far, only to turn back now, they declared stoutly, and he knew he could not in good faith ask again. They deserved better than that from him; and so now he set about preparing them instead for what they would face, explaining how he planned to infiltrate the ranks of the SoulEaters and what he would expect from his followers.

His training of Rhiannon grew so intense, so urgent that she sometimes thought he meant to drive her to the breaking point. He eyed her progress so dispassionately, corrected her mistakes so harshly that she began to wonder if she had but dreamed those fervent kisses on the deck of the *Frostflower,* the highly charged emotions that had leaped between them, the love she felt they shared, though neither of them had ever spoken of it in so many words. At other times she sensed that it was fear that made Iskander cruel, fear that his quest would be the death of her—the knowledge of which would be unbearable to him.

"'Twill not be like the slaying of the trolls, Rhiannon," he told her one evening, "which was grievous enough to ye. I tell ye now, so ye will not be taken unaware, what Cain and Ileana said to me before I left Mont Saint Christopher: Because ye are Chosen, because ye have Power, ye will be able to see what those ungifted do not when the UnKind die. For a moment, horribly, ye will see them as they were when they were Kind, and they will cry out to ye, piteously begging ye to spare their lives. No matter how this rips at your heart, ye must not be moved by it, Rhiannon, for 'tis but some hideous trick of the senses to lure ye unto your own death. Do ye understand?"

"Yea," she said, shuddering at this terrible revelation.

Observing the expression on her face, he hissed, "Ye are too soft-hearted, Rhiannon! Despite that I have warned ye, ye will listen to their UnKind cries and ye will die!"

"Nay, Iskander, nay," she protested, but she saw he did not believe her.

"Ye shall fail me," he said coldly.

"Nay, Iskander, I shall not, I swear."

"And what if I fail ye?" His thought was so fierce, so anguished that she heard it in her mind, and she stretched out one hand to him imploringly, laying it upon his arm. But roughly he shook off her touch. Upon his face were pain and anger both as he snapped, "Do ye see how ye tear at me so I doubt myself, so I hesitate to do what I must do? By the moons! I curse the day I first beheld ye, agreed to take ye and the others with me! I must have been mad! Utterly mad!"

Rhiannon gasped, stricken, her hand flying to her open mouth as though he had brutally hit her, knocking the wind from her. Tears filled her eyes, and after a moment, stunned, she turned and ran blindly into the woods. Swearing heatedly, Iskander followed, wroth and ashamed that he had hurt her for what was no fault of her own—but his. Catching her arm in a savage grip, he yanked her around to face him, inhaling sharply as the light of the sickly Blue Moon illuminated her fair countenance. Her unbound hair was sodden, dark as auburn fire in the moonlight. Her golden eyes were luminous; tears and rain clung to her long, thick lashes and mingled upon her cheeks. Mauve circles of exhaustion ringed her eyes. It came to him how thin and pale she had grown again, how their hard, tension-fraught journey and his pushing the limits of her Power had sapped her strength. Yet she had borne it all uncomplainingly, refusing to forsake him.

"Rhiannon," he whispered, his voice choked with

emotion, "I'm sorry. I did not mean it. Ye must know that I did not. 'Tis my fear for ye, for us . . . it eats at me—Rhiannon . . ."

The Wheel of Time turned—and kept on turning. She did not know how fast, how far, as she stood there in the copse, enfolded in Iskander's embrace, his mouth hard and hungry upon hers, while the rain spilled down upon them through the leaves of the trees. She knew only that she loved him with all her heart—and feared, as he did, for their future. And so, feverishly, she clung to him, her lips yielding to his, her senses dizzied by his onslaught, wanting more than what he gave her, wanting to give more than he took. His hands cupped her face, his fingers twined through her hair as he kissed her, while her hands, splayed, pressed against his broad chest, feeling his heart beat within, in harmonious counterpoint to the steady tattoo of the rain. It seemed they were alone in all the world, the wind weaving about them a gossamer cocoon of mist. If only for this moment, nothing mattered to either but the other as each touched and tasted, brimming with emotion and longing unfulfilled.

But then a dark cloud scudded across the face of the Blue Moon, and slowly Rhiannon became aware of another kind of light, another kind of mist curling insidiously around them, its forked tongues venomously foul as those of snakes, thin and pallid.

"Iskander," she breathed, horrified. "Your sword— Nay, do not draw it," she warned as, spying the vaporous celadon tendrils that swirled about them, he reached over his shoulder to slip free the ring that held the Sword of Ishtar in its scabbard at his back, to pull the blade from its sheath, whence the trailing yellow-green wisps emanated. "How can this be? 'Tis not even keyed," she noted softly.

"It has Power of its own," he reminded her, "vested

in it by the Custodians of the Citadel of False Colors, wherein it laid before Ileana brought it forth from the crystal flames of truth; and Cain and Ileana left their own imprint upon it, too, as well we both know, the residue of their own Power of the Elements."

"It senses something, Iskander. Something has caused it to awake, its Power to manifest . . ."

"The UnKind!" he exclaimed quietly, knowing intuitively that this was so.

Even as he spoke the words, there stepped from the shadows of the trees a group of the SoulEaters, hemming man and woman in on all sides. Rhiannon gasped sharply at the sight of them, for even the decaying corpses of the UnKind she had spied in the tall grasses edging the shore of the River Knotted had not prepared her for the impact of the creatures in the living flesh.

From head to toe they were absolutely black—not just the dark, tea-colored hue of many of the Gallowish and Nomads she had seen, but black as the night sea when the moons did not shine and the stars were obscured by mist. Though all the SoulEaters were tall, their heads seemed too large for their torsos, even so, as though the flesh covering their craniums had somehow swelled all out of proportion. They were completely bald, their foreheads ridged at the center with two vertical knobby protuberances that seemed to be like eyebrows, then swept up into short, hornlike protrusions that jutted from the top front halves of their bulging heads. These, Rhiannon correctly assumed, were the horns the Scalie Scalpers hunted for bounty money. The bottom ends of the ridges continued down the UnKinds' faces, melding and forming what appeared to be their broad, flat noses. On either side of these, wide-set, were their eyes, slitted and red as hot embers, black-pupiled, devoid of lashes. Their mouths were grim black slashes, their teeth like fangs, dripping saliva. Their long, square jaws narrowed to small, triangular chins that were almost nonexistent, disappearing into throat fans. Their ears were tiny and pressed close to their heads.

All were naked, their bodies well formed, muscular, and extremely powerful, both fingers and toes ending in razor-sharp talons. At the navel of each, Rhiannon knew, though these were currently retracted, were long umbilical cords that could lash out like whips to pierce the flesh of their enemies, infecting them with the dread disease that afflicted the SoulEaters. No external genitalia were visible, but this meant nothing, since, as the plague progressed, the hard, tough black hide covered with barklike scales that formed on the skin gradually encased the entire body. At the base of each of the UnKinds' spines was a truncated tail. All of the creatures were heavily armed.

A few of the SoulEaters had what were plainly hellhounds at their heels, for the beasts did indeed bear a startling resemblance to Anuk, except that each bore a pair of horns upon its head, the other prize sought by the Scalie Scalpers. The hellhounds wore menacing spiked collars and appeared as vicious and unnatural as their perverse masters.

Ringed by the UnKind, there was no escape for her and Iskander, Rhiannon saw, her heart racing, her mouth dry, her palms damp. Even if she and Iskander managed to alert the camp, the SoulEaters would be on them before help could arrive. Like it or not, Iskander would have to draw the Sword of Ishtar; they would have to fight.

"Well, what have we here?" one of the UnKind rasped in Tintagelese, in a low, ghastly, sibilant voice, causing the fine hairs on Rhiannon's nape to prickle. "SSSpiesss? Or SSScalie SSScalperssss? Or both? What? No anssswer? Well, no matter. 'Tisss certain ye are no friendsss of oursss, elssse ye would not ride ssso furtively through thessse hillsss and build sssuch sssmall campfiresss in thisss missserable weather. Ah, yea. We know all about ye. We have been watching your warrior band for daysss now, waiting to catch at leassst one of your number alone—and now we have. We wanted ye alive, ye sssee, ssso we could interrogate ye about your plansss before we sssend word to our Imperial Leader of your tressspasssssssing in our land of SSSalamandria. Ye two ssshall do nicely for our purposssesss." Without warning the SoulEater turned to the others, ordering savagely, "SSSeize them! Bind them! Do not let them essscape!"

During this discourse the Blue Moon had reappeared, lending the color of its smoky blue light to the Power issuing from the Sword of Ishtar, so it had seemed as though the chartreuse tentacles were nothing more than mist shot through with moonbeams eddying about man and woman. Thus the UnKind were taken unaware when Iskander yanked the blade from its scabbard, loosing its terrible Power while at the same time calling up his own.

Blinding brightness exploded in the coppice, a gigantic pinwheel of spangles and flame and color, Rhiannon's aura adding its own coruscation to Iskander's as she, too, encased herself in a protective barrier of blue fire. The initial burst of Power fried six of the UnKind in their tracks. Shrieks of agony split the night as the bodies of the creatures were ignited like torches, making Rhiannon shudder uncontrollably, for she knew, horribly, as Iskander had warned her, that the screams were Kind. Then, little by little, as their shiny reptilian hides burned away like melting wax, the SoulEaters appeared to metamorphose back into what they had once been, and Rhiannon saw their faces—Kind faces—racked with anguish, begging pitifully for assistance.

"Help me. Help me," their mouths seemed to cry,

though she knew that the words rang only in her mind. Their glowing red eyes bulged and ruptured, ichorous matter streaming down their gruesomely distorted visages; but still, their cindery, hollow eyesockets continued to stare at her imploringly. *"Help me. Help me."*

Rhiannon tried to close her eyes and ears to the entreaties, but at last, unable to bear the heartrending pleas a moment longer, she began to stretch out one trembling hand to the blazing corpses. Then, at the last minute, some instinct warning her, she quickly jerked it back, forcing herself to remember—to believe—that the seemingly Kind appeals were but a trick to deceive her into lowering her guard. And she dared not permit even a single chink in her wall of warding, through which a lethal UnKind umbilical cord could slip to penetrate her skin, infecting her with the dread disease it transmitted. For this reason she did not even attempt to wield her morning star against the SoulEaters, knowing that it would do little damage against their armorlike scales.

Instead, she stood at Iskander's back, shielding him as his own aura repeatedly shifted and rived as he wrestled determinedly with the Sword of Ishtar, compelling its putrid poison outward, up the blade. Horrendous balls of fire belched from its tip. The smell of roasting flesh filled the air, making Rhiannon long to retch, as more and more of the UnKind were set ablaze, their hearts exploding in their chests, ripping open their torsos so blood and pulp flew in every direction, spattering the trees and the ground. Rivulets of crimson trickled across the sodden earth so that the SoulEaters slipped on their own blood as they fought hideously, like rabid animals, to prevail, gnashing their teeth and slavering madly as they came on, despite their swiftly dwindling numbers.

They had, in a fit of frenzy at seeing their ranks so

depleted, cast away their shields and weapons and were now attempting with bared fangs and claws alone to assault man and woman, while the hellhounds, ruffs standing on end, barked and snarled and did what they could to help their masters. Rhiannon gasped as one UnKind after another slashed at her inviolable aura, then fell back, shrilling with pain at the resulting burns they experienced. Still, even knowing that she was safe from the SoulEaters' reach did not prevent her from cringing each time they approached, looming over her, faces dark and macabre beyond the blue barrier. But her months of training with Iskander held her in good stead. She instinctively moved when he did, covering his back and wondering how much longer he could control the Sword of Ishtar before she must help him as she had before.

She understood now, from Iskander, that the previous clashing of their auras had been due to neither knowing the exact colors and patterns of the other's, and though he had tried to compensate for this, most of his concentration had been riveted on battling the Sword of Ishtar. So his attempt to meld their auras had not been successful; nor, strangely enough, had he shown her how it was done. Still, sensing the drain on his Power as his wall of warding began slowly to flicker and evanesce, she tried.

Taking a deep breath and turning her impenetrable back on the UnKind, she slowly stepped into Iskander's aura, prepared this time for the jolt when their blue barriers collided. As before, a violent shower of sparks sprayed from the impact, so Iskander knew she had joined him. But this time he made no protest, accepting—even grateful for—her aid; for the deaths of the abominable creatures seemed to be having a most peculiar effect upon the sword, heightening its balefulness and nearly overwhelming him. His and Rhiannon's auras wavered wildly before desperately she did what she could to stabilize them. Then slowly, from behind, she slid her arms around Iskander's waist to grasp the hilt of the blade, feeling a thrill shoot through her as her hands closed over his own strong, sure ones. Reaching deep into the dark, inner reserves of her Power, she linked her mind to the weapon, searching for the essence that was Ileana—and finding it, that unknown but loving spirit who seemed somehow to be guiding her through the sword. Exultation filled Rhiannon's being, a pure white light that welled up inside her to blaze forth like fox fire, enveloping the hilt, combatting the blade's bane as together she and Iskander stood firm against the evil that threatened to overpower them.

Then suddenly, like a volcano erupting, the malignant celadon radiance spewed in a burst of massive flame from weapon, seeming to turn the grove into an inferno. Kind scream after Kind scream reverberated agonizingly as the SoulEaters were consumed, wrenching Rhiannon's heart. Even the hellhounds were destroyed—though it seemed to Rhiannon that some shadows at the edges of the trees slipped away, eluding the conflagration. Her heart lurched at the thought, for if any of the UnKind had escaped, they would warn their Imperial Leader of the questers' presence in Salamandria and bring an army against them.

Abruptly the skirmish ended. The Sword of Ishtar dimmed. Rhiannon's and Iskander's auras winked out, and gasping for breath, they fell into each other's arms, unmindful of the rain that continued to drench them. Before they even had a chance to speak, however, more explosions suddenly shook the night and flare after flare rocketed through the trees. Sparing but an emotional glance for each other, Rhiannon and Iskander broke into a run, fearful that the camp itself was now being assailed. Frantically they raced from the copse, weaving through the tangle of woods and undergrowth to where they came upon Yael, Sir Weythe, Kaliq, Hordib, and several other warriors waging the last of a brief but deadly fray with a handful of SoulEaters who had indeed somehow managed to flee from the terrible might of the Sword of Ishtar. Yael's battle-ax and Sir Weythe's sword had already ended the lives of three hellhounds; and in their hands Kaliq and Hordib held Bezel Boomers, which were still discharging, setting two bolting SoulEaters afire, the flames rapidly devouring them.

"Well, let's hope that was the last of them," Kaliq declared grimly after a moment. "Are ye all right, Lord? Lady?"

"Yea, shaken and exhausted—but unharmed," Iskander panted as he struggled to catch his breath. He gestured toward the bodies on the ground, those of the UnKind still incinerating from the Boomers. "'Twas fortunate ye arrived when ye did, else those few might have got away."

Kaliq nodded soberly, his brow knitted in an anxious frown.

"Yea, we saw the sorcerous light, Lord, and heard the growling of the hellhounds. That's how we knew that ye were under attack. We came as quickly as we could, but it *is* possible that there were those who escaped us, Lord. If so, they will doubtless come back with reinforcements—and even if they do not, the magic auras . . . the strangely colored fires . . . the burning of the corpses will have been visible from a great distance, Lord, despite the rain. Other Scalies will surely arrive to investigate."

"My own thinking exactly," Iskander concurred, looking grave. "For that reason we must get out of here . . . now . . . tonight. Let us return to camp at once. I want us packed and ready to ride in less than an hour. We dare not delay any longer than that."

They discovered that the camp was already on the alert. Chervil and Anise had taken a small party of Bezel warriors to determine whether an army of SoulEaters was come upon them and to assist Iskander and the rest, if necessary; the others were, under the surprising direction of the feisty Gunda Granite, hurriedly preparing for a pitched battle in case they should be assaulted. Upon learning that the UnKind had been bested but that there was a chance that one or more had eluded capture, the companions began hastily to gather up their belongings and to strike their tents, loading all onto their horses. Then they resumed their arduous journey, all of them driven now by a sense of urgency.

Because of this, they no longer stopped, except for brief respites to rest the weary horses; there was no building of fires or making of camps. Food was eaten in snatches along the way. All dozed—when they could—in their saddles as the small party wound through the hills and deeper into the trees that grew ever taller and thicker the farther south the travelers ingressed into Salamandria. Beneath skies not their own, under stars some of them had never before seen, through wind and mist and intermittent but seemingly ceaseless rain, they rode, sodden and miserable, numb with exhaustion. Anuk still scouted ahead, ripping the throats from two hellhounds he flushed from the brush, whence they had been spying upon the questers. Fiercely Kaliq scalped both the creatures, hanging their horns from his belt, along with their spiked collars, from which the Scalie Scalpers frequently fashioned their gauntlets. Rhiannon shuddered each time her eyes fell upon the grisly trophies. But far worse was the dread she felt as she listened to Iskander at her side, practicing the abhorrent role he must take on once they reached the SoulEaters' stronghold.

Over and over, he repeated the words the UnKind had spoken in the copse, mimicking that sibilant voice until it rang so true that Rhiannon's hair stood on end. She did not know how Iskander could bear to speak so, how he would ever bring himself to assume that UnKind shape. Yet he must, for how else could the heart of the Darkness be penetrated, its innermost secrets be ferreted out, and it be struck a mortal blow? There was no other way, she knew. But still, she kept on desperately hoping otherwise—right up until the terrible moment when at long last the questers emerged from the Hindrance Hills and saw what awaited them at the end of their toilsome journey.

THE FALLING

The Sacred Scroll

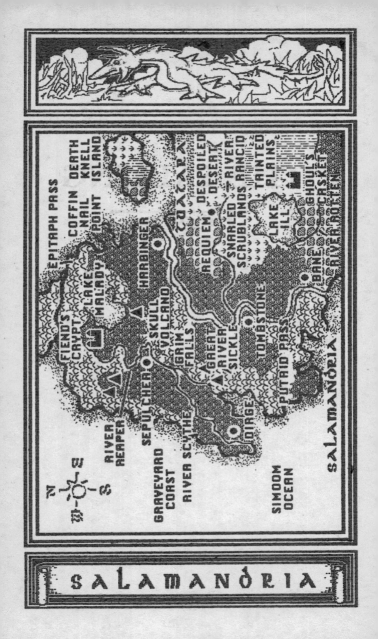

SALAMANDRIA

Chapter 23

*It was a canker on the land, a monstrous raw,
gaping wound turned gangrenous and oozing putrefaction. I had never before beheld anything like
it. I hoped—I prayed—never to see the likes of it
again. Iskander had named it truly: the heart of
the Darkness.*

*I stared at it in utter horror. We all did. For there
was not a single one among us who thought we
would come out of it alive.*

—Thus it is Written—
in
The Private Journals
of the Lady Rhiannon sin Lothian

The Hindrance Hills, Salamandria,
7276.1.29

THE DAWN WAS PALE, FOR IT WAS A SICKLY SUN THAT CREPT
above the eastern horizon, dimmed by pewter clouds
scudding across a lowering sky that threatened further
rain. But a wind smelling of the distant sea had blown
away the early morning mist. So now, as they crested

the last of the Hindrance Hills, the companions could spy clearly what lay below, and as one, they drew up short, aghast.

As far as the eye could see, the land was despoiled as though some prodigious blight had swept ruthlessly across it, ravaging all in its path. For miles in every direction, the trees had been destroyed, chopped down by UnKind hands for a purpose that was only too plain. In the midst of the ruin was a great lake, black and putrid with slime, and upon its scummy waves floated four ominous-looking ships nearing the final stages of completion—ships about half as large as the mighty windjammers of the East but obviously designed to carry an army. Beyond the southern shore of the lake rose an immense volcano with a cranium-shaped peak. A little way down its slope, facing the travelers, were three fathomless cave openings, situated in such a way that the volcano appeared to be a gruesome skull gaping at them. From its maw, like a horde of army ants, an endless string of SoulEaters came and went, plying an array of materials between the volcano and the lake, where other UnKind swarmed the vessels, busily measuring, hammering, and sawing.

All around the site, where the forest had not yet been decimated, the dense trees grew tall but twisted, trunks and branches torturously contorted and be-fouled with rot. Wisps of stringy, sticky, pallid gray-green moss hung from the limbs; fungus mottled the green leaves splotched with yellow and edged with brown, for it was summer here in the southern hemisphere, the rainy season, when all ought to have been abloom and bursting with life and color but was not. Lichen encrusted the bark of the trees and scabbed the dank earth.

A long, wide river tainted as the lake whence it originated snaked its way through the woods—to the

Simoom Ocean, Iskander correctly surmised, for the four ships were surely intended for the sea, and how else to get them there except to sail them down the waterway? And thence across the ocean to the East. Like a blow, the realization struck him as he recalled the skeleton of the SoulEater that had, years ago, washed up on the coast of Bedoui. The UnKind must be planning to invade the East—and it seemed likely that this would not be the first time they had made such an attempt. Iskander was more determined than ever to succeed in his quest. He dared not permit the SoulEaters to finish their vessels, to go beyond the places they had already conquered.

At the eastern edge of the lake stood the massive UnKind stronghold, a towering monstrosity, menacing in appearance. Built entirely of black rock, its battlemented walls, studded at each corner with turrets and lined with hideous gargoyles, soared fifty feet or more into the air. From their heart the coronate keep rose, its many spires like needles, threaded by the dark, roiling clouds that obscured the wan rising sun. Being almost entirely surrounded by the lake and the river, the castle had no moat. There was only one way in or out: through the iron portcullis and the stout shadow-oak doors on the southern side.

This view of the donjon was initially blocked from the travelers' line of sight by the fortress itself. But after carefully, furtively, working their way through the foothills skirting the lake's western shore, they were able to get a good look at the keep's single portal. It was while they were studying this that a figure on horseback trotted beneath the stone arch, heading toward Skull Volcano. To the questers' profound shock, it was—incredibly but definitely—a man.

"Let me see that spyglass, Kaliq!" Sir Weythe hissed, fairly snatching the small telescope from the mercenary's hands. With trembling fingers the old soldier jammed the brass-rimmed lens to his right eye and peered through it at the red-robed man astride the black steed. "Nay, I don't believe it! It can't be!" He gasped. "But it is. Somehow it is—Lord . . . Lord"— he turned, ashen-faced, to Iskander—"'tis the Prince Lord Gerard's brother! 'Tis the wicked Prince Lord Parrish!"

"The one who murdered their oldest brother, the Prince Lord Niles, and caused Gerard to be banished from Finisterre? But—but how can that be?" Iskander asked, puzzled. "I thought he was taken prisoner by the SoulEaters years ago."

"He was, Lord," the swordsman confirmed, frowning. "He was. That's why at first I believed I must be mistaken. . . . But I'm not. 'Tis him, all right—the bloody bastard." Weythe spat upon the ground. "After all the evil he wrought upon the House of Ashton Wells, Lord, I'm not likely to be forgetting him, let me tell ye. 'Tis him. I don't know how. But 'tis him—the scurvy necromancer!"

"There is your answer, Weythe," Iskander pointed out soberly. "He is a practitioner of the Black Arts. That is why he has not been 'Poxed,' as those who hunt the horns call it. Somehow the Prince Lord Parrish has found a way either to avoid becoming infected by or to cure the disease that afflicts the UnKind. Or else, when he was captured, he managed somehow to persuade the SoulEaters he could be of more use to them as a wizard than a lizard," Iskander observed dryly but darkly. He paused, his visage troubled. Then he continued. "I had not expected this . . . a necromancer in their midst, the extent of whose Power is unknown to us. . . ." His voice trailed away. For a long moment he was silent, thinking. Then finally he said, "Come. We must find a secure place in these hills to hide. After twilight falls I will try to get inside the castle—and then we shall see what we shall see."

After much stealthy and desperate searching, the companions came at last upon a cave deep in the western hills, along the shore of the Gulf of Uland; and here, they concealed themselves and their horses, sheltered from the rain for the first time in many a long night. With the blue fire of the Druswids, Iskander and Rhiannon heated the stones within. Gratefully the travelers boiled tea and cooked food for their supper, ravenously devouring the hot meal, more than welcome after so many evenings of naught but cold rations.

Then, their bellies replete, their garments drying, the small party gathered around to hear Iskander's plans; for while the rest had looked for a hiding place, he and Anuk had secreted themselves in the foothills, watching the comings and goings of the UnKind. Neither man nor beast had seen any further sign that there were any Kind left in the whole of Salamandria save for the Prince Lord Parrish; and it seemed unlikely that those inhabitants who had not managed to flee north to safety had somehow escaped both the SoulEaters' detection and disease. The land the Bezels had known as Sylvania was gone—utterly. The travelers could not expect that in the donjon there would be those of their ilk who would help them. This had been a slender hope at best but one that had heartened them; and now that it was extinguished, they must face the fact that they were well and truly on their own, totally alone in a hostile land, where even death was a fate kinder than what they would suffer at the hands of their enemies.

The questers could not even be certain that if by some miracle they eluded the UnKind here, they would not find the creatures waiting for them at Epitaph Pass; for it was likely that the skirmish that had lighted the night sky some weeks ago had attracted the attention of the SoulEaters. Perhaps even now the creatures were engaged in a vicious battle with the army of Scalie Scalpers who had remained behind to hold the pass. In the bluish light cast by the radiant stones, the faces of the companions were somber at the thought. Still, even if such had occurred, there was nothing to be done about it right now, so they forced themselves to address their most pressing concerns.

"At least four of ye are to watch at all times," Iskander instructed. "No one—not even those on guard duty—is to leave the cave for any reason. As we all know, the UnKind are much more active at night, and we dare not risk being spotted by any of them, lest we have them all up here, combing these hills for us. I myself will not attempt anything other than a trial run tonight, to determine whether I can pass muster, whether I can indeed infiltrate their ranks undetected. I'm sure I do not need to tell ye that if I fail, if I am apprehended, the SoulEaters will leave no stone unturned to learn if others accompanied me here. So if a sudden hue and cry should be raised, ye must assume I am taken, and ye must escape with all speed. Absolutely *no* foolhardy attempt to rescue me is to be made. Is that clear?" he questioned sharply, staring hard at Kaliq and Hordib, especially, the latter of whom flushed a dull red. "I'll have your word on it," Iskander insisted when they made no response.

"Ye have it, Lord," they stated reluctantly.

"Very well." He nodded, satisfied. "Then I will prepare to go."

So saying, he stood. Slowly he shrugged off the harness that kept the Sword of Ishtar sheathed at his back. He loathed leaving the blade behind, but there was no help for it. If he wore it within the vicinity of the UnKind, its Power might manifest itself again, drawing unwelcome attention to him. He started to hand the weapon to Rhiannon, but she refused to accept it.

"Nay," she said, determined in her denial, though her voice trembled a little at the thought of what she meant to do, of Iskander's wrath shortly descending upon her. "Give it to Kaliq. I cannot take it."

"Why not?" he asked, thinking that she had begun to fear the terrible Power of the sword; but the answer, when it came, stunned, angered, and frightened him.

"Because I am going with ye, Lord."

"What?" he cried, his heart lurching sickeningly in his breast at the sudden and horrible vision that filled his mind, of Rhiannon in the clutches of the SoulEaters. "Are ye mad? By the moons! Ye cannot possibly hope to ShapeShift into one of the creatures, much less to sustain the image! I am not sure that even *I* can do it—and I am a twelfth-ranked Druswidic priest, with more than two decades of proper training at Mont Saint Christopher!"

"Do ye say ye have not trained me properly, Lord?" Rhiannon shot back, indignant. "Nay, I did not think so, because we both know that ye have. Even so, I was not thinking of roaming about as a SoulEater, Lord," she explained quietly, though her face was pale at Iskander's outrage, "merely a hellhound at your heels —and *that* image I *can* ShapeShift into and sustain. After all, 'tis basically that of a lupine with horns and a spiked collar—no offense intended, Anuk."

"None taken, khatun," the lupine replied. *"Indeed, with a set of horns and a spiked collar, I myself could accompany ye, also."*

"Ye are both of ye moonstruck!" Iskander asserted, his face harsh.

"Nay, khan. In truth, we are behaving more sensibly

than ye," Anuk declared. "*We cannot remain camped here indefinitely, while ye ferret out the UnKind's strengths and weaknesses, which might take days or even weeks. Every moment we delay here is another moment that puts us all at risk. The three of us together can cover much more ground than ye alone,* khan— *and ye know it. By thinking with your heart instead of your head, ye imperil us all, not just yourself or the* khatun *and me.*"

"Damn it, Anuk! When I want your advice, I'll ask for it!" Iskander growled, but he knew that the lupine was right; and despite all his misgivings, and much against his better judgment, he was forced to agree to their going with him.

At hearing this poor Moolah fell upon his knees and, drawing the hem of his gallibiya up over his head, began to wail and pray softly; for he had grown quite attached to Rhiannon, believing that her and Gunda's knowledge of medicinal lore and skill with herbs had miraculously prevented him from being infected with the UnKind disease from the Poxed trolls. It was not true. Neither woman understood in the least how he had somehow managed to escape the affliction. But their protests had done nothing to diminish his affection for them.

Young Lido, too, at learning the news, burst into tears, for fear that Anuk would be captured. So the mood of the small party was decidedly glum as they did what they could to assist with the preparations.

With some black leather thread they unraveled from the hem of Iskander's sable cloak, Gunda and Anise tied firmly atop Anuk's head a pair of the horns Kaliq had scalped from one of the dead hellhounds, carefully concealing the bindings in the lupine's fur. After that the two women fastened one of the spiked collars around his neck, then stood back to survey their handiwork. Even Iskander was compelled to admit that Anuk would fool all but the closest and most discerning of inspections.

Meanwhile Rhiannon had stripped down to her leather etek and shaksheer, the shirt and breeches, providing her greater freedom of movement than she would otherwise have had. She had both her morning star and dagger belted at her waist; and Iskander had exchanged his sword for Kaliq's.

"I must tell ye that do ye find it necessary to use the blade, Kaliq, and it keys itself, ye will not be able to control its Power. In truth, I believe that ye will die, that what the weapon contains will kill ye," Iskander warned.

"Well, we all must do what we must, Lord, for Tintagel—and for the Light," Kaliq rejoined.

"For Tintagel and for the Light." The others, one by one, took up the chant, as though it were a talisman, and spontaneously they stood and joined hands, forming a circle, without beginning or end. "For Tintagel and for the Light. For Tintagel and for the Light!"

It was a deeply moving moment. There were tears in Rhiannon's eyes as she gazed at the faces of those who surrounded her, who had come so far and dared so much for their world, their Kind, and the Immortal Guardian, who had bestowed upon them the greatest gift of all, the gift of Free Will, the freedom to choose between right and wrong, the Light and the Darkness. She was proud beyond measure to be one of their number.

"Take care, Rhiannon," Yael whispered as he hugged her close.

"Count on it," she said, trying bravely to smile even as her eyes searched his face intently, in case this were the last time she ever saw him. "Yael, ye know—ye know why I must go with him, do ye not?"

"Yea, I have known for some time, Rhiannon,

though ye have never spoken the words to me. Ye love him—as a woman loves a man, as once I hoped ye would come to love me. But it was not written in the stars for us—at least, not in this LifePath. Ye have a greater purpose here, as I have come to understand and to accept; and if ye could not be mine, then I am glad ye are his, for in truth, methinks he is a prince among men. Ye have chosen well, Rhiannon. Go now. Your place is at his side, where ye so long to be, where ye belong; and somewhere out there your destiny awaits. I feel in my heart that this is so."

Nodding her thanks, unable to speak further, such was the emotion that welled up inside her at Yael's words, Rhiannon turned to follow Iskander and Anuk out into the night. As they stepped beyond the confines of the cave, the wind swept in from the sea, enshrouding them in a thin veil of mist, so they were quickly lost from sight; and then the rain came, as though even the heavens wept for the valiant three.

Chapter 24

To whosoever may find this record, let it be known that a great and terrible evil has been wrought by Men, and its name is Biological Warfare. It was at the Torrido Military Institute of Science and Technology that scientific research and development for other than peaceful purposes was conducted for years, the most dire of which was a top-secret experiment assigned the code name of Operation Snakeskin.

This experiment, in layman's terms, involved the altering of certain strains of bacteria through the introduction of genetic materials taken from external sources, specifically from the Class Reptilia, Subclass Lepidosauria, Order Squamata, Suborders Sauria and Serpentes, and the Subclass Archosauria, Order Crocodylia. The initial goal of the experiment was the production of a plague that would attack the epidermis and destroy the skin cells, simultaneously preventing their renewal, thus effecting the death of the victim. Other formulas, however, producing various different results, were also tested.

I record this information, in this archaic, handwritten fashion, because during the Intergalactic Wars, the Torrido Military Institute of Science and Technology was bombed and suffered a direct and devastating hit from a nuclear missile. As a consequence, the integrity of at least two or more of its laboratories, despite their being far below ground, was compromised, and the deadly bacteria isolated therein were inadvertently released. It can be assumed that these bacteria will, in future, not only undergo a mutation process, but perhaps will crossbreed, the results of which contamination and adulteration, in addition to exposure to radiation and chemicals, are currently unknown.

The holocaust and subsequent nuclear winter we feared are upon us. All power and communications systems are disrupted or failing. Yet all this is the least of my worries. I am exhibiting all the symptoms of radiation sickness and chemical poisoning, and I know I will not live much longer, perhaps a day or two at most. I am very weak. Before I die, however, I must do what I can to warn those who survive, if any, of the lethal bacteria that have escaped. I write this record in the hope that someone, somewhere, somehow, will find it.

I was one of the scientists at the Torrido Military Institute of Science and Technology. My work was in the field of medicine, specifically the research and development of drugs and other therapies that would counteract the effects of all known and suspected biological weapons, including those of the top-secret experiment Operation Snakeskin. . . .

—**Thus it is Written**—
in
The Sacred Scroll
by an UnKnown Old One of Torrido

HIGHLY SKILLED AS HE WAS, IT NEVERTHELESS TOOK ISKANder three tries before he was able to assume the shape of a SoulEater, and even then his abhorrence of the unnatural form was such that he did not know how long he could sustain it. Because of this, he knew they must move swiftly. Rhiannon and Anuk padded noiselessly at his side, twin hellhounds, as they all three made their way down to the lake, dark as an onyx beneath the hazy light of the dim moons and the few, unfamiliar southern stars.

At the water's edge, grimacing, Iskander knelt and doused himself liberally with the malady-ridden muck, while Rhiannon and Anuk dipped their paws deep into the sluggish waves, all of them praying that the scum would not cause them to become Poxed; for it appeared to be the same oily residue that coated the bodies of the UnKind and perhaps the reason why they instinctively feared fire and could be ignited like torches. The three questers applied it to themselves in the hope of masking their natural scents, which the real hellhounds would otherwise surely sniff out as being Kind and lupine and not belonging in Salamandria. Because of this, for the first time Iskander was glad of the rain, which would help to wash away the traces of the companions' earlier passage through the hills to the cave.

"Well, we're as ready as we'll ever be," he communicated mentally to the other two. *"Let's go. And remember: Stay close! We must try to keep one another in sight at all times, in case one of us should run into trouble."*

Rhiannon and Anuk nodded. Then they all continued on around Lake Malady until they reached the steep, narrow track that led up to the cavernous eyes and mouth of Skull Volcano. There, much to their relief, arousing no suspicion, they surreptitiously joined the long line of SoulEaters who toiled ceaselessly, it appeared, day and night, night and day, trudging back and forth between the volcano and the lake, where the four ships bobbed gently upon the waves.

"SSSo we go/Heave, ho!" the UnKind chanted gutturally, sibilantly, as they marched along in orderly procession, like a well-greased mechanism of the Old Ones, their hellhounds trotting at their heels. "SSSo we go/Heave, ho!"

Iskander joined in the song, while Rhiannon and Anuk studied the hellhounds and copied their behavior. Slowly the three ascended Skull Volcano to enter its gaping mouth.

As in the catacombs of Labyrinth, it was a blast of heat that struck them first. The interior of the volcano was like an inferno, hissing with steam and trickling with rivulets of molten lava that cast an eerie red glow on the black basalt walls. Forges gleamed red-hot as coals, belching smoke and soot and sparks into the stifling air. The immense chamber was crawling with SoulEaters too numerous to count, all busy at work. Instinctively Rhiannon shrank against Iskander, terrified by the sight of so many UnKind in one place at one time.

The noise was deafening. Iron mallets pounded constantly on anvils, where weapons of every kind and other articles were being fashioned. A loud and unrelenting, high-pitched whine filled the air, and as Rhiannon glanced about for the sound's origin, she spied things she had never before seen in her life: huge steel boxes with knobs and teethed rings and other protrusions sticking out all over them, from which long rubber cords snaked across the floor of the volcano, ending in unknown devices that rotated so fast they made her head spin, ripping through logs like a knife through butter, sending wood chips and sawdust flying. Other rapidly whirring objects punched holes in boards quicker than an awl through leather.

"*Iskander, what are all these awful things?*" she asked, stricken.

"*Generators and other machines of the Old Ones,*" he replied grimly, knowing with certainty from the descriptions of them in the Holy Book, *The Word and The Way*, that they could be nothing else. "*The SoulEaters must have stumbled onto them, unearthed them from someplace, and somehow figured out how to make them run. If we do naught else, we must destroy these infernal mechanical devices. We dare not permit them to remain in the hands of the UnKind— especially with our not knowing for what other wicked purposes the machines might be used besides the building of boats with which to invade the continents of Aerie and Verdante again, or the lands of the East. Come. We have seen enough here for now. Let us go—and quickly!*"

Before they could slip away unnoticed, however, Iskander was approached by one of the SoulEaters, apparently an overseer of some kind.

"Hey . . . ye, there . . . yea, ye," the creature snarled in the Common Tongue at him. "What are ye ssstanding around like a pile of dragon ssshit for? Nobody told ye to take a break, did they? Well, then, pick up thossse planksss and get them down to the ssshipsss! Unlessssss, of courssse, you'd like to haul your asssssss up to the Crypt to explain to the Prince Lord Perisssh your reasssonsss for mooning around here, asss though ye were only half ssscaled, when there wasss work to be done? Nay? Then ssshake your tail, sssoldier!"

Taking up the stack of boards as instructed and hoisting them onto his shoulder, Iskander hurriedly rejoined the queue egressing the volcano, glad to escape from the scowling SoulEater. In the future he would have to be more careful not to draw attention to himself, he thought. Still, the UnKind overseer had evinced no mistrust of him, had not ordered him seized and carted off to the castle for interrogation; and there was a great deal to be said for that, Iskander reflected, not without pride that he had succeeded in fooling the creature—and at such close quarters.

Rhiannon and Anuk following behind, he headed back down to Lake Malady, where he unloaded the planks, getting, in the process, a good look at the four vessels. They were, as he had surmised, definitely warships, capable of transporting a large army and complete with catapults, mangonels, and ballistas. All this, too, would have to be demolished, he knew, an idea as to how to accomplish the deed already forming in his brain, though nebulously. He was tired, he realized. Projecting the perverse image of a SoulEater had proved even more of a strain than he had expected. There would not be time to investigate the fortress tonight.

"Rhiannon . . . Anuk . . . I grow weary . . . terribly weary, of a sudden. We need to return to the cave right away," Iskander told them, barely able to transmit the words.

Knowing the dangers if they delayed, neither Rhiannon nor Anuk put forth any argument. Instead, deeply concerned by the weakness of his TelePath, they glanced about warily to ensure that none of the UnKind were paying them any heed. Then, utilizing the cover of the mist that wafted along the lakeshore, they sneaked away into the darkness, Rhiannon leading the way, her every sense alert to the unforeseen presence of any SoulEaters patrolling the area, though there had been none earlier. Anuk brought up the rear, watching to make certain they were not followed.

The three had got away not a moment too quickly, for they had no sooner begun to wend their way through the foothills than Iskander lost the Shape-

Shift, reverting to his usual Kind form, whereupon he groaned and sank to the ground, shuddering with horror and fatigue. Hurriedly Rhiannon resumed her own Kind shape, kneeling beside him, laying her hands upon his arms.

"Iskander, are ye hurt?" she asked, her voice sharp with fear for him, for he had his head cradled in his palms, as though he were blinded by pain, and his shoulders shook uncontrollably.

"Nay," he gasped, "just—just drained, utterly drained of all my Power. . . . The ShapeShift . . . such an—an alien, evil image to project. . . . All of a sudden it was as though—as though I were . . . all twisted up inside, warped somehow—"

"Shhhhh. Do not try to talk anymore," she said, her eyes meeting Anuk's worriedly. "Iskander, we dare not linger here. Do ye think that ye can stand?"

His breath still coming hard, he nodded, and Rhiannon helped him to his feet. His arm flung about her shoulders so she supported a good deal of his weight, they staggered toward the cave, making it as far as the sandy beach that edged the Gulf of Uland before, moaning, Iskander collapsed. His eyes fluttered briefly, then closed—and did not reopen. Frantically Rhiannon pressed her head to his breast, relieved to find he still breathed, while, pausing but an instant to ascertain that his master lived, Anuk raced on ahead to fetch assistance.

Anxiously, while she waited for the lupine to return, Rhiannon did what she could with the waves rushing in upon the shore to cleanse the lake muck from her own and Iskander's bodies. Her heart pounded with fear, for he shivered so badly that she believed he must have caught a chill or, far worse, been Poxed by the black slime. This last thought was like a dagger in her belly, and she scrubbed him all the harder, splashing him with the seawater she cupped in her hands, then rubbing him vehemently with her knuckles in an effort to get rid of what not even the rain had washed away. She had no care for herself, only for Iskander.

She was never so glad to see Yael in her life as when he appeared hard on Anuk's heels, Kaliq and Hordib following behind. Among them the three men lifted Iskander gently and bore him away to the cavern, where they laid him upon his sable cloak, spread upon the stone floor of the chamber. Hastily Rhiannon drew upon her Power to heat more of the rocks scattered about, while, squeaking with alarm, Gunda scurried away to retrieve her sack of medicines and Anise set tea to boiling.

"What happened?" Kaliq queried as he hunkered beside Rhiannon, bent over Iskander's still figure.

"The strain of the ShapeShift must have been unbearable . . . such a wicked and aberrant form— It took every ounce of his Power. He just gave until he had nothing left to give—" Rhiannon broke off abruptly, her voice catching on a sob. "Oh, Kaliq, priest or not, he is only a man, *one man,* and the Druswids asked so much of him—too much. . . ."

"Hush, Lady! 'Twill do no good for ye to become distraught," Kaliq pointed out logically. He paused for a moment, then continued. "I am the first to admit that I do not understand much of this strange Power of his—and of yours. But from what ye and the Lord have explained to us, it seems reasonable to me to assume he merely exhausted his magic and needs but to rest to renew it. He does not appear to be unconscious or injured, only deep in slumber. Priest, mage, whatever ye call him, his Power is not unlimited, Lady. But it *is* considerable. That is why his people, these . . . Druswids, believed in him, why we all believe in him, why we are here now.

"Ye are frightened for him because ye love him— we would all have to have been blind not to have seen this. But do ye have more faith in him, Lady. He is strong; he is a survivor. He could not have come so far or done all he has managed to do if he were not. So do ye also believe in him, Lady. Believe in us. Believe that no matter what happens, some of us will get through this. By all that is holy, this I swear: Some of us *will* get through this! We will live to tell others of the lands beyond Bezel's shores, of the Power, and of the Light. Thus will the Word and the Way of which the Lord has taught us spread; and hearing of these, so will more and more of us fight to hold back the Darkness. And in the end isn't that what it is all about, Lady?"

"Yea," she replied softly. "Yea. In the end that is what matters above all."

And as she gazed at the impassioned, determined faces of those in the cave, Rhiannon knew that it was true. Somehow, some way, some of them would survive, and they would tell the tale of Iskander's quest, as she and Yael, Chervil and Anise, and Sir Weythe sang the song of the Strathmore Plains; and there would be those who listened and who took up the battle against the Darkness that had come upon their world, the battle for Tintagel and for the Light.

For this had they overcome their innate fear of Iskander's and Rhiannon's Power, had they followed him unto the very Gates of the Darkness, despite how he had warned them that he surely led them to their doom. Because there was that worth dying for—to keep Tintagel free, to keep the flame of the Light Eternal forever burning.

In the beginning Rhiannon had thought selfishly only to learn of her Power, to find her homeland. And in the end she had learned of her Power, yea. But she had also learned of truth and honor, of love and sacrifice; and she had found that home was wherever the heart lay—and hers was forever in Iskander's keeping. It no longer mattered to her if she never saw Vikanglia, the land of her ancestors, set foot upon its distant shores. It was not important now; it never had been. She knew that now. For here, at Iskander's side, among the hodgepodge of the many friends who surrounded her, she had made a place for herself; she belonged. There was peace in that—and hope in Kaliq's words.

She would hold on to that hope. It would see her through, come what may—it and her love for Iskander. Tenderly she pressed her lips to his brow.

"I believe, my love," she whispered fiercely. "I believe."

Chapter 25

How do I speak of those days and nights that followed? Except to say that they were the worst of my life, amid which, like that tiny patch of paradise that flourishes at the heart of the despoiled Strathmore Plains, I experienced the greatest joy I ever knew. . . . For there is always a light to guide one through one's darkest hour, as I have come to learn, does one but have faith.

But I get ahead of myself—perhaps because I do not like to dwell on what was so agonizing that even now the pain of it is as real and intense as though born of a new-made wound, raw and wide and deep. To this day I do not know how Iskander ever bore what he did, what he had to do to fulfill his quest. Time and again he played that role so repugnant to him and, in the guise of an UnKind, walked among the vile, hideous creatures, ferreting out their strengths and weaknesses, unearthing their darkest secrets.

And time and again did he collapse afterward, utterly drained of his Power. My heart ached for him. Lines that had not been there before engraved his handsome face; shadows haunted his eyes and lay like crescent moons beneath his lashes. At times he seemed almost feverish, maniacal, as

*though he were naught but an entity of pure
energy, consuming himself, burning himself up.*

*And still, he drove himself, urgently, mercilessly,
eating and sleeping only in snatches—and then
just long enough to fill up the well of his Power.
Even I could not reason with him. He was a man
obsessed, spurred on by his fear that the necromancer, the Prince Lord Parrish—or "Perish," as the
SoulEaters, with their penchant for the macabre,
referred to him—would uncover our presence in
Salamandria before our mission could be brought
to fruition.*

*On all the few occasions when we had dared to
venture close to the dark wizard, he had appeared
to sense something out of the ordinary and he had
glanced about sharply, his cruel black eyes so
piercing, so probing that inwardly I had trembled,
lest he should penetrate Iskander's false image or
my own.*

*All magic leaves a mark in its wake, as Cain's
and Ileana's Power of the Elements had left its
imprint on the Sword of Ishtar; and so it was just a
matter of time, we knew, before the necromancer
would discern that faint ethereal trace born of my
and Iskander's Power of the Earth—and would
know that sorcerers other than himself were
abroad and at work in Salamandria.*

—Thus it is Written—
in
The Private Journals
of the Lady Rhiannon sin Lothian

IT WAS CALLED FIEND'S CRYPT. THEY KNEW THAT NOW,
just as they knew every twist and turn of the anfractu-
ous castle's maze of long, narrow corridors and, for
the most part, airless, windowless chambers furnished

with a bizarre and ghastly array of tables and chairs fashioned from bones, oil lamps created out of skulls, and other trappings equally gruesome and wholly repulsive. Rhiannon never entered the keep without feeling a shiver tingle up her spine, making her yearn to flee the fortress with all possible speed. But she never did, just as she did not now, concentrating instead on maintaining her projection of a hellhound's image as she slunk through the passages alive with eerily dancing shadows cast by the flickering flames of the iron cressets, basketlike sconces attached to the stone walls and filled with the same putrid oil that polluted Lake Malady.

In the week that had passed since she, Iskander, and Anuk had made their initial foray into Skull Volcano, they had between them covered every inch of the UnKind's habitat, including the donjon itself, observing and absorbing all they could about their enemies, then returning to the cave to report their findings to the others and to lay their plans.

Fortunately, except for their few unnerving brushes with the Prince Lord Perish, the three had had only one close call—when one of the SoulEaters, grumbling under his breath, had spied Rhiannon, in her hellhound guise, nosing around one of the outbuildings and had led her off to the kennels, where he had chained her to a post. She had endured what had seemed an eternity of apprehension, fearing that Iskander's Power would fail him before he could arrive to release her, that she would be forced to revert to her true shape to get free of the chain, thereby setting off a baying frenzy among the real hellhounds, which would prompt the UnKind to investigate the cause of the disturbance. But luckily Iskander, pushing his Power to its absolute limits, had reached her in time to avert the disaster that had threatened, and they had got away. Later, much to their horror, they had discovered that the outbuilding was full of Kind, mammalian, and reptilian corpses—the SoulEaters' larder, in effect. The UnKind kept the hellhounds away from it, else the voracious beasts would devour its grisly contents.

Tonight Iskander had wanted to make one final attempt to sneak into the Prince Lord Perish's rooms —the one place neither he nor Rhiannon nor Anuk had so far managed to search. So here they were, prowling about the castle for what they hoped and prayed would be the last time before carrying out the plans they had made.

Now, as Rhiannon and Anuk took up guard posts at either end of the stairs that led to the necromancer's tower, Iskander bent his ear to the door of the Prince Lord Perish's antechamber. Hearing naught to deter him, he quietly turned the knob and went in. Once inside, where none could see him, he gratefully dissolved his ShapeShift, both to conserve his Power and to prevent his leaving behind him any vestiges of magic that would alert the necromancer to the fact that his private sanctuary had been encroached upon. Skull oil lamps blazed within, illuminating the room. But to his dejection, after a cursory inspection Iskander saw nothing to interest him. The antechamber was merely a sitting room, obviously used to receive arrivals, hold audiences, and entertain favored guests.

Beyond it, on one side, lay Perish's bedchamber. Here, too, skull oil lamps burned, and to Iskander's surprise the room actually possessed a single Gothic window with lozenge panes of lead glass. Through them he could see the horde of vampire bats that, after nightfall, winged their way from the uppermost reaches of the keep, in search of prey. Shuddering at the sight of the bloodsucking creatures, he turned away, rifling the contents of Perish's chests and coffers as swiftly but carefully as possible. Again there was naught to capture Iskander's attention.

Returning to the antechamber, he tiptoed across the floor to the door he surmised led to Perish's study and his alchemic atelier above. Iskander had just laid his hand upon the knob when there reached his ears the sound of heated voices coming from behind the portal.

"I am quite sssure I do need not to remind ye that I am *mossst* disssspleasssed by thisss interminable delay, Perisssh. I do not undersssstand why a necromancer of your inordinate knowledge and talentsss hasss not yet managed to decipher the SSScroll."

"Perhapsss it isss sssimply becaussse hisss knowledge and talentsss are not ssso great asss he hasss led usss to believe, Imperial Leader," another voice chimed in slyly. "After all, he did not foressee the dessstruction of our vassst army on the SSStrathmore Plainsss of Finisssterre, did he? A mossst curiousss and highly lamentable oversssight for sssuch an illussstriousss wizard, would not ye agree, Imperial Leader?"

"Damn ye, Ghoul!" Perish spat. "I warn ye: Ye shall not lay that fiasco at *my* door! If anyone is to be blamed for the crippling loss of so many of our Imperial Forces, 'tis ye. I told ye that Woden was unfit to command. He was not only brutish, but maniacally aggressive, untempered by either intelligence or cunning. But did ye listen to me? Nay, ye insisted on placing him in charge of the invasion of Aerie and Verdante anyway!"

"Yea, that decisssion wasss mine," the First Leader, the Lord Ghoul admitted, with some annoyance, which he speedily masked. Then, more confidently, he went on. "But dessspite your claimsss to the contrary, Woden wasss a good sssoldier, Perisssh. After hisss induction—a *willing* induction, I might remind ye—into our ranksss, he wasss judged by none other than the SSSecond Leader, the Lord Goblin, to demonsssstrate potential, and he wasss brought to SSSalamandria accordingly. Once he had achieved hisss full ssscalesss, he wasss trained by Goblin himsssself before being returned to Aerie. Do ye sssay that Goblin isss an idiot? *Faugh!* Woden would have ssserved our caussse admirably, I tell ye, if not for that inexpugnable sssorcerer—whossse presssence on the field of battle ye ssso conveniently failed to divine, Perisssh!"

"That was not my fault!" Perish insisted. "The Demons are both deceitful and malicious, and those I summoned to my circle of magic spoke in dastardly riddles, of a man and of a beast of the Darkness who were one but not the same. Of course I surmised that the Demons referred to one of our own and a hellhound—a natural mistake."

"A foolisssh blunder, ye mean," Ghoul asserted smugly.

"Enough!" the Imperial Leader, the Lord Fiend, snarled suddenly. "Time Passst cannot be changed. 'Tisss Time Future to which we mussst look—and thisss SSScroll of the Old Onesss may prove of value, jussst asss their machinesss have. Why elssse should it have been ssssealed in that metal cylinder and ssso carefully cached? I asssk again: Why have ye not deciphered it, Perisssh?"

"I am doing my best, Imperial Leader, I assure ye," the necromancer answered smoothly. "But recently I have had other priorities—"

"SSSuch asss?" Fiend lifted one knobby eyebrow demonically.

"Imperial Leader, some weeks ago, from the towers of the Crypt, I observed a strange, erratic blue-green fire in the Hindrance Hills—"

"Faugh! 'Twasss nothing more than a couple of Bezel Boomersss, Imperial Leader," Ghoul scoffed, "the resssult of a brief ssskirmisssh between one of our raiding partiesss and thossse pathetic rat droppingsss who dare to hunt usss for our hornsss."

"Then why has the raiding party not returned from across the border?" Perish demanded.

"Perhapsss becaussse they are ssstill raiding?" the First Leader suggested with a contemptuous smile. "After all, 'tiss winter in Montano, and the Kind have retreated like frightened mice behind their high wallsss. . . ."

"And what, then, of the faint traces of ether I discovered just this morning—not only inside Skull Volcano and around the shore of Lake Malady, but here, in the very Crypt itself? What of those, Ghoul? I tell ye that a sorcerer has come among us—"

"May the Demonsss dine on your inssssidiousss tongue, Perisssh, for assssssuredly I have no ussse for it!" Ghoul sneered. He turned to the Lord Fiend. "Imperial Leader, firsst, when it isss of the utmosst conssssequence, thisss would-be wizard ssseesss no sssorcerer at all; and now, when there isss naught in the leassst to fear, he sssseesss one in every corner— the resssult of too much palm wine, I have no doubt! I beg ye, Lord: Do ye rid usss of thisss poor excussse for a mage before, in hisss ineptnessssss, he dropsss his crysssstal ball and doesss our feet sssome mortal injury!

"He isss either mad or a fool to think that a sssorcerer walksss freely among usss, with none of usss the wissser! I asssk ye, Lord: How did he get here, thisss great and unknown sssorcerer? Did he fly like a witch on the wingsss of a giant bat to elude our guardsss posssted at Epitaph Passssss? But sssurely *one* among usss would have noticed sssuch an extraordinary arrival, would ye not agree, Lord? And hasss he sssome incredibly powerful magic ssspell, thisss mysssteriousss sssorcerer, that hasss rendered him ssso invisssible that not even our hellhoundsss have managed to sssniff him out? *Faugh*, I sssay!"

"Ghoul, I am going to find this sorcerer," Perish avowed through clenched teeth, "because no matter what ye say, he's here—here in this very Crypt, I tell ye! I've seen his spoor. I can feel him in my bones. And when I find him—and I *will* find him—I am going to use every single Black Art at my command to reach inside your pea-brain, Ghoul, take hold of your soul, wrest it from your body, and put it into that of this same sorcerer so ye will learn just how real he is! Meanwhile I intend to do what I ought to have done in the first place instead of listening to ye when I saw that blue-green light in the hills: trust both my instincts and my better judgment and dispatch troops to Epitaph Pass to find out what is wrong there—and hope that it is not too late to prevent your stupidity and your conceit from proving the ruination of us all!"

"Why, ye insssufferable—"

"SSSilence!" Fiend thundered, enraged. "I have heard all I wisssh to hear from the both of ye! By all meansss, Perisssh, sssend our Imperial Forcesss to Epitaph Passssss if 'twill eassse your mind, and continue your sssearch for thisss sssorcerer ye ssseem ssso certain isss prowling about the hallsss of the Crypt. But do ye get that SSScroll deciphered ere my temper growsss ssshort and I lossse all patience with ye! I have tolerated your endlesssssss delayssss and feeble excusssesss for far too long asss 'tisss!" His red eyes glowering, he turned to the First Leader. "And asss for ye, Ghoul, your progressssssss on my warsssshipsss leavesss much to be desssired asss well! Do ye get them completed before sssummer'sss end, elssse ye ssshall find yourssself posssted to Frigidia inssstead of the Casssket! Do I make mysssself clear?"

"Yea, quite clear, Imperial Leader," Ghoul ground out, prudently bowing to hide the fact that he was both angered and frightened by this threatening reprimand.

"Then, Lordsss, ye have your ordersss!" Fiend snapped. "Do ye sssee that they are carried out at once. The propagation of our tribe isss paramount. We ssshall sssweep like a fearsssome tide acrosssss the world, and all in the landsss ssshall bow down to me asss their Imperial Leader. The whole of Tintagel isss mine for the taking, and I ssshall not ressst until every sssquare inch of it isss under my control! That isss all."

With that, his bloodred silk cape swirling like mist about his scaly black calves, Fiend whirled about and, after striding furiously across the room, ripped the door open wide. Iskander barely had time to send a mental warning to Rhiannon and Anuk and to conceal himself hastily in a nearby armoire before the two SoulEaters and the necromancer advanced into the antechamber and then out into the corridor beyond, disappearing down the wending passage. For a moment Iskander could only heave a sigh of relief that Perish's agitation had been such that he had not sensed an intruder's presence.

Quickly, not knowing how much time he had before Perish returned, Iskander emerged from the wardrobe and slipped into the study, where he spied upon the necromancer's desk the Scroll he had overheard the three discussing. Immediately he realized why Perish was having such difficulty deciphering it. The Scroll was written in the Old Tongue. Iskander himself recognized only a few words, but these so excited him that he was sorely tempted to snatch the Scroll then and there and run with it. Caution prevailed, however, for he knew that should Perish return to discover the Scroll missing, he would leave no stone unturned or spell uncast to find the culprit responsible for its theft; and Iskander could not be certain that he, Rhiannon, and Anuk would be well away from the fortress before that happened.

So reluctantly he compelled himself to leave the Scroll where it lay. Moving from the desk, he conducted a brief but particular examination of both the necromancer's study and alchemic atelier, astounded and appalled by the number of arcane books Perish had collected, all having to do with the Black Arts and many of them quite old. Iskander's fingers itched to burn the tomes to cinders, not knowing what doors to evil knowledge they might open for the necromancer. But in the end the books, too, he forced himself to let alone, comforting himself with the thought that like the Scroll, the most ancient of the volumes were also written in the Old Tongue, which Perish plainly did not comprehend.

The necromancer's alchemic atelier was even more dismaying. It was full of an assortment of creatures— bats, toads, lizards, snakes, even a baby dragon in a cage—and deadly plants, such as mistletoe, nightshade, and poisonous toadstools, all employed, Iskander felt sure, in the casting of wicked spells and the summoning of foul Demons. There was an array of colored-glass flacons that contained lethal gases, putrid powders, and magic potions; and all sorts of mortars and pestles, crucibles, alembics, matrices, and caldrons littered the shelves and floor. A large, inky crystal ball perched in a brass stand in one corner; a silver cheval mirror stood in another. There were pendulums and witching sticks, staffs and wands. The place was a veritable warehouse of wizardry. Iskander touched none of it, not knowing what he might accidentally unleash.

At last, sensing how rapidly the Wheel of Time turned, he exited Perish's chambers and, resuming the loathed UnKind shape, rejoined Rhiannon and Anuk, who were skulking in the shadows at either end of the stairs outside. As unobtrusively as possible, the three egressed the Crypt and returned to the cave, where Iskander elatedly informed the others of his discovery of the Scroll.

"Mind ye, I could read almost none of it," he reported, "for 'twas written in the Old Tongue. But it seemed to me that it spoke of ways to combat the SoulEaters' dread disease. We simply cannot leave here without that Scroll. If I'm right, and Perish succeeds in deciphering it, the Lord Fiend will order it destroyed, and we may never learn how to rid ourselves of these unnatural creatures once and for all!"

"Then, of course we must steal it," Kaliq agreed. "What do ye suggest, Lord?"

Late into the wee hours of the morning, the questers talked, carefully going over and refining their plans. Five of their number were gone, having saddled up and ridden out in the hope of reaching Epitaph Pass in time to warn the army of Scalie Scalpers stationed there to expect shortly the arrival of the Imperial Forces, even now preparing to march northward, by order of the necromancer. For Perish had lost no time in dispatching the UnKind troops. The castle was ablaze with torchlight as the SoulEaters readied themselves for their journey—and battle.

Beyond the mouth of the cavern, through the brush with which the companions had hidden the opening, Rhiannon could see that the rain was still falling. But though she was heartily sick of the drizzle, still, she thanked the Light for it; for it and the muck from Lake Malady were what had kept the hellhounds from scenting the presence of herself, Iskander, and Anuk during their forays, what had prevented Perish from discovering until this morning the ethereal traces of her and Iskander's magic, and what even now thwarted him in his attempts to locate their origin. The rain had muddied the faint marks, and the slime had further obscured the imprints, making it difficult to discern that they came from not one, but two sources of Power. She thought that the necromancer must be deeply frustrated, trying to unravel the maze of magical residue that crisscrossed the keep and its vicinity, at knowing that a rival sorcerer had penetrated the fortress but being unable to prove it, to pinpoint whence or how. Perish must further be greatly baffled by the fact that despite the traces of ether he had found, no magic to which he could actually point had been performed. Since the ability to ShapeShift was a rare gift, it seemed likely that the necromancer, for all his erudition and talents, was unaware of the skill, else it would surely have occurred to him as the only possible answer to all his questions. Still, she and Iskander would need to be even more vigilant now, Rhiannon knew, for Perish was certain to be devising any number of traps with which to catch them.

She was especially troubled by the threat he had made to the First Leader, the Lord Ghoul, for being ignorant of the extent of the necromancer's Power, she did not know if he was truly capable of transferring a spirit from one body to another, as he had claimed. Assuming he was, however, she felt he posed a real menace to Iskander, whose own Power was so severely drained by his transforming into such an unnatural shape that he would be highly vulnerable to BodySnatching.

"What if it was not an idle boast?" she pressed him worriedly a few evenings later. "What if Perish does indeed possess both the Power and the knowledge to effect such a transfer?"

"That is a risk I must take, Rhiannon," Iskander

replied. "I must have that Scroll. I feel in my bones that this is so."

They sat in a sheltered niche in the hills above the cave, from which vantage point they could spy upon the donjon. A rocky outcrop above the lunette nook kept the worst of the drizzle from them, and a gently swaying green lattice of trees and bushes shielded them from the prying eyes of the UnKind and the hellhounds below. Twilight had fallen. The hazy light of the rising moons came mottled through the canopy of branches, dappling the sodden earth and Iskander's resolute visage with splotches of luminescence. Stars whose names Rhiannon did not know glimmered in the melanotic welkin. In the distance a hellhound bayed at the moons, an eerie, mournful sound. The wail set Rhiannon to shivering, as though the Grim Reaper himself had, with his icy fingers, caressed her.

"It has been three days now since ye learned of the Scroll," she pointed out, "and in all that time, Perish has not once to our knowledge left his private sanctuary in the Crypt. The Wheel of Time turns, Iskander. The Imperial Forces march north to Epitaph Pass, and each hour we delay here strengthens the chances that our only escape route shall be cut off by a terrible pitched battle when we reach it. We cannot go on lingering here, hoping that an opportunity for ye to seize the Scroll undetected will arise. Ye said that the Lord Fiend's patience with Perish has worn thin. What if the necromancer does not leave his tower until he has deciphered the Scroll? What then, Iskander?"

"Then I must take the Scroll from him," he stated flatly, his tone making it clear that he would brook no further argument; but Rhiannon was not to be deterred.

"And what of Perish's threat to put Ghoul in your

body?" she queried sharply. "Even if the necromancer has not the Power and the knowledge to accomplish such a feat, he will surely attack ye in some fashion. Ye cannot possibly hope to ward off his assault and to sustain your UnKind image at the same time. To fight Perish ye will have to revert to your own shape, Iskander; and even should ye defeat the necromancer, perhaps ye will lack the strength to resume the form of a SoulEater. Drained of your Power, unable to pass as UnKind, ye will never make it out of the Crypt alive. The SoulEaters and their hellhounds will rend ye limb from limb—and the Scroll will still remain in their possession."

"Perhaps all will indeed happen as ye say," Iskander conceded. "But then again, perhaps it will not. With each passing day my body has grown more accustomed to the perverted demand I have placed upon it. Mayhap my Power will prove strong enough that I can both prevail over Perish and manage my escape."

"And what if it does not?"

"It must. There is no other way."

"Isn't there, Iskander?" Rhiannon prodded.

"What do ye mean?" he asked, his eyes narrowing.

"I mean that I think that there *is* another way and that ye know what 'tis—though why ye have not spoken of it eludes me, I confess, unless 'tis because of what lies between us. But that is wrong, Iskander, and in your heart ye know it; for did not ye tell me that we two were nothing when all Tintagel was at stake? That has not changed. I am not a child, Iskander. I do not need your protection. Other things I would ask of ye, yea, if our lives were different. But here, now, I ask only for your honesty. Tell me the truth: Is there not some way, as I believe, to combine our Power, to merge our auras so they become one, a single shape sustained by one of us, defended by the other?"

He was silent for such a long time afterward that she thought he did not intend to answer. But at last, his voice low, he admitted, "Yea, there is a way—a way for each of us to learn the exact colors and patterns of the other's aura, the other's Power, as truly and surely as we know our own. But it involves the . . . deepest of intimacies, Rhiannon, the giving of what a woman can give only once in her life, a man take from her only once. I am an honorable man. How do I know I have the right to ask that of ye? That—the Immortal Guardian help me—I ask it for Tintagel and for the Light, and not for myself? Oh, Rhiannon, in truth ye know so little of the world ye would call home—of the East and of Vikanglia—so little of men— Your feelings for me . . . perhaps they are born only of my having been the first man of your own kind ye ever really knew. How do ye or I know otherwise? What if we survive this and I take ye to the East, to Vikanglia, where there are men of your kind beyond counting? Perhaps there ye will come to regret what we did in the heat of this moment, when it seemed the only way and our future was so uncertain, our need so desperate. Ye have given so much of yourself to this quest. This, then, I would spare ye. I would not spoil ye for another of your choosing. I would not have ye despise me—as ye might come to do someday when the only darkness ye know is that which follows the dusk and is lighted by the stars. . . ."

"Do ye truly believe that, Iskander?" she asked earnestly. "That I could ever come to hate ye? Tell me: In all Tintagel how many men are there who are my kind? Who have been Chosen? Who have that rarest of gifts, are ShapeShifters, like me? Who know what it means to fly like a bird, unfettered, across the night sky amid the stars? How many, Iskander? A handful? Less than that? And of those few, who among them will know what it is to travel to the ends of the earth?

To be cold and wet, hungry and tired, huddled miserably around the scant warmth of a hearthstone, beneath the meager shelter of a tent? Who among them will know the feel of the tundra snow beneath their feet when the long, dark time of the winter comes to an end? The sound of the wind as it sweeps across the Groaning Gorge to dance amid the RingStones? The sight of a sickly Blue Moon hanging low over the black mountains of Labyrinth? The smell of a Bezel Boomer when the fuse is ignited? Who among them will know what it is to leave behind all that is dear and familiar, to brave the very heart of the Darkness—for Tintagel and for the Light?

"In all the world there is only ye, Iskander, and even were there a thousand such men, ye would still be the only one for me. For are we not each but a half, made whole by the other? I have never doubted your honor. Do not ye doubt my love. Once, aeons ago it seems now, I offered myself to ye out of desperation. Now I offer out of my love for ye, Iskander—a love that is true and certain and everlasting. Not only for Tintagel and for the Light, but for myself, for us. Is that so very wrong, so very selfish of me, of ye? I think not. For I do not believe that the Immortal Guardian, in Its infinite wisdom and understanding, would be so cruel as to deny us one stolen moment for ourselves. So, will ye not have me, then, Iskander? Please." Her voice was soft, entreating, her face white as snow in the moonlight, etched with all the love that filled her to overflowing for him.

"Yea, with all my heart and soul, beloved," he said then, knowing that it would be so—and wanting it, wanting her, with every fiber of his being.

The rain came harder, but they neither knew nor cared. For them the Wheel of Time had stopped. In all Tintagel there was only now, there was only each other.

Slowly he shrugged off the Sword of Ishtar and laid it to one side, close at hand; for even now they did not quite forget that the Darkness encompassed them, that they had dared to trespass upon Its domain, and that there would be a price to pay for that. But that belonged to tomorrow—if tomorrow ever came. And so they would not think of it now, this night, which was theirs, only theirs, for so long as the moons ruled the sky.

Iskander spread his sable cloak upon the damp earth of the sheltered niche and drew Rhiannon down upon its warm, velvety fur, his hands gentle upon her—but so sure that she trembled from the wealth of emotion that welled inside her, strong and sweet as the Power when it swept through her body, an engulfing tide of want, of need urgently seeking release. His mouth was as soft and warm as his cloak, and like a scarlet bud unfurling, her lips opened to his, yielding eagerly to his tender onslaught. Lightly his tongue traced the outline of her mouth, then probed the moist recesses within, twining with her own tongue, touching, tasting, while the night wind wove about them a gossamer cocoon of mist and mizzle. But Rhiannon felt not the gusts that blew in from the sea, trailing spindrift in their wake; for Iskander had laid her white mantle over them, and beneath it, he shared the heat of his body with her. So she was warm as though a fire burned in the crescent nook instead of in her blood, setting her ablaze with passion and desire.

She was like the tundra at the winter's end, and Iskander was the sun, thawing, waking her. She melted against him, molding herself to fit the long, hard length of him as he clasped her to him, his hands roaming where they willed, arousing within her a thousand exquisite sensations she had never felt before. She had not known that it would be like this, as though a fever had come upon her, making her dizzy and weak, so she felt fragile as an alpine flower, its delicate petals laid bare to the wind and the snow. Iskander's mouth was upon hers, giving, taking, seeming to drain the very life and soul from her body, and then to pour it back in. Roughly his fingers burrowed through her hair, tearing at her braid, loosing it, enveloping them both in a web of silken flame. Groaning, he buried his face in the coppery tresses and wrapped them about his throat, as though to bind himself to her forever. Her hair smelled of herbs and wildflowers, mist and rain, scents of the earth, intoxicating him. Deeply he inhaled the fragrances that mingled with the heady perfume of Rhiannon herself, making his loins tighten suddenly, sharply, with exigency. Spurred on by his ardor, his lips slanted across her upturned face to find her mouth again, hungrily, demanding now. Fervently she kissed him back. They breathed as one, oblivious of all but each other.

The drumming of the steady drizzle matched the tattoo of their quickening heartbeats. The wind was a breath primeval as their own as they strained against each other, breast to breast, thigh to thigh, their bodies sleek and supple as the leather garments they had cast away in the heat of their desire. Naked, then, they lay, sweat sheening their skin, she fair as the pale moonlight, he dark as the dusky night, their embrace a complement perfect as the heavens and the earth; for what was one without the other? Children of Ceridwen they were, and all that the Keeper embodied.

Rhiannon's unbound hair was like a snarl of thick autumn gorse, russet branches ensnaring Iskander, drawing him down to her. Her breasts, swollen with passion, were soft hills to be explored by his palms. His breath was like the wind upon their crests and the valley between them, his tongue moist as the mist that drifted and curled in the hollows of the land, tasting the salt of her skin, clean and damp as spindrift. Every line, every curve of her, he mapped, until there was no part of her he did not know, had not claimed as his as he showed her what it was to be loved by a man and, in return, taught her of his own passion and desire.

She reveled in the feel of him, his flesh smooth as clay in places, hard as horn in others, where old scars marked his bronze body. Like tall grass in a soughing breeze, the muscles in his broad back and arms and thighs rippled beneath her fingers. The fine black hair on his chest was soft as moss against her hands and against the highly responsive peaks of her breasts as he brushed against them, a feathery caress that made her inhale sharply and moan low in her throat until with his lips he swallowed the sound and her breath, scattering her senses as though they were but seeds to be tossed to the wild wind. After that she could no longer think, could only feel, every inch of her so incredibly alive, so utterly sensitive that his every kiss, his every touch was a flare of lightning pulsating through her body.

Somewhere time passed, far beyond the vignette that ringed man and woman, lost in a place as timeless and dark and atavistic as the earth's beginning, a place where flesh and emotion ruled, where mouths and tongues and hands unstill worked their mellifluous, savage will, weaving a sorcerous spell that honed desire to a keen, serrated edge. Rhiannon's body throbbed at its secret heart with an unbearable hollow ache, so she longed urgently for Iskander to fill her, as he so yearned to do. She writhed against him, crying out, driven by blind, primitive need; and at last he took her.

She gasped at the shock of his entry, the deep, hard, sudden thrust, the sharp, sweet pain that made of her a woman and of him her lover; for she had never truly grasped until now this absolute invasion and surrender, this stretching and molding of oneself to accept the other as two bodies melded into one. It was as though Rhiannon no longer belonged to herself at all, but had become a part of Iskander. His hands were beneath her hips, lifting them to meet his own as he plunged into the warm, nectareous core of her; and in that moment the world spun away into nothingness as she reached for some nameless thing she felt she must find or die.

Of its own volition her Power erupted inside her, surging and swelling, flowing forth in a torrent of light and color and pattern as she soared to the stars and beyond, wingless, ethereal, unfettered. From far away, it seemed, she felt Iskander's fingers tighten on her painfully, his nails digging into her skin, heightening the intensity of what she knew. The kaleidoscope that exploded within her and about her was twofold, bursting with the brilliance and profusion of Iskander's own Power spilling rapturously into hers, taking her breath away. Abruptly the earth tilted on its axis, the moons fell from the sky into the sea; and in that instant, as Rhiannon's and Iskander's bodies had become one, so now did their hearts, their minds, and their souls. The aura that enfolded them fused in a perfect whole, lights and colors and patterns blended in a harmonious union, without beginning or end, pure, beautiful, unrivaled, unconditional, the shining essence of love.

Then slowly . . . very slowly, their glorious flight ended, Rhiannon and Iskander fluttered down to the earth, became once more a part of it, whence their Power sprang, as they were a part of each other now—for all time. They did not speak. They had no need of words between them. The bond they shared was all-encompassing, spanning time and space—and even death, should it come for them tomorrow. That thought they banished, however; they would not think of it now, while the night was yet theirs. Gently he withdrew from her and pulled her into the cradle of his arms, where she laid her head on his shoulder.

Beyond the niche, the rain continued to fall as the stars glimmering in the black-velvet firmament began to wink out one by one. Presently, on the far horizon, the dawn came, pale and leaden.

Chapter 26

Let it be known to all Men that in the Year of the
Light 7276, by the Common Reckoning, there did
come to the land of Salamandria, once known as
Sylvania, the Lord Iskander sin Tovaritch and his
beloved, the Lady Rhiannon sin Lothian, both
True Defenders of the Light, and with them
twenty-three warriors constant and brave, to strike
a mortal blow at the heart of the Darkness.

For this did they dare to trespass within Fiend's
Crypt: to steal from the evil necromancer the
Prince Lord Parrish, called "Perish," of Finisterre,
the Sacred Scroll and to wreak havoc and ruin
upon the Scalies, that Tintagel should be saved
from annihilation and the Light should not be
extinguished, but should continue to burn forever,
an eternal flame of hope and promise for all Kind.

—Thus it is Written—
on
a cave wall in Salamandria
carved by the Scalie Scalper Kaliq set Rubyatta

HE HAD NO RIGHT TO MAKE OF HER A DRUSWIDIC
priestess; this he knew. Whether she was worthy to
take her Final Vows, to have the mark of the moon set
upon her brow, and to be given the Collar of First

Rank was a test she herself must pass or fail at Mont Saint Mikhaela by summoning the barge *Swan Song* and guiding it through the mists to the cloister—or not. But in his heart Iskander knew that had Rhiannon been trained at the nunnery, as she ought, the title of priestess would already be hers, that she was, in truth, deserving of the honor; and he was fiercely, stubbornly, determined that she should have it before they embarked upon the severe trial they would face this bleak night.

Now, as he gazed down at her kneeling at the center of the ring he and the eleven others she had chosen for her initiation rite had formed around her, Iskander deliberately pushed from his mind the fact that he had no authority to perform the impending ceremony at which he intended to officiate. Other than that, the ritual would be as proper as he could make it under the circumstances. He had drawn the necessary circle, symbols, and runes upon the ground; and torches burned all around. From silver chain links the Scalie Scalpers had proudly contributed from their mail, Gunda and Lido had lovingly fashioned the prescribed crescent-moon torque with its single line that denoted the First Rank of a Druswid. Iskander himself had, from the sea, gathered the mollusks whence came the Tyrian-purple dye for the ineradicable tattoo that was the irrefutable, lifelong sign of a Druswidic priestess. And if those who surrounded Rhiannon were not of the Sisterhood and the Brotherhood, they were her sisters and brothers in spirit, meriting more than anyone in all the world, he thought, the privilege of standing at her side, of vouching for her worthiness.

Glancing about at the rest of the faces that surrounded him, Iskander reflected wryly that those in the cave, who waited solemnly for the rite to begin, were so diverse and ragged a lot that they might have been mistaken for a band of brigands. In truth, Rhiannon, garbed in her leather etek, shaksheer, and white fur mantle, scarcely looked the part of a novice about to take her Final Vows but, rather, a mercenary girded for battle. Those at Mont Saint Mikhaela would be shocked and appalled by the sight of her, Iskander knew. Still, if he and she survived their quest, he meant somehow, no matter what it took, to compel the cloister to recognize and bestow its blessing upon this night's work. About that he was firmly resolved.

So thinking, he slowly lifted his palms and, in a voice low and melodic, started to chant in the ancient language, the Old Tongue, words he knew only by rote from ceremonies such as this. Gradually his aura began to radiate from his being, holding spellbound those who watched; for this was a summoning of the Power unlike any they had ever before observed. The blue fire that haloed Iskander's body now was somehow different from usual, they realized—shot through with a thousand pastel streaks of color, like a rainbow arching across an aquamarine sky. But only Rhiannon, kneeling at his feet, knew that this particular aura was born of the love they shared, was his half of the whole they had made between them last night. Emotion filled her to overflowing as she understood that what illuminated Iskander's being was not what it should have been for this ritual, but was for her alone, so she would know how much he loved her.

In the flickering torchlight her face was so luminous that those who attested to her ritual thought she must be, in truth, the embodiment of Ceridwen, the Keeper of the Earth. Her joyous voice rang so softly and sweetly as she chanted the appropriate responses Iskander had taught her that it was as though the strings of a harp echoed in the cavern. It was a rite of mystery and beauty, of passage from woman to priestess, never before beheld beyond the high walls of the Mont-Sect cloisters, never to be forgotten by those who witnessed it now, who would carry the memory of it to their graves, never speaking of what they had seen; for they had not the words to describe it. The Power that Iskander called forth was so delicate yet so potent that it spun about them the silken skeins of a tapestry, the gossamer threads of a dream, so they knew not if they were awake or slept.

Only Rhiannon saw truly, knew that it was real, felt the burning of Iskander's hands as he laid them upon her, scorching the mark of the Tyrian-purple crescent moon into her pale brow; felt the molten heat of the silver torque against her bared skin as he hung it about her swanlike neck; felt the searing of his lips upon her cheeks as he gave her the Kiss of Peace, and then pronounced her a Druswid, a Priestess of the First Rank, a True Defender of the Light. All around them the rainbow fire blazed high, at its heart a joining of another sort as he raised her from her knees to stand before him, her hands clasped in his—not man and woman now, but priest and priestess, pledged to honor, serve, and defend the Light, whatever the cost. Tears glistened on her lashes at the thought of the price the two of them might have to pay. Gently Iskander's hands cupped her face; his mouth kissed the salty droplets away. For a long moment his eyes held hers, pressing like a flower into the pages of his memory every last detail of her countenance.

Then he said, "Come. It is time, beloved," and as one, they stepped from the light into the darkness, where fate stood waiting and death lurked in the shadows.

All around him in the tower of Fiend's Crypt, skull oil lamps flickered, bathing his study in dancing shades of umber and crimson, ocher and citrine, making the inky runes on the Scroll before him writhe as though burning alive. His obsidian eyes were filmed with red. He had had little sleep the past four nights—and that had been fraught with nightmares, dreams of foreboding that had left him troubled and restive, for he did not know what the ominous omens portended. Three times he had summoned the Demons, and three times, as once before, they had spoken in riddles—of a man and of a beast, who were one but not the same. Did the Demons foretell of the same sorcerer, then, as that of the Strathmore Plains? He who had once been the Prince Lord Parrish of Finisterre shuddered at the thought. Yet he could not deny that he had sensed an alien presence in the Crypt; he had seen the mark of magic that could have been made only by a sorcerer. Was it the same one who had destroyed the Imperial Forces in Finisterre? He did not know; he could not be certain, for tonight there had been an added twist: *First man and beast, and then will come she. When two are one, look to see three.* What did it mean? Perish had asked himself over and over, racking his brain and cursing the malice and cleverness of the Demons. But no matter how hard he had tried, he had not learned the answer to his question. His crystal ball, his silver mirror, his magic wands . . . all in his alchemic atelier had availed him naught. Yet some instinct told him that the missing piece of the puzzle lay plain before him.

The drugs he had taken in the hope of enhancing his murky visions had left him on edge, and the palm wine he had consumed had done little to soothe him. Inside, he felt coiled tight as a snake, filled with venomous rage at the failure of his dark Power to enlighten him further; at the smug mockery of the First Leader, the Lord Ghoul; and at the megalomania of the Imperial Leader, the Lord Fiend, that blinded him to all but his ambition to conquer the world. The necromancer could not shake the black depression that had come upon him, the feeling that they were all poised on the brink of disaster.

There is a sorcerer come among ye, a sly and insidious voice inside his mind whispered tauntingly.

Yea, but how? *How?* And then, of a sudden, Perish knew—but by then it was too little too late. The hellhound was upon him.

They were one heart, one mind, one shape, moving in perfect unison as they trod the narrow halls that wended through the Crypt, prudently keeping to the eerie shadows cast by the flickering cressets on the walls. No one paid them any heed. The lone black-furred, grey-eyed hellhound they were raised no suspicions, gave no cause for alarm. But still, there was always the chance that one of the UnKind might take their presence amiss, might lead them outside to the kennels and, there, chain them to a post. That was a calamity they could not afford. tonight. If they had to reveal that they were not one, but two—and Kind— they could not hope to live long afterward. They could afterward. not hope then to do what they must do: steal the Sacred Scroll before the profane Perish deciphered and destroyed it.

Time harried at their heels. Swiftly they ascended the steep, winding stone stairs that led to the upper-most reaches of the castle, then padded along the short, curving corridor that ended at the door to the necromancer's private sanctuary. A hairy paw that momentarily had longer toes and a good deal more dexterity than it ought turned the knob, and they went in, quietly sliding the bolt into place behind them. Careless, Perish was, they thought, to leave his door unlocked—and were heartened by the notion.

He was there, as they had known he would be,

sitting at the desk in his study, almost as though he were waiting for them, expecting them. Yet even so, at first there was upon his pale, handsome but dissolute face a look of uncertainty, of confusion, as though they were not at all what he had anticipated, had envisioned. It was only a hellhound, nothing more, he thought, oddly downcast. And yet he felt in his bones the Power of the beast. No ordinary animal, this. Of that the necromancer was suddenly certain. But his brief moment of doubt, of indecision, cost him dearly; for without warning, a low growl issuing from its throat, the hellhound lunged at him.

Instinctively Perish held up his hands to ward off the attack, a vile yellow-green fire shooting from his fingertips. A shower of sparks erupted as the serpentine tongues of ichorous flame encountered the barrier that protected the beast, the blue aura, invisible until now, that abruptly materialized from the force of the impact. He had believed that the animal meant to rip out his jugular vein. Instead, with its razor-sharp teeth, it seized the Scroll lying upon his desk.

In that instant the necromancer knew that whatever was written therein must not leave the tower. Marshaling his wits, scrambling wildly onto the top of his desk, he flung himself with all his might at the hellhound. Rhiannon staggered back violently at the brutal blow, her head reeling at the savage clash of chartreuse fire and blue. She fell—hard—dragging Iskander with her, knocking the wind from them both; and while they were momentarily stunned, Perish penetrated the thin veil of their aura and grasped the answers to the Demons' riddles. *ShapeShifters*. Two who had somehow merged their Power to become one. An enormous greed for that Power devoured him, even as he recognized the dangerous threat it posed to him.

The woman was the weaker, he sensed, though only

because she was the less skilled; and with a feral cry, the necromancer summoned the full strength of his Power, tearing his ethereal essence free of his body to assault Rhiannon with every Black Art at his command. She cringed, horrified, as the corrupt black soul sought ingress into her body and her mind, bent on the vicious, pitiless rape of all she knew and was. Scream after scream exploded from her throat, reverberating through the keep—the unholy baying of a hellhound. The beasts in the kennels heard the sound and echoed it; and soon the night was alive with wailing, so the questers, who waited tensely in the hills knew that the strike at the heart of the Darkness had begun.

"Think of the Light, Rhiannon! Think only of the Light!" Iskander's voice, Iskander's essence, filled her mind as he entered into a desperate battle with Perish for possession of her being. *"Trust me, beloved! Do not fail me in this—when I need ye most!"*

I will neither ask for nor expect any quarter from ye. I will do my share of what needs doing, and more; and I will bend my Power to my will or die trying. For always at the back of my mind will be the thought that when ye need me most, I must be there without fail, come what may—for your sake, and all Tintagel's.

The words she had once so earnestly pledged to him came back to her now, as he had intended, giving her the strength she needed; for she knew what he asked of her.

Trust me, beloved! But before Rhiannon could act, there rang in the chasms of her mind other words Iskander had once spoken, now cruelly dredged from her memories by the evil necromancer. *I do not know where I go or into what dark peril or at what cost—only that I must do what must be done, no matter what. For this I would give my own life—and yours as well, if such ever became necessary. Do ye understand me?*

*The whole of Tintagel is at stake, and I cannot afford to
be merciful if ruthlessness is all that will serve me.* Her
brain resounded abominably with Perish's wicked,
mocking laughter. *Trust me, beloved!*

Strangely she thought then of Ileana, who had
trusted, of Cain, who had chosen—because there was
always a choice; and in that moment Rhiannon made
hers. With all the love in her heart she channeled her
Power to the sustaining of the hellhound's image,
trusting that Iskander would defend her body and her
mind, would not let Perish snatch them from her.
Dropping the Scroll, she bared her fangs and leaped
for the necromancer's throat. Sensing the peril to his
being, Perish was compelled to divide his Power,
weakening it, as he was assailed on both fronts, mental
and physical. His slender hands, surprisingly strong,
shoved at the beast's massive chest, holding the animal just inches from his jugular vein as he thrashed
his head from side to side in a frantic attempt to avoid
the hellhound's snapping, crushing jaws, while he
continued his perverse attack upon Rhiannon's body
and mind.

Iskander's essence shone like frost as he torturously
twisted and twined it about the necromancer's black
soul, seeking to choke the life from it, to keep it from
the rape of Rhiannon, only dimly aware of how she
assaulted Perish physically, tiring him. All about the
three of them, their auras blazed, Iskander's and
Rhiannon's blue fire now white-hot, Perish's yellow-
green flames now veined with ragged streaks of black,
as though oozing with putrefaction. Again and again
fiery spangles spewed from the colliding walls of
warding that constantly rived and shifted from the
jarring born of their violent contact. Gradually, as the
barbarous conflict wore on, the sparks became thin,
jagged forks of lightning that scorched the chamber in
all directions, shattering the lozenge lead-glass panes

of its single window and stabbing the melanotic night sky with terrible tridents of coruscation.

Alerted by the frenzied baying of the hellhounds, though as yet uncertain of its cause, the UnKind, upon seeing the unnatural flames shooting from the necromancer's tower, came running, for fire alone was their mortal fear. From Skull Volcano and Lake Malady, from the outbuildings and kennels of the fortress, they came, hissing and rasping as they stared at the inferno that was the tower. Secretly frightened of Perish, thinking him half mad, they hung back until their commanders began barking orders, sending them scurrying right and left for the hides with which they must smother all blazes, the scummy water of Lake Malady, with its oily substances, only fueling any fire, their hoard of rainwater precious, for drinking only. Inside the donjon itself, the Imperial Leader, the Lord Fiend, sat upon his bone throne, peremptorily issuing directives. Bowing and scraping, the First Leader, the Lord Ghoul, hastened from the great hall to do as he was bidden, only to discover that the stout door to the necromancer's private sanctuary was bolted fast.

"Get an ax!" he demanded of one of his subordinates. "Fetch asss many peltsss as ye can find!" he cried to others. "Hurry! *Hurry!*"

Within Perish's study the furious combat raged on, hellhound and necromancer both fighting for their lives. The chamber was a shambles, bone furniture splintered, skull oil lamps smashed, their contents spilled, seeping in rivulets of flame across the floor. Tongues of fire had begun to lick up the walls; acrid smoke filled the air. From the alchemic atelier above came the shrieks of terrified creatures, scrabbling desperately to break out of their cages. Perish's crimson silk gallibiya hung in tatters, shredded by the hellhound's nails. Blood dribbled from the punctures in his flesh where the beast's teeth had bitten him. His Power was fast waning. In his black heart he knew he could not prevail. His attempt to snatch Rhiannon's body, to seize control of her mind, was unsuccessful; nor could he invade those of Iskander, whose essence gripped his own soul in a stranglehold from which the necromancer feared he could not escape. And all the while the hellhound mauled him, sapping his strength as they rolled and grappled their way across the room.

Determinedly Perish called forth every last ounce of his gangrenous Power, and in a sudden burst of horror so repellent that Iskander and Rhiannon both recoiled from it, he wrenched himself free of all that constrained him. For a moment, gasping for breath, he glanced about wildly for the Scroll. Spying it, he would have grabbed it up, but the hellhound was quicker. Its jaws closed around the Scroll, snatching it from his reach. Shooting the beast a look of utter hatred that fairly shouted of his resolve to gain his revenge, the necromancer whirled and darted up the stone steps to his alchemic atelier, wrath and terror goading his exhausted, bloodied body. At the top of the stairs, he disappeared into a cloud of smoke, though whether this was from the fire enveloping the study or was some aberrant creation of his own, neither Iskander nor Rhiannon knew. They knew only that Perish had vanished—was, ominously, still alive.

But however much that seemed to bode ill for the future, there was no time to pursue him. The chamber was a holocaust, and the crash of the door beyond warned them that the portal had been breached. A streak of black fur, the hellhound bounded from the tower. Ghoul and the rest of the UnKind who accompanied him paid no heed to the beast, thinking it frightened of the flames. It was Perish who concerned them, the necromancer whom Fiend had ordered them to save at all costs. Coughing and gagging on the smoke, the creatures slowly braved the inferno, only to be driven back by a terrible explosion from the alchemic atelier. With a great creaking of timbers, its wooden floor collapsed into the chambers below, pinning the SoulEaters beneath its fiery wreckage. Only Ghoul, who had wisely remained near the door, was spared. A shrill cry of agony split the night as Perish fell with his atelier, a burning shard piercing his right eye, his gallibiya aflame as he struggled to haul himself from the blackening ruins.

"Accursed sorcerers," the necromancer moaned, as, through the insufferable pain that ravaged him, he sensed Ghoul's presence and weakly stretched out one trembling hand in supplication. "ShapeShifters . . . that was how . . . they managed it—damn them. I should . . . have guessed— They took . . . the Scroll. . . ."

For an instant Ghoul stared with naked loathing at him, despising him absolutely for his pathetic attempt, even now, to insist that the Crypt had been invaded. It was Perish, drunk, drugged, whose own Power had somehow gone awry, who had not been able to control whatever Demons he had summoned, and who had fabricated this wild story to conceal the fact that his magic was impotent, had failed him, that he could not decipher the Scroll. Abruptly the First Leader turned on his heel, abandoning the necromancer to his fate.

As though pursued by the Foul Enslaver Itself, they raced from the blazing castle and across its grounds, still damp and muddy, sucking at their four paws, as though to drag them down into the very bowels of the earth. Behind them they heard the horrible cracking that was Perish's alchemic atelier giving way. But still, they did not look back. Hard and fast around the mucky shore of Lake Malady, they ran, their swift, strong legs pumping in perfect harmony, eating up the ground.

And then at last they reached the foothills; and there, the final remnants of their Power drained, the hellhound they had been evanesced without warning. In place of the one beast stood two Kind, man and woman, separate, apart, naught but the love in their hearts for each other—and the Sacred Scroll they held between them—binding them. For a wordless emotional moment, their eyes met and locked, their hands clasped tightly. Then, Iskander tucking the precious Scroll safely inside his kurta, they climbed on, wending their way quickly through the Hindrance Hills to the cave overlooking the shore.

From his vantage point in the niche, Yael saw them coming. Incredible joy welled within him, his eyes filled with tears, and a lump rose in his throat, nearly choking him. He swallowed hard.

"They made it!" he shouted elatedly to the others as he scrambled down from his perch. "By the moons! They made it!"

"All right. This is it," Kaliq announced grimly to the rest as he heard the cry, though his eyes shone with a triumphant light. "Ye know what must be done. Go with the Light."

Mounting up, leading Iskander's and Rhiannon's horses, the companions rode from the cave to meet the two on foot. His strong hands gripping her waist, Iskander lifted Rhiannon into her saddle, then flung himself into his own, catching in one hand the Sword of Ishtar that Kaliq, an unholy, exultant grin splitting his dark visage, tossed to him. The rising night wind cool against their skin, whipping their hair back from their faces, the small party galloped forth to execute the plans they had laid. Splitting up, half headed toward Skull Volcano, while the rest made for Lake Malady, its black water agleam with the red-yellow light cast by the burning Crypt. The baying of the hellhounds had reached a feverish pitch; and now the attention of the UnKind was drawn by the riders silhouetted against the moonlit horizon. With a start, outraged, the SoulEaters realized they were under attack. Like the hissing of a thousand snakes, their voices rose, a ghastly clamor that was their call to arms.

Inside the keep Ghoul, hearing the dreadful din, felt deathly cold and sick, of a sudden. A foreboding clutched his heart, as though to rip it from his breast. Was it he after all, and not Perish, who had been the fool? He did not know. Still, sweat beaded his horned brow. He broke into a run, taking the narrow stairs two or more at a time, skidding on the stone steps as he so rashly descended them. Rushing from the keep, he drew up short, stricken at the frightening scene that met his eyes. All was chaos. Everywhere he looked, fires blazed, devouring the Imperial Forces, who ran about mindlessly, UnKind torches, shrieking with agony as the flames consumed them and their hearts exploded in their chests.

Boom! Boom! A thunderous noise rang out, splitting the night, as though it were the bursting bodies of the SoulEaters themselves making the monstrous sound. But Ghoul had heard this particular cacophony before; he knew what was causing it—Bezel Boomers. Turning, he spied in the distance the invaders at last. Like a madman, he yanked at his horns and gnashed his teeth, slavering rabidly at the sight, at the certain knowledge, then, that he had been wrong, that Perish had been right. Perversely the First Leader would have given much in that moment to have had the necromancer standing at his side.

Mounted on horseback, the interlopers were battling their way through the ranks of the UnKind who had somehow managed to escape the fires raging beyond control, and who now fought tooth and nail. Ghoul could see two of the rat droppings, the Scalie Scalpers who hunted the SoulEaters for their horns, kneeling upon the slope of Skull Volcano, lighting the fuses of the Boomers. But this was no ordinary Bezel raiding party, the First Leader recognized. He spotted two pick-wielding gnomes splitting open the skulls of the Imperial Forces and a giant and two elves, all armed with bows, sending their fiery arrows flying.

Lake Malady was now ablaze, and as Ghoul watched, his gut churning, he saw the first of the four ships go up in flames. Fury and fear such as he had never felt before roiled inside him, spewing forth in a sibilant roar of curses as finally his eyes fell upon the man—the sorcerer—he somehow knew instinctively was the impetus behind the destruction being wrought upon Fiend's Crypt and all that surrounded it. Beside the man, like an avenging angel, rode a woman so bold and beautiful that had he been Kind, she would have taken Ghoul's breath away. Even now, feelings long suppressed stirred within him, memories of what he had once been, buried deep somewhere in the chasms of his mind. Deliberately he squashed them back down into the silt of his brain. Sometimes the metamorphosis was incomplete; the mind could not be reconciled to the transformation. Even those who were fully scaled had been known to go berserk of a sudden. The First Leader did not intend to be overtaken by madness. His red eyes glowing, he stared at the man—the sorcerer—dark as the night on whose wings he had come, and at the woman, whose unbound hair was like fire. What had Perish gasped out in his last moments?

They took . . . the Scroll. . . .

The necromancer's words returned now to torment Ghoul; the specter of his execution at the hands of the Lord Fiend rose to haunt him. Abruptly he pivoted, his cape whirling like a shroud about his tall, scaly form as he strode toward the armory and the stables.

Both the Bezel Boomers and the flaming arrows continued to wreak their havoc as the questers struck savagely again and again at the heart of the Darkness. Employing their weapons ferociously against the UnKind, the Scalie Scalpers formed a protective ring about Kaliq and Hordib, so, unmolested, they could send the Boomers rocketing into the yawning eyes and maw of Skull Volcano. Blast after blast resounded within as the generators and other machines caught fire and exploded, rocking the inside of the cavern trickling with lava until at last, deep within the bowels of the earth, a low rumble started, gradually increasing in intensity so that the ground quaked violently.

Rhiannon's steed, running at full gallop as she swung her morning star around and around to bring it smashing into a SoulEater's ugly face, was thrown off balance by the sudden shifting of the earth and stumbled to its knees, pitching her from the saddle. She screamed, as afoot, her advantage lost, she was immediately swarmed by the UnKind, their red eyes like hot embers, their fangs bared, drooling saliva as they lunged toward her, intent on rending her limb from limb. Despite her morning star, she was no match for the hideous horde of circling creatures. Fear overwhelmed her. She knew she was but a heartbeat from death; for she had exhausted her Power during the desperate conflict with Perish, and now, though she summoned it frantically with every last ounce of her will, it failed her.

And then somehow Iskander and Sir Weythe were there, their steel blades glittering in the moonlight, stabbing, slashing, driving the SoulEaters back. Poisonous tongues of chartreuse light licked along the Sword of Ishtar, unkeyed by any save its own magic, for Iskander's own Power had been drained, too. In some remote corner of her brain, Rhiannon thought that he ought not to have unsheathed the weapon. But there had been no help for it, she knew. All around her the UnKind writhed in the throes of death, their shrill, horrible cries mingling with those of her horse, which thrashed sickeningly upon the bloodstained ground, its flanks ripped wide open by the SoulEaters' long, sharp claws. With one arm Iskander yanked her up before him atop his nervously prancing steed, while mercifully Weythe sliced his sword downward to put a quick end to the torment of Rhiannon's poor beast. Within moments, even as they had surrounded their own fallen masters, the hellhounds closed in, snarling and yapping at one another as they tore frenziedly into the dead animal, quarreling over its meat and entrails, slipping and sliding on its blood and guts. Choking back with difficulty the gorge that rose in her throat, Rhiannon closed her eyes to the gruesome sight, trying to keep from fainting by breathing deeply.

But smoke and blood and death befouled the night, as though every grave in the universe had opened to vomit up its contents and every urn had turned upside down to strew its cremations upon the wind that keened like a legion of ghosts. As she inhaled the putrid air, Rhiannon abruptly clapped her hand to her nose and mouth, pinching her nostrils tightly shut and trying hard not to retch. Beneath the hooves of the horses, the earth crawled with parasitic worms and maggots that, attracted by the bodies that littered the ground, had slithered from their slimy burrows to join the hellhounds' feast. The pools and rivulets of blood that covered the damp earth, heated by the scattered flames, boiled and bubbled like the baleful brew in some witch's caldron; and fox fire glinted on the UnKind corpses.

From where she perched on Iskander's saddle,

trembling in his soot-streaked arms, Rhiannon could see Yael sitting like a megalith astride his steed and, beside him, Chervil and Anise, all of them deploying their fiery arrows as best they could to shield the rest of the companions from the SoulEaters. Kaliq and Hordib had regained their mounts, and now furiously they and the other Scalie Scalpers bolted down the incline of Skull Volcano, which shook and grumbled menacingly.

"Come on!" Iskander yelled urgently. "Come on! 'Tis going to blow!"

He had no sooner got the words out of his mouth than it was as though the earth suddenly cracked wide asunder. With a massive, bone-jarring roar, the volcano erupted, its mouth spitting great globs of lava, lava streaming from its eyes, lava spraying like a pulpy mass of damaged brain from its cranium. Crying out with terror at the bloodred fire that gushed from the monstrous skull, the Imperial Forces fled for their lives, as did the questers. Muck flying from the hooves of their horses, they galloped toward the foothills on the western shore of Lake Malady, where Moolah and Anuk waited anxiously. Both had been left behind, Moolah to lay the trap that the companions hoped would ensure their escape, and Anuk not only to guard Moolah, but to be hidden away, lest he be mistaken in the melee for a hellhound and accidentally slain.

"Lord!" Kaliq shouted to Iskander, who rode at their fore. "We are pursued!"

Glancing over his shoulder, Iskander observed bleakly that they were indeed—by none other than the First Leader, the Lord Ghoul himself, and the horse soldiers of the Imperial Forces, numbering more than a hundred and all of them mounted on fresh steeds.

"Moolah, light the fuses!" Iskander ordered sharply, once the questers had safely passed the snare that tangled along the earth, lying in wait for their pursuers.

The merchant did not need to be told again. Torch in hand, he wheeled his horse about, dashing along the trap he had laid, leaning from his saddle to ignite the long fuses that the Scalie Scalpers had fashioned earlier and that he had twisted together and strung along the ground from one Bezel Boomer to another. Sparking and sputtering, the fuses caught, thin trails of flame blazing across the earth. Seeing that the fuses were alight, Iskander cried, "Ride! Ride!" and spurring and lashing their mounts forward, the companions obeyed. Soon the Hindrance Hills loomed all around them, while behind, the UnKind came hard on their heels and Skull Volcano bellowed its anger, spewing its lava so high into the night sky that it seemed as though the heavens rained fire or blood.

Ghoul was lucky. He was already past the Boomers when they began to explode, panicking his troops, throwing them into utter chaos as several of them were killed outright and others were set aflame. White-eyed, snorting, and whinnying with fear, the SoulEaters' horses reared and bucked, biting and kicking one another, creating further pandemonium. Yanking brutally upon its reins, Ghoul brought his own steed under control.

"After them! After them!" he shrieked, feverishly flicking his whip in the direction the questers had taken. "They mussst not get away, do ye hear? They mussst not get away! They have ssstolen the SSScroll!"

A short while later the companions heard on the track behind them the pounding of horses' hooves and knew that the Imperial Forces had been slowed but not stopped by the Boomers. Those who had hunted the horns were now themselves the hunted. Grimly they pressed on into the gloomy night as, far above them, a shadow winged its way across the Blue Moon.

Glancing up at the silhouette, Rhiannon remembered the baby dragon in Perish's alchemic atelier, small but big enough for a desperate man to ride, and she shuddered. She drew her white mantle more closely about her, noticing for the first time that it was spattered with ichor and blood. She swayed a little in the saddle, grateful for Iskander's arm about her waist, steadying her, as he had steadied her during their terrible struggle with the evil necromancer, defending her against the ruthless rape of her body and mind.

The tower had been an inferno, she told herself. It was not possible that the necromancer had somehow managed to escape. It was only the wind that echoed in the chasms of her mind. It was only the wind, nothing more.

Overhead, its skeletal wings beating evenly, the dark, amorphous creature passed from the halo of the Blue Moon to be swallowed up by the night, while at Iskander's back, the now-sheathed Sword of Ishtar spat celadon flames.

Chapter 27

*Rhiannon dreams of the necromancer, the
Prince Lord Perish; and the Light help me, much
as I love her, I cannot stop her nightmares from
coming.*

—Thus it is Written—
in
The Private Journals
of the Lord Iskander sin Tovaritch

THE QUESTERS RODE OUT OF SALAMANDRIA AS THEY HAD
ridden into it, through wind and mist and rain, day
and night, sleeping in their saddles, never pausing for
any longer than it took to rest the horses and to snatch
a mouthful of what little food remained to them,
though fresh rainwater was plentiful. For behind
them, relentlessly, rode the First Leader, the Lord
Ghoul, and the horse soldiers of the UnKind. But
though exhausted, the companions traveled swiftly,
being but fifteen now, having that night of the battle at
Fiend's Crypt lost five of those courageous warriors
who had hunted the horns. Three had been slain by
the SoulEaters, and two, their skin punctured by the
creatures' infectious umbilical cords, had honorably
fallen on their swords, as was the duty of any Scalie
Scalper so unfortunate as to become Poxed.

414

It was into an uncertain future that the questers journeyed, for they did not know what lay in store for them at Epitaph Pass, whether the five of their number they had sent ahead some days back had got through to warn those holding the pass of the northward march of the SoulEaters that Perish had dispatched. It might be that the companions had escaped from Fiend's Crypt, only to find themselves crushed between two Imperial Forces. The thought lay like a pall upon them all. Hungry, tired, dispirited, they spoke little, only glancing now and then uneasily at the tentacles of celadon light that continued to curl from the Sword of Ishtar, though upon their Power's being renewed, Iskander and Rhiannon had attempted to purge the blade.

"I believe that its Power is sentient," he said once, tersely, to hide his disquiet, "that because of the Lord Cain's unintentional warping of it, it reflects the evil it senses around it."

And ahead and behind—and perhaps all around—were the UnKind. The threat of ambush dogged the travelers' every step. In the hills, eerily, there was only silence, save for now and again the dripping of the rain, the rustling of the trees, and the howling of the wind—until that morning when the screams and moans of those dying at Epitaph Pass shattered the hush.

The mist had only just begun to lift from the hills, so it was like blind men that the questers galloped down the narrow, winding track toward they knew not what, though they imagined a thousand scenes of horror, each more terrible than the last, the reality worst of all as, foam flying up from the deep chests of the horses, they rounded the bend into the pass and saw in the harsh grey light of the dawn the slaughter. A mountain of dismembered corpses, disembodied heads, arms and legs sticking out all over, blocking the trail . . . the steep, high walls awash with ichor and blood . . . a river of blood coursing through the pass— It was only a fleeting impression of such images that filled Rhiannon's dazed mind before Yael shouted, "Lord, Ghoul and the horse soldiers are come upon us!" and there was no way to go forward, no way to go back, and the SoulEaters pressed them from all sides.

And then the Sword of Ishtar was in Iskander's hand, a swath of yellow-green fire swirling away from the blade's tip as he cried out and dug his spurs into the sides of his horse, charging straight toward the carnage and the UnKind even now turning with bared fangs and claws to meet his wild assault. Without warning, the wind rose, wailing; and suddenly, to her horror, Rhiannon realized that the walls of the pass were channeling the Power of both man and weapon, forcing it inward, warping it somehow. The mist whirled away and, with it, the SoulEaters, black dust on the wind. Her mantle streamed back from her shoulders as, white-eyed, whinnying shrilly with fear, the terrified horse plunged on, blood spraying up from its hooves, flecking her face. And still, Iskander and the sword worked their terrible will. His left arm gripped her waist. His heart pounded against her back as he drove with his heels, cruelly roweling the frothing steed forward through the pass, the others coming hard and fast and frightened in his wake—Ghoul and his horse soldiers but lengths behind, among them only the First Leader having some inkling of the unnatural sorcery that devastated the Imperial Forces ahead.

Stunned men and women, numbed by days of unrelenting battle, shrieked in mindless panic, not knowing what had come upon them—only that it broke the ranks of the UnKind, and for that alone was a thing to be feared. Some flattened themselves against the walls of the pass; others ran as though they could outstrip the blinding, dread flame.

"Iskander! The warriors!" The words were ripped from Rhiannon's mouth; she did not know if he had heard them or not, if he understood.

But he must have, for abruptly, to her relief, he swung the blade up as they thundered past what remained of Kaliq's band, then hauled up short, reining hard about as he fought to control the anxiously prancing horse, the savage, unpredictable weapon. The struggle was brief on all fronts. The steed was weary to the bone. Both the sword's Power and Iskander's were spent, exhausted by whatever unknown thing had seized them in the pass. The blade was cold and dark. Dismayed by what had happened, Iskander slid the weapon into its scabbard.

"Are ye all right?" he asked Rhiannon, cradling her against him.

"Yea," she said, "only tired, so very tired."

But there was no time for either of them to rest. The others had caught up with them; and now Ghoul and his horse soldiers were streaming through the pass, brutally trampling several of the paralyzed warriors who obstructed their path.

"This is where my men and I leave ye, Lord," Kaliq announced fiercely as he gazed back at the tattered remnants of his brave and loyal band. "Go. My warriors and I will do what we can to hold the rest of that horde here, to buy ye whatever time may be bought—Lord, nay." He held up his hand, forestalling Iskander's words. "I already know all that ye would say, and I beg of ye: Do not attempt to dissuade me from this course of action. Go—while ye still can. No doubt 'tis indeed death, as ye would warn me, that awaits me back there. But even if it were the Foul Enslaver Itself, they are my men and my women—"

"Yea, I understand," Iskander said quietly. "My

thanks, Kaliq. 'Tis little enough for all ye have done, but 'tis all I have to offer. Leave me, then. Go . . . go with the Light."

"I will not forget, Lord. None of us will ever forget," Kaliq declared as he and Iskander clasped each other's forearms in the way that men do to show their respect and affection when they cannot find the words to express their emotions. "Ye brought us light in our hour of darkness. 'Tis enough. 'Tis more than enough. Those of us who survive will remember. We *will* remember, and we will tell the tale of the quest for the heart of the Darkness. We will sing the song of Fiend's Crypt. And we will spread the word of the Holy Book so all who would hear us will learn of the Light. By all that is holy, Lord, this I swear."

Right fists clenched tightly over their hearts, Hordib and the other three warriors saluted Iskander. Then, bidding the rest of the companions farewell, they wheeled their mounts about and galloped back to join their band. The First Leader spared them barely a glance; at his nod a handful of his troops broke away to engage the five men. The rest of the horse soldiers came on, undeterred.

"'Tis me they want," Iskander observed softly. "'Tis my head Ghoul means to take with his sword. Somehow he knows that I have the Sacred Scroll."

"What shall we do then, beloved?" Rhiannon queried, for she had no thought of leaving him; nor did he ask her to. "What shall we do?"

"We must go to the place we know best," he said, "a place where I do not think the SoulEaters will follow, and where we stand the greatest chance of losing them if they do. We must go north, beloved . . . north to the tundra."

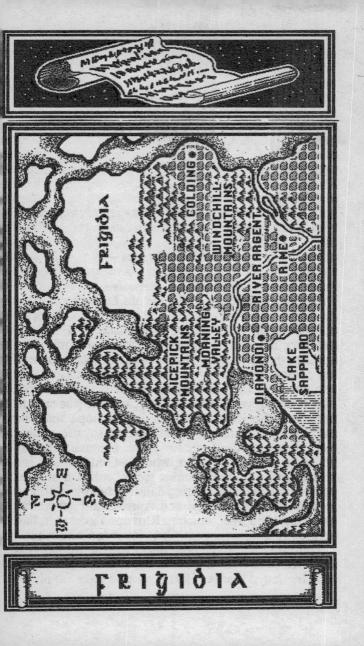

FRIGIDIA

Chapter 28

We ran until there was no place left to run, until at last, inevitably, our time ran out. . . .

—Thus it is Written—
in
The Private Journals
of the Lady Rhiannon sin Lothian

AS ONLY FOUR HAD LEFT THE SNOWY LAND OF BOREALIS, so, after many long weeks of travel, had only four come to that of Frigidia, home of the trolls. The rest of the companions were gone. Iskander had insisted that Moolah take them across the River Copper to seek haven in Rubyatta, there to wait until it was safe to approach the River Knotted, in the hope that the Labyrinthian Watchers of Baffle would spy their signal light and send the ferry for them. From Baffle they could go on to Imbroglio, where—Gunda and Lido had promised—the gnomes would make a stab at turning their clever, crafting hands to boat-building so Sir Weythe and Chervil and Anise could get home. Only stubborn Yael, much to Rhiannon's despair, had refused to go, staying with her, Iskander, and Anuk.

Following the rough map that a tearful Moolah had sketched before leaving them, the four had journeyed over the Jaded Plains of Bezel, around Lake Sapphiro, and into the Emeralde Forest, where, by means of a crude raft they fashioned from logs, as they had done once before in the Groaning Gorge, they had crossed the River Argent into Frigidia. Three times along the way, at the Bezel towns of Amethyst, Pearl, and Diamondi, they had managed to halt briefly for supplies. But though they had longed to remain behind the sanctuary of the towns' high walls, to bed down at an inn for many long nights, they had not dared to linger, knowing that Ghoul and his troops harried at their heels, and would attack the innocent towns, if necessary, to obtain the Scroll. Barricaded behind the high walls vigorously defended by the Bezel Boomers, the companions would doubtless have been safe for as long as the town folk could have withstood an UnKind siege. But unless Iskander could get it to the East, to the Mont Sects, where its secrets could be unraveled, the Sacred Scroll was useless to him, to the Druswids, and to Tintagel, his quest for naught. And so the weary travelers had moved on, disheartened by the fact that Ghoul and his horse soldiers were advancing in shifts, so all in their ranks would have an opportunity to rest, while the questers did not.

Only because the First Leader was wary of the Bezel towns—known to burn the plains at the sight of the SoulEaters—had the companions had any respite during the day. For then the Imperial Forces, all too aware of the havoc that could be wreaked upon them by the Bezel Boomers, had lain low, biding their time until nightfall, when they had stealthily and rapidly progressed across the land.

Abandoning their exhausted horses at the River Argent, knowing that the beasts would be useless to them in the forbidding mountains that had loomed ahead, the travelers had pressed on afoot, trekking through the Moaning Valley of the Icepick Mountains, and thence to the tundra, where none knew better than they how to live off the land, how to survive. But still, Ghoul and his troops had followed, their hellhounds—indeed some breed of lupine, Iskander now felt certain—taking to the tundra as though belonging there, decisively sniffing out the scent of their desperately fleeing quarry.

Now, as they stared at the endless snow and sea that stretched before them on all sides, the questers knew they had no place left to hide. The Sea of Clouds, which Iskander had prayed to find still frozen, was a mass of roiling waves strewn with the stars that glittered and the Moonbow Lights that danced in the northern night sky, so achingly familiar, so poignantly bittersweet, so very far from home. The spring thaw was under way. The companions' last hope of escape was irrevocably dashed. In the distance they could hear the baying of the hellhounds, and they knew that it was only a matter of time now before the UnKind overran them.

"It will be as it was upon the Strathmore Plains," Iskander stated bleakly as he thought of dying in this foreign land, though not alone—a grief far worse to him now than the solitary death he had, at the lonely beginning of his quest, feared and envisioned, a death he would gladly welcome now, would it spare the rest. "The SoulEaters will come at us in waves—until my and Rhiannon's Power is utterly drained and we have nothing left to give. And then we will all of us be at their mercy; we will all of us be finished." He turned to Rhiannon. "Oh, beloved, that I should have brought ye so far, to such a cruel end, when all was nearly within our reach—I could weep for that."

"Oh, Iskander," she breathed, her heart in her eyes as she gazed up at him, "do not ye know that my life was nothing until ye came into it, that it would be nothing without ye? My place is at your side, my heart in your keeping, for always—come what may." She took his hand in hers, and with her other she clasped Yael's. Sensing what she wanted of them, they each laid their free hands upon Anuk's head, so they all formed a circle, without beginning, without end. "Do not ye regret! Do not ye for one moment regret! We did what we had to do—for Tintagel, and for the Light," she whispered fiercely, as they had all of them done that night in the Salamandrian cave, as though the words were a talisman—or a prayer.

It was then that, with a horrendous boom that jarred them to the bone, the ice upon the shore began to crack apart beneath their feet, sending them abruptly scrambling for safety. As they watched, shivering, the fissure widened slowly, filling with sluicing water until at last a small, snowy glacier floated on the waves.

"The current!" Iskander exclaimed suddenly. "The current might take us to Persephone, the northern polar cap, and if we could reach that, we would be home free; for I've my sled and provisions cached there—Rhiannon, get on the iceberg—"

"Are ye mad?" Yael cried, horrified. "You'll be washed away, drowned! And even if by some miracle ye are not, you've no guarantee that the current will take ye in the right direction. It might change course —ye could drift for leagues, for days. Ye will never survive. Ye will die, I tell ye!"

"We surely shall if we stay here," Iskander declared grimly, "and I'd rather take my chances with the sea than with the UnKind. At least this way we'll *have* a chance—and that's more than we had before."

"The iceberg is not large; nor can we depend upon its being solid," the giant pointed out in a last, futile attempt to dissuade him from the rash plan. "I do not think that it will hold us all or that, even so, our enemies will be deterred by the sea from their pursuit of us. They are mad and will stop at nothing to retrieve the Scroll"

The sudden hope that had lighted her eyes dying, her heart sinking, Rhiannon recognized that all this was no less than the hard, bitter truth. One of them would have to remain behind—and they all knew it.

"I will stay here, khan," Anuk volunteered promptly. *"Of us all, I am the one most likely, alone, to escape from the SoulEaters; for why should they bother with me, a mere beast? If fate is kind, I can hold them at bay long enough for the rest of ye to escape."*

Heartsick, even as he nodded his thanks to the lupine, knowing that it was the only way, Iskander reluctantly announced, "Anuk has said he will remain."

"That makes no sense," Yael protested. "He is not so big or so heavy as I. None of ye is. It must be I who stays. For all her Power, Rhiannon is not the warrior I am, and Iskander must protect and guide her to the East." Then, before anyone could argue against this, he snatched the lupine up and tossed it onto the floe. "On ye go, Anuk." The iceberg rocked wildly for a moment, drifting a little way from the shore before steadying, bobbing gently on the waves. The Boreal turned to Rhiannon. "Now, ye, Rhiannon."

"Yael, this is madness," she averred, tears blurring her eyes as she stumbled into his outstretched arms, stricken by what he did for love of her. "We can all go. We will manage, somehow—"

"Shhhhh. Hush. No regrets, remember?" He hugged her close. "Though I pray not, I fear that ye are doomed as surely as I am. So what difference does it make which of us goes and which of us stays? At least this way ye might have a chance—and I would that it were a fighting one, who have been my love, my only love. . . . Kiss me, Rhiannon, before ye leave me. Kiss me just once as ye would have done had ye ever been mine. I do not think that Iskander will grudge me that."

Nay, he would not, she knew; and so she put her arms around Yael's neck and kissed him deeply—for all the years they had been brother and sister, for all the shared memories of their youth that was gone now and would never come again, for all the love she held in her heart for him, though it was not the love he had hoped for. Weeping, she clung to him. He tasted her sweet mouth and the salt of her tears upon his lips; and before he could change his mind, Yael murmured, "Goodbye, my dearest love. Wherever ye may go, go always with the Light," and picking her up, he cast her onto the glacier.

Falling to her knees upon the rime, Rhiannon wrapped the fingers of one hand tightly in Anuk's thick fur to balance herself as the iceberg tilted precariously for an instant, then leveled itself, rising and sinking rhythmically as the ocean surged and swelled beneath it. Yael thought he would never forget the beautiful but forlorn sight of her kneeling there upon the starlit frost, her unbound hair aflame with the Moonbow Lights, her golden eyes raining tears, her mantle white as snow, as the mist that drifted about her, so she seemed to be rising like some ancient goddess from the crystalline ice, the frothy sea.

"Guard her and keep her well, my friend," the Boreal said gruffly to Iskander, embracing him as he would have a brother.

"With my life and all my heart, for so long as I live. By all that is holy, Yael, this I swear," Iskander vowed, his throat choked with emotion at the giant's noble sacrifice.

"A man could not ask for more than that. Do ye go now, my friend. Hurry!" Yael urged. "The UnKind come, and I would know that she is well away from here, from them, ere I die."

Iskander, too, could see the SoulEaters now—their horses long abandoned—striding row after row across the tundra, Ghoul at their fore, the hellhounds running eagerly ahead, sensing they were closing in on their prey. For a moment his eyes locked with Yael's; and then, knowing there was nothing more to be said or to be done, Iskander turned and leaped across the broadening gulf of the sea onto the floe, fighting to steady himself as the glacier heaved yet a third time. All that had remained in the questers' possession Yael quickly pitched to the three who were even now beginning to glide far beyond his reach. He kept naught for himself; he needed nothing but his mighty battle-ax for what he must do.

The last Rhiannon ever in her life saw of him, he was shouting, *"Uig-biorne, märz ana!* War-bears, march on!"* the battle cry of the valiant giants, a thousand warriors strong, who had perished to the last man upon the Strathmore Plains, as, swinging his massive battle-ax, he ran forward to meet head-on the ferocious charge of the UnKind. They would not take him easily, she knew. But still, for a wild instant she wanted to jump into the sea, to rush somehow to his side. Yet there was nothing to be done. Even the Sword of Ishtar was useless now, for in cutting down the SoulEaters, it would also surely smite Yael; and Rhiannon could not bear to throw away any chance, however small, that he might somehow, some way, survive that terrible assault that took him from her so she, Iskander, and Anuk might be spared.

After a moment, slowly, she stood, knowing of a sudden that there was after all something she could do, must do, for Yael. In a voice strong and clear, so he would hear above the sounds of the battle, she began to sing, the words coming not from her memory, but from her heart. She told the tale of the quest for the heart of the Darkness and of the hero, Yael, who had stood fast against all odds, in the Name of the Light. Rhiannon had never loved Iskander more than she did then, when, understanding what she did, he knelt and, cupping his hands before her, brought forth the blue flames of the Druswids so there might be a fire for Yael.

The moons and stars of Tintagel gleamed in the night sky, where the Moonbow Lights were the colors of the aura she and Iskander had made between them; and that love, too, welled inside her. Sweet as the tears that froze upon her cheeks, her voice echoed on the wind as the iceberg swept forth across the dark and cold, unending sea.

DARK STAR

The Moonbow Lights

Chapter 29

The Sea of Clouds, 7276.5.34

I never knew for certain if Yael lived or died. I like to think that he survived, though in my heart I feel he has gone through the Gates to the Light Eternal, to join those courageous Boreals of the Strathmore Plains. At night I look up at the stars and the Moonbow Lights in the sky, and I fancy he is there, somewhere, among them, watching over me, as he did since I was a child.

Where I go, where this floe and the sea take me, if to Persephone, the northern polar cap, as we three hope and pray, or to a watery grave, I do not know. I know only that Iskander, my beloved, is at my side and that wherever we are destined, we go together.

It is enough. Now. I do not ask for more.

—Thus it is Written—
in
The Private Journals
of the Lady Rhiannon sin Lothian

Here ends
BEYOND THE STARLIT FROST
Book II of The Chronicles of Tintagel